The Sleep of the Furies

The Sleep of the Furies

ROBERT L. GAEDE

authorHOUSE®

AuthorHouse™
1663 Liberty Drive
Bloomington, IN 47403
www.authorhouse.com
Phone: 1-800-839-8640

First published by AuthorHouse   08/30/2011

ISBN: 978-1-4567-9579-5 (sc)
ISBN: 978-1-4567-9578-8 (ebk)

Library of Congress Control Number: 2011915120

Printed in the United States of America

"She had once picked up, in a house where she was staying, a translation of the *Eumenides*, and her imagination had been seized by the high terror of the scene where Orestes, in the cave of the oracle, finds his implacable huntresses asleep and snatches an hour's repose. Yes, the Furies might sometimes sleep, but they were there, always there in the dark corners, and now they were awake and the iron clang of their wings was in her brain."

—Edith Wharton, *The House of Mirth*

PART ONE

CHAPTER 1

Pat Lott was sure he would've seen the little girl standing on the upstairs terrace if she'd been there when he first drove into the motel's parking lot. Even if he'd only caught a glimpse of her out of the corner of his eye as he went past, he'd've noticed, he believed. So she must've been someplace other than at the very edge of the overhead deck until after he pulled into the parking space, turned the car's engine off, and got out.

As soon as he locked up the car and turned toward the stairwell that led to his room on the second floor, he saw her. There was no way he could avoid it. She was a flash of ivory white in the middle, and streaks of off-white above and below that, with a black mop atop it all, standing by the wrought iron bars that supported the metal railing that were the only things separating the walkway from the twelve-foot drop down to the concrete barriers at the head of each parking space below. The bars were spaced about eight inches apart, and each stood three feet high. Between two of the bars the little girl stood, a full foot shorter than the supports and slim enough that she could slip between them. The splash of snow white that'd attracted Lott's attention was the plastic outer covering of her disposable diaper; the off-white portions that sandwiched it the bare legs and bare torso, arms, and face of the toddler.

Lott stopped frozen in place as soon as he realized it was a kid clinging to the edge of the terrace.

As the kid thrust its head forward to peer down at him from the parapet, Lott expected at any moment that an adult's hands'd grasp the youngster from behind to anxiously whisk her away. Lott stayed planted where he was, directly beneath the toddler, and he ran his eyes across the expanse in front of the second-floor rooms: there was no one else anywhere to be seen. All eight doors were closed. The curtains of five of the rooms were drawn back, the way the maids left them to show they'd been cleaned that morning. Lott's room, 202, the second from the far end and four doors from the stairwell, was one of those in which the curtains were drawn—because he rented his room by the week, the maids only cleaned and changed the linen once a week and it wasn't his day for housekeeping.

Lott shifted his eyes back to the kid. She had very dark eyes that looked black at a distance, and there was a noticeable cleft in her chin. She put her hands up to grasp the balustrade rail above her head and swung one foot out in front of her, as if exploring the wide open space she'd fall through if she were to let go.

"Oh, no, sweety!" Lott said quickly. He threw his hand up, fingers and thumb extended and palm out in a halting gesture. "Don't do that! That's dangerous, sweety!"

He tried to keep his voice from sounding too alarmed, or expressing anger. He didn't want to startle her, since that might cause her to let go of the railing and lose her balance.

The little girl placed the foot she'd lifted back down on the walkway carpeting. She looked at Lott, tilting her head slightly to one side with curiosity, but she didn't move away from the edge of the terrace or take her hands from their perch above her head.

Lott warily watched for a moment to see if she was going to stay where she was, and when he was satisfied that she wasn't preparing to step forward, he dropped his eyes to check the ground floor rooms. There was no one outside any of them, either. Every one of the doors on the first floor was shut. He could see the flickering blue-gray light of a television screen through one uncurtained window several doors away from where he stood, but he saw no one inside.

"Jesus H. Christ!" he muttered between clenched teeth, carefully keeping his voice low enough so the little girl wouldn't overhear him and become frightened by his tone. "Where's the kid's mother?"

With no one to call on for help, Lott found himself in a dilemma: he could stay where he was to be ready to catch the girl if she fell, or leave her unwatched for the thirty seconds or so it'd take him to get to the stairwell and rush up the steps to snatch her from the precarious position she was in. If he tried to call someone from one of the rooms to assist him, he risked agitating the girl so much that she might lose her balance and do exactly what he was trying to stop her from doing in the first place.

"Goddamn it!" he told himself after he'd stood in place indecisively for another ten seconds and no one'd come out of any of the rooms.

"Listen, sweety," he called up to the girl coaxingly. "I'm gonna come up to get ya, okay? Ya just stay where ya are. Don't go any closer to the edge, all right? Ya might fall and hurt yourself. Stay right where ya are. Right there. I'll be up there in a flash. Wait there."

The little girl turned a bright-eyed look of interest toward him as he spoke. Lott didn't know if the kid could understand anything he said to her; she hadn't said a word the whole time, so he couldn't tell if she was old enough to talk yet or not. He hoped his soothing tone'd convey enough of his message, but all the way upstairs he had an image in his mind of the little girl taking one awkward step too far while he was *en route* so that he'd arrive on the walkway only to find her lying down below with the soft spot of her head pierced by a rusting piece of iron T-bar that anchored one of the concrete abutments on the parking lot. He shot up the stairs, listening for any sound from the toddler but hearing only his own harried footsteps echoing weirdly off the stucco sidewall of the building.

After he reached the landing, he made it around the corner that hid the walkway from his view and stopped. The narrow corridor that ran in front of the rooms was empty.

His heart, already pounding from the effort of racing up the steps, throbbed even harder. His pulse resounded in his ears like a trip-hammer. He was faced with the same predicament as before, only this time in reverse: should he race back down the stairs to begin administering first aid, or investigate further. In a flash, he made his choice. He strode three brisk paces to where the girl'd been standing when he'd seen her last, and looked over the railing. He'd already twisted his face in a grimace of distaste at what he expected to find: the tiny body splayed on the ground, her arms and legs cocked at odd angles and her skull shattered like an eggshell.

He leaned over the parapet and peered down. There was nothing to be seen. No body, nothing but his own car two slots over where he'd left it. The metal of the engine still ticked loudly as it cooled.

Lott ran his gaze across the patch of asphalt below him. He bent over the balustrade as far as he dared to glimpse the concrete walkway of the first floor, but he grew dizzy and thought he felt the railing giving under his weight, so he pulled back. There was no sign of the little girl.

The padded patter of small bare feet on the carpeting sounded to his right. He turned to look, and there she was, just outside the opening to the alcove in which the ice machine was kept. She gave him an enigmatic La Gioconda half-smile; then she covered her mouth with one hand and bent over at the waist as though stifling laughter before she whipped around and dashed back into the recess.

Relief flooded over him.

He strode to the opening of the alcove. He stopped there and smiled at the girl while his breathing and his heart rate sank back to normal.

"So, ya think that's funny, do ya?" Lott asked the little girl, giving her a sidelong glance.

She pushed her face forward, widened her eyes, and laughed silently.

"Well, I guess it was a pretty good joke on me," Lott admitted.

She lifted one of her chubby legs and pressed the instep of her bare foot against the knee of her other leg. Standing on one foot, she put her hands over her head and rested them on top of her short crop of black hair. Then she straightened her cocked leg, put the bare sole of her foot on the ground, and turned to the ice machine. Along the edge of the door-flap, on the lip of the angled metal, she'd carefully set a dozen M&Ms in a row. She took a green one between her thumb and forefinger and popped it into her mouth. She pushed her lips out as though she were sucking the flavor from it, and then closed her eyes ecstatically, clearly enjoying the ultimate pleasure life'd yet tendered her.

It lasted only a second. She opened her eyes, still sucking on the candy, picked up a yellow M&M that was next in the row she'd laid out, and held it toward Lott.

Lott approached her as he would a wounded bird he found lying on the ground. He held out his hand cautiously for the candy she was offering him. He wondered what the proper etiquette'd be when taking candy from a baby; he had no desire to eat it, but he didn't want to offend her by refusing it. She didn't take her eyes from him, and she seemed to be watching him expectantly, so finally he slipped it between his lips.

"Mmmm-mmm," he said to indicate he was enjoying it as much as she'd appeared to enjoy her own. Satisfied by his response, she turned to pick up another M&M, put it into her mouth, and then she took one more and gave it to Lott. Lott histrionically relished that one as well before he said, "I'd love to stay here and eat M&Ms with ya all day, but I think I'd better get ya home. Why don't ya pick up the rest of these and bring 'em with ya. Okay?"

The little girl said nothing, but she seemed to understand, for she began dropping the M&Ms into her left hand one by one until they were all clutched in her fist. Without Lott having to volunteer, she grasped his hand with her own empty one. Together they walked downstairs. He had to wait for her as she struggled to lower herself down every step, her legs awkwardly resisting the bends they needed to make in order for her to swing her feet to get from one to the next. To lower herself the last few risers, she simply sat and slid on her bottom. She took his hand again when they reached the ground.

He knew she must live on the first floor. The rooms downstairs were the only ones ever rented to families with children, the three or four at the very end being set aside for families renting on a weekly basis; Lott knew she belonged in one of those four rooms, but he didn't know which one—he never paid much attention to the occupants down that way.

"Where do ya live, huh?" Lott asked her. She looked up at him with bright, intelligent eyes, her lips in a half-smile, but she said nothing.

"Oh, won't talk, eh?" he said in his best impression of Moe of the Three Stooges.

She blinked her dark eyes up at him but still said nothing.

He smiled at her, and she broadened her smile back at him.

"Well, let's try this one," he said, and led her to the door of the room he'd seen the television screen lit up in earlier.

He knocked and waited. When the door was opened, a large black woman filled the doorframe.

"Hi. I found this little girl on the upper deck, and I'm tryin' to take her home. Do ya know where she belongs?"

The woman looked at the toddler and an expression of shock spread over her face. "Was she out by herself?" the black woman asked, her face crumpling up in wrinkles and lines like a much-used brown paper bag. "I swear, her mother! That woman—" She shook her head, as though exasperated by her own inability to think of words strong enough to express what she felt. "That's Denise Carleton's baby, she down in 109. She never do what's right fo' that little girl. And that baby—oh, she's the most precious thing in the world, she is. How're you, Morinda?"

The woman turned her full attention to the toddler. The girl was pleased to be recognized, and she beamed. She let her hand fall away from Lott's, dug an M&M out of her fist with the hand she'd freed, and offered the candy piece to the woman.

"Oh, no thank you, honey!" the black woman said. "That's the last thing in the world Lucille needs, she got too much on her as it is, honey!" The woman laughed and patted her own hefty thigh to illustrate her point. To Lott, Lucille said, "This little girl'll give half a anything she has fo' you even ask for it. She musta learned it straight from God in Heaven 'fo' He sent this angel to earth, 'cause she shore never learned it from that gutter-trash crack-head mother a hers."

Lucille bent, facing Morinda, and placed her hands over the preschooler's ears. "You didn't hear me say that, baby, I'm sorry I ever did in front a you." With her hands still holding the sides of Morinda's head, Lucille looked up at Lott and said in a low voice, "But it's all true, so help me God!"

Morinda twisted her head out of Lucille's grasp, and the woman groaned as she stood up again.

"Down here in 109, ya said?" Lott asked.

"That's right. At least till CPS come and take her 'way. Which I wouldn't wish on a dog, but—" Lucille shook her head woefully as she looked at Morinda "—but it might be fo' the best fo' this poor little thing."

Lott didn't immediately recognize the abbreviation. When the woman said CPS, he ran through his mind the possibilities the initials might stand for. It took him a while to come up with Child Protective Services.

He nodded his head, then said, "Thanks for the help."

"Hmm-hmm," Lucille said. She didn't close her door; she stood in the doorframe watching Lott escort Morinda past the door of 108 to room 109.

He could hear the moans of a couple having sex coming from the room, and for a split second he considered leaving with Morinda and returning later. But when he remembered the danger the youngster'd been in by being allowed to wander around the upper floor without any supervision, and what Lucille'd told him about Morinda's home-life, he decided he didn't much care what he was interrupting. When his knuckles rapped on the door, it swung in on its hinges as far as the security chain'd allow, leaving a gap large enough for Morinda to've squeezed through. To Morinda, Lott said, "Somebody left the gate open, huh?" Morinda nodded her head bemusedly.

Lott heard a man's voice issuing a complaint, and then rustling sounds. Oddly, the moans of sexual gratification continued unabated. Lott waited for a few seconds. When no one came to the door, he knocked again, louder and more urgently.

A woman muttered gruffly, "Awright, awright." Then a face was pressed to the space between the door's edge and the jamb.

"What?" a hoarse voice on the edge of sleep demanded.

"Are you Denise?"

"Yeah," the woman croaked.

"I found your kid up on the deck of the second floor. Hangin' off the railin'. About to fall."

In the middle of his report, the woman's eyes glanced down to see Morinda at Lott's side. The security chain rattled and the door opened, revealing Morinda's mother. She was young, not more than twenty, Lott judged. But the pupils within her blue irises were constricted so that they were barely larger than pinpricks, giving them the look of madness so often found in chronic crack smokers. And she'd given up using makeup or brushing her hair long ago. She'd thrown on a housecoat that opened down the front; she clutched it together at her throat, but the halves hung open in a V that showed she wore nothing under the robe. Lott clearly saw the patch of black pubic hair between her legs. The woman might once've been reasonably attractive, but she'd become so slatternly in the meantime that the idea of even contemplating her as a sexual being made Lott's stomach roil. He hastily moved his eyes up and kept them fixed on the space beyond the woman.

A queen-size bed took up most of the floor space of the room. The thin, worn bedspread, the single blanket, and the top sheet were rumpled and soiled. The man who'd groaned when Lott first knocked lay under the covers; he rolled over so that Lott could see only his bare shoulders tattooed with the name "Roxanne" in inch-high Gothic lettering. There was a lot of clutter around the bed: a box of disposable diapers was open, its contents spilled across the floor and over the single armchair; there was a rank, sour smell of ammonia and fresh shit that told Lott that some of the disposable diapers scattered about were soiled and never thrown out. Articles of adult clothing, some belonging to a man but mostly those of a woman, were dropped as though they were rags no one cared about. In one corner were stacked several cardboard boxes, one precariously perched on top of another, and each stuffed to overflowing with clothing, kitchen utensils, children's toys, and food items. The boxes'd been stacked in one place so long that the sides of those on the bottom were crushed in on themselves.

The television was on, turned to channel 4, the motel's closed-circuit channel on which were shown a constant stream of cheesy X-rated movies. A woman who was having her clitoris licked by what appeared to be a disembodied tongue in extreme close-up was issuing the series of moans that Lott heard coming from the room; he could hear the accompanying generic synthesizer music of the video's sound track, something he'd missed earlier.

"Morinda?" the woman said. "What're *you* doing out there?"

Morinda'd finished eating all her M&Ms. She waved her hands in good spirits, then brought them together in a silent clap. A second later, she repeated the gesture.

"Ya need to keep this baby someplace ya can watch her," Lott said in a peremptory fashion. "She's outside like that, she gets in the parkin' lot. People drive through, and she could get run over. Or she'll find a way back up the stairs, and she could fall."

Morinda'd walked into the room and now stood a few feet away from her mother, facing Lott.

"I told her," the woman said. "I told her not to be out there. I told her not to go up them stairs."

Lott stared at the woman for a moment, attempting to comprehend what the woman was saying, trying to make sense of it in relation to the child she was talking about.

Finally he said, "Well, if ya told her not to do it, and she did it anyway, that's just willful disobedience, isn't it?"

The woman's face twisted like a dishrag being wrung out. "Huh?"

Lott glanced toward Morinda. The little girl smiled at him, stood on one foot, lifted her arms above her head, and shifted her eyes merrily from side to side, giving the appearance that she'd gotten the joke that her mother hadn't.

"Ya need to watch this baby. She's gonna get hurt." Lott cocked his head to the bed. "Is that her father?"

Denise seemed surprised by the question, as though she'd forgotten there was anyone else in the room. She snapped her head around.

"Him? Oh, no. Morinda's daddy ain't with me no more. He's—that's just a friend, that's all."

The man on the bed kept his back turned to the commotion. He was either asleep or pretending to be.

The woman on the television set was now on her knees giving head to the man who'd been servicing her before. The man pumped his penis into her mouth as she greedily sucked at it. Lott's face curdled into a scowl.

"Ya shouldn't have that on when your kid's here to see it."

"Huh? What?"

Lott glanced at the man in bed. He lay inert. Lott pushed past Denise to the TV and pushed the on-off button. The screen went dark.

He returned to the doorway and squatted to look Morinda in the eye. "If ya ever need anything, ya let me know. Anything. Okay?"

She made no response, just looked gravely at him.

"But don't come upstairs by yourself. That's dangerous, sweety. I don't want ya to hurt yourself. All right?"

He stood and, without saying another word, he left.

The black woman, Lucille, loitered in her own doorway, making no effort to hide her curiosity about the confrontation. Lott rolled his eyes, pressed his lips together, and shook his head slightly as he went by her. Lucille hummed her agreement: "Hmm-hmm."

He reclimbed the stairs to his room.

CHAPTER 2

Several weeks later Lott was called to the door of his motel room by a knock to find Denise holding her daughter by the hand. He'd seen neither of them since he'd discovered Morinda on the second-story terrace and taken her to her mother's room, and the few times he'd given any thought to the matter, he wondered if they'd moved.

Morinda wore a wrinkled cotton print dress with several large stains deeply embedded in the fabric. Her mother wore a pair of slacks that seemed oddly ill-fitted for a woman's form; Lott guessed they were originally meant for a man, and for one who was bigger across the hips than Denise'd ever been.

"Hi," Denise said. "Remember me?"

Lott said nothing. He kept his face a blank.

"Ya brought Morinda back that time she got out, remember? Well, I come by to see if maybe I could borrow ten dollars."

Lott found himself reaching for his billfold and opening it before the thought struck him: She's begging door-to-door. That, after all, was what it came down to. And dragging her baby around with her while she did it.

Still stunned by Denise's effrontery, he checked his wallet, finding that the smallest bill he had was a twenty. It was that, and the realization this'd certainly not be Denise's last visit to his room for the same purpose, that made him say what he did.

"I tell ya what," he told her, his hand inside his wallet holding the corner of a bill. Denise stared at the contents of the wallet, but she unwillingly lifted her eyes to look at Lott's face when he hesitated in drawing the money out. "I won't *loan* ya ten dollars—I'll *give* ya *twenty* dollars."

Denise's eyes widened at the offer. Callously, Lott added, "On the condition that ya never—and I mean *never*—ask me for money again. Don't come back here asking for a loan, or a handout, or anything else."

He pulled the twenty out and held it in Denise's direction. She'd started to reach for it when he was only half-finished stating his condition; her hand froze in mid-air as he completed the proviso.

"I was only askin' to borrow ten . . ." she retreated.

"And I already said no to that. Ya don't understand 'no' in English? I'll say it in Spanish: No! What I'm offerin's twenty—not as a loan, it's an out-and-out gift. But only if ya promise that you'll never come around beggin' for more in the future. Deal?"

Denise winced when Lott baldly stated the word 'begging.' Her right hand clutched the smaller hand of her daughter. Her left hand, which she'd raised to pluck the bill from Lott's grasp, slowly sank to her side. "Ah, now, it's not like that—"

"Whatever it's like, however ya wanna think of it, that's okay with me. But what I'm offerin's right here—the twenty dollars's yours if ya want it. Just tell me ya won't be back askin' for more."

Her left hand slowly, reluctantly, rose from her side and accepted the money. She said nothing by way of thanks or goodbye, merely crumpled the bill in her fist and turned with her daughter in tow toward the stairwell.

Lott closed the door behind them, satisfied that he'd handled the situation the best way he could. He'd been cruel, but only in order to be kind. Denise had no business dragging her baby around with her if she was going to panhandle from people she scarcely knew. He'd only done what he needed to do to keep himself from being plagued by further imploring visits: he'd cut the parasite off early, before it became too firmly attached.

A week later, Denise knocked at his door; again she had Morinda with her. As if she had no memory of the promise he'd extracted from her, she boldly asked Lott for six dollars.

"It's not for what ya think!" Denise hurriedly added when she saw Lott's face darken. "I need it to get Morinda some Pampers."

"I thought we had a deal."

Denise stared at him as if she had no idea what he was talking about.

"I gave ya twenty dollars on the express stipulation that ya never—ever—ask me for anything again," Lott explained. "You agreed to that. Ya promised me ya wouldn't ask me for more money. But here ya are now, beggin' for more."

"I know," Denise began, a whine creeping into her voice, "but it's for Morinda, she needs—"

"No, no, no, that's not the point. The point is, we had a deal. I said I'd give ya the money *if.* Ya then took the money. That's a contract. Ya took the money. And now you're violating the terms of our agreement."

"Morinda needs Pampers," Denise doggedly repeated, as though it were something other than a *non sequitur.* "And I don't have the money. It's not for what ya think it's for, I swear."

"What'd ya do with the twenty dollars ya got from me last week? Ya use it to buy crack? Ya blow all at at the rock house?"

"Ya *gave* me that money, ya said. It was mine, I could use it for whatever I wanted."

Lott rolled his eyes to heaven. "Give me strength!" he said, then turned his attention back to Denise. "I gave it to ya on the condition that ya wouldn't ask me for any more. And here ya are, a week later, askin' for more."

"But I need *this* money to buy Pampers."

"If ya hadn't wasted the money I gave ya a week ago at the rock house, you'd have it to buy Pampers today, wouldn't ya?"

Denise looked helplessly to the toddler beside her. Lott's glance followed hers down. As soon as his eyes met Morinda's, the little girl's face lit up. Lott couldn't help himself: he smiled back at her. She glowed with the attention he paid her. Lott kneeled so his face was level with hers.

"How've ya been, sweety?"

She beamed at him and clapped her hands together.

"They treatin' ya all right around here?"

She put her hands on his knee and stretched her face upward toward his, as if she were planning to kiss him, but she danced away from him, turned on one foot, and almost fell on her bottom when the balletic movement proved too difficult for her to carry through. Lott reached out to grab her and hold her up, but she regained her balance on her own. She looked chagrined, and Lott stood to face Denise.

"Where were ya plannin' on buyin' these Pampers?"

"They got 'em at the minimart," she said, pointing in the direction of a convenience store around the corner from the motel.

"Just over here?"

"That's right."

17

"Then let's go over and get 'em."

He hastily checked his pocket for his room key, closed the door behind him, and stepped around Denise so that Morinda was between them. Denise took Morinda's hand in hers, and as if it was the most natural thing in the world to do, Morinda raised her other hand and placed it in Lott's.

When they reached the minimart, Denise proceeded to the aisle on which the baby supplies were shelved, leaving Morinda with Lott by the magazine counter. Morinda let Lott's hand go; she went directly to the lowest level of the display rack, squatted down, and picked up a children's book with a gaudy picture of a gingerbread man with a clock's face and forks for hands on its cover. She pointed at the picture with her forefinger, and looked over her shoulder at Lott with an expression of amazement. Lott smiled fondly, and she turned again to the book, fascinated.

Denise reappeared carrying a large package of disposable diapers in her arms. She set it on the counter and then snatched a pack of generic brand cigarettes from a stand by the cash register and put it on top of the Pampers. The clerk started to ring the two items up. Denise turned to Lott expectantly, saw that he was watching Morinda, turned to see what her daughter was doing, and in her grating voice called out, "Morinda, put that back! Ya don't need that!"

Impelled by Denise's tone more than anything, Lott said, "Sure she does. Bring that over here, sweety, and I'll get it for ya."

Morinda carried the book held flat, pressed between the palms of both her hands, to Lott. He patiently explained to her, "We have to pay for this, but as soon as we do, it's yours. Okay?"

She surrendered the book to him. He put it with the Pampers and the pack of cigarettes Denise finagled him into paying for. The clerk rang up the new item. On impulse, Lott picked up a package of M&Ms for Morinda and had the clerk add it to the bill. "Anything else?" the clerk said before he totaled everything again.

On the way to the motel, Morinda ambled between the two adults. She used both her hands to take pieces of candy from the bag and pop them in her mouth. Lott asked Denise, "How's your boyfriend?"

"Who?"

"Your boyfriend. When I took Morinda to your place that time, there was a guy there?"

"My boyfriend? Oh, him!" Denise waved her hand dismissively. "I don't even remember his name. He was just there, is all, just the one time, ya know?"

Lott knew. He let the matter drop.

Lott wasn't quite sure how it came about, but he started seeing more and more of Morinda. The little girl'd be standing in the open doorway of her motel room when he drove into the parking lot, and he'd stop to talk to her, which usually led to him taking her with him to the minimart to buy her some M&Ms and perhaps a book, or if Denise made him feel guilty by mentioning that Morinda needed something else, he'd get it for her. Morinda always showed such obvious and immense pleasure in whatever it was he gave her that it was better than receiving any half-hearted, and probably insincere, thanks from Denise.

Sometimes when Denise had to "run an errand," as she put it, or she was entertaining one of her "boyfriends" in her room, she'd bring Morinda by Lott's room and ask if she could leave her daughter with him for a little while. He knew Denise used every other permanent resident in the motel in the same way, but he liked having Morinda around, and he always said yes whenever his schedule allowed.

Morinda loved to be read to; she always brought along one or more of the books he bought her when she came to stay with him, and he kept a stack of others at his place for her visits. By that time, Morinda'd begun to speak, and from memory she could mouth something similar to most of the words Lott read aloud. He'd pause before the last word or two of each sentence, allowing Morinda to finish it, and when she did, he'd coo encouragement to her, telling her, "You are so smart! You are just a smartybutt!" and pressing his forefinger into her stomach until she giggled with delight. Morinda'd then fold her legs in toward herself so she could grab her bare toes in self-satisfaction while Lott lauded her with even more praise.

They'd finished going through a stack of books one afternoon and she'd fallen asleep on the couch. Lott sat next to her watching television with the sound turned down low so it wouldn't wake her. The door to his room was propped open so he could spot Denise as soon as she returned to the motel. A shadow fell over Lott like a cloud moving across the sun.

The doorway filled with the form of Al Thibodeaux, Lott's boss. As always, Thibodeaux was dressed conservatively, but expensively and very fashionably. His lips were thin, and his nose came to a sharp point. He held a cigar in one hand. The smell wafted to Lott a second after he realized he had a visitor. Thibodeaux's eyes swept the room for a few seconds as he stood in place. He jerked his head back skeptically and said, "What the hell's this?"

His eyes rested on Morinda's sleeping figure, draped across the sofa cushion in a posture that suggested she'd died melodramatically in battle.

"Hey, Al. How ya doin'? This's one of the neighbor's kids. I'm kinda watchin' her for a while. C'mon in," Lott invited.

Thibodeaux stayed where he was. He cocked his head to watch Morinda out of the corner of his eye. Then he raised his cigar and put it in his mouth, clamping his teeth on the butt. He puffed several times, the upward swirling smoke coiling in front of his face.

"We don't pay ya enough, ya gotta do babysittin' to make ends meet?"

"No, it's not like that," Lott laughed. "I'm only helpin' the kid's mother out."

Thibodeaux puffed at the cigar. A new stream of smoke veiled his face.

"Ya tryin' to get with the mother, or what?"

Lott looked as if he'd just taken a mouthful of milk that had turned. "Please!" he said.

"All right, all right. I was just askin'. She's that bad, huh?"

"Worse. But the kid's really neat."

"Yeah, kids are great," Thibodeaux said perfunctorily. It was obvious he had no interest in children.

"So, what brings ya to this neck of the woods, Al? Slummin'?"

"Workin' for a livin's more like it. I need ya at the club tonight."

He was referring to the Delaware Club in Gardena. Gardena, a small city in the greater Los Angeles area, has no local ordinances prohibiting wagering at card games. Poker's played at several casino-style clubs in the city, as is the more exotic Oriental game of Pai Gow, which attracts thousands of the immigrants from China and Southeast Asia who'd flocked to Southern California.

"Dealin'? Or ya want me to shill?"

"Dealin'. But I got good news for ya."

"A place as pit boss opened up?"

Lott'd been working at the Delaware Club as a dealer; he'd been angling for the better-paid and more responsible position of pit boss ever since he'd started.

"Even better. We're takin' ya out of the club, though. Tomorrow, you and me are gonna take a ride. Up north. Collectin'. I'm gonna get ya started on that."

Lott knew there were two sides to the business he'd been recruited into: the legitimate end of things, which involved working at the Delaware Club, and the other, a sports book operation that had bookmaking offices scattered throughout the state of California. He was being shifted from one to the other.

"Okay. What do I gotta do?"

"Just be ready to go first thing in the mornin'. Meet me at the club at nine, we'll take my car from there. We'll be goin' over the Grapevine, then up the Central Valley. Make about half a dozen stops till we get to Sacto. Pick up the money, then bring it back. You'll be ridin' shotgun."

"Shotgun?" Lott's face sagged and the muscles between his shoulders tautened.

Thibodeaux shifted his cigar from one side of his jaw to the other without touching it with his hands. "Hey, ya knew the job was dangerous when ya took it!"

"Yeah, sure," Lott said with no real conviction in his voice.

Thibodeaux chuckled bemusedly, removed the cigar from his mouth, and added, "Don't worry, it's just an expression. You'll just be along for the ride this trip. Ya won't need any firepower. All we do's collect, we don't hafta shoot it out with nobody."

Lott's shoulders dropped and he breathed a sigh of relief. "That's good to know."

"Looks like your partner there's comin' to life."

Morinda was awake. She sat up with her grouchiest face on. She looked balefully at Thibodeaux, then crawled over to Lott and piled into his lap, where she plopped as if preparing for a long stay. He put his hands under her armpits to shift her around to a more comfortable position for him, and she angrily flapped her arms to keep him from succeeding with the maneuver. Lott tried to soothe her by cooing and stroking her, but she refused to be placated. She slapped at him until he gave in and left her where she wanted to be.

Thibodeaux watched the scene impassively. He puffed on his cigar and said, "Yeah, kids are great, it says here in fine print. I'll see ya at the club tonight. Ya should be there by seven."

"Sure thing."

Thibodeaux left. Morinda's captious attitude vanished as soon as the visitor was gone, and she became playful, standing beside Lott on the sofa to twist his hair gently into knots and pull his cheeks and chin out as though they were made of rubber, laughing at the funny changes this made in his appearance.

CHAPTER 3

Lott went along with Thibodeaux to learn the locations of the various bookmaking operations in the the widely scattered cities of California's Central Valley, be introduced to those who ran them, and collect the week's take from each. As they drove north on Highway 99, crossing the Tehachipi Mountains by means of the Grapevine, Thibodeaux lectured Lott on procedure.

"Ya can start down here and do Bakersfield first, or Las Noches, either one, it's up to you. And if ya start here, ya go straight up 99, boink, boink, boink, to Modesto, Madera, Fresno, Stockton, and then Sac. Or ya can drive on up, maybe even take Interstate 5, it's faster than 99 but it's boring as all hell, and start in Sacto then double back, Stockton, Fresno, Modesto, Madera, to Bakersfield and Las Noches, whichever, before ya head home to L.A. Either way, it's up to you.

"Ya go to each store, ya pick up the money they got waitin' for ya. Ya put the money in the trunk. Ya lock the trunk. The money never goes in the front of the car. It always goes in the trunk. Ya always lock the trunk. The money stays in the trunk, and the trunk stays locked. The only time the trunk's unlocked's when ya open it to put the money from the next stop in, or when ya get back to L.A. and ya pass the money over. Or sometimes when ya gotta make a stop overnight. Sometimes ya gotta do that. Then—and only then—do ya take the money out. Ya got a place to stay. The place'll be reserved for ya ahead of time, it'll be a motel. Ya take the money out—ya listenin' to me?"

"Yeah, I'm listenin'."

"Ya don't act like you're listenin' to me."

"I'm listenin', I said."

"Okay, don't act like you're listenin' while ya really got your mind on gettin' laid or some shit. Really listen. Where was I? Oh, yeah. If ya stop at a motel, I'll let ya know which one to stop at. Everything'll be set up. When ya get there, ya take all the money—that's *all* the money, I said—outta the trunk, and ya take it into the room with ya. Ya sleep with the money. Ya don't leave the motel to go out and get a drink. Ya don't pick up some bimbo and bring her to the room. Ya don't leave the money for any reason. Ya don't have anybody else in the room with the money. Ya stay with the money and ya make sure nothin' happens to it."

"Right, okay."

"You *must*—I stress the word *must*, and I hope for your sake you are truly payin' attention to every word I utter—show up with every dime of the money ya pick up at each and every stop. There must be no discrepancies between the amount of money ya collect and the amount of money ya bring back. Don't dip into one of the bags for change for a parkin' meter. Don't help yourself to an advance to buy a pack of cigarettes. If you're broke and ya run out of gas on the way, better use your Oklahoma credit card and suck it out of somebody else's tank before ya try dippin' into the bags ya picked up. 'Cause every one of them bags's been checked. It's been added up by the guy who runs the book in each town. And the tape that guy ran was double-checked by Sid the bookkeeper over the phone before the money was put in the bag. And the tape the guy who runs the book added up, and was double-checked by Sid, has been sent to L.A. by UPS. And if the tape shows up, and it don't match the money that's supposed to be in the bag, guess what?"

"My ass'll be in king-size crack."

"Well, it could be the guy who runs the book, who's been workin' with Jack for umpteen years and has never taken a penny that he didn't have comin' to him, just this one time made a mistake. Or maybe Sid, who's been workin' for Jack since about ninety years before God was born and has never, ever, come up missin' a red cent, suddenly lost his mind and ran amok. Or it could be that you, who've only been workin' for Jack for all of a few months and are therefore so far down the food chain that you are plankton—and I mean by that that you are an absolute bottom feeder and lower than pond scum, should push ever come to shove—it could be that you, my friend, will take the rap. I hope ya understand me when I say this."

"I understand."

"So don't fuck with the money. Say that back to me."

"I won't fuck with the money."

"No, no, no. You're not sayin' it with conviction. Ya gotta say it so ya make me believe ya mean it."

"I won't fuck with the money."

That finally seemed to satisfy Thibodeaux. At least, he said nothing further on the subject.

They visited many different locations in as many different towns, up and down Highway 99. Each of the books they stopped at had a cover business that disguised the bookmaking operation. In Fresno, the sports book was a caterer; in Modesto, an auto wrecking yard.

When they got to Sacramento, it was already dark. Thibodeaux pulled into a small strip mall and parked in front of a barbershop. The storefront was lit up, and there were several customers inside along with a white-haired man dressed in a white smock holding a gleaming straight razor in his hand. A bell tinkled as they pushed through the door, but no one in the place paid any special attention to the newcomers except that a boy of about eighteen who was standing with a janitor's broom in his hands disappeared out of sight down a short corridor as soon as he noticed Thibodeaux's arrival.

The barber, who was well past sixty and possibly in his seventies, was saying, "Get in the chair, Dave, and I'll show ya what it's like to get a real shave."

A man rustling through the different sections of a newspaper while he lounged in a chair by the wall said, "I know how to shave myself, thanks. I'm not letting anybody else hold a razor to my throat."

"Shave yourself!" the barber scoffed. "Use one of them cheap throwaways. Safety razor, my ass! It's safe because it can't cut anything. Leaves stubble like a clear-cut forest. Ya want smooth, ya come to a pro."

"I don't want smooth," Dave said, pulling the Sports section of the newspaper out and unfolding it. "I wanna stay alive. How do I know what you're gonna do with that damned thing once ya got me in that chair? I wouldn't even be able to watch where it's going once ya got down around my neck, and I wouldn't be fast enough to stop ya if ya went for my throat. I saw a guy get hit by shrapnel so it severed his carotid artery in the war. Blood just went pfft! shootin' outta him at about a hundred miles an hour. He didn't live longer than three seconds. Massive blood loss, instant death. I'll stick with my Schick."

"Stick with my Schick!" the other customers repeated appreciatively to each other. "That's a good one, Dave."

Dave ignored the praise and coolly spread the Sports section open to the second page.

"Aaw, you're cryin' before you're hurt," the barber insisted.

"It'd be a little too late to cry after ya got finished shortening me, Walt. Besides, you're too damned old to be workin' on people's sensitive parts with that cutthroat razor. Your hands shake, Walt. They won't let ya drive anymore, I don't know why they let ya pretend ya can still shave anybody who'd be stupid enough to climb in that chair and let ya go at 'em. It's time for ya to give it up."

"My hands don't shake!" Walt the barber said. "Look at this—rock steady." He held the hand with the razor in it straight ahead of him, pointing at Dave. Dave didn't bother to glance up from his paper.

"What's the line on the Redskins' game?" one of the other customers leaned over and asked Dave in a low voice.

"When I was in barber school learnin' my trade, I had to shave a balloon clean of shavin' cream before they let me graduate," Walt said. He lifted the razor in the air and began to demonstrate. "It had to be done gently, ever so gently, since the slightest prick of the skin of that balloon and I'd've been out on my ass in the street, flunked out of barber school, earnin' my livin' loadin' crates of spinach on a truck at the market. So I made a swipe, barely touchin' the blade to the rubber, only givin' it a hint of the steel. A mere whisper to take off that layer of cream, not more than kissin' the rubber with the edge. I swept that steel around the curves like a toreador with his cape, the razor flowed in my hands, I skimmed the lather off and left that balloon shaved clean—and unbroken. I was like a surgeon. And I still am. This razor's capable of holdin' an edge ten times sharper than any 'safety razor' you'll ever buy at the five-and-dime, and in the hands of a master barber, this's an instrument that can provide ya with a shave beyond compare. But if ya fuck with the man who holds it—"

Walt flicked the straight razor's blade out and down. It slashed through Dave's newspaper, slicing it so that he held two halves of what'd once been a whole, one part in each hand.

It took Dave several seconds to realize what'd happened, and his eyes went wide as he did. He dropped both parts of the Sports section on the floor and lunged out of the chair to stand with one foot forward, his chest thrust out, and his arms bent at the elbows, as though prepared for a fight.

"Ya crazy bastard! Whattaya think you're doin'?"

Walt was serene. "I was showin' ya the advantage of an institutional razor over those flimsy pieces of shit you're used to usin'."

"Ya coulda killed me!"

"Never! Not unless I wanted to."

Dave held one of his hands up with the palm facing him to examine it, waggling the fingers to make sure they were all there. "I almost lost fingers," he said in wonder at his luck. "If I hadn't pulled my hand away in time, they'd be callin' me Lefty."

"Aaw!" Walt dismissed the possibility. "If I wanted to take your fingers off, I'd've aimed for your nose."

"You're nuts, Walt! You've got fuckin' Alzheimer's!"

The other customers were wheezing with laughter, and Thibodeaux joined them.

"This isn't funny!" Dave said indignantly. He looked around from one person to the next for support. "This crazy son-of-a-bitch carries a nigger-knife like that, and he's ready to use it on anybody who walks in here, how's that funny?"

"He didn't use it on *any*body," Thibodeaux pointed out. "He used it on *you.*"

"Yeah, well, wait till he gets around to you guys, then see how long ya laugh. Try laughin' with your throat cut—it don't work!"

Dave stalked out of the shop. The bell tinkled as he opened the door, and then again when the door swung shut behind him.

"Jesus, this place never changes!" Thibodeaux said.

The man who'd been sitting next to Dave and asked about the line on the Redskins' game eased himself up and slid into the empty chair Dave'd occupied so he was nearer Thibodeaux. He diffidently touched Thibodeaux's elbow and said, "Al, whattaya think of this new guy the Redskins put at quarterback?"

"I think he must be getting his hair cut by Walt, here," Thibodeaux said, raising chuckles from the loafers around the shop: the Redskin's new quarterback's bad haircut was legendary. Walt sneered at the imputation.

"No, I mean it, Al," the man persisted. "Ya think he's gonna hold up, or is he gonna fall apart again. Ya know, he had all those fumbles a couple of seasons back. And he's kind of slow and sloppy."

"But he's been playin' without injuries so far this year, and that makes up for a lot," one of the other customers pointed out.

"A sixth-round draft pick when he came into the NFL," the customer who'd raised the subject in the first place said dubiously. "Nobody had much faith in him right out of college."

"He's been puttin' points on the board," Thibodeaux said. "Ya put up more points than the other team's defense allows and they gotta name for ya. They call ya a winner."

The bell tinkled as Dave came back in. He ignored Walt and squeezed between Thibodeaux and Lott to return to the chair he'd been sitting in before Walt cut his newspaper.

"That was my chair," he told the man who'd taken it.

The man who'd so deferentially importuned Thibodeaux's opinion about the new Redskin's quarterback was unsympathetic. "You got that right—it *was* your chair. Now it's mine. Ya shuffle your feet, ya lose your seat."

A murmur of subdued laughter at Dave's expense, mixed with approbation of the rhyme, swept through the shop.

Dave reacted with a degree of petulance. "Oh, I see how it is around here! It's only the big-time *losers* get treated with any respect. If ya drop a bundle, then everybody's your pal. But if ya win your bets, they wanna get rid of ya fast. All you suckers, you're putting Walt and Murray's grandkids through college with the bets ya drop." Dave swept his eyes around until they came to rest on Walt. He raised his hand and pointed an accusatory forefinger at the old barber. It shook with rage as he exclaimed, "And you owe me for my paper!"

He stomped out of the barbershop one more time.

The boy carrying the push broom returned. He slid into his old place by the wall next to the opening of the corridor.

"Murray back there?" Thibodeaux asked the boy.

The boy nodded and hooked his thumb over his shoulder.

Thibodeaux turned to Lott and said, "Why don't you go ahead and make the collection from Murray? He's down the hall to the left, behind that door marked 'Private.' He knows we're here, so it should be ready for ya when ya get there."

He returned to his conversation with the others without waiting for Lott's assent. Lott did as he'd been told.

He knocked when he came to the closed door, not entering until he heard a voice calling from the other side, "It's not locked!"

He turned the knob and went in.

A man sat at a desk across the room. Lott assumed this was Murray. Murray had his back to Lott, and the only part of him Lott could see besides his white hair was a pair of bony shoulder blades sticking out from a blue barber's tunic since he had both his elbows cocked and resting on the desktop in front of him. The air of the room was hazy and smelled of stale tobacco smoke. A trail of fresh smoke zigzagged to the ceiling from a cigarette Murray held in his hand and occasionally lifted to his mouth.

Lott paused, waiting for Murray to acknowledge him. But Murray never looked his way. He had a pensive air, as though he was deep in somber thought and couldn't bother to rouse himself from his cogitations to attend to minor matters such as the comings and goings of other people. Lott was about to clear his throat to remind Murray of his presence, but before he could, Murray said, "It's ready. You know where it is," in a tone of voice that conveyed a lordly disdain.

Lott replied, "Uh—no, I don't."

The old man spun around at the sound of his voice, and his bushy white eyebrows jerked up and down in surprise. "Say, I'm sorry. I thought you were someone else."

"Al sent me back to get the collection," Lott said. He felt he was an intruder in a private drama that he was embarrassed to find himself not only a witness to, but also an unwilling participant in.

The old man at the desk said, "Oh, yeah! You're the one Jack hired who's working for Al."

"I'm the one."

Murray raised his bushy eyebrows archly. "The way your life's going, ya don't need me givin' ya an extra ration of shit. I'm really sorry about the way I acted when ya came in."

"No harm, no foul. Forget about it."

"No, I feel bad. C'mon over and have a seat. I'll buy ya a drink by way of apology."

"Sure," Lott said, and he took the empty chair beside the desk.

"You a bourbon drinker? I haven't got any branch water, but there's the water cooler over there if ya really think ya have to."

"Bourbon's fine. No water—I know what fish do in that stuff."

Murray crushed his cigarette out in an ashtray and pulled a fifth of whiskey and two glass iced-tea tumblers out of a drawer. He poured an inch of bourbon into their bottoms and gave one of them to Lott, then lifted his own glass toward his guest and said, "*L'chayim*." Lott tilted the rim of his tumbler at Murray before he sipped from it.

"So, how'd ya manage to get hooked up with Jack Kilby and Al Thibodeaux? I'm sorry, I don't recall your name—I know someone told it to me on the phone, but—" he tapped his nicotine-stained index finger against the side of his head "—it's gone. Gettin' old's a terrible thing."

"Pat Lott."

"So, how'd ya get mixed up with the Hole in the Wall Gang, Pat Lott?"

"It's kind of a weird story."

"Are there any other kind? I mean, any other kind of *true* ones."

"A few months ago, I met Jack in a bar. We got to talkin' 'bout one thing and another. The next thing I know, he offered me a job. I needed work, so I took it. He started me off dealin' poker. I thought he had me pegged to take over as a pit boss, but Al's started me at this instead."

"Aah! Jack's classic recruiting method!"

"He's done this before?"

"All the time. Were you in the service?"

"Army."

"Ya mentioned that to Jack durin' your conversation at the bar, I take it."

"It probably came up. I think he started talkin' about it."

"That explains a lot."

"Not to me."

"Jack likes to bring young guys like you into the business, especially if they've been in the service. He thinks he can trust 'em better. He's always got one or two of 'em, 'bout your age, workin' for him. I think of 'em as Jack's surrogate sons. Ya know he's got two daughters, Jack does? Never had any sons, so he finds protégés to bring into the business, and he looks after 'em, and some of 'em stick with it and get promoted and do all right."

Murray tilted his head back and raised his eyebrows inquisitively. "Jack told Al to put ya on under him, did he? That's gotta make Al happy."

"As a matter of fact, it does seem to bug him. I couldn't tell if he's that way with everybody, or if he just doesn't like me."

"What Al doesn't like's havin' Jack push ya on him. It's nothing personal. It's probably not personal, that is. But it worries Al 'cause Al doesn't know if you've been put in place by Jack just to keep an eye on him or not. And even if ya aren't around to spy on him, he doesn't like havin' anyone who isn't his own picked underling workin' for him. It makes him nervous."

"Ya don't seem to like Al much."

"Oh, that's not completely accurate, Pat. May I call ya Pat? Or do ya go by Patrick? That's not a really accurate assessment of the situation, Pat." He lifted his glass and sipped. When he lowered it again, he said coolly, "I don't like Al at all."

"Hm."

"Ya may think I'm tellin' tales out of school. But I'm an old fart, and I don't care what anybody thinks any more, and I've seen and heard a lot of things in my time, and I get tired of just lettin' those memories run round and round in my own mind, so sometimes I feel the need to pass the wisdom of the ages on to someone else. Ya know how Jack came to own the Delaware Club?"

"Uh, ya know," Lott said evasively. "I heard a few things. Rumors, like. Nothin' definite."

"Two years ago, it belonged to a guy named Larry Keane. Keane was a *schmuck*. He lost money hand over fist. He had some other business interests, on which he also lost money. He was going tits up fast. Al Thibodeaux was a friend of Keane's, and Al convinced Keane he should try the bankruptcy scam, and Al brought Jack Kilby into it. Ya know how the scam works? No? Keane went out and borrowed to the hilt from every lending institution he could, and then he made an arrangement with Kilby so that Jack took him to court and got a judgment against Keane for more than two million dollars. This was recorded in the judgment book of the county clerk's office of the superior court. A few months later, Keane declared bankruptcy. Keane's creditors were then supposed to divide up whatever assets he had left among themselves in order to recover partial payment for their debts. But Jack had a secured prior lien which legally had to come first out of whatever funds were available before any of the other creditors could get a dime. Jack was supposed to return this money to Keane after he took out his cut for helpin' him in the scam. That's the way Al arranged it with Keane. What Keane didn't know was that Al'd made a totally different arrangement with Jack, and Jack gave Keane *bupkus*. Jack took over the Delaware Club to pay off Keane's secured lien, and Al got the job he now has as a reward for screwin' his former friend."

"Sounds pretty Byzantine."

"Byzantine's Al Thibodeaux's trademark. He'd rather go around three corners to come up behind ya, stab ya in the back, and lose money in the process than meet ya face to face, shake your hand, and have ya give him a grocery sack full of newly minted bills for nothin'. He's got the loyalty of a border-town pimp and the ethics of a snake in the grass. Al raises the interesting question of how something with no backbone whatsoever can manage to stand erect—I think he does it by blood engorgement, like any other prick.

"Now Jack Kilby's a whole different kettle of fish," Murray went on. "That low-life *momser* Al's sneaky, and he thinks he's shrewd, which is what leads him to pull this pathetic chicanery. Jack's a lot more straightforward. Downright blunt. If he's got a problem with ya, he'll deal with ya right to your face, no bullshit. Ya may not want him to, but that's the way he'll handle the problem. I tried to warn him about Al after that bankruptcy scam went down, told him that anybody who'd steal for him'd steal from him, but he didn't wanna hear it. Just laughed it off, thought the whole thing was funny. Well, that's Jack's look out. He's a big boy, he can take care of himself. Ya met Jack, ya know what I mean about him."

"He's a character," Lott admitted.

"That he is! He's big and bluff, and he's a blowhard. He talks a lot of crap, but don't take most of it too seriously. He'll shoot off his mouth and run down the coloreds, and Mexicans, and Italians, and Jews, and the Polish, and women. He'll tell ya he hates fags, and he hates hippies, and everything else under the sun. But the fact of the matter is, none of those things really matter to Jack. Ya look at his businesses, and you'll see blacks and women and gays and even Jews such as myself workin' in 'em. Even runnin' 'em, sometimes. The truth is that Jack only respects one thing, and that's money. If ya make money for Jack, he doesn't care what ya are or what else ya do. He's the most completely democratic person I've ever come across. Jack doesn't care if you're Kunte Kinte and like to dress up like Little Bo Peep and fuck German shepherds—as long as ya do your job and make him money, he's gonna look the other way. But steal from him—that's the one thing ya do not *ever* wanna do. Ya don't even wanna be suspected of stealing from Jack Kilby. Kilby's a *gonif*, but he won't allow *you* to steal from *him* under any circumstances."

"I think I heard this already today," Lott said.

"Ya can't hear it enough times, believe me. Jack's serious about his money. And he's a dangerous man to cross."

"Ya seem to know a lot about these guys."

"Ohh, I've known Al and Jack for a lot of years."

"You've been working for 'em that long?"

Murray smiled ruefully. "Not workin' for 'em, no. But when you've been runnin' a book as long as I have, ya get to know a lot of people. I ran my own book here in Sacramento for thirty years. Never affiliated with anyone else, just me and a few guys under me. But Jack set up his own book in L.A. a while ago, and he started rollin' up the state, setting up a syndicate. He established books in towns that had nothin' goin' on, and he came in to towns that already had some action where he'd either buy somebody out, or swallow 'em up, or he'd go into competition and drive 'em out. When he got here to Sac, he made me an offer to merge with his operation, and I took it. I was too old to fight him, and I've only got a few years left anyway, so I figured what the hell? Workin' with Jack, I don't make quite as much as I used to when I ran it myself, but he takes some of the headaches out of it. He pays off the cops and the DA out of his nut. If we get busted, he's got lawyers on retainer. Stuff like that. There's a down side to workin' for Jack, though. Things I don't like, but Jack wants 'em done that way. I don't get involved in any of that personally, so I try not to think about it."

"Things like what?"

"Oh," Murray said, heaving a sigh. He leaned back in his chair and lit another cigarette. "Like collectin' bad debts. See, when I had my own book, I never had to worry too much about it 'cause I didn't let anybody get in too far over their head. A guy owed me a couple of hundred, he never paid me, I wrote it off to experience. And I never let him bet with me again. But I figured I could afford to lose a yard or two more than he could afford to lose a bookie who'd front him. But Jack, he says that discourages the big players. 'People who think nickel and dime, stay nickel and dime,' he says. So he tells me to raise the bar. Now we're lettin' guys go as high as a few grand before we call in their debts. If they don't pay up, Jack eats the loss. But he sends people out to get the money. It comes out of his end, but—"

Murray shrugged his shoulders fatalistically.

"Like I say, I'm an old fart, and I've only got a few more years left. It's not the way I ran the business, I never had to use no strong-arm, but it's out of my hands at this point."

Someone pounded furiously on the door, and it made both Murray and Lott jump in their seats.

"C'mon!" Thibodeaux shouted from the other side. "It's time to go!"

Lott gulped the rest of the bourbon that was left in his tumbler, set the empty glass on the desk, and stood.

"His master's voice!" Murray said, smiling wryly.

"I've gotta make the collection," Lott said apologetically.

"Sure, sure." Murray rose from his chair and walked to a filing cabinet next to the desk on the side opposite where Lott'd been sitting. He slid open the bottom drawer and removed a canvas bank bag. "I got it out of the safe earlier. I keep it in here until Al comes for it. Or until *you* come for it, if that's gonna be your job from now on."

Passing the bag to Lott, he said, "Welcome to the funhouse."

"Thanks for the drink," Lott said.

Murray waved the thanks away.

Lott took the bag to where Thibodeaux waited.

As they went to the car, Thibodeaux commented, "Ya see how many people they got comin' and goin' in this place? And only about one in five ever gets a haircut. Damned barbershops are dying right and left, put out of business by all those damned hair stylists, but this place does a land-office business if ya judge by the walk-in traffic."

They stopped at the rear of the car. Thibodeaux said, "So where's the money go?"

"In the trunk," Lott promptly replied.

"So why isn't the money there yet?"

"'Cause—you got the keys?" Lott guessed.

"Exactly right," Thibodeaux said, pulling his jingling key ring from his pocket. "You may get the hang of this yet."

There was no light in the parking lot, and Thibodeaux fumbled about as he tried to insert the key into the keyhole.

"They oughta put some hair around the damned thing so ya can find it in the dark," he muttered. "Ah, there it goes!"

Lott dropped the canvas bag beside the others, Thibodeaux slammed the trunk lid, and they drove back to Los Angeles.

CHAPTER 4

On a Monday morning in late January, Lott was finishing up at his bathroom sink when he heard a knock at the door. He ran tap water over his razor and pulled a towel off the rack to wipe his face clean of the remaining shaving cream. He left the towel draped over one shoulder as he crossed the room.

"Oh, hi, Denise," he said. Then he glanced down. Morinda stood next to her mother wearing only a disposable diaper, crushing a book against her bare chest with both hands. The bottom of her right foot rested on the side of the knee of her left leg, but she dropped the foot to the ground as soon as she saw Lott so she could dance a little jig of happiness.

"Hi, sweety," Lott said to Morinda, and he kneeled so he could speak to her face to face. "Did ya bring a book to read? Which one is it?"

He reached out to take the book from Morinda's bosom so he could see the title.

"Oh, boy!" he said, giving Morinda a sly look. "This's a good one!"

Morinda beamed at him.

"We'll read this one together, okay? Soon as I finish gettin' ready to go."

Lott stood and the joy left his face.

"What's up, Denise?"

She looked bad, Lott thought. Her skin tone was unhealthy, her face drained of color leaving it with a sallow cast to it and its flesh puffy and bloated. Her eyes were evasive, shifting from side to side and never actually coming to rest upon him even though he stood directly in front of her.

"I wanted to talk to ya. It's not about what ya think! I'm not here to ask ya for anything."

"Well, that's a first."

"I wanted to talk to ya."

Not bothering to mask his impatience, Lott said, "Ya said that already. And you're already talking to me as it is."

"Can we go in here?" She pointed beyond Lott to the interior of his room.

"Yeah, Cmon in. But I gotta tell ya, I got somebody comin' over in a few minutes, so I don't have much time."

He turned his attention to Morinda and he spoke with solemn courtesy to her. "If we don't get to read your book today, I'll make sure we get to it tomorrow, okay?"

"Oh, ya don't hafta go out of your way," Denise insisted.

Lott measured Denise with his gaze. "Yes. For her, I do."

He left the door open when the mother and child entered.

"You're always so good to Morinda, Pat. You've always been real good to her. I know ya really like her and everything. That's what I come to talk to ya about."

Lott waited.

"And she really likes you, Pat. Everybody sees that. How much she likes ya. People even ask me if you aren't her daddy."

Denise laughed, while Lott said nothing.

"'Cause of how you're so good with her, I mean. Not that anybody thinks there's anything goin' on between you and me. I don't mean that. It's just that ya get along with her so good, and ya help her with stuff, buyin' her books, and Pampers, and toys, and everything. I mean, it's like she was your own, some ways. Ya treat her better than her daddy did. Her daddy, he—well, ya know, I told ya before, he left me a few weeks after she was born, just up and ditched me. We stopped at this gas station to use the facilities, but when I got back out the car was gone with him in it. He left me there in a gas station in the ass-end of nowhere—"

"Denise—is there a point?"

"Yeah, sure there is. Sorry. I didn't mean to get off the track like that. I was thinkin' how nice ya been to Morinda, and I thought—I thought maybe you'd like to have Morinda, ya know, for your own. All the time. Ya see what I'm sayin'?"

Lott frowned in annoyance at Denise's vagueness. "No, I don't see it at all. What the hell are ya talkin' about?"

"I was wonderin' if—if maybe you'd want to take Morinda over. Like adopt her, sort of. Not a legal kind of thing, where we'd have to go through a judge and stuff. But it'd be like a real adoption. She'd be yours, and ya could have her like your own. See? And ya could—ya could maybe pay me, ya know, some money, ya see, 'cause I'd be givin' her up, I'd be havin' to do without her myself. So the money'd be for me, to pay me for havin' to do without her."

"Let me get this straight," Lott said. "What ya wanted to talk to me about is—is selling Morinda? Ya want to sell me your baby?"

"For a thousand dollars. I know ya make good money, so ya can afford it. And you'll be able to take care of her better than I ever could. And, and—"

"And ya need to get high," Lott finished for her. "And you've got nothin' else to sell. I thought you'd hit rock bottom, Denise, but ya amaze me. You've actually found some place even lower to go, a new depth to sink to."

Too exasperated to express himself, Lott fell silent and simply shook his head.

"Ya could take her clothes and stuff, too," Denise continued desperately. "That'd be part of it. I wouldn't charge no more for that."

Lott stared at Denise in consternation for several seconds, then he felt compelled to look at something else. He looked to Morinda. The little girl was following the interchange between him and Denise by turning her head from one to the other as they spoke, like a spectator at a tennis match. Her face showed how seriously she took the whole affair, leading Lott to wonder how much of what was being said Morinda understood. She couldn't yet put more than two words together in a sentence, but she had an almost uncanny grasp of what others were saying at times.

Lott raised his voice for the first time above the conversational level. "Denise—did somebody shit in your brain and forget to flush it?"

Flustered, she let her lower lip droop. "Ya don't hafta talk like that to me, Pat."

"Apparently I do. There doesn't seem to be any other way of gettin' through to you. Normal people do not go around tryin' to get rid of their kids, Denise. Normal people love their kids—they fight to keep their kids. Therefore, Denise, this whole scene's not normal. You are not normal. You are out of your fuckin' mind, is what you are."

"I came to you first, Pat," Denise said defensively. "I didn't try to sell her to some stranger or somethin'. I came to you."

"First? Ya came to me *first*? Ya mean to say you're gonna try peddlin' her around town, sellin' her to the highest bidder, or something? Is that what you're tellin' me?"

"What difference does it make to you? You don't want her, I guess."

"I don't want her? Did I hear ya say that, Denise? I don't want her?" Lott turned his face to the ceiling in an appeal, then back again to Denise. "Ya don't have a clue, do ya? Every morning ya wake up to a whole new world. It's like there's no connection with anything that's happened up to now for you. You have this beautiful baby—this girl who's so bright, she's scary. You have her, this kid who could—who could change your life, Denise. Who could make everything different for ya. Who could make you into a better person than you've ever been. Who could make you into what ya should be. If you'd only let her do it. And she could do it, Denise, if you'd only do for her what ya should be doin'. If ya could pull your head away from that crack pipe long enough to see what ya have here."

"That's easy for you to say, Pat. You, with your good job, and the money ya make, and everything. Me? I got nothin'. What can I give her, Pat? I got nothin' even for myself. So what can I give her?"

"Always puttin' yourself first, aren't ya, Denise? Ya know, if ya tried puttin' Morinda first and yourself second, you'd find that ya both come out way ahead."

"I can't even get Welfare for her, Pat, ya know that. She's got no birth certificate, no Social Security card, nothin'. And that's what I got—nothin'," Denise averred stubbornly. "Morinda's got nothin'. And ya add nothin' and nothin' together and ya got a whole lot more a nothin'. And I don't wanna live like that. Not no more. I can't do it. I gotta find some other way."

"I'll tell ya another way, Denise."

"What's that?"

"Stop smokin' that fuckin' rock! Stop fuckin' guys for money! Get a job! Take some responsibility! Act like Morinda's mother! Like the mother she deserves!"

"I am her mother, and I do the best I can for her! But I can't do it no more!"

"I don't have time for this Denise! I got things to do today! I got people who count on me to be where I say I'll be, when I say I'll be there! So you're just gonna hafta take care of your problems on your own! And I'd better not hear about you tryin' to sell Morinda to one of those dope fiends ya hang out with!"

Morinda listened intently to the debate until the two adults started to yell, and then she stepped away, turned her back, and covered her ears with her hands, shaking her head from side to side in an effort to exorcise the demons. She ran across the room to the far wall, and then, when the noise of the angry voices didn't abate, she dashed to the door. She was already outside when Lott saw her fleeing.

"Go take care of your kid, Denise!" he commanded, pushing her ahead of him by her shoulders, sending her in the same direction Morinda'd gone. "And make sure nothin' happens to her!" he called to Denise's back.

Morinda came to a stop on the walkway fifteen feet away. She still had her hands over her ears. She looked terror-stricken, and she stood on one foot at a time, hopping from one leg to the other. Denise went to her and picked her up, tucking Morinda under one arm to carry her away. Morinda refused to cooperate, making her whole body stiff, not relaxing a muscle. Denise lugged the weight of her child to the stairwell and started down.

Lott stood in his doorway to watch them go, and at that moment Thibodeaux appeared on the landing. He passed Denise and Morinda on the way, and he cast a puzzled glance backward as he came into Lott's view. When he got to where Lott waited, he scratched his ear and said, "Was that the same kid I saw over here before?"

"Yeah," Lott answered sourly. "And the mother."

"Trouble in paradise?"

"Same as it ever was. I'm ready to get the hell out of here, Al. When do we roll?"

"Not gonna be any 'we' about it, *amigo*. Ya been promoted. As of today. You're no longer my assistant. Now you're chief cook and bottle washer—the whole shootin' match. You're gonna take care of the Highway 99 run all on your lonesome. Is your car runnin'?"

"Yeah, sure. Why the change in plans?"

"Got some problems in the east. I'm gonna hafta fill in for the guys who usually do San Berdoo and Riverside. And we can't blow it off and let the money accumulate, not the day after Super Bowl Sunday. All the bets are gonna be paid off, and the cash flow's gonna be a flood. We gotta pick up the extra and bring it back alive. Don't wanna leave that kinda money layin' around. It's too much of a temptation for some people. So ya make the run up north, same as we always do, 'cept this time you're on your own."

"Okay."

Lott bent to pick up the book Morinda'd dropped during his dispute with Denise. It was *The Little Engine That Could*. He tossed it to the side so that it fell in a plastic crate filled with toys he'd bought to keep on hand for Morinda whenever she came to visit.

"You're not gonna be comin' back tonight," Thibodeaux said. "You'll stay up in Sac and drive home tomorrow. That way ya can get today's receipts on the way up, and whatever comes in before ya get there tomorrow on the way back down. There's a room already reserved for ya. Here's the name and address of the motel." He handed a slip of paper to Lott, who tucked it into a pocket in his pants. "Make sure ya stay where I'm sendin' ya, Pat. Don't go cancelin' the reservation there and headin' off someplace else. I need to know where ya are if I wanna get hold of ya."

"Okay."

Thibodeaux looked at Lott sidelong. "Don't mess this up, Pat. Make everyone of the stops. Keep the money in the trunk. Ya stay tonight at the place I told ya."

"Right."

"And I want ya to call me from Sac. As soon as ya get to the motel. Not before, not after, but as soon as, so I know everything's okay."

"Got it."

"There's no phones in the rooms at this place I'm sendin' ya. You'll need to use a pay phone. Find one around the motel. Not someplace else. Right around the motel. Make sure ya do."

"Will do, Al."

"This's your big chance to prove your worth. Don't choke in the clutch, Pat."

"Ya can count on me, Al."

"I hope so."

Lott made the collections along Highway 99. It was dark when he finally got to the end of the run in Sacramento, and he was exhausted from the day-long drive. It was with a sense of relief that he pulled into the parking lot in front of Murray and Walt's barbershop for the last pick-up of the day. The same collection of loquacious loafers as always were inside: some of their faces changed from week to week, but the conversation never did. No one paid Lott any special attention when he entered.

"Hey, Walt," one of the idlers asked. "I been wondering—why's this the only barbershop in the world that's open on Mondays?"

"'Cause if I let you guys go two days without payin' what ya drop here, I'd never see any of it. None of you'd have two nickels to rub together if I gave ya an extra fifteen minutes to bet it at another book."

"How much'd ya lose, Dave?"

"Lose? I didn't lose nothin'! All I did was pay tuition. For my education. It cost me six hundred clams to learn never—ever—to trust those pathetic dirtbags to win the big game. They've broken my heart for the last time. I've learned my lesson well. No more! Never again!"

"A better lesson to learn from this's never to bet on a team with no defense. Great offense and no defense equals many disappointed fans. Wailing and the gnashing of teeth. Alas! Alackaday!"

"So how much'd you come out ahead? Ya must've made out like a fat rat."

"I did better than you, which's as much as I'm prepared to disclose about the state of my finances. Ya see, the trick to success is: always bet on the winnin' team. Otherwise, ya lose."

"Gee, why didn't I think of that? That must be what I've been doin' wrong up to now. Since ya put it that way, it's so obvious."

"No—don't thank me. If I'd known it'd take so little to set ya right, I would've done it years ago."

"God, I hate it when you win! Ya get so damned smug! Fortunately, it only happens about once in a lifetime, so I probably won't ever hafta listen to ya gloat again."

Lott had to admit Thibodeaux was right about one thing: nothing ever changed at the Sacramento book.

He stuck his head in long enough to say hello to Murray, take the bank bag out of the file cabinet, refuse a drink, ask directions to the address

Thibodeaux'd given him for the motel at which he was supposed to have a reservation, and leave.

He drove to a section of frontage road that paralleled the highway that had green road signs advertising it as "Motel Row," a one-sided street filled with garish neon signs lit up in bright, primary colors.

"Cheap bastard!" he muttered to himself as he passed the Flamingo Lodge, the motel where Thibodeaux'd gotten him a reservation.

Lott pulled into a space at the curb, took the key from the ignition, and stepped out on the sidewalk. The neon lights gave the atmosphere a weird, otherworldly glow. He didn't bother going to the office to check in; he was supposed to find a pay phone nearby to let Thibodeaux know he'd arrived.

The only public phone he could see was two blocks up from where he left his car. It was an actual booth, like those Superman used, and it stood outside a vacant building that was once a restaurant, its large windows now covered with sheets of plywood splashed with spray-painted graffiti. The glass that'd formed the walls of the booth'd long since been smashed out; the panels on the sides were empty.

Lott was three steps from it when a dark figure advancing from the other direction moved out of the shadows next to the deserted restaurant and snaked into the booth ahead of him. It was a Mexican teenager wearing a silver and black Raider's jacket with his hair slicked straight back from his forehead and held in place by a hair net. He used the phone booth only for its interior light, which for some reason'd never been vandalized. He used it to read a slip of paper and jot further notes on it with a pencil.

Lott looked up and down the street, trying to spot another phone. There were none visible. He started walking, but'd only gone a block when he decided to retrace his steps and try his luck the other way.

At an alley several blocks from the motel, they were waiting for him. There were two of them, and before Lott could tell what was happening, they'd dragged him off the street and into the darkness. The taller one stood in front of him while a complicated piece of metal he carried in his hand flashed and clicked; it took only a second before it folded in upon itself and then back out again. When it'd gone through its metamorphosis, Lott recognized it as a butterfly knife. The man held it so the tip of its blade was less than an inch from Lott's eye. Though his mind was focused on the blade that gleamed in the half-light, Lott couldn't help but notice the homemade tattoos on the back of the hand that wielded it: the standard three dots which stood for "*Mi Vida Loca*," or "My Crazy Life"; a *pachuco* cross, being a Latin cross with four detached oblique rays emanating from the arms; and a large 13.

Lott spun on his heel preparing to make a run for the lighted street, but the other one'd circled behind him. He dangled a man's sock halfway to the ground; it had an ominous bulge at the bottom. When the man with the sock began to spin the weighted end, Lott realized it could be used as a sap to knock him senseless.

"My wallet's got about twenty-five dollars in it," Lott said. "There's some gasoline credit cards and a Visa card in there, too. The watch's a Timex. Let's make this easy on everybody, okay? It's a pain in the ass gettin' another license, so if you'd just leave the ID with me . . ."

"The car, *ese*," the tall one with the knife said.

"You're gonna jack my car?" Lott asked incredulously. "Are you guys new at this? My car's a six-year-old shitbox."

"Ya got the keys?"

Lott put out his right hand with the fingers splayed so the thugs could see he was doing nothing threatening, then he slowly eased his fingers into his pocket and withdrew his key ring. He held it toward the man with the knife so that it hung by his forefinger.

The one with the sock spoke in Spanish to his partner: "Which *carrucha, carnal*? We didn't see him come in, *ese*." Lott spoke Castilian Spanish fluently, and he mentally translated all the words he understood into English.

"Which one's your ride?" the man with the knife said to Lott in English.

"Sure, right. It's the—"

Lott stopped himself in mid-sentence when he realized his best chance for survival was not to identify the car for his attackers while he was still at their mercy in the dark alley, but to actually take them out on the street where they'd be much less likely to kill him.

"It's over here by the curb." Lott turned so he was facing the street. "I can show it to you."

"He said to get everything out of the trunk," the man with the sock-sap said to his partner in Spanish.

Lott was prepared to give them the car in exchange for his life, but a warning signal flashed inside his mind when he heard the *cholo* specify the trunk. How did they know there was anything of value there? And who was the "he" who'd told them to clean it out?

"Get the keys," the man who was now behind Lott carrying the knife said to his partner.

The sap-wielding man took the cluster of keys from Lott. Metal tinkled against metal as he fingered through them looking for the square-headed one that went to the ignition and the matching round-headed one that went to the trunk.

The tip of the knife poked Lott in the back, an inch above his belt. "Let's go find the car, *ese*," the one with the knife said in English, "and don't give us any shit."

The three exited the alley together and moved down the sidewalk. That was when the teenager in the Raider's jacket wearing the hair net who'd snaked the phone booth from him stepped out with his hands in his jacket pockets and started toward the group made up of Lott and the two thugs who'd accosted him. He strutted in an exaggerated manner as though his body's center of gravity'd been surgically altered by shifting his hips forward three inches and his shoulders back half a foot in the *cholo* stroll affected by Mexican gang members. As he approached, he squinted, frowned, and cocked his head to the side to study the group ahead of him. When he was ten feet away, he removed his hands from his pockets and began flashing gang signs at the others. His fingers twisted and bent in bizarre shapes as he turned them up, down, and to the sides.

The men escorting Lott stopped; the firm grip they kept on Lott's arms brought him to an abrupt halt as well. The man with the sap let Lott's elbow go and he stepped away. He dropped the sock filled with sand he'd been using to intimidate Lott and raised his own hands with the fingers dangling limply, as if he was about to throw hand signals back.

"Don't signify, *ese*," the one with the knife admonished his companion. When the other replied, he spoke in *caló*, a bastardized mixture of Spanish, English, and street slang, and the conversation between the thugs continued in argot. Lott understood some of what was being bantered back and forth, but there were many things he could only guess at.

"Man, I'm not letting this *pinche cabrón* throw his bad looks at us and then signify without givin' it back to him! I hate these *pinche norteños*, man!"

"Let it pass, man," the one holding the knife said. "We're not in L.A. This *puto* could have his *compas* around. We gotta job to do, we don't wanna hafta mess with his *clica*, too."

The boy wearing the hair net who was confronting them grew impatient when they didn't respond. He took another pace closer, snapped his chin up, and called out, "*Donde?*" which Lott translated as, "Where are you from?"

The one who'd had the sand-filled sock strutted two steps toward the other *cholo*, stopped, and said, "*Doscientos trece*," he said, identifying the 213 area code that covered central and east Los Angeles. "*Y'que?*" "What are ya gonna do about it?"

The boy in the hair net sneered, and almost spit out the words in *caló*, "*Catorce rifa!*" "Fourteen rules!" Then, without warning, he reached beneath his Raider's jacket and brought a revolver from the waistband of his baggy khaki pants.

The one who'd so ostentatiously been swinging the sand-filled sock only a few minutes before also reached under his outer clothes and drew out a pistol, this one a semiautomatic.

Lott froze in place. The barrel of the gun in the hand of the boy with the hair net came up, and Lott dropped to the ground and wrapped his arms around his head. A gun blasted more times than Lott could count, and with each crash that echoed along the empty street, Lott expected to feel the searing heat of a bullet ripping through him. But he felt nothing. He winced at each shot, and his hands shook from fear, but he experienced no pain. He could smell the acrid cordite from the expended shells, and he was deafened by the sound, but he was unharmed as far as he could tell.

The shots came in rapid succession, then abruptly the reports ended. Lott kept his head covered for what seemed like a long time. When he finally dared to look up, he saw the hair-netted man still standing in place, smoke curling from the snub-nosed barrel of the pistol in his hand. The two who'd been intent upon mugging him seconds before now lay crumpled like dolls abandoned on the sidewalk. The one who'd pulled his own gun to defend himself never got off a shot.

The *cholo* wearing the hair net swung the muzzle of his revolver toward Lott. He held it trained on him, saying nothing. Lott awaited death, the same death that'd been dealt to the punks who lay on either side of him, but for some reason even he couldn't explain since he never consciously considered making an act of obeisance in order to save his life, he met the eyes of the gunman and said, "*Catorce rifa.*"

The last remaining *cholo,* apparently accepting this as a suitable act of homage, said, "You got *that* right, motherfucker," dropped the gun down by his side, turned, and ran from the scene.

Lott pushed himself to his feet. He glanced at the bodies on the sidewalk, and he bent to retrieve the keys that were clutched in the fingers of the dead gangbanger. Only then did he glance around to see what sort of attention the shooting might've attracted.

No one came out on the street from any of the nearby buildings; there wasn't a living soul to be seen on the street in either direction.

Lott gave only a second's thought to the matter, and he decided the best thing for him to do was to get as far away, as fast as he could.

He stumbled to his car in a daze. He slumped in the front seat behind the steering wheel in a state of near stupefaction. He'd never before come so close to being killed. He'd previously been mugged twice, but neither of those experiences left him feeling as wrung out, as drained, as empty, as the attempt this evening. He knew he should call Thibodeaux and tell him what'd occurred, explain why he wasn't staying in Sacramento at the motel he'd been ordered to go to, but he'd had enough: he planned to return to Los Angeles immediately, take the money to Thibodeaux as soon as he possibly could, and quit this job.

No more, he told himself, no more of this for me.

CHAPTER 5

Lott headed to the freeway on-ramp, then took the turn-off to Interstate 5 going south, which'd be faster than returning to Los Angeles by Highway 99. He passed the job of driving to the lower parts of his brain that controlled autonomic motor functions while the upper levels of his mind grappled with the meaning of what'd occurred earlier.

The two *cholos*, or Mexican gang members, who'd set upon him in the alley were from Los Angeles, probably members of the 18th Street Gang, the largest Hispanic street gang in the country and far more numerous than the better-advertised Crips and Bloods. The Mexican gangs in California split neatly into two geographical groups: those in the south, who wore blue and identified themselves with the number 13, and those in the north, who wore red and identified themselves with the number 14. The dividing line between them took place at about McFarland, a small farming community in the Central Valley. As the interaction between the three *cholos* showed, the opposing sides despised each other. So what were the two *sureños* doing so far from their home base, intruding deep into *norteño* territory in order to pull a simple mugging and car-jacking?

And how'd they know he was carrying anything worth stealing? And know exactly where it was, in the trunk of his car? Had they been watching him and Thibodeaux coming and going from the bookmakers for the past few weeks, planning on ripping them off, perhaps even scheming to make the big score after the collection following the Super Bowl, when the greatest take of the year'd be available? Even if that were the case, how'd

55

they know he'd be stopping at this particular motel? They might've trailed him from the barbershop after he made his last pick up, but the assault'd been prearranged, it seemed to Lott, not just opportunistic happenstance. They'd been waiting for him in the alley, and they couldn't've followed him or they'd've known what his car looked like. So they must've known ahead of time where he was going to be, and they'd prepared an ambush.

Then there was their weapons. They'd used a knife and a sock-sap when they accosted him in the alley, but the one'd been carrying an expensive semiautomatic pistol he'd drawn only when he was threatened by the revolver of the rival *norteño* gang member. Why use such crude and unreliable devices when they had at least one semiautomatic pistol in their possession?

An answer to this question entered his mind as though another person'd whispered it into his ear: *In case anything went wrong.*

Lott shook his head, wondering: What the hell does that mean? But he figured it out without any further prompting from his subconscious. The two *cholos*'d been told to rely on the unsophisticated weaponry they carried rather than guns in case the plot went awry and Lott escaped alive. Then he'd be able to say only that he'd been mugged on the street by a couple of punks. On the other hand, if everything went as planned, Lott was to be killed so he could say nothing at all to anyone, ever again. The money he carried'd disappear, as would Lott, and it'd seem that he—who'd only worked for Jack Kilby for a few months, and only entrusted with the important job of collecting the large sums of cash due to an emergency situation that'd arisen so that Thibodeaux was forced to rely on Kilby's young protégé—had succumbed to the temptation to make off with it. And that'd explain why Lott—and the money—were never seen again.

Lott's imagination obligingly provided him the scenario of Thibodeaux breaking the bad news: "No, Jack, the son-of-a-bitch didn't come back. Took off with the cash, is what it looks like. Probably headed to the Caribbean. I always told ya—remember me sayin' it, Jack?—that ya couldn't trust him. I never wanted ya to stick me with that *putz*, but you insisted, Jack. He's some guy ya met in a bar, and it turns out he's a low-life rip-off artist. Well, live and learn, huh, Jack?"

The more he thought about it, the more convinced he became that Thibodeaux'd set him up as a patsy. Only Thibodeaux knew where Lott was going to be after making his collections that day. "Make sure ya stay where I'm sendin' ya, Pat," Thibodeaux'd said. "Don't go cancelin' the reservation there and headin' off someplace else. I need to know where ya are if I wanna get hold of ya."

"But there aren't any phones in the rooms at the motel ya sent me to, Al," Lott said aloud to himself. "How were ya gonna get hold of me? Jesus, I didn't even think of that till now!"

More memories arose in his mind: "He said to get everything out of the trunk," the one *cholo*'d told the other. Who else could've given those instructions besides Al Thibodeaux? "He's got all the loyalty of a border-town pimp and the ethics of a snake in the grass," Murray'd told him once, describing Thibodeaux.

"If I'd only listened to ya, Murray," Lott said.

So what he'd have to do was take the money directly to Jack Kilby when he got to L.A., and tell Kilby everything he'd figured out about Thibodeaux. How Thibodeaux'd planned to rip Kilby off and fix the blame on Lott, the new guy. He'd explain that Thibodeaux thought he'd get away with it because he'd proved himself loyal to Kilby by helping him get title to the Delaware Club, while Lott'd be the scapegoat for the theft since he'd only been working for Kilby for a short time. "You've gotta see it, Jack—you think you're runnin' Al, but Al's runnin' you," he'd tell him.

He knew the plan was hopeless as soon as he formulated it. Another memory intervened, a memory of Thibodeaux telling him who'd be assigned the blame for any fiscal irregularities: "Well, it could be the guy who runs the book, who's been workin' with Jack for umpteen years and has never taken a penny that he didn't have comin' to him, just this one time made a mistake. Or maybe Sid, who's been workin' for Jack since about ninety years before God was born and has never, ever, come up missin' a red cent, suddenly lost his mind and ran amok. Or it could be that you, who've only been workin' for Jack for all of a few months and are therefore so far down the food chain that you are plankton—and I mean by that that you are an absolute bottom feeder and lower than pond scum, should push ever come to shove—it could be that you, my friend, will take the rap. I hope ya understand me when I say this."

His heart sinking, Lott muttered to himself, "Yeah, Al, I understand ya when ya say that. Translation: I'm fucked. No matter what I do, I'm screwed, blued, and tattooed."

If he took the money to Kilby, by-passing Thibodeaux in the chain-of-command, and told Kilby his story, he wouldn't be believed. The whole thing'd be dismissed as a paranoid fantasy. And then Thibodeaux'd have a grudge against Lott that'd virtually guarantee that Lott'd be killed. He might be allowed to live for a few more months, or even years, but if he stayed working for Kilby, Thibodeaux'd sooner or later get rid of him. He'd scarcely avoided death this very night, how could he hope to steer clear of it when Thibodeaux had all the time in the world to act? He was a dead man if he stayed in L.A., Lott knew, if he remained working for Jack Kilby in any capacity. Even if he said nothing to Kilby, and acted as though nothing strange'd occurred during his time in Sacramento, Thibodeaux'd know that Lott knew who was behind the plot, and it'd only be a matter of time before Thibodeaux eliminated the problem. Lott'd have to live out his final days waiting for the axe to fall. It wasn't a pleasant future to look forward to.

He could think of only one alternative: take the money and run. Run fast and run far. With the money in the trunk of his car, he'd have a chance to hide himself, something he'd never be able to do if he played it straight. There was certainly a risk in stealing from Jack Kilby, he knew, but he muttered to himself, "There's a risk either way. I may as well be hanged for a sheep as a goat."

By the time he got back to his motel, his decision'd been made.

When Lott pulled into the parking lot, he slowed only enough to avoid hitting the masonry half-columns that were set on either side of the entrance. His car bounced twice as the front wheels and then the back passed over the speed bump. After he cleared the obstruction, he pressed the gas pedal and accelerated, screeching to a halt in the empty parking space nearest the stairwell. The night manager, a short Asian man with his hair trimmed in a sugar-bowl haircut who wore black-framed eyeglasses, stuck his head over the counter in the office like a baby bird importuning its parents for a worm to see what was causing the disturbance, and then stood and put his face nearer the glass barrier to get a better look. Lott ignored him. He got out and quickly went around to open the trunk, from which he scooped the canvas bank bags into his arms, then elbowed the trunk lid shut before jogging to the stairwell and up the steps.

Once in his room, he dumped the bags on the bed, locked the door behind him, then slid the security chain in place. He grabbed a paring knife from the kitchenette and pierced a hole in one of the canvas sacks. The knife wasn't sharp enough to saw through the thick material, so he tried a bread knife, slid it into the hole the paring knife'd started, and hacked a ragged line around in a complete circle. Then, holding the container upside down, he dumped the contents out. Bundles of bills of different thicknesses, from half an inch to three inches, held together with rubber bands, poured out. Some of the bundles held fives, some tens, most of them twenties, fifties, and hundreds.

He used the two knives to slash open the rest of the bank bags, and poured what they held on top of the pile. It made a pyramid two feet high, the base of which covered the bedspread of the queen-size bed.

From the closet, he brought out a several suitcases. He pulled clothes from their hangers, folded them without much care, and stuffed them in one of the bags. He took a smaller case into the bathroom. He slid his hand along the top of the medicine chest, scooping the pill bottles off and into the open mouth of the case he held to catch the falling items. Once the top was cleared, he flipped the mirror door open to do the same to the three shelves inside.

In the middle of his manic burst of activity, he was brought up short.

He thought he heard someone knock. He stood in silence, not moving, just listening.

Three taps sounded again, definitely coming from his door.

He left the small suitcase sitting on the sink and took one step forward so he was in the frame of the bathroom door and could see across the room.

The first thought that entered his mind was: Thibodeaux!

Thibodeaux knew where he lived. If Thibodeaux now knew the rip-off'd failed, and that Lott was still alive and in possession of the cash, he might've sent someone to watch Lott's motel in case he showed up here. And if that was true, then Lott was about to be dead. There was only one way out of the room, and that was through the door.

But if there were killers outside, Lott reasoned, why were they so polite as to knock first? They'd have to've seen his car downstairs, seen the light on in his room, so why didn't they simply kick the door in and enter with guns blazing? It made no sense.

The more he thought about it, the more he doubted that killers sent by Thibodeaux lurked outside. Maybe the motel manager'd come to give Lott a warning about racing so recklessly through the parking lot.

He moved stealthily across the room, pausing long enough to throw the bedspread over the pile of money, then went to the corner and pressed himself against the wall next to the door.

"Who is it?" he called.

He heard a muffled voice, but couldn't make out what it said. The voice was too high-pitched to be anything other than a woman's.

"Who?" he asked a second time.

The voice, slightly more amplified, said, "It's me—Denise from downstairs."

Lott warily opened the door as far as the slack of the chain latch allowed.

Denise stood outside. She was alone. She didn't look at Lott. Her eyes glanced anxiously about, turning from one side of the walkway to the other on either side of the door. Her hair looked as though she'd slept on it so that it had a wild, thick clump sticking off to one side in a cowlick.

"I don't need this shit right now," he muttered to himself as he slipped the chain lock, making no attempt to keep Denise from overhearing him. Once the door was fully open, Lott demanded, "Whattaya want this time?"

"Hey," Denise began, "sorry to bother ya. I know it's real late, and everything. But I saw ya drive in, and—"

"Yeah, and I'm about to head right back out again," Lott said with undisguised truculence. "What is it?"

"Well, ya see—ya see, it's Morinda."

Lott scowled. "What about her? Is she sick?"

"No, no. It's not like that."

"Did ya leave her alone in the bathtub again, Denise? To come up here? 'Cause I swear to God, I—"

"No, no. She's in the room. She's okay. She's asleep. She's sleepin'. everythings okay with her, honest."

"Then what's it about? I haven't got all night."

"I wanted . . ." she began, but her voice faltered. Her pupil-less Little-Orphan-Annie eyes gave her the appearance of a madwoman. She shifted them to the right as she gathered her courage to get to her point. "I wanted to see if maybe you'd—ya know, changed your mind? About what we talked 'bout this mornin'. It was this mornin', wasn't it? Or this afternoon, I guess, maybe."

Lott was flabbergasted. So much'd taken place since his conversation with Denise earlier that day that he could find no place to focus, no point of reference to grasp what it was she was alluding to. He simply stared at her in complete bafflement, waiting for her to connect what she was talking about with something that made sense. But she offered him nothing else to go on.

"Look, Denise, my time has some value, even if yours doesn't. Whattaya want? Spit it out and let me get the hell out of here, will ya?"

"About Morinda," she said, finally turning her eyes to look fixedly at him, though Lott couldn't be certain what she could actually see with them: they were circles the size of dimes of nearly pure blue. "I know ya said ya didn't want, didn't wanna—ya know, to buy her from me when I asked ya before. But, ya know, I thought maybe you'd had enough time to think about it and maybe have a change of heart. 'Cause you'd give her a better home than I can, is what I thought. That maybe you'd reconsidered it and everything, like."

Only then did Lott recall distinctly Denise's proposal to him that morning that he buy Morinda from her. Lott stared at her while his mind churned. He began to formulate his feelings in words, preparing what he'd say, but the only thing he could articulate on the spur of the moment was the prefatory remark, "Anybody who wants to sell their own kid . . ." He could get that far, but he couldn't complete the thought. One part of him wanted to finish with the ultimate put-down, an absolutely crushing *bon mot*, but there was another part of his mind that urged a different response, something he couldn't quite translate into words. There was something he intended to say after that, but it wouldn't come. "Anyone who wants to sell their own kid . . ." The same phrase circled round and round in his mind, though the sentence'd arrive at no conclusion.

Then, like the ball falling into the slot of a spinning roulette wheel, he knew what he was trying to say: "Anyone who wants to sell their own kid," it suddenly occurred to him, "*should*."

Aloud, he said in a staid, measured manner far different from the harried tone he'd used before, "All right, Denise."

"So ya think—?"

"Yeah, Denise, yeah. Ya want me to take Morinda? For a thousand dollars? You're on. It's a deal."

"Yeah?"

"Yeah. She's downstairs, ya said? Go get her. Bring her to me. Bring anything of hers you're not gonna need anymore. Diapers, her bottle, her toys, her clothes. Put everything in a box. Oh, and the car seat I bought for her, too. Bring that out. Leave it there by my car."

"The money," Denise said. "I told ya—I told ya a thousand, didn't I? A thousand. Ya have that—ya have that much—ya have that much with ya? Ya got it now?"

"Oh, yeah. I've got it. In cash."

"Hold on," she said. "Hold on. I'll go get her. You wait here. I'll be right back. Wait right here, right here. I'll be back—"

She vanished from his sight, but he could hear her shoes clattering along the walkway and then banging on the steps of the stairs.

Lott closed the door and returned to the bed. He tossed the bedspread aside and began stuffing the bundles of bills into an empty suitcase. He kept out a stack of hundreds, and from that he counted out twenty bills that he laid on the wooden table by the window. The rest of the bundle he shoved in his pants pocket. Then he carefully closed the clasps on his luggage and took the two cases to the car. He opened the trunk and placed them inside. Denise was hauling a cardboard box filled with Morinda's things from her room, walking backward while the bottom of the box dragged on the ground. She got it to where Lott waited for her, and he picked it up and put in the trunk along with his luggage.

"Is that everything?" he asked.

"'Cept for the car seat," Denise said. "I'll get that in a second."

"Okay. Be sure ya do. I'm gonna need it. Just put it in the front seat, and come to my room. I'll pay ya then."

He didn't even bother looking at Denise as he spoke. He turned and walked away.

Lott did a fast search of his room to make sure he wasn't leaving anything important behind, but he found nothing he couldn't easily replace. He heard Denise downstairs opening the door of his car, and then closing it. A few minutes later he heard her hustling up the stairs. She entered the room with a sleeping Morinda draped over her shoulder. Morinda hung almost in half, her head and torso and both limp arms dangling behind Denise, and her bare legs suspended in front. Lott took the toddler as soon as Denise brought her into the room. Morinda didn't awaken.

"Where's—where's the money?" Denise asked.

"Right there."

Lott pointed toward the table.

Denise twisted her head to see it, took one quick step in its direction, then slowed her pace. She approached the money with much less alacrity than her previous eagerness would've led Lott to expect. She went to the money like a pilgrim to a shrine, almost reverentially.

"Is that it?" she asked, without yet having touched it. "The whole thousand?"

"I decided not to pay ya a thousand, Denise. I'm gonna make it two. Two thousand dollars. Two whole grand. To make things fair."

"Two thousand?" she said.

He didn't so much as nod his head, and she didn't take her eyes from the money to look at him.

"Two thousand?" she repeated in a low, hushed tone. This time she reached out to touch the bills. She leafed through them.

"Ya know why I'm givin' ya twice what ya asked for, Denise? Ya remember the last time?"

"What—?"

"It means, Denise, that you should never—ever—ask for Morinda back. There won't be any refunds or exchanges on this deal. Don't ever expect to have Morinda again. Once ya take that money, Denise, Morinda's mine. That's why it's two grand, Denise, instead of one. Ya take that money, don't come to me later and tell me ya changed your mind. Don't think I'll give Morinda up after this. Ya understand that?"

"Yeah." She cleared her throat. "Yes. I understand."

"So—there's the money."

"Okay," Denise said. She folded the bills in her fist, gave a last glance toward Morinda asleep in Lott's arms, and said, "I've gotta get somewhere."

"Don't let me stand in your way."

She left Lott's room and scurried down the stairs.

Lott waited a decent interval, enough time to allow Denise to get out of sight, and then he turned off the lights in his room, carried Morinda to the car, put her in the car seat, and left.

He drove to the freeway where, once he got to an on-ramp, he turned the car to the south, heading for San Diego and the border.

PART TWO

CHAPTER 1

He was following them again.

He was a year or two older than the girls, perhaps fifteen or sixteen. He was tall and slim, with broad shoulders, his wavy black hair combed back from his high forehead, and his face graced with classically carved features. He followed Morinda and her friend Maria Elena as they strolled through San Estaban, just as he'd done the last few times they'd come to town. He always stayed far enough behind them so that he could believe he was being inconspicuous and that the two girls hadn't noticed him, but they'd spotted him and remarked on him from the first.

"There he is," Morinda told her friend in Spanish.

"I know," Maria Elena said, also in Spanish. "I saw him a minute ago when we went by the car lot. He slowed down when you stopped to write something in the dust on that car's windshield so he wouldn't have to go past us. My sister says his name is Felipe."

The two girls looked very much alike, although Morinda's black hair was longer; Maria Elena's fell below her waist, but Morinda's went nearly to her knees, and Morinda was slightly taller than Maria Elena besides.

"What is it you do that gets these boys to follow you through the streets this way?" Morinda said.

"Me?" Maria Elena cried. "It's you! He's following *you*!"

Morinda gave her friend a meaningful look. "All I know is that every time I see him, I'm with you."

"Well, every time *I* see him, I'm with *you*!"

Their reciprocal accusations set them both giggling until Morinda's face grew serious and she said, "Come on! Let's go in here!" in a breathless rush.

They were passing in front of the CONASUPO, one of the government-owned supermarkets to be found in the smaller communities in Mexico. The town of San Estaban on the Pacific coast of Baja Norte where they lived was too small to support one of the larger CONASUPERs, so it had to make do with the scaled-down version. Morinda grabbed Maria Elena's arm and tugged her into the store. They ducked to the side and peered out the picture window at the street beyond.

"Is he coming?" Morinda asked.

"I can't tell. I think—I think he's over there, still walking. Is that him? Going by the sign?"

"Maybe. I don't see him anyplace else. It must be."

Maria Elena's eyes grew big and she said, "I just remembered! I have to get that soap my mother wanted."

"Then get it!" Morinda said. "Go on! I'll wait here and keep watch."

Maria Elena went down one of the aisles and vanished.

Morinda waited by the window, her face an inch from the glass, her gaze fixed on the street outside so that she didn't notice the American man and woman when they entered the store behind her. She glanced at them only when she heard them speaking English to one another, then quickly snapped her head around so her face was hidden as soon as she recognized the couple as the Blowfelds.

"I hope whoever runs the meat department here knows how to cut a T-bone steak," Mrs. Blowfeld complained, as she was wont to do. "I can't believe these people! When we went to that butcher shop, that what-do-they-call-it?"

"*Carnicería*," Mr. Blowfeld said.

"Yeah, that. And the man there didn't have a clue what I was talkin' about. Calls himself a butcher, and he doesn't know what a T-bone steak is! And the meat they sell—lean, tough. I can't believe they get away with it!"

"It's an international disgrace, Martha, that's what it is." He spoke as if he were above it all. "They think they can do things their own way just because it's their own country."

"I've got to find some meat for a change, Steve. All this fish we've been eatin' since we've been here! I've got to eat some red meat." They'd paused inside the door to banter back and forth the shortcomings of Mexico. Morinda kept her back to the couple, hoping they'd leave soon so she could escape. But Mrs. Blowfeld asked her husband, "What are all these skulls and skeletons and evil, nasty things, anyway? Is it for Halloween?" She was pointing at the decorations taped to the store's window facing outward. Mr. and Mrs. Blowfeld took several steps closer to Morinda.

"The Day of the Dead, Martha," Mr. Blowfeld said. "It's a big deal here. It's on November first."

"Why'd they have a holiday the day after Halloween? It doesn't make any sense."

"It's like *Cinco de Mayo*, Martha. They celebrate the Fourth of July on the wrong day of the wrong month, and they can't get Halloween right, either. Wrong day of the wrong month. I think I see a pattern developing. Maybe Mexicans are calendrically challenged. That should be looked into."

The Blowfelds'd been in San Estaban only a week; they were staying at the RV park Morinda's father owned, and Morinda'd seen and heard enough of them that she had them pegged: Mrs. Blowfeld was one of those *norteamericano turistas* who disliked everything about Mexico and the Mexican people, and who groused continually about every little thing that was different from the way they were at home, leading Morinda to wonder why she didn't stay where she'd come from. Mrs. Blowfeld's ignorance of the customs and traditions of the country she was visiting were abysmal. Mr. Blowfeld, on the other hand, always had a cryptic half-smile on his face. He was far more intelligent than his wife, and though he always seemed to support her steady stream of captious remarks, he never initiated any himself. Morinda sometimes had the idea that Mr. Blowfeld was laughing up his sleeve at his wife's stupidity, but at other times he appeared to be wholeheartedly endorsing her rude, shallow comments. Morinda thought that if she could ever be certain that Mr. Blowfeld was being sardonic, she might've liked him; but because she couldn't tell for sure whether he was secretly amused at his wife or was in full agreement with her, she mistrusted him as much as she detested Mrs. Blowfeld.

Then the words Morinda dreaded most to hear issue from Mrs. Blowfeld's lips came:

"Don't I know you?" she asked sharply.

Morinda had to acknowledge Mrs. Blowfeld then; Mrs. Blowfeld had her cornered. Morinda turned and smiled weakly at the woman but said nothing.

"I know ya, don't I? Ya work at the RV park."

"She was at Snidely Whiplash, too," her husband observed.

"That's right. Ya were workin' at the bar the other day." Mrs. Blowfeld narrowed her eyes suspiciously and demanded, "Don't they have child labor laws in this country?"

"Child labor laws?" Morinda asked innocently. It was then that she saw her situation less as a predicament and more as an opportunity. "Oh, I don't work because the law makes me! I'd work whether the law told me I had to or not. I work because the only other ways I have to make money—well, they're wrong."

"Other ways of making money?" Mrs. Blowfeld repeated.

"I think she means being an Herbalife distributor, Martha," Mr. Blowfeld contributed from the side.

Mrs. Blowfeld ignored him. "Aren't ya supposed to be in school?"

"Oh, I was in school." Morinda turned her eyes to stare wistfully into the distance. "Many years ago. That was when I lived on our little farm. With my father and my mother and my thirteen brothers and sisters. I went to school then. For two years. Until my mother got too sick, and she couldn't pull the plow any more. That's when my father came to me and said, 'Morinda, you will pull the plow from now on.'" Morinda's chest swelled and her face glowed with pride as she related the event. "So I left school, and I took my mother's place pulling the plow. I haven't been to school since then."

Mrs. Blowfeld was aghast. "That's disgraceful!"

Morinda's face fell. "I wasn't that bad at pulling the plow, really I wasn't! I wasn't as good as my mother, that's true. But I tried. I tired as hard as I could. But you're right—my father could see that I was never going to be as strong as my mother had been, so he sent me here to work. To make money. To try to save the farm from the *banditos* who come out of the hills every fall, just after the harvest, to seize our crops. So I was sent to work here at the RV park and at the bar."

"This's horrible!"

"It's not so bad, really," Morinda said. "In fact, it was a lucky thing for me. I was here working when the earthquake destroyed our village and killed my mother and most of my brothers and sisters. And my father and the two others who were left alive after the earthquake, they caught cholera because the water supply went bad. So if I'd been here, I'd probably have died along with the rest."

Her mouth agape, Mrs. Blowfeld demanded of her husband, "Can you believe this, Steve?"

Mr. Blowfeld considered Morinda while the corners of his eyes and lips raised almost imperceptibly. "I have to admit, it does strain credulity."

Mrs. Blowfeld asked Morinda, "So ya don't have any way to get out of this?"

"I get a day off once a month." Her face brightened. "In fact, today is my day off from work! And this morning, my fa—*Señor* Tavia, I mean, he sent for me and said, 'Morinda, it's your day off. Since you won't have anything else to do today, I want you to go into town and do some things for me.' That's why I'm here. I'm running errands for Mr. Tavia."

"So he's got ya workin'—on your day off?"

"And working for *Señor* Tavia, it's better than it was on the farm," Morinda assured her. "On the farm, all of us, my mother, my father, my thirteen brothers and sisters, and me, we lived in just two rooms. But here, with *Señor* Tavia, I have a room of my very own. I don't have to share it with anyone else. I can sleep there, and sometimes, when no one is looking, I sneak away and I can sit there by myself and think."

"I should hope he'd give you a room to yourself!"

"It's very nice." Morinda's expression became dreamy. "Small. Dark. Lots of clothes . . ."

"A closet?" Mrs. Blowfeld sputtered. "He makes ya stay in a closet?"

"It has plenty of room for me, though. If I bend my knees, I can sleep, and there's still more room off to the side. If I could only think of how to use all of the room so I could stretch out without having to bend something . . ."

"Oh, this's too much!" Mrs. Blowfeld said. Her face went red. Her nostrils flared. "This is—this's the end! I'm gonna do something about this! I swear, I'm gonna do something!"

Maria Elena eased in next to Morinda and touched her elbow to get her attention. When she saw her friend was ready to leave, Morinda told the Blowfelds, "I have to go now. Please don't tell anyone that I complained!" Her eyes went wide with terror. "Please, don't tell them I said anything was wrong! Please? You don't know—you don't know what they'll do to me if they hear something like that!"

Morinda hurriedly left, and Maria Elena followed her.

"Who were those people?" Maria Elena asked in Spanish when they were outside. Maria Elena spoke English, but her knowledge of the language was limited to the rather formal constructions taught in the classroom. When it came to colloquial, idiomatic English as used in most daily conversations, she often got lost.

"Some people staying at my father's RV park. They wanted to know how people in Mexico live, so I was telling them."

"The woman, she seemed very angry."

"I noticed that, too. I think maybe she was a little confused."

Well aware of her friend's proclivity for fictionalizing, Maria Elena said, "You really shouldn't do that to people, Morinda."

"She deserved it. They've been here a whole week now, and they almost never come out of their RV. And when they do, she does nothing but complain. She doesn't like the food, she doesn't like the roads, she doesn't like the people. She should just stay home, except the people there probably made her leave because they couldn't stand Mrs. Blowfeld, either."

"You said things to her that weren't true because she deserved it?"

"That's right."

"And will you be there to do something good for her when she deserves that?"

Morinda stopped and put her hand on the other girl's shoulder. "Maria Elena, you always make me want to be a better person." Morinda sighed deeply. "But you're my best friend—so I forgive you." And before Maria Elena could chide her again, Morinda changed the subject. "Is your mother going to cook a big meal for the Day of the Dead?"

"Just like every year," Maria Elena said.

"Will she let us help? Like last year?"

The flesh between Maria Elena's eyes squiggled and her lips crumpled into a weak smile. "*Let* us help? You call that *letting* us help? She drags us out of bed at five in the morning and marches us down to the kitchen before we've even had a chance to wash. We start cooking before we've eaten breakfast."

The girls resumed walking.

"I like your mother," Morinda said. "She's fun."

"I don't think she's fun," Maria Elena said. "She yells."

"But she yells at *every*body!"

"That's what I mean!" Maria Elena turned her face away, as if from embarrassment at the thought of her mother's perpetual bad temper.

Morinda remembered the times she'd been allowed to help cook with Maria Elena's mother for the Day of the Dead differently, although Maria Elena hadn't distorted the objective facts. *Señora* Ramirez trooped her six daughters and Morinda to the kitchen before dawn, exactly as Maria Elena said. Once there, she issued a constant barrage of commands, keeping the girls scurrying to the pantry, to the shelves, to the range oven, to the market, to the garden, to the neighbors, and all points in between, while she herself conducted the most important aspects of preparing the numerous dishes that'd be served not only to the living but also to the spirits of those who'd died in the house who'd be accommodated when they returned later that night. *Señora* Ramirez was ruthless when it came to running the staff of her kitchen. She ordered them about as though they were privates in her personal army; she always had a task for each of them to keep them busy, and she brooked no delay in carrying out the assigned duties, or any clumsiness in executing them. The whole day one could hear her shouting, "Maria Isabel, get up you lazy thing! Bring me the pepper mill! *Rápido*! Maria Elena, can't you go any slower fetching those eggs? Haven't they hatched yet? I thought you knew I wanted them so I could fry the hens once they're grown! Hurry up! Morinda, I set you to keep that sauce from turning rock hard—stir, stir! Ah, these girls, these girls! They can't cook, they can only eat!" It went on as long as they were in the kitchen, until the family sat down to dinner that night.

All of that was true, as Maria Elena'd said. But *Señora* Ramirez also frequently interrupted her badinage and, without warning, hugged one of the girls to her ample bosom and said, in just as loud a voice as she used to harry them into action, "Ah, *mija*, you are my best helper! That's the way to make *mole*!" And she'd then plant a kiss on the cheek of whatever girl happened at that moment to've earned it. And it didn't matter which of the girls it was; *Señora* Ramirez was as indiscriminate in passing out her encomiums as she was in handing down imprecations. Each of the girls was graced many times during the day with the unexpected compliments and busses from the matronly *Señora* Ramirez, Morinda being treated no differently than the others, as though she were another of *Señora* Ramirez's brood. For Morinda, the best part was having *Señora* Ramirez call her *mija*: she liked being called *mija*.

"She doesn't mean it when she yells, Maria Elena," Morinda said. "It's just her way."

Their stroll brought them to a small street lined with shops. The warm, yeasty aroma of freshly baked goods filled the air.

"Cookies for the Day of the Dead!" Morinda said, and she clutched Maria Elena's arm and turned her into the entrance of the bakery. "Let's go in here!"

The side of the shop nearest the doorway was filled with customers, mostly stout women holding babies in their arms while their older children clung to the hems of their skirts or, the ones who were older still and more adventurous, squirmed through the legs of the adults to fight their way forward so they could press their noses against the glass case that held the loaves of *pan de muerto* decorated with meringues of different bright colors and shaped like skulls and skeletons. From the back room of the bakery wafted the heated air from the Dutch ovens, warm and thick and sweet like the breath of a panther, when the bakers opened them to take out the finished goods with wooden battledores before refilling them with doughy white uncooked lumps. The air of the shop was so saturated with the odors of yeast and flour that merely to stand inside was to taste them.

Maria Elena leaned her head back and breathed in the rich scent; the ends of her long black hair almost brushed the linoleum tiles of the floor. "I'm going to own a bakery when I grow up, so I can smell this whenever I want," she said. "This smells almost as good as my mama's kitchen when she makes bread. Mmmm, I love it!"

"Or you could live next door to a bakery," Morinda suggested. "Then you could smell it whenever you wanted, and you could be a dancer and an actress besides."

"I'll be a dancer and an actress and I'll own a bakery, too," Maria Elena said. "That way, I can have the people who work for me bake bread day and night so I can smell it all the time."

"Good thinking," Morinda affirmed.

A slight break in the crowd in front of them opened, and the two girls stepped forward half a pace to fill it. There was no real line formed by the people waiting to be served, so it was a matter of jostling ahead as those nearest the counter were served and then bulled their way through to the exit.

"Should we get some candy after we buy the cookies?" Morinda asked.

"We could. But only some for us, for today. My mama wants to wait until nearer the Day of the Dead to get most of the candy. Are you coming to our house on the first night?"

"Sure. We don't have any children who've died in our house, so I'll spend the first night with you. It's okay with your mama and papa, isn't it?"

"Oh, yes. And my sisters, too. Everyone wants you to come."

"Your sisters—Maria Teresa, Maria Gabriela, Maria Isabella, Maria Magdalena, and Maria Sophia? All the Marias?" Morinda laughed with delight as the list of names of Maria Elena's sisters rolled off her tongue.

Maria Elena twisted her mouth into her peculiar crinkled smile and crunched her forehead in its usual accompanying frown. It was her customary expression for miscellaneous emotions: any feeling that wasn't overt joy or panic or heartfelt sorrow was shown by Maria Elena in the same way. That each of the surviving children of Maria Elena's parents were daughters named Maria was a perpetual source of mirth for Morinda; Maria Elena never understood why. Morinda always referred to Maria Elena and her sisters collectively as "the Marias." She'd tell her father, "I'm going over to see the Marias," before she walked to the house across town.

Maria Elena said, "We'll set a place for my brother Rafael, and my cousins Guadalupe and Angel, and my niece Dolores." These were dead children whose passing was remembered on the first night of the Day of the Dead.

"What about the second night?" Morinda asked. "I'm going to set up an altar for the second night. For my mother. So I'll stay home then. Maybe you could come over to my house."

"We're going to go to Mass the second night."

Morinda sighed. "Well, I'm going to keep watch the second night. It'll just be me. And my mother, if she shows up."

"Your papa, he doesn't . . . ?"

Morinda frowned, a more earnest frown than the tentative expression Maria Elena used. "He and my mother—" she began, then stopped. "He doesn't like to talk about her. They must have had fights, or something, before she died. He—" she shook her head. "He acts like he's mad at her. But I'll set a place for her. I always do."

When they reached the counter, they each bought a half dozen cookies and had them put in bags made of white waxed paper. Then they pushed their way out of the bakery and onto the street. As they walked away, the odors of baking dissipated, and the scents of the sea grew stronger. Gulls soared overhead, calling raucously to one another and drifting down to feed on garbage wherever the pedestrian traffic thinned enough to give the birds the time to scavenge in peace.

Morinda removed a red and yellow frosted cookie and took a dainty bite. She stopped in mid-stride. Maria Elena paused beside her. Morinda made a "mmmm" sound, closed her eyes rapturously, and held the cookie toward Maria Elena's lips for her friend to share. Maria Elena obligingly nibbled a corner off, and licked her lips to get the crumbs.

Out of the corner of her eye, Maria Elena saw something, and she turned her head to look along the street the way they'd come. Then she snapped her head back around to lock eyes with Morinda.

"There he is again," Maria Elena said in a stage whisper.

Morinda glanced casually the same way her friend'd just looked. There were people crossing from one side of the street to the other. Morinda could pick out Felipe in the crowd without too much trouble: he was tall enough that he stood several inches above most of those around him.

"I told you he was following you," Maria Elena said. Maria Elena cocked her head to give a sly glance at the boy, then again turned to Morinda to say, "I think he likes you."

Morinda heaved a sigh, then set her face as though preparing to solve a difficult problem in mathematics. She watched Felipe for several seconds before she announced, "I think he likes *you*."

Morinda set her bag of cookies on the green painted sill of a shop window. She clutched her friend's arm and spoke fervidly. "It's you, Maria Elena. You're the one he's following. He's fallen in love with you. He's only seen you from a distance, but it was love at first sight, and now he wants you to be his *novia*."

Morinda lowered her voice and huskily intoned, "Maria Elena, my love, my life. I cannot go on this way. I've been driven mad by your beauty. From the first moment I saw you, I knew that I would make you mine, or I would die. Your eyes, your hair, your lips—everything that is you cried out to me from across the space that separated us, calling to me, telling me that I must come nearer, that I must approach you, that I must reach you, that I must touch you, that I must press my lips against yours. Aah, Maria Elena, I more than love you—I adore you! I must convince you that my love for you is true. I must convince you to express your love for me. You must be mine, Maria Elena!"

Maria Elena's eyes widened; she retreated to the wall of the nearest building as Morinda, playing the role of her ardent suitor, crowded her backward. Morinda's passionate proclamations continued, and Maria Elena's smile formed, then widened, until finally a small chirp of laughter escaped her.

"Aah, Maria Elena, you are so cruel!" Morinda exclaimed. "I profess my love for you, and you laugh in my face! You entice me with your beauty, and then you heartlessly mock my deepest feelings! You are like a flame, and I am but a moth! In spite of your jeers, I cannot help myself! My love is too deep, too wide, too—too something else I cannot even think of, I am so dizzy with my love for you!"

Maria Elena tittered. Her cheeks turned red from her efforts to suppress her laughter.

"Maria Elena, have pity on me! I follow you through the streets of town like a dog. Yes, like a dog! Hoping only that you will give me one look, one smile, one small token that you might return my love! I must have a sign from you that—"

In the distance, a sharp smack resounded, and Morinda jumped, letting out a yip of surprise. A second later, a whole series of similar pops echoed. Realizing it was only a string of firecrackers echoing from a nearby street, Morinda let her shoulders slump. But the game she'd been playing with Maria Elena lost its zest, and she didn't return to it. She continued to hold her friend's elbow in one hand. She picked up the bag of cookies she'd set on the window case of the building and tugged Maria Elena's arm as she set off along the street again, pulling her friend along with her as she went.

They'd gone only a few steps when Morinda leaned her head toward Maria Elena's and murmured, "Is he still behind us?"

Maria Elena craned her head around. Morinda's hand released her arm as she did. Felipe'd gotten nearer in the time Morinda'd spent imitating a character on a *telenovela*, and now was only twenty feet away. Maria Elena began speaking before she turned around. "Yes, he's—"

Morinda was no longer beside her. She was running ahead, and was already five paces from where Maria Elena stood. Her long black hair streamed behind her as she raced away, and her laughing face glanced backward to Maria Elena.

CHAPTER 2

Maria Elena started from a standstill, but Morinda wasn't seriously trying to outrun her friend so Maria Elena caught up with her by the time Morinda came to the next corner, and while they both continued to dash along the street that was too narrow for vehicular traffic, she put her arm through the crook in Morinda's arm so that they were interlocked and could hold each other up as they spun around the turn, skidding and nearly falling and shrieking with laughter. Elbows linked, they encouraged each other to hurry, to run faster, and each pulled the other back into the race when one stumbled and slowed to recover her footing, all the time giggling and crying out in mock horror of their pursuer. They passed people, mostly older women carrying overstuffed shopping bags by string handles who kept their eyes turned down to watch the pavement ahead of them as they trudged homeward, never bothering to glance up as the two silly girls sped by them.

The street ended where it abutted on a small plaza on two sides of which were set up the wooden stands of vegetable and fruit sellers shaded by canvas awnings. Scores of people crowded around the stalls, pinching, thumping, and handling the different items for sale in order to judge their ripeness and quality. The girls veered to the left, away from the throngs, and ran to a building that, like the others surrounding the square, was of whitewashed stucco. Propped against the wall was the hull of an eighteen-foot fishing boat. Its bottom was patched in several places and its paint faded nearly away over most of its planks; there was a large, ragged hole in the bow. A bunch of metal barrels sat in a patch of grass growing near the damaged fishing smack. A transparent brown liquid that'd curdled and hardened permanently like tree sap turned to amber clung to the rims of the barrels, frozen in place.

The girls charged across the plaza in their awkward fashion, running as if they were tied together in a three-legged race except that they were joined by their elbows rather than their ankles. They dropped to their knees once they were on the berm next to the building, and together they crawled behind the thirty-two gallon drums to lean against the stucco wall.

"Oh-oh," Morinda said, turning to Maria Elena with her eyes widened, sputtering with laughter that promptly set Maria Elena giggling uncontrollably as well. Felipe entered the square still running for several paces before he slowed to a more dignified walk as he found himself the object of public notice, then finally coming to a complete halt. He lifted his chin and turned his head from side to side, examining every part of the plaza as though he found everything there of great interest.

Morinda inched forward on her hands and knees to where she could press her forehead against two of the metal drums and peer out through the space between them. She spied like this for only a few seconds before she fell back against the wall beside Maria Elena and said, "He must *really* like you!"

There was an opening through the stucco wall a few yards away from them that led to a staircase; from it the girls could hear a saw huffing as it sliced through wood, and a hammer pounding. Mixed with the smell of sawdust was the tangy petroleum odor of shellac.

A boy much younger than the two girls came out of the entrance. He was only six or seven, though he had broad shoulders from which swung long, ape-like arms so that he had the appearance of a dwarf out of Teutonic mythology. He wore a green workman's apron fitted to his small form; it was covered with sawdust and daubs of dried paint of different colors. His face, beneath his short-cropped head of black hair, was heavily freckled. He stopped at the berm, looked one way and then the other, then his gaze fell upon Morinda and Maria Elena. He shuffled over to them, his broad shoulders swinging his arms from side to side as he came.

"Shhh!" Morinda said, her forefinger held to her lips as a caution. Her eyes flashed out to the plaza and then back to let the boy know the danger was in that direction.

"What?" the boy asked, crouching and letting his own eyes follow Morinda's to scan the plaza. "Are you hiding?"

"Yes," Morinda said in a rough whisper, though Felipe was too far away to've heard anything she said even if she'd spoken in her normal voice. "Don't let him know we're here, okay?"

The boy raised himself on tiptoe and peered over the tops of the metal barrels. "Which one is it?"

"The boy, the tall one in the white shirt. There, that one," Morinda said. She'd leaned forward again to look between the barrels.

"Oh, him," the young boy said. He lowered himself to his ordinary height by setting his heels on the ground. "You want him to leave you alone?"

Morinda gave Maria Elena a sidelong glance, while Maria Elena did the same to her. Neither of them answered. The boy took their silence for consent.

"I'll take care of him, no problem," he assured them.

He shifted himself around and began to skirt the screen of barrels. Morinda reached up and grabbed him by his arm.

"Wait! Don't let him know we're here!" she hissed shrilly.

The young boy turned to face her and used both his hands to pat the air in front of him.

"Don't worry," he said. "I'll ask him who he's looking for. When he tells me, I'll say I saw you going that way."

He pointed a dirty finger across the square before he spun on his heel and swaggered out into the plaza. Only then did Morinda notice the string of blue and white ladyfinger firecrackers the boy carried in his back pocket; they hung like a tail that swayed pendulously as he walked.

Both the girls leaned forward and pressed their faces against the barrels to see what'd happen. As the young boy approached to within a few feet of Felipe, Morinda heard Maria Elena say in a quiet voice from the side, "He likes *you*!" Morinda was about to respond, but at that moment the boy reached Felipe.

The girls couldn't hear what was said, but they saw that Felipe ignored the boy who planned to misdirect him on their behalf. He blithely continued to scan the plaza, moving his head slowly and deliberately from one side of the square to the other, his gaze gliding smoothly over the head of the little boy who called up to him without effect. The little one, frustrated, waved his arms above his head to attract Felipe's attention, but Felipe still paid him no heed; he even turned his back, acting as though he didn't know the youngster was there. The little one grew so mad, he seemed about to kick Felipe. Morinda said aloud, "No, let him go, *mijo*! He's looking the other way!" for Felipe now also had his back to the girls. But Felipe went around in a complete circle, surveying the people in the plaza as he did so. Not able to find who he was seeking, he finally deigned to notice the little boy in the workman's smock standing at his knee.

Felipe and the aproned boy spoke to each other. Each of them gestured: Felipe wagging a forefinger at the little one, the small one shrugging elaborately and then pointing off to the side. Felipe faced the way the little one indicated, keeping his eyes locked in place for a while as he stared thoughtfully, then he shook his head as if dismissing the idea suggested to him. The boy nodded his head with vigor and expostulated, arguing vehemently. But Felipe wagged his head from side to side and then seemed to lose further interest in anything the boy had to say. The youngster stamped his foot in anger, making him look even more like a dwarf from Teutonic legend, like an illustration of Rumplestiltskin Morinda'd once seen in a book of fairy tales.

Felipe shifted his gaze until he was looking directly at the barrels behind which Morinda and Maria Elena hid. His eyes stared steadily at them for a long time, and Maria Elena gave out a short gasp. Felipe's eyes narrowed, and he took a tentative step forward. The little boy glanced over his shoulder anxiously, then he again spoke to Felipe, who again ignored him. Felipe cocked his head to one side and peered ever more intently at the barrels. Then he strode determinedly toward them.

The little boy ran after him, calling as he went, but he could do nothing to halt or deflect Felipe. Seeing that he was about to fail in his mission, the young one reached up and tugged at the bigger boy's shirt. Felipe didn't stop or even slow down; he idly waved his hand behind him, as if he were brushing away a fly.

Discouraged, the little boy stopped in place and glared at Felipe's retreating form. And then it was as if a light bulb went on over his head. In a flash, his face changed from showing total dejection to beaming with delight. From his back pocket he tugged the string of firecrackers. From another pocket he took out a large wooden kitchen match that he expertly lit with a single stroke across its phosphorus tip with his thumbnail. The match flared, and he set the fuse of the first ladyfinger burning. Then he ran forward with the string to shove the end farthest from the lighted fuse into Felipe's pant waist. Now the firecrackers dangled from Felipe like a tail. Felipe did not so much as look around to see what it was the little boy'd done.

The faces of the two girls grew solemn at the same time. Together, without any consultation, Morinda and Maria Elena stood to get a better look. As their heads rose over the tops of the barrels, a smile of recognition spread over Felipe's face.

His happiness lasted only a moment. The first of the firecrackers went off. When it exploded, Felipe jumped a foot in the air, twisting around in a half circle as he did so. Before he landed again on the ground, others of the string erupted in a rapid-fire cadence, and Felipe began madly flapping his hands across his backside while he spun and twirled in contortions to try to get at the source of the blasts. Every time he flipped sideways to grab for the string of firecrackers, the centrifugal force of his own motion swung the string away from him and he missed with each frenzied effort.

The sound of the firecrackers, and Felipe's antics, attracted the attention of the people shopping at the fruit and vegetable stalls. A group of boys aged from a few years younger to a few years older than the aproned one who'd set the string alight, who'd all been gathered together to watch one of their number make a skeleton puppet dance and shake on its strings, now ran to gawk at Felipe's impromptu show. They quickly surrounded Felipe. The square rang with their catcalls and jeers as they facetiously compared Felipe's herky-jerky performance with that of the toy skeleton.

Nowhere near as amused as the gaggle of boys, Morinda and Maria Elena also watched Felipe bat frantically at the firecrackers while he lurched at every painful discharge. The noise of the string died down, and Morinda said hollowly, "I don't think he likes either one of us very much right now."

The two girls looked at Felipe lying supine on the ground, then exchanged glances with each other showing expressions of dismay. Each grabbed the other's arm as they had earlier, and they ran, though this time they didn't laugh. Once they were safely out of the plaza, they slowed to a funereal pace.

"Do you think he's really hurt?" Maria Elena asked.

"I don't know. We didn't actually have anything to do with it," Morinda said. "It was the little boy—he's the one who put the firecrackers in his pants. We didn't tell him to do anything like that."

Maria Elena shook her head. "My papa, he won't take that as an excuse."

Morinda words were equally strained. "Neither will mine," she decided.

"I hope he's not hurt."

"So do I."

"We shouldn't have done it."

"But we didn't *do* it."

"We were there."

"I know."

"And he wasn't doing anything so wrong. He was just following us."

"I know."

"And he's handsome. Don't you think?"

"He's all right, I guess."

"And my sister says he's very nice, very polite."

Morinda said nothing.

"We shouldn't have done it," Maria Elena concluded.

"I know. I feel bad."

They plodded morosely to Morinda's house, a large five-bedroom Spanish-style structure around a central courtyard attached to the office of the RV park her father owned. The girls entered through the living room.

Encountering no one inside, Morinda led Maria Elena to her bedroom. Morinda picked up a copy of her favorite book that she was rereading for the fourth time, *Silas Marner* in the original English, that lay open on the bed. She was careful to keep it at the place where she'd left off as she put it on top of the volumes of the Spanish-language *Enciclopedia Barsa* in the bookcase in the headboard. Both girls immediately plopped themselves on the bed, Morinda clutching a stuffed cat to her bosom while Maria Elena picked up a large, plush teddy bear to hold. They'd barely gotten settled when they heard a door slam, and then Morinda's father calling from the living room, "More! Morinda!"

"What do you think?" Morinda asked her friend. "Should we pretend we don't hear him and hope he goes away?"

"He lives here, Morinda. So do you. You're going to have to talk to him sooner or later."

"'Later' sounds good."

Three knocks struck the bedroom door.

"So much for 'later,'" Morinda said resignedly. "I'm in here, Dad!" she called.

Pat Lott, twelve years older than he'd been when he fled Los Angeles, stuck his head and one shoulder into the room. He looked at Maria Elena, then at Morinda. Then he pushed the door open and stepped inside.

"Ladies," he said in English, nodding his head to acknowledge Morinda's friend.

"*Buenas tardes, Señor* Tavia," Maria Elena said, addressing him by the name he'd adopted when he came to Mexico and by which he was known in San Estaban.

"*Buenos tardes*, Maria Elena." Then he reverted to English. "Have you girls been here all day?"

Morinda lifted her eyebrows, quickly lowered them, and frowned. "No."

"Were you in town?"

"For a while . . ."

"What'd ya do there?"

Morinda's eyes shifted over to Maria Elena, whose woeful look gave her no encouragement. Then she hesitantly suggested, "Nothing?"

"That's not what Mrs. Blowfeld says."

Morinda saw this mention of Mrs. Blowfeld as an opportunity to be exploited, and she immediately determined how best to deal with the situation. She tightened the corners of her mouth and furrowed her brow to show her father she was taking the matter very seriously. She gestured with her forefinger as she said, "She's not always right, you know. I've heard Mrs. Blowfeld say a few things that were downright inaccurate."

"Well, that wouldn't surprise me a bit," Lott said. "Let me rephrase the question: Is she right *this* time?"

"I guess it's *poss*ible," Morinda admitted. Then, knowing she didn't want to hear the answer but feeling obligated to pose the question nevertheless, she asked, "What did she say?"

"Did you tell Mrs. Blowfeld I make ya sleep in a closet?"

"Not—not exactly," Morinda said.

"Hm."

"She must've misinterpreted. People do that. They don't pay attention to what I say, they just assume. And they get everything mixed up. You know?"

"Yeah, sure. Like the time when ya were eleven and ya told me you'd gone to see the circus and asked me would I give ya what it cost for a ticket? Except I found out later you'd only gone and looked at the circus, you'd never actually gone in? Or paid the entry fee?"

Morinda looked pained. She turned her eyes away to examine the floor, embarrassed at this reminder of an occasion that hadn't been her finest hour.

"Well—technically—that was true," she pointed out. "I did *see* the circus, and it *did* cost twenty pesos to get in. All I did was ask if you'd give me the twenty pesos—"

"'Technically!'" Lott cut her off. "'Technically!' Ya sound like a lawyer, now."

"You take that back!" Morinda demanded.

"Ah! Ya don't mind talkin' like a lawyer, ya only resent it when somebody points out to ya that that's what you're doin'. *There's* some lawyerly hypocrisy on top of the legalistic hairsplitting!"

"Words are very exact tools," Morinda said, the conviction her voice carried eroding. "They're precision instruments. I choose my words very carefully, and if someone else doesn't listen carefully, it can seem as though I said something completely different than what I actually did say."

Lott lifted his chin, lowered it, and peered down his nose at Morinda as though from a great height. "It's lying," he said.

"It was not a lie," Morinda answered, in high dudgeon. "It was the truth. You just . . . missed the point?"

"You picked your words deliberately so as to lead me to believe something that wasn't true. Ya knew I thought ya meant something else. And a sin of omission's as bad as a sin of commission—deliberately leavin' someone with a false impression's the same as tellin' a bald-faced lie. Is that similar to what ya did to Mrs. Blowfeld?"

Morinda said nothing.

"Well, she came stompin' into the bar in a huff. She said she was gonna go to the *delegación*, and after that she was gonna take it to Amnesty International and UNICEF if she didn't get any satisfaction from the stupid Mexicans who run this country. She and her husband are checkin' out of the RV park this afternoon, she said, and they're never comin' back. Morinda, when ya tell my customers things like that, they get mad. They get mad, and they leave. They leave with their money, so they don't pay me any more of it. If I don't have the money, I can't spend it on you. Or on me. Or anybody else. Because I don't have it to spend."

"It was only meant to be a joke," Morinda said. "I'm sorry."

"Ya don't sound sorry," Lott said. "Ya don't look sorry."

Morinda lifted her shoulders, breathed in a huge amount of air, then let her shoulders sag as she exhaled. She turned her eyes back to the ground with a hangdog expression and said contritely, "I'll go to Father Rodriguez and confess. He'll give me an act of penance."

"You're not Catholic," Lott reminded her.

Morinda refused to rise to the bait. "I'll convert," she said dolefully. "I'll cut off my hair and take the veil. I'll become a bride of Christ. I'll live a sequestered life."

Lott gave her his patented what-am-I-gonna-do-with-you look, shook his head, then said indulgently, "You're a good kid—when you're asleep. Don't cut your hair. Don't renounce the world."

She considered the alternatives for less than a second, and then brightly answered, "Okay!"

"But this's the last time, Morinda. Ya understand? If we have another repeat of this, I'm gonna have to ship ya off to military school."

It was Lott's repeated threat, and it'd become a standing joke between them: that her father brought it up now was an indication to Morinda that the lecture was over.

Morinda drew another long face. "The Hermann Goering Academy for Wayward Youth in East Jesus, Nebraska?"

"That's the one," her father said.

"I—I don't know how to march in a goose-step," she said.

"Then it's about time ya learned. They'll teach ya there. They'll break ya down, and build ya back up again. They'll make a man out of ya."

She appeared unsettled. "Couldn't they make a woman out of me?"

Lott considered. "Doesn't say anything about that in the prospectus they sent. Just said they'd make a man out of ya. Apparently, one size fits all."

"They wear uniforms there . . ."

"Thick, scratchy wool on the inside," Lott agreed, "hot, tacky-looking polyester on the outside."

"I think I'm allergic to—to everything they make their uniforms out of. It gives me hives, or nosebleeds—I can't remember which. Probably both."

"Then you'd better straighten up your act, huh?"

He put his arm around Morinda's shoulders and rocked her back and forth.

"Forget about it," he went on. "Mrs. Blowfeld's a status-seekin', social-climbin' geek! When they registered, she gave their address as Manhattan Beach. Manhattan Beach! Who are they tryin' to kid? I know the street they live on—that's El Segundo!

"We'd be better off if people like Mrs. Blowfeld stayed the hell out of Mexico. I told her that—and that I didn't want her comin' here again, anyway. But it'd've given me a lot more satisfaction to've told her the same thing if she hadn't had reason to think I was abusin' you. Jesus!" he muttered, shaking his head as he released his hold on Morinda. "A closet! Where do ya come up with this stuff?"

"Was there—any other news from town?" Morinda asked.

"Why? What else were ya up to? Never mind—I don't wanna know." He turned to face Maria Elena and spoke in Spanish. "Are you staying for dinner tonight, Maria Elena? If you are, make sure you tell Erminia, More, so she can make enough."

Erminia was the cook.

"Can you stay?" Morinda inquired of her friend.

"I can call my mama and ask," she said.

"Okay."

"Oh, More," Lott said, still speaking Spanish. "I need you to keep an eye on the RV park office till Lupe gets back from *siesta*. He's off till 4:30, so you'll need to be here to take care of any business that comes our way. Make up for the customers you drive away."

"Oh, Dad! Who's going to show up here to do anything during *siesta*?" Morinda objected.

"Most of our customers are Americans. You know, those people who think everybody in the world has air conditioning, so they don't worry about anyone having to take a break in the heat of the day? Lupe gets the afternoon off, I have to look after things at the bar, and guess who that leaves to run things around here?"

Morinda angrily slapped her hand into the stuffed animal she was holding.

"Look on the bright side," Lott said, this time in English. "It'll give ya a chance to get out of your room." He waved his hand. "Which, I might add, is in desperate need of cleanin'. As soon as Lupe gets here, you're free to go. Just don't go too far. And let someone know where you're going. And be back by eight for dinner."

Morinda was already bopping her head from side to side to mock his litany of commands, so Lott stopped issuing them. He said, "Are ya listenin' to me, More?"

"I'm always listening to you, Dad."

"Meanin' that I nag too much, and I should shut up, go away, and leave ya alone."

"I never said that!"

"No—'technically,' ya didn't. To the untrained ear, the words, 'I always listen to ya, Dad' and 'I'm always listenin' to ya, Dad' sound very much alike even when they're pronounced, as they were, with a tinge of teenage sarcasm. But the professional Morinda observer, such as myself, notices a subtle difference in meanin' between those two statements. If anybody else'd said it, I might assume it was merely a slip of the tongue. But those of us who are exposed to her on a day-to-day basis've learned to our peril that, to Morinda, words are exact tools, precision instruments, which she chooses very carefully."

"Hoist with my own petard. My own statements turned against me." Morinda fluttered her eyelashes, melodramatically pressed the back of one wrist to her forehead, languidly fanned herself with her other hand, and said, "I feel a sick headache coming on. May I be dismissed to my closet now? I—I need to lie down."

Lott said to Maria Elena in Spanish, "How do you put up with her?" On his way out of the bedroom, he called, "Listen for the bell from up front," added, "Goodbye, Maria Elena," and left.

"Trapped here!" Morinda hissed to Maria Elena in Spanish as soon as her father was gone.

"We weren't planning on going anyplace else, were we?"

"That's not the point," Morinda said. "Whose side are you on, anyway? Oh-oh. My eye—my eye, Maria Elena, it's feeling the urge—the urge to sing." She lifted her hand to her face, putting her thumb on the bottom of her eye and the forefinger on the top. She began crooning a Spanish-language version of *Achy Breaky Heart* while her thumb and finger worked together to make the eyelids move in sync. It was *schtick* that Maria Elena always found hysterically funny, and in a few seconds she was rolling across the bed, collapsed with laughter, pleading with Morinda to stop.

Morinda's father'd been gone not much more than half an hour when the two-note ringer sounded through the house, indicating that someone'd entered the RV park office. Morinda and Maria Elena were talking about a movie they wanted to see when the interruption came, and Morinda dropped her stuffed cat and growled, "Aagggh!" She got up and made a major production of her dislike for the job she was being called upon to perform.

Morinda entered the RV park office through its rear door. She walked to the counter and stopped, Maria Elena a few discreet steps behind her. Two men waited to be served.

One of them was in his mid-thirties, at least ten years younger than his companion. He was slim, his thinness accentuated by his height, and blonde with very fair skin. His nose was too large, and his chin too weak, for his face to be considered movie-star handsome. He wore a red and blue warm-up jacket with a hood that draped across his shoulders. He stood by the side wall on which hung the licenses and certificates issued by the various levels of the Mexican government—local, state, and federal—for the RV park, examining the documents displayed in their cheap frames covered in glass, so Morinda saw him only in profile. He squinted at the official paperwork, moved his face closer to the wall to read one of the framed certificates, and finally took a pair of glasses out of his jacket pocket along with a piece of Kleenex, rubbed the tissue over the lenses, and then placed the spectacles on his nose.

The older of the men was shorter and stockier in build. He wore a yellow tank top that revealed thick arms and shoulders: the upper part of his body was fleshy and looked strong, but had little muscle definition. The man was in his mid-forties, with three long horizontal frown lines running across his forehead, a bald dome on the top of his head surrounded by a fringe of black hair, and a thick black soup-strainer mustache. The stocky man waited at the counter.

"*Buenas tardes*," he said with a strong Midwestern American accent.

"Good afternoon," Morinda said. "Looking for a site for your RV?"

"Hey, ya speak English! Yeah. We need a place to park. It's a forty-five footer. Got a space big enough?"

"That is big. But we can fit you in. Electrical hookup at the site. There's a liquid petroleum gas yard about a kilometer away, on the road into town. Coin-operated washers and dryers around the side of this building, over here."

"How much?"

Before Morinda could answer, the tall one by the wall read aloud, "Ernest Tavia." He removed his glasses, let them dangle from his fist, and faced Morinda. "Who's that?"

"That's my father," Morinda said. "He owns the business."

"Ernest Tavia," the tall one repeated as if he were comparing the sound of it to something he'd heard before. "Ernest Tavia. And he's your father, ya say?"

"That's right."

The stocky one at the counter grinned. "Are you two sisters?" He looked from Morinda to Maria Elena. Maria Elena demurely lowered her eyes when the man spoke of her.

"No," Morinda said. "This is my friend. Her father is the *delegado* of San Estaban."

The tall one asked the stocky one, "*Delegado*?"

"Town bigwig. The mayor, sort of," the stocky one with the mustache explained. "Grand high mucky-muck."

To Morinda, the man in the warm-up jacket said, "But that's her father who's the *delegado*, ya said? Not yours. Your father's this Ernest Tavia?"

"That's right. Ernest Tavia."

"What's your name?" the tall one asked.

"Morinda."

"Morinda," he repeated. "Morinda Tavia. Pretty name."

"Thank you," Morinda said cautiously.

"Ernest Tavia," the tall one near the wall said, turning to read one of the licenses again. "Tavia—that's Spanish. But his name's here as 'Ernest,' not 'Ernesto.' Is he Mexican, your father?"

"No. He's American."

"I mean, is he Mexican—ya know, by descent?"

"No."

"Aah. Your father—did he ever go by any other name?"

Morinda frowned. A hint of asperity entered her voice. "Why would he use another name?"

"No reason. Ya look familiar, and I thought maybe you and your father resemble each other, but I don't know anybody named Ernest Tavia."

The stocky one standing across from Morinda put his hands on top of the counter that stood between them; the gleam of a gold wedding band on the ring finger of his left hand caught Morinda's eye. Speaking over his shoulder to his companion, he said, "She does look familiar, doesn't she? Who's she look like? I know—like that girl on the television show! What's her name? She looks just like her, doesn't she? Ya know the one I mean! She was in that movie, too. Ooh, what was her name? Anyway, she's the spittin' image."

Morinda's face flushed.

"Is your dad around?" the tall one asked.

"Not right now. He's in San Estaban, at his other business. He should be back any time."

"How about your mom? Is she here?"

"No."

"No one here but us chickens, huh?" the younger one said. Then he smiled. "We wanna get checked in."

"I can do that," Morinda said officiously. "Here's the registration form. I need to see your driver's license and your tourist cards."

"Do ya have cable TV here at the park?"

"Of course," Morinda said off the top of her head as she wrote the names and addresses of the two men on her register. "Where do you think we are, Timbuktu? We even have indoor plumbing in San Estaban. Had it for years."

"Indoor plumbing *and* electricity!" the stocky bald one with the mustache whose name Morinda saw was Lou Helmholtz said. "Dee-luxe! Is there a video store in town, or's that too much to ask for?"

"Yes, there's a video store," Morinda said. "You Americans, you come down here and you have this stereotyped image in your minds about Mexicans. You all think they're lazy, stupid, and living in the nineteenth century!"

"*All* of us Americans stereotype Mexicans?" the tall, thin one said. "Isn't that stereotypin' Americans?"

Morinda looked up from her work. The corners of her mouth turned up ever so slightly. "That was irony," she announced.

The man laughed softly and said, "Aah! Now I recognize it." Then he laughed aloud. "You're funny," he said.

"What?" Lou asked his companion. "What'd I miss?"

The other man said, "Never mind. If ya have to explain a joke, it isn't funny anymore."

Morinda said, "Your name's—Flower Child Ashland?"

"Yeah. One of the worst forms of child abuse, I'm afraid. Ron and Carol Ashland were a couple of Deadheads and Rainbow-Coalition followers who thought the name 'Flower Child' was 'groovy,' 'farm out,' and 'out-of-state.' I been payin' for it ever since. What's the fishin' like here?"

"Shore fishing, or are you going to charter a boat? You'll need to get a fishing license, either way. You can do that at any of the bait and tackle shops in town. It's a little late in the year, and I hear some of the fish are starting to move south to warmer water, but there's still plenty out there. You can't catch more than ten a day per person, but the good fishermen are still getting the limit."

"How far south would ya have to go to catch up with the fish?" Flower said.

"Past Bahia Magdalena the water stays pretty warm the whole year round," Morinda said. "But like I said, there's still plenty of fish right here. Don't think I'm trying to run you off."

"Oh, no," Flower said. "Right here's where we plan to stay until we finish up what we came to do."

"Good. I have the perfect space to put you in," Morinda said, smiling brightly. "The Blowfelds just moved out of it!"

CHAPTER 3

The walk along the beach south of San Estaban in the early morning hours was one of Morinda's favorites. The strip of sand was framed by an arc of cliffs that towered a hundred feet high on one side, with the sea on the other. Flocks of gulls hovered above the ridge and glided down to skim across the surface of the water, constantly on the search for food. There were usually fishermen casting from shore or wading in the surf, but never many of them; most of the fishing around San Estaban was done from the decks of the scores of boats that set out before dawn each day from the town's harbor to the north.

When she first began her walk that morning, the sea'd been like glass and the tide at its lowest. By the time she doubled back toward her house, the tide'd turned, and breakers were rolling in higher and higher. She'd had to change her path to avoid the rising surf, walking ever farther to the east to keep her shoes from getting soaked. Someone'd left a fishing pole stuck in the sand next to a tackle box and a metal ice chest; the flood tide surged to within a few inches of the equipment. Morinda stopped nearby and searched for their owner to see if he'd be returning soon to keep them from being washed out to sea. There was only a single fisherman in view, and she kept him in sight for several seconds before she realized it was the man named Flower—or Flora, as Maria Elena called him.

He was dressed in black hip-waders held up by suspenders slung over his shoulders. He was thirty feet from shore, in water deep enough to reach his knees even in the trough of the waves. He splashed slowly through the rising tide, concentrating completely on his fishing, for he didn't so much as glance toward the beach. In his two hands, he held the cork-lined butt section of his rod. He watched the incoming waves, and Morinda could follow what he was thinking by his actions: the surf swirled over a shallow sand bar, and there was calmer water just inshore of the bar that had a darker color than the rest of the sea that meant this was where a school of fish were feeding. The water, though roughened by the fresh breeze blowing off the ocean that rippled its surface, was clear. Flower drew back his pole like a batter waiting for a pitch and cast ahead of him with a whip-like motion. The silver lure at the end of his line flashed through the air, then plunked into the water and plummeted downward. He'd dropped it just ahead of the dark shapes of the school he was stalking. It was only a couple of minutes before he had a strike. He worked the rod back, and then reeled in his catch. He labored efficiently, with no wasted motion; when he brought the fish out, he held up the monofilament nylon line and carried it along with the pole to a craggy boulder the waves crashed against. The fish writhed and struggled to free itself as Flower grabbed it by its tail. He raised it to shoulder level, then swung it to bash its head against the rock. The fish ceased to squirm and hung limply from Flower's hand. He turned and waded through the waves to the beach.

"Mornin'!" he called to Morinda when he was still fifteen feet away. "Or *buenos días*, I guess I should say!"

"Good morning!" Morinda replied. "I was going to move your things if you didn't get them pretty soon. The tide's coming up, and it'll take everything."

"Thanks," Flower said. He nestled the butt end of the rod he carried into the sand next to the extra pole already there. He proudly held up his catch for Morinda's inspection.

"Man, I've never seen fishin' like this!" he said. "I caught a croaker and a dolphinfish earlier. Then I ran across a school of these feedin' right over here 'bout half an hour ago, and I caught three of 'em bam! bam! bam! They've really been goin' for this silver spoon lure!"

Morinda politely admired the fish he showed her. "*Papagallo*," she said.

"Is that what they're called? How was that again—papawhatsit?"

"*Papagallo*," she repeated. "Roosterfish, I think they say in English."

"*Papagallo*. Are they any good to eat, do ya know?"

"Oh, yes."

"Good. I hate to think I'd gone to all that trouble for something that's not worth eatin'."

Flower opened his tackle box and took out a rusty pair of needlenose pliers. He pried the mouth of the fish open and reached inside to grasp the hook between the jaws of the tool. Once he forced the hook loose, he dropped the pliers into the tackle box then opened the lid of the ice chest to reveal the rest of his day's catch. The beady, unmoving eyes of the dead fish stared out. Flower draped the roosterfish on top of the crushed ice inside and let the lid fall back into place.

"I guess I'd better start getting this stuff out of here," Flower said. "Tide's comin' in pretty fast now. I'll need to make a couple of trips to get everything. Maybe—" he looked behind him. "Maybe I should drag it up there, higher up the beach, to get it outta the way."

"No, look," Morinda said, "we can get it all in one trip. You carry the poles, and I'll get your tackle box. And you take one handle of the ice chest and I'll take the other one. See?"

She bent from the waist to secure the lid of the tackle box, snapping shut the tabs that held it to the body. She tucked the box under her elbow and grasped the handle on her side of the bulky metal ice chest; to test its weight, she hefted her half an inch or so off the ground.

Flower looked dubious. "Ya sure about this? That's awful heavy, ya know."

"It's not that heavy! We can stop and rest on the way if we have to. Come on!"

Flower picked up both poles in one hand, tucking them under his arm, and grabbed the other handle.

"So you've been using lures?" Morinda said. "Have you tried live bait?"

"No, the lures've been bringin' me luck so far. What kinda bait do they use here?"

"All kinds. Bloodworms are good. Squid and mussels. Sometimes crabs and shrimp. Right now, they're mostly catching croaker and corvina. That's what the fishermen say. Of course, most of the fishing is out in the ocean. On boats. Did you bring a trolling rod for deep-sea fishing?"

"I've got two with me, but—"

"That's where the big ones are. Marlin and swordfish."

"Yeah, I know," he said sourly.

"You don't like to go out on the ocean?"

"I tried it a few times. But I get sea sick," Flower admitted. "Bad. Pukin' my guts out all day long. I'm one of those people that Dramamine does nothin' for. But you sound like an expert. How many swordfish've you brought back?"

"Me? I've never caught a swordfish. But I've caught tarpon. And dorado. I've only been out a few times. With my father, when he goes. He's caught swordfish. And sailfish. And marlin. You know, if you get sick on boats, maybe you should do what my father taught me to do. I used to get sick when he first took me out, but he told me how to get over it.

"You see, when you're on the land, you look at the things around you and they stay still, they're fixed in place, so you get used to being able to keep your balance by seeing where you are in relation to everything else. You're accustomed to doing that, checking out the things around you to tell you exactly where you are and if you're standing upright and the rest of it. You use landmarks to figure out if you're right-side up. On the land that works.

But when you're on a boat, and everything's moving, you can't get a fix on where you are in relation to other things. When you try to do it, it makes you sick. What you're really doing is tricking yourself into being sick, because you don't have to use your surroundings to tell you where you are and that you're upright and okay—you already *know* where *you* are. You're right there. You know that. You can feel it inside you. You always know exactly where you are. It's only when you try to orient yourself by looking at everything else that you get thrown off, you feel off-balance.

"So what you do is, instead of paying any attention to what's around you, trying to make it seem solid and not moving—you tell yourself, over and over again, 'I'm me. I'm right here. This is me. I'm right here.' You keep reminding yourself that you're right there, and you're balanced and standing upright and that there's nothing wrong with you no matter what weird things are happening around you. And in a few minutes, you'll stop being sick."

"That works, huh?"

Morinda raised her eyebrows then let them drop. "It worked for me. I stopped being sick, and I've never had a problem with it since."

"Maybe I'll give it a try. It'd be a shame to drive all this way to Baja and not go out for some deep-sea action."

"If you want, I can tell you who the best captains in town are."

"Hey, that'd be great. Appreciate it."

They'd reached the site where Lou and Flower's RV and the car they'd towed behind it were parked. They set the ice chest near the door. "May as well leave it here," Flower said. "I've gotta clean these fish before I take 'em in."

He leaned the fishing rods against the side of the RV, slipped the straps of his hip waders off his shoulders, and stepped out of the leggings. Then he took the tackle box from Morinda.

"Could ya hang out for a minute? I wanna get somethin' to write down the names and addresses of those guys ya were telling me about. The ones with boats. Hold on, let me see if it's clear."

He pushed the door to the RV open and called out, "Hey! Lou! Ya in here?"

There was no response.

Flower said to Morinda, "He must've gotten up and gone somewhere. Go on in."

Morinda entered ahead of Flower. He brought the tackle box in after her, carrying it to the galley area to set it on the floor next to the refrigerator cabinet.

"You've really been a lot of help, Morinda. It was Morinda, right? Let me give ya one of these fish. As a way of sayin' thanks."

"You don't have to do that."

"No, really. We're not gonna be able to eat all this, and it'd just spoil by the time I got it home."

Flower ignored her protests and pulled apart the sections of a newspaper that lay on the table. He stepped outside and took the largest of the roosterfish he'd caught and when he returned to the RV he wrapped the Business section of the paper around it, tucking the ends into the folds so the whole thing held together as a container. He lay the package on the table.

While he washed his hands under the tap in the sink, he said, "So, ya seem to know almost everybody in San Estaban. Ya lived here your whole life?"

"Well, not my *whole* life. I wasn't born here. But I've been here ever since I can remember."

"Where ya from originally?"

"Los Angeles."

"Really?"

"That's what my father says."

"You're mother doesn't agree with him?"

"My mother's dead."

"Oh, sorry. You're American, then. Ya must be about—what? Sixteen?"

"Fourteen."

"Fourteen?" He appeared thoughtful for a moment. "Ya seem more mature than that. And then ya moved here with your dad. Your dad bought the RV park. And ya said he owns another business in town, too?"

"A bar. It's called Snidely Whiplash."

"Like in the old Dudley Doright cartoons! Cool! He must be doin' all right for himself. What kind of work did he have when he was in L.A., do ya know? Was he in business there, too?"

"I don't really know what he did then. He—"

A door down the hallway opened and Lou's voice carried to the galley as he called out, "Aaah! There's nothin' so overrated as a piece of ass, and nothin' so underrated as a good shit!"

Lou appeared in the opening that faced on to the galley, shirtless and shoeless, stretching his arms and bending his torso to limber up. He let his arms droop by his sides and stood erect when he noticed Morinda.

"Oh, hey, sorry about that. Didn't know ya had company."

Morinda turned to Flower and said, "I have to go. I have some things I have to take care of."

She walked toward the door, but before she'd gone two steps, Flower called to her. "Hey! Don't forget the fish!"

He'd picked up the bundle in the newspaper and was holding it out for her to take. She stopped, reached for it, and then hurried out of the RV.

Lou pressed his lips together as he watched Morinda leave. "Mmm-mmm-mm," he said with approval. "Not much by way of tits, but what the hell—more than a mouthful's wasted. And she's got a great ass! Didn't realize ya were puttin' the make on her, or I wouldn't've cock-blocked ya. How close were ya to gettin' her in the sack?"

Flower stared at Lou, his expression clearly showing his annoyance. "I was in the middle of gettin' some information from her."

"What kinda information? Like, is she a moaner?"

Lou laughed harshly.

"She's a nice kid," Flower insisted. He used a paper towel to sop up the melted ice he'd spilled on the floor when he'd brought the fish in to give Morinda.

"Yeah, sure, Flower. Guess what? They were all nice kids before some degenerate low-life like you or me managed to get 'em out of their panties. After that—" he made a noise imitating a plane in a steep dive and the resulting collision with the earth while he mimicked the coinciding action with his hand. "Crash and burn. If ya ain't a virgin, you're a whore. If they do, they're no good, and if they don't, what good are they? Ya get that one and that friend of hers, the one she was with yesterday—get them together in the sack and make a sandwich. Yee-hah!"

A staccato series of engine backfires sounded outside the RV, and Lou used one finger to pry apart the slats of the Venetian blinds on the window beside him.

Flower said, "The one she was with yesterday—ya mean the mayor's daughter?"

"The *delegado*'s daughtero," Lou said, jocularly emphasizing each syllable while he peered out. "I wouldn't mind getting somethin' straight between me and that one, too."

"That'd be all we need. Like we don't have enough trouble as it is."

"Whattaya mean?"

"Ya don't remember night before last? What happened then?"

"Sure, I remember." Lou seemed to be concentrating more on what was taking place outside than on the conversation. The backfires'd given way to the stuttering gasps of an engine; then the cranking of a motor that refused to start. "I just don't recall anything that happened that's any trouble for us. Check this out! He ever gets that thing goin' again, I bet it'll do seventy—if he pushed it off a cliff!"

Flower went to another window to see what Lou was talking about. There was an ancient, battered pickup truck in the cul-de-sac that ran past the space their RV was parked in that was painted three different colors of primer and on the bed was something written in Spanish in crude lettering that hadn't been applied with benefit of a stencil.

"What's that say on the side?" Flower asked.

"'Four Seasons of Life and then Heaven.'"

"What's that mean?"

"They name their trucks here." Lou shrugged. "What's it mean? How the hell would I know? He's some delivery guy who can't afford anything better than that deathtrap, and he figures givin' it a classy name makes up for how crappy it runs."

An old Mexican man with white stubble covering his chin sat behind the wheel of the stalled pickup, futilely turning the key in the ignition.

"He's gonna run that battery down," Flower said. "He oughta push start it. That can't be an automatic, can it? It's gotta be a stick shift. Let's help him get it movin'."

"What? I'm not gonna push that thing! He got into this by himself, let him get out of it by himself."

But Flower wasn't listening. He hastened out the door and was calling to the old man in the cab of the pickup, "Hey! I'll push ya! Pop the clutch! Okay? Pop the clutch!" He motioned with his hands to show the clutch pedal jumping off the floorboard.

The old man seemed to understand and he smiled, showing wide gaps of missing teeth, and waved one shaky, liver-spotted hand in agreement. Flower got behind the tailgate and shoved. It only took a few seconds to get the truck up to five miles per hour, the driver engaged the transmission, and the pickup's engine started to life. The truck lurched, then pulled away from Flower, the old man in the cab once more lifting his palsied hand to wave thanks. Flower waved back.

"I never had you pegged as a bleedin' heart," Lou said when Flower returned to the RV.

"Well, that's one of the reasons I did it."

"Huh?"

Flower shrugged. "I don't like people thinkin' they got me figured out. Like you, just now—ya thought ya had me figured out, ya thought ya knew me so well that ya could predict what I'd do, that I'd say to hell with the guy."

"Asshole should do some maintenance on that rollin' piece of shit," Lou muttered.

Flower smiled. "The old guy just needed a hand, so I helped him. And I don't like people thinkin' they know me, like I'm somethin' that's so basic they can always guess how I'm gonna act under any given set of conditions. I don't want people assumin' they already know everything there is to know about me, thinkin' about me like they can bet on a race when the fix's in. People do that to me, it makes me feel—I dunno, it makes me feel like I'm some kind of simple life form, like I'm only a *thing* that can't be anything except what it is, instead of a human with free will. That bothers me." Flower turned his hands over to look at the palms. They were covered with dirt from touching the truck. "Ya finished in the biffy? I wanna take a shower after I clean and scale what I caught."

"I'm done for now."

"We gotta go into town as soon as I get ready. I'll need ya along to translate."

CHAPTER 4

Lott came into the dining room of his house and saw the altar set up in the corner that Morinda'd made for her mother for the Day of the Dead, which was actually two days, the first and second of November. The altar was a set of boxes in the shape of a pyramid covered with a tablecloth on which were spread *papel picado*, or paper cutouts, candles, and sugar candies in the form of skulls. The Day of the Dead was still a ways away, so Morinda hadn't yet put out the fruits, vegetables, and loaves of *pan de los muertos*. It was a tradition Morinda took part in every year in memory of her mother, whom Morinda couldn't truly remember at all. Lott never interfered in her celebration of the holiday, though he himself never participated. When she first began to take an interest in *El Dia de los Muertos*, when she was about seven or eight, Morinda asked him what her mother's favorite foods'd been so she could put them out at the place at the table that was set for the deceased on November 2, when the spirits of adults who'd died were supposed to return. And the last few years, Morinda'd tried to wheedle more information about her mother from him: she'd begged him for pictures of her mother so she could use them to decorate the altar. But Lott made it a habit, whenever Morinda inquired about her mother, to turn his face into an expressionless blank and look away and not reply. The only response he'd ever given Morinda to questions about her mother was a shake of his head and the words, "I dunno. I don't remember." He hoped she'd come to believe the subject was too painful for him to want to recall, and his daughter'd eventually accept the fact that he wouldn't discuss it. So far, that hadn't happened.

He heard someone entering through the kitchen door, and then Morinda talking to Erminia, the cook. He followed the voices to their source.

Erminia was unwrapping a fish from a folded newspaper at the sideboard while Morinda watched.

"Hi, Dad," she said when he entered the kitchen.

"Hi. Where'd that come from?" he said, speaking in English as Morinda'd done.

"Those men I told you checked in yesterday, the ones in that big old RV? One of them gave it to me. Hey, Dad, I wanted to ask you—what kind of work did you do when you lived in L.A.?"

"When I lived in L.A. which time? I was in L.A. off and on for a lot of years."

"Oh, I mean when Mom was still alive. When I was first born. Right before we moved here."

Lott answered warily, fearing this was nothing but an overture by his daughter toward an interrogation about her mother. "I was in sales."

"What did you sell?"

"Life insurance. Door to door. It was a pain in the ass. Why? What's with this sudden interest in ancient history?"

"Oh, the guy who gave me the fish asked me something about it."

"Why'd this total stranger wanna know about my work history?"

"He was just making conversation. Don't get all weird about it, Dad."

"I hafta go into town. I'll be at the bar if anyone needs me."

"If no one needs you, won't you still be at the bar?" Morinda asked.

"No one likes a smart ass."

"I know—it's the family curse." She clutched her father's arm in both her hands and gushed, "Papa! You never should have laughed at the old Gypsy woman's magic and *dared* her to make life a living hell for you and all your descendants till the end of time!"

"Where do ya get this stuff?"

Releasing her father, she said, "If it didn't happen that way—it should have."

"What are you gonna be doin' today?"

Morinda answered a bit more prosaically, "I have an assignment to work on. 'Write two thousand words on local history, the topic of your choice.' Slaving over a hot computer the whole day, typing my fingers to the bone." She waggled her two forefingers to show which ones'd be wasting away. "Does life get any better than this?"

"Not for you, it doesn't. Enjoy it while ya can."

"Four or five hours of staring at the computer screen, digging up facts about Baja on the Internet."

"So long, honey. I'll see ya later."

He kissed her on the cheek.

"Bye, Dad."

When Lott arrived in San Estaban, he parked in the gravel lot behind his bar. He intended to enter through the rear entrance, but he spotted some scraps of paper littering the narrow strip of Bermuda grass that grew along the side of the building. He policed the area, picking up even the few discarded cigarette butts he found, carrying the trash with him so he could dump it in a wastepaper basket inside. When he rounded the corner at the front, he glanced up the street. He saw Enrique Espinoza's squat form standing outside his bait and tackle shop three doors away while he talked to two men Lott presumed were American *turistas*: one of them in his mid-thirties, tall, lean, and wearing a red and blue team warm-up jacket; the other ten years older, shorter, fleshier, bald with a fringe of black hair, and sporting a mustache. The man in the team jacket was facing Lott, and he tracked Lott with his gaze.

Lott noticed Espinoza turning to see what the American was so intent upon, and he shifted the litter he held into his right hand so he could wave to Espinoza with his left before he went inside.

He made a quick survey as soon as he entered. There were four people seated at the bar, and no one occupied any of the tables—a typical crowd for this time of day. Guillermo, the daytime bartender, was on duty. The television behind the bar was tuned to ESPN, but no one was watching the stock car race. Lott pushed the swinging half-door that blocked access to the space behind the bar, found the thirty-gallon trash barrel under the counter, and dropped the papers and cigarette butts he'd collected into it.

Guillermo joined him, and Lott asked in Spanish, "How is business?"

The bartender shrugged indifferently. "Slow."

"Don't worry. Tips will get a lot better soon," Lott promised. "The Baja 1000's next month, and the tourists will start swarming."

The Baja 1000's an off-road race sponsored by SCORE International held each year in November. It's centered on Ensenada, and on most occasions it's kept strictly within Baja Norte, but every few years the course's extended to run the full length of the peninsula, from Ensenada to La Paz. The event's one of the major attractions drawing tourists to the region, and it's looked forward to by all the area business owners and shopkeepers, as well as by those of their employees who supplement their earnings through tips.

Guillermo smiled in anticipation, then he said, "Hey, boss. There were a couple of guys in here earlier. Americans. They were asking a lot of questions about the business. I told them they should talk to you."

"What guys?"

"I don't know their names. They said they were staying at the RV park, though, so you could find out easy enough. One's wearing a Clippers jacket. The other one's bald, with a mustache."

Lott recognized them as the men he'd just seen.

"What did they want to know?"

"Oh, they were asking how an American can get a business started here. Whether you can buy the land, or if you have to lease it, if you need to put up a bond, what it costs to get a liquor license. They sounded like they were scouting the place out, like they wanted to set up their own business. I told them they should talk to a chamber of commerce to get the story straight, since they'd have to join one to run a business here anyway."

"I think I saw the guys you're talking about, standing out there with Enrique Espinoza. I hadn't noticed them around before. They're staying at the RV park?"

"That's what they said."

"Huh."

"I told you about them because they might be trouble for you, boss."

"Why do you say that?"

"They first started asking questions about how to get a business going. What you have to do in Mexico to get licenses and stuff. What kind of taxes you have to charge your customers, and what you have to pay to the government. Things like that. Then they started to get nosy. About you. Asked me if you were a Mexican or an American. Where you were from. When you opened the bar here. How much money you paid for it. How much money the place makes. Things I didn't think were any of their business. So I shut up and told them they'd have to ask you about any of that, if you were willing to tell them. You better watch these guys, boss.

They sound like maybe they want to open a bar in San Estaban. Maybe they want to drive you out of business. The one, the mustache one, he doesn't seem too bright, but the other guy, the one in the Clippers jacket, him—"

Guillermo closed his right hand into a fist with the little finger held out and lifted it to make the *colmillo*, "the fang," by drilling the little finger into his jaw to show the man he was referring to could really screw someone in a deal.

Lott pondered the possibility that the two men were planning to open an American-type bar in competition with his in San Estaban, and the thought worried him. Twelve years before, when he first arrived in Mexico, Lott'd bought the RV park, and a year later he purchased a small *cantina* he then fixed up and converted into a classy American-style bar he named Snidely Whiplash. The place attracted American college students on spring break as well as the tourists who stayed at the RV park. It'd done well for him, though it wasn't as well-known or as prosperous as Hussong's Cantina in Ensenada or the Giggling Marlin in Cabo San Lucas, but then San Estaban wasn't Ensenada or Cabo San Lucas. The bar's main attractions (or conversation pieces, which was how Lott thought of them, since no one ever actually used them for longer than about five seconds) were the several tanning lamps at tables in the back; the bar's advertising slogan was, "Go home from Baja tan and fit—and never leave Snidely Whiplash!"

Lott's small American bar did well because it dominated a niche market in tiny San Estaban, but the population of the town was growing, and far more Americans were stopping on their way to and from Cabo and Ensenada and the other tourist hotspots in Baja. Perhaps, Lott thought, he'd grown too complacent, and he should take seriously the threat of competitors moving in on what he'd come to consider his exclusive piece of turf. Another American bar in town could seriously cut into his profit margin. He filed the thought away in the back of his mind that he should keep a wary eye on the two visitors who seemed so interested in his business affairs.

Later that afternoon, Lott took an unopened bottle of tequila from behind the bar and paid a neighborly visit to Enrique Espinoza at his bait and tackle shop up the street. Fewer fishers came to Baja Norte as the seasons changed and winter approached, and Enrique was loafing in front of his business, sitting in a rattan chair he periodically moved to keep it permanently in a sunny spot as the day wore on. He was in his late sixties or early seventies, Lott guessed, and though he'd once been a hardy outdoorsman who captained a boat and owned several others besides that were chartered by parties of deep-sea anglers, his hands'd become so crippled with arthritis that his sons'd taken over the more active aspects of the business. Now, Enrique only managed the shop. He spent most of his time when he wasn't waiting on customers dozing on the porch beside the bottled-water cooler that was kept there so the old man didn't have to get up to get a drink when he needed to wash down more of the numerous pills he'd been prescribed for his failing health.

Enrique had his head turned away, so he didn't see Lott coming. The old man rubbed one hand in the palm of the other, soothing the aching joints of his knuckles while grimacing at the discomfort they caused him. Lott knew the old man was too proud to show anyone that his arthritis slowed him in any way, so he paused ten feet from where Enrique sat and ostentatiously stamped his foot on the concrete walkway as though he'd gotten something on his shoe and was attempting to remove it. He kept his eyes turned downward, giving Enrique time to react to the warning. Enrique forced a smile and let his one hand release the other as Lott finished wiping the sole.

"Hello, my friend!" Enrique said. "Good afternoon!"

Lott held the bottle aloft. "I know you can't leave your post, so I thought I'd see if I could talk you into having a drink with me."

"It would be an insult to my honored friend to refuse such a gracious invitation," Enrique said expansively. "Pour, my friend, pour!"

Lott cracked the seal around the mouth of the bottle while Enrique pulled two paper cups from the dispenser attached to the bottled-water cooler. Lott carefully filled each of the shotglass-sized cups, handing one to Enrique and keeping the other for himself. The two men toasted each other and said, "*Salud!*" at the same time before they drank.

Lott asked after Enrique's health, and wondered how his wife and sons were, and how the fishing'd been, and how the bait and tackle shop was doing; Enrique asked after Lott's health and well-being, and how his beautiful daughter was, and how his bar and RV park were flourishing.

"I saw you talking to two men earlier," Lott said, after the polite preliminaries were out of the way. "They looked like Americans."

"Oh, yes. The one does not speak any Spanish, and his friend does the talking. But the one who does not speak, he asks the questions."

"Which one doesn't speak Spanish?"

"The tall blonde one, the one who has no mustache."

An image of the two men flashed into Lott's mind; the one who'd been watching Lott that morning was the brains behind the operation, then, as the bartender Guillermo'd said.

"What kind of questions was he asking?"

"Oh, they saw you cleaning up around your building. They wondered who you were and asked about your bar. I told them how that place used to be such a dump before you came here. When it was that trashy dive of a *cantina*, before you bought it from that *cabrón* of a *gachupín*. That filthy pig of a Spaniard! But you came and bought his place, and changed it into a clean, respectable place where a man can drink without having to worry about getting crabs from some *puta* he'd never so disrespect his *verga* by putting inside her! I told them of the disgusting *putas* who used to be found in the place in the old days, before you took it over, and they were amazed!"

"It was in bad shape when I bought it," Lott agreed.

"It was the asshole of the world!" Enrique declared. "I do not deny it, I thought then that you were a fool to have saddled yourself with that pest hole! And when I asked you then what you planned to do with it, and you told me you were going to make it into a decent bar, I told you it could not be done! I told you—and I am ashamed to say it, I blush to repeat it—that you can't shine shit, my friend! And look what you have done with it! It has been transformed! The two who were here, they wanted to know how long it took you to change it from the barnyard it was when that pig-fucker of a Spaniard owned it. I told them that you bought it eleven years ago—that I was proud to have been your friend ever since you first came to San Estaban, and that the two of us have worked together as neighbors for that long, but that you had pulled down the shit heap of a building you bought from the Spaniard as soon as you got it, and that you created this piece of art of a new building only a year after you arrived."

Enrique was already on his third drink. His fulsome praise for Lott's accomplishments was embarrassing, and his garrulity could only be expected to get worse as he drank more. Lott smiled indulgently, and said, "So they were interested in my business, were they?"

"Oh, my friend, they wanted to know everything I could tell them about you, the man who brought such a wonder into being! They were surprised that you, a successful businessman, had been able to raise a daughter on his own—without having a wife to help him!"

"They asked about Morinda?"

"Certainly! They met her when they checked in at your RV park, didn't they? And the one who does not speak Spanish, he met her on the beach this morning when he was fishing. He bought his license from me yesterday, you know."

It clicked in Lott's mind: the one who'd met Morinda on the beach must've given her the fish, so he was the one who'd questioned her about what sort of work he'd done in Los Angeles before he came to Mexico.

"Did you get the idea they were scouting around to see about setting up their own business here in San Estaban?"

"Those two?" Enrique seemed shocked by the suggestion. "Those two settle here in San Estaban? No, my friend. They're not going to be staying anyplace as small as this. They're from the city, you can tell. And they will only fit in in a big city. They would never move to a small town. It's not their nature. They remind me of those who come here to hire a boat for a day or a week to fish. The ones who think they want to relax on the ocean, to get away from it all. But as soon as they're on the boat, they pace from one end to the other, and they scowl at the water like it's played them a dirty trick, and they have to give orders to everybody on the boat like they're still in their office in Los Angeles or San Francisco or New York until I tell them to be quiet and fish or I'll throw them the hell off the boat and they can swim back. The kind of men who can't wait to return to the city."

Lott had one more drink with Enrique, but then he excused himself. He insisted on leaving the rest of the bottle with Enrique, and he returned to Snidely Whiplash.

That evening when he went home, he stopped off in the office of the RV park and checked the registrations from the past few days until he found that of the two men who were asking so many questions about him in San Estaban: Flower Child Ashland, with a home address in Santa Monica, and Lou Helmholtz, home address given as Torrance.

The next day as he drove through San Estaban, he saw the same two leaving the office of Victorio Flores, Notary Public. Lott knew Flores well. In Mexico, a Notary Public's not merely a minor functionary who witnesses signatures on documents and graces them with a seal to verify they've been duly completed in the manner prescribed by law; a Notary Public in Mexico's an attorney with advanced training before one of whom every transaction involving land such as a mortgage has to be executed, and Flores had a graduate degree and so was appropriately addressed not simply as *Señor* Flores, but as *Licendiado* Flores. *Licendiado* Flores was the attorney who'd aided Lott when he arrived in Baja a dozen years before in gaining title to the RV park.

When the Transpeninsular Highway was first built to provide direct access from the United States to every part of Baja, the Mexican government assumed it'd attract large numbers of American tourists, so they threw up many RV parks along its route. But most of these were cheaply built, and lacked the amenities American travelers wanted, so they languished and fell into disuse and disrepair before ultimately being abandoned. The RV park Lott currently owned'd been in the possession of a *paracaidista*, a parachutist as they were known, who'd taken over the site by the simple process of squatting on it. Lott, as a foreign national, couldn't legally own real estate within thirty miles of the coast, so he'd had to wend his way through a maze of intricate judicial technicalities to establish himself as the owner of the RV park, and later of the *cantina* he'd rebuilt into Snidely Whiplash. *Licendiado* Flores served as his legal guide through the purchase of both.

Recognizing the men he now knew as Flower and Lou exiting the lawyer's office, Lott did a double take. Neither Flower, the one who spoke no Spanish but who seemed to be the leader of the pair, nor Lou, the one who did all the talking, noticed him as he went by. He slowed to a crawl and watched them in the rearview mirror: they ambled to a small Japanese car parked on the street, got in, flipped a U-turn, and drove westward, probably returning to the large, expensive RV they kept docked at Lott's RV park.

Lott made a snap decision and whipped the wheel of his own car around. He drove to the front of the sandstone building in which the attorney conducted his practice and stopped. He went inside and asked the receptionist if *Licendiado* Flores'd be able to see him without an appointment. He was admitted to the inner office in only a few minutes.

Flores, as always, was elegantly and conservatively dressed in a black pinstriped three-piece wool suit that was totally unsuitable for the climate of Baja, but which didn't appear to cause him any degree of discomfort in his air-conditioned offices. Flores rose from his place at his desk to shake hands with Lott, and then he invited Lott to take one of the chairs on the other side of the desk.

"What can I help you with today?" Flores asked.

"There were two men who just left your office. Their names are Ashland and Helmholtz, I think."

Flores didn't respond, not even with so much as a nod of his head to acknowledge he'd heard what Lott said.

"Are they setting up a business here in town? Is that why they came to you?"

Flores leaned back in his chair and contemplated the ceiling. "It would be a grave ethical violation for me to discuss with another the affairs of someone who has consulted me on a legal matter. I could not properly speak to someone else of the matters you and I have talked about concerning your businesses, nor would it be appropriate for me to tell tales out of school about what another client has discussed with me. It would not even be possible for me to tell a third party that you and I have had conversations of a legal nature. Nor would I feel it right to mention to you the same thing about another. I hope you can understand that it is not my intention to be in any way disrespectful to you, *Señor* Tavia. But on a delicate matter of this kind, I do not feel I can respond in any other way to your question."

"Maybe you can advise me on a matter of business, then."

"If I can, I would be happy to help you."

"If someone were to set up a new bar, say in San Estaban, would they still have to file a license with the *subdelegación*?"

"Of course."

"If a foreigner—an American, for example—were to take a lease on land for a business in San Estaban, would they need to take care of the paperwork before a Notary Public?"

"That is the law, yes."

"Filings for business licenses are public records, aren't they? Anyone can see them?"

"Absolutely."

"I guess I should go over to the *subdelegación* building, then."

As Lott started to rise, Flores spun about in his swivel chair to face him. Something in Flores's expression told Lott the attorney had something further to convey, so he dropped back into his chair and waited.

"Since you are here, I wonder if perhaps you could help me with a minor matter. A task that has recently been given to me by—a new client."

Initially, Lott was piqued by the lawyer's temerity. Flores'd blown him off when he asked for a favor, but he immediately turned around and asked Lott for help. His first reaction was to tell the lawyer to forget it, but he thought better of it and instead smiled, and said, "If I can."

"This problem was presented to me, as I said, very recently, and it was a stroke of good luck that you should happen to visit me when you have. Because you are the perfect person to provide me with the information I require. You see, I have been asked to make inquiries—discreet inquiries—about a man who might possibly have been here in San Estaban. One who might still be living in San Estaban, or who might have passed through at some time in the past. An American. And since you own the RV park where many Americans stay when they come to Baja, and you also own a bar to which many Americans go when they visit, I thought you would be the best source of information for this, that if anyone would have heard of this person, it would be you."

"It depends on who it is. What's the name?"

"The name I was given is—Patrick Lott."

Lott made an effort to keep his face impassive.

"He is supposed to be in his early forties," Flores went on, speaking in a conversational tone that gave no hint that he placed any special emphasis upon his words. "About your age, I believe. He might have come here for the first time about twelve years ago."

"Patrick Lott, you said?"

"Yes."

"It doesn't sound familiar. No, I don't think I've ever heard the name."

Flores nodded his head and again leaned back in his chair. "I had never heard the name, either, but I was asked to find out what I could. As I said, this was meant to be investigated so that word of the inquiry does not get spread around as gossip. So if you would not mention it to anyone else, I would appreciate it."

"Of course," Lott said blandly.

"Well—" Flores stood and reached across his desk to shake hands with Lott. "I thank you for your assistance. And I'm very sorry that I was not able to answer your questions about the—the other subject. It's a matter of confidentiality. I hope you understand."

"Yes. Thank you. I understand perfectly. Perfectly."

Lott walked through the lobby then out to the street where his car was parked, understanding *Licendiado* Flores perfectly. Flores'd said that a new client'd very recently asked him to find out about Patrick Lott, a name Lott hadn't used since leaving the United States a dozen years before; and the two men Lott'd seen leaving Flores's office'd been making inquiries about him, seeking to establish precisely when he'd arrived in San Estaban, and asking about Morinda, ever since they'd showed up in town two days before. Flores was telling Lott, in as forthright a manner as he dared, that Flower Ashland and Lou Helmholtz hadn't been in the attorney's office that day in order to get advice about setting up a business; they'd been there asking about him, only this time they'd let slip the name of Patrick Lott, which gave their whole game away: it told him precisely why the two strangers were in San Estaban.

"That bitch, Denise!" he growled to himself. "She never could hold up her end of a deal!"

CHAPTER 5

Lott parked his car behind Snidely Whiplash and entered through the rear. There were half a dozen people drinking in the bar. They were all Americans, most of them staying at his RV park. His attention was drawn to the far side of the room where the stocky, baldheaded man with the thick mustache, Lou Helmholtz, was playing the old-fashioned Bally pinball machine with lots of body English, vigorously hip-checking and jolting the corner of the device with the palms of his hands and issuing loud cries of triumph interspersed with moans of disgust. At a table near the pinball machine, nursing a drink, sat his companion, Flower Child Ashland. Flower kept his eyes trained on Lott from the moment he came in.

Lott retreated to his private office, closed the the door, and settled into the chair behind his rosewood desk to brood. He remembered something that'd taken place when he'd been in Mexico only a couple of years. Morinda'd gone through a stage when she was about four when she frequently awoke screaming. Her nightmares were different each time: once she was being chased by a giant spider; another time she was trapped on the roof of a building while hungry lions and tigers circled her. One night Morinda yelled so loudly that both her nursemaid and Lott rushed to her room to see what the trouble was. When he realized his daughter was only suffering from another bad dream, Lott sent the *nana* back to her own room and sat on the edge of Morinda's bed to help Morinda through the crisis.

"They're coming!" Morinda cried frantically in English. After two years in Mexico, she spoke Spanish and English with equal facility, and she used them interchangeably. "They're after me!"

"Who's comin', sweety?"

"Bad men! They're after me!"

"Shh, shh, shh," Lott said to calm her. She lay on her bed, her dark hair that'd grown to her shoulders spread across the pillow. Lott put his hand on her back and patted her. "It was just a dream, sweety," Lott went on. "It was only a dream, and now it's over."

"They're coming," Morinda said, her voice still quavering with terror, but no longer so loud that it carried to other parts of the house. "The bad men."

"What bad men, honey? Was it somebody ya know?"

"No. I don't know. I didn't see them. But they're coming. They want to catch me. And if they catch me, they're going to hurt me."

"Shh, shh. No, baby. No one's gonna catch ya. No one's gonna hurt ya. I promise, sweety. No one can hurt ya while I'm here. And I'll always be here. See? So everything's gonna be fine. It was only a dream. It wasn't real. You're in your room, in our house, and I'm right here. So nothing can get ya. The bad men, they can't do anything to ya."

"They'll hurt me."

"No, sweety. No one's gonna hurt ya. I promise. If someone ever tried to hurt ya, they'd have to go through me first. All right?"

Morinda's head was still nestled on the pillow, but she turned her dark eyes up to look at her father and said in a tearful little voice, "What if they go through you?"

Lott half-smiled at the ingenuous egotism of the four-year-old's question, but he rubbed the grin away with his hand and kept his facial expression and his tone of voice very solemn as he answered, "If they go through me—*then* you should worry. But not until then. Until then, ya let *me* worry. Okay?"

She sighed heavily and snuggled her face into the bedclothes. "Okay," she whispered, and she closed her eyes.

Lott leaned forward and kissed her forehead. She did not open her eyes again. Lott, with his hand still resting on Morinda's back, began to sing to her in a low, crooning voice a song his own mother'd used to sing him to sleep. He patted Morinda in time with the rhythm:

> I love you a bushel and a peck,
> A bushel and a peck,
> A bushel and a peck.
> I love you a bushel and a peck,
> A bushel and a peck,
> A bushel and a peck . . .

By the time he got to the third stanza, she'd fallen asleep again.

It'd been twelve years since Lott'd bought Morinda from Denise and fled with her to Mexico. The Furies'd been sleeping from that time, but they'd since awakened; the bad men had come. And it was time for him to fulfill the promise he'd made to his daughter.

He left his office and returned to the bar, proceeding directly to the table where Flower sat. Flower had a drink poured in a twelve-ounce highball glass in front of him; Lou, still at the pinball machine, had left a beer in a pilsner glass resting on the table in front of his vacant chair.

"Everything all right here?" Lott asked.

Flower watched Lott as he approached; his cool, detached expression didn't change except to take on a slightly bemused edge at Lott's words.

"Fine as frog's hair. And that's pretty fine."

"I hope I'm not disturbin' ya."

"I can always spare some time for a fellow American," Flower said. "That sounds like something out of B. Traven, doesn't it? *The Treasure of the Sierra Madre*. Ya ever read Traven?"

"No, but I saw the movie. I prefer Malcolm Lowry. *Under the Volcano*."

"I found Lowry to be—incomprehensible. Couldn't follow him. But I liked Graham Greene's *The Power and the Glory*. At the end, when the whiskey priest's about to be shot by the firin' squad, and he realizes in the face of his own death how easy it'd've been to be a saint—that's great stuff."

"Everybody's got a different image of Mexico. Mind if I sit down?"

Flower waved his hand toward an empty chair and said, "Ya own the place, don't ya?"

"Yeah, I do, as a matter of fact. Ya seem to know a lot about me."

"You're a prominent citizen in a small town. And there aren't many Americans who live here in San Estaban year-round, so ya stand out."

Lott asked bluntly, "Why are you here?"

Flower shrugged. "Why does anybody come to Mexico?"

"Different reasons," Lott said. "But why are *you* here?"

Flower turned away and smiled wistfully, as though his thoughts were on something else entirely. "For the fishin'. For the water sports. For the sun tan." Flower flicked his head toward the tanning lamp tables and then watched Lott ironically over the rim of his glass as he sipped his drink.

Lott shifted in his chair and hunched his shoulders closer to Flower, leaning several inches further across the table. "I know why you're here," Lott said, lowering his voice as though revealing a confidence.

"Ya should," Flower said, his reserved demeanor unchanged. "I just told ya."

"No. I mean why you're really here. I know."

Lou came back to the table, loudly announcing, "Great machine, man! Not like those pussy video games they've replaced the pinball machines with in the States. If ya can't tilt the machine, it's not a game of skill, I say!"

He picked up the glass of beer and drained it, then set it on the table noisily and said, "What's up?" looking from Flower to Lott and back again.

Lott remained silent. Flower said, "Nothin' important. We're just talkin'."

"Ya need me for anything?" Lou asked.

"No, I don't think so. Mr. Tavia—?" Flower gave a significant glance toward Lott, his eyebrows arched. "Mr. Tavia speaks English."

Lou shrugged his shoulders, turned, and strolled back to the pinball machine. He dropped a quarter in the coin slot, the lights and bells came to life, and he returned to his play.

"Maybe we could go to my office to talk," Lott said. "There'll be fewer distractions there, and the booze's better."

Flower drained his glass to the bottom. The crushed ice at the bottom rattled when he set it down. "Sure."

Lott led Flower to the private room at the rear of the building and shut the door behind them. He waved Flower to a seat and said, "Sorry about the clutter. We're having a temporary storage problem."

Lott's office, although comfortably furnished, had dozens of cardboard boxes filled with cases of liquor stacked five-high around the walls.

"I should have such problems!"

"You a Scotch drinker?"

Without waiting for a reply, Lott cracked open a case and removed a bottle from it.

"This's a good single malt here. It's good straight. Or I can get some ice if ya want."

He poured the Scotch neat into old-fashioned glasses for both Flower and himself. Then he settled into his chair at the desk.

"You've been askin' questions about me all over town. Askin' about Morinda."

Flower didn't rise to the bait. He sipped his Scotch and looked at Lott expectantly, as though waiting to be told the point of the conversation.

"There's only one reason ya can be here: Morinda's mother sent ya to find her. To take her back. Denise must've gotten clean and sober someplace along the line, huh? And then decided to welsh on our agreement. Yeah, that's pretty much her style.

"Since you're looking for Morinda, ya must be either cops or private detectives. And I figure if ya were cops, you'd've gone to the state police first, and they'd've sent ya through the *subdelegación*, and ya wouldn't've had to waste a lot of time fooling around questioning my neighbors and employees. So you've got to've been hired by Denise to find Morinda. Which means she's not only gotten clean, she's come into some money, too. I know you guys don't work cheap. What happened, somebody die and leave her an inheritance? She get lucky and win the lottery? Marry some *schmuck* with a big life insurance policy on him just before he kicked off? And now she wants Morinda back—is that it?"

"I couldn't say," Flower said. "I honestly couldn't tell ya."

"Yeah, sure, you've gotta protect your client. Cover your ass. Some sort of code of ethics thing for you guys, huh? Well, let me tell ya about the woman ya wanna take Morinda back to. When I first met Denise, she was turnin' tricks out of her room at the motel she was stayin' in. Morinda wasn't even two years old then, and she had the kid in the room with her while it was goin' on. Except for the times Denise got so high she forgot about her kid, and then Morinda'd wander out into the parkin' lot by herself. Which happened—a lot. If Denise couldn't pick up some john, she used to go around the motel beggin' people for money. So she could blow it at the rock house. She'd take Morinda with her when she made the rounds, 'cause people felt sorrier for her when they saw her. They thought maybe some of what they gave Denise might actually go to the kid. Fat chance! Like that was ever gonna happen!

"Something else ya should consider. Denise's got no proof Morinda's even her kid. Did ya know that? She told me once she had Morinda in the back seat of a car. She was too scared to have the baby at a hospital 'cause they'd've found out Denise was a crack head. Afraid they'd bust her for endangering the health of her baby. So there's no birth certificate. Nothing to prove she's ever even been born. Try taking her back to the States, and I'll throw so many legalities at ya, ya won't know whether to shit or go blind.

"Let me tell ya the kind of—person—ya wanna take Morinda back to, okay? Denise told me this one day. Just out of the blue. Some guy she'd had shacking up with her for a couple of nights woke her up by pissing on her face while she was still asleep in bed. Pissed on her face to say goodbye, then took off. With Morinda in the same room with 'em, the guy she'd hooked up with, another crack head, does this to her. He thought it was funny.

"Whattaya think of a woman who'd let a guy into her place who'd do something like that? With her kid in the same room? Whattaya think of a woman who'd do that? I'm askin' ya."

Flower swirled the Scotch in his glass. He pursed his lips and said, "Not much."

"Yeah. And not only does she let it happen, which's bad enough, but then she walks around the neighborhood, carryin' her kid with her, *tellin'* everybody about it. She admits it. I mean, the woman's got no shame!"

Flower's face remained impassive, though he seemed interested in every word Lott said.

"I can't let ya take Morinda back to that," Lott said. "I don't care if Denise's cleaned herself up. I don't care if she's convinced you she's made herself over into Rebecca of Sunnybrook Farm, it's only on the surface. Deep down inside, she's still what she always was: a worthless piece of garbage. And I won't let her destroy Morinda's life."

Lott leaned forward in his chair. "I'll match whatever Denise's payin' ya. In fact, I'll double it."

Flower took in a deep breath, held it for a moment, then exhaled softly.

"Ya don't wanna tell me what you're chargin' her?" Lott said. "Then how's this. Let me put my bid in at twenty-five thousand. Twenty-five grand. That's American dollars. Paid in cash. No receipt necessary. Whattaya say?"

Flower placed his half-finished glass of Scotch on a coaster on Lott's desk and said, "I'd say that's very generous. Or I might—if I knew exactly what ya expect me to do for the money."

"That's simple. I expect ya to leave San Estaban. Vanish. Go back to the States and forget whatever you've found out about Morinda and me. Ya never heard of us here. Whatever ya came lookin' for, ya didn't find. We're two other people than who ya thought we were. We're not the man, or the girl, Denise's lookin' for after all."

"That's a hell of a lot to pay just to get me to go home, which's something I'm gonna be doin' anyway, and forget a few things."

"Ya need to discuss this with your partner?"

"Lou? He's not my partner. He's just hired help. Don't tell him I said that, it'd hurt his pride. He likes to think he runs with the big dogs. Ya know. But he wouldn't be part of this agreement in any manner, shape, or form."

"Got it," Lott said. "Then I deal strictly with you."

"That'd be best."

"Good. Makes it simpler. So, whattaya think? We have a deal?"

"For twenty-five grand? I gotta admit, the offer is—tempting. Very tempting."

"You're a detective. If ya think I'm lyin' about Denise, if ya think I made this stuff up, look into her background. The woman isn't fit to keep a dog, much less raise a kid. The situation I took Morinda out of was—unbelievable. It was a disgrace, the way she was bein' brought up. Morinda's so much better off here with me—I, I can't even start to express it. Ya gotta see that. Takin' her back to Denise'd be—" Lott broke off, unable to dredge up words that could convey his meaning.

"Can ya see what I'm sayin'?" he ended lamely.

"I can see what you're sayin'," Flower said. "And ya make some good points. I'll give what ya told me some consideration."

"Don't take Morinda away from me. Don't take her back to Denise."

"I really couldn't say for sure what I'm gonna do," Flower said. "I mean, I can see ya feel strongly about the whole thing. And as I said, ya raised some issues I'd like to mull over. And then—there's the money."

"Twenty-five grand," Lott emphasized. "It's all yours. Just say the word."

Flower stood, and Lott rose as well.

"I'd better get back," Flower said. "It's been—interesting."

Lott shook Flower's hand and hurriedly crossed the room to the same cardboard carton from which he'd earlier taken the bottle of single malt they'd been drinking.

"Here, here—take some of this with ya." He pulled another fifth of the whiskey out and passed it to Flower. "It's the best we've got. Ya can't get any better in San Estaban, I guarantee it."

"Well, hey, thanks. Appreciate it."

"Let me know what ya decide. Give me a day or two to get the cash together. But it'll be yours. Don't worry, I've got it. Ya can find me here at the bar, or if I'm not here, I'm at home. Ya know the house attached to the RV park office? Just c'mon up. Let me know."

Flower left the office and went to where Lou sat waiting at the table. Lou'd ordered another beer and halfway finished it. When he saw Flower coming, he gulped the remainder of the glass down. The two left the bar together, going out the front to their car.

As they went, Lou said, "What was that all about?

"I dunno. He was goin' off about what a rotten bitch his ex was and why he divorced her no-good ass. Whenever anybody starts runnin' down their ex, I don't pay a lot of attention. I just zone it out. Why does anybody think the rest of us wanna hear that crap, anyway? But he thinks we're a couple of detectives sent to look for his daughter."

"Why's he think that?"

Flower lifted his shoulders and twisted his face into an expression of total bafflement. "Hell if I know," he said. "But he gave me this free bottle of Scotch!"

CHAPTER 6

Flower leaned the twelve-foot fiberglass pole against the side of the RV, then scaled and cleaned the barred perch he'd caught earlier. With a curved-bladed knife, he first scraped off the gills and then ran the point down the fish's white belly so that a thin stream of red appeared where it opened the meat. He levered the viscera that clung to the interior walls of the body cavity with the knife's tip into a plastic bucket he kept outside for that purpose, and when he'd finished he washed the blood and organs off his hands in a second bucket filled with sea water.

He pulled the suspenders that held up his waders from his shoulders before he sat on the ground in order to tug the leggings off. Thick streaks of white salt where the brine'd dried crumbled beneath his fingers as they skidded across the surface of the rubber. He turned the suit upside down and pounded the sand from each boot, then draped the hip-waders across the aluminum pole that held the awning over the side of the RV.

His eyes burned red from the salt and flecks of grit the wind'd blown into his face and the glare of the afternoon sun reflected off the water; the muscles of his calves ached from fighting the resistance of the water. He hadn't realized how tired he was until he returned to the RV.

Lou was somewhere out of sight when he entered. He could hear Lou speaking animatedly, his voice carrying from the bedroom where he must've taken the cellular phone. Lou nearly shouted, his booming voice only modulated by proximity as he paced back and forth and his steps took him nearer to, or farther from, the open door at the end of the corridor.

"It's almost done down here, and I'll be headin' home . . . That's what I'm sayin', Tawny. I'll have it. I *will* have it . . . Tawny, listen to me, baby—I'm tellin' ya I'll have the money. Just tell 'em to wait a few more— . . . No, no, no. I know they've heard the same thing before, baby, but this time I'm gonna be able to make it right. I'll have the money . . . Oh, c'mon, Tawny, don't you start on me, too. Don't tell me that. Please, baby, please. I'll get it. I promise . . . Oh, no. Don't say you're gonna do that. Please, baby, give me a chance. I'll get this thing together, you'll see."

Flower made a sour face. This was the second time he'd overheard Lou begging his wife. On the drive from Los Angeles to Baja, they'd stopped at a government-owned PEMEX service station to fill up the RV's tank, and Lou placed a call home from a pay phone; Flower inadvertently caught a portion of that discussion as well, and it was almost an exact duplicate of the one he was listening to now, until Lou's wife, Tawny, hung up in the middle of Lou's abject importuning. Each time he was exposed to it, it made Flower feel dirty.

"Don't let 'em take the car," Lou said. "Look, don't—don't—look, don't let 'em get the car, okay?" Lou went silent for a moment, then he said, "Honey, don't—don't talk like that, okay? I'll get the money. Yeah, I know. That's what I'm doin' here. I told ya, there's a good chance this deal'll go through, and I'll be back with enough money to hold everybody off. The guys at the collection agency, the repo people, everybody'll get some. They'll be off our backs. Just don't let 'em take the car. Keep it parked off the street, keep it in the garage so they can't get to it, okay? Yeah, yeah, I know—I hate this stuff, too. But it's only for a little bit longer, and everything'll be okay, I promise."

Flower turned away. On the table across from the galley lay a cluster of objects that belonged to Lou. Lou's Game-Boy was there, and his wallet, along with the solid-frame Smith and Wesson .38 revolver he'd smuggled into Mexico. The pistol was broken open with the hinged cartridge wheel laying to the left. Beside the gun was a can of sewing machine oil, a cylindrical brush for cleaning the barrel, a short metal ramrod with an eye like a needle at one end through which a piece of oiled rag was thrust, and an open box of cartridges. Flower, after he'd washed the fishy smell off his hands with the plastic squeeze bottle of lemon juice at the sink, sat at the table. The petroleum scent of the sewing machine oil, pungent but sweet, mingled with the lingering odors of fish and lemon.

In the bedroom, Lou was saying, "Oh, no, baby, don't say that! Don't say you're gonna leave me! I couldn't live without ya, baby, and that's the truth."

Lou's pleading grew even more shameless, and Flower grimaced with distaste. His eyes turned to the worn leather billfold on the table. It was open, showing photographs in clear plastic covers. Flower picked it up and flipped through the pictures. Some of them were of Lou and a woman, and more were of the same woman standing by herself, and Flower knew this had to be Lou's wife, Tawny.

He was almost shocked. From the way Lou so ignominiously groveled at her feet, Flower assumed Tawny was some bleached-blonde tramp twenty-years younger than Lou who'd used him to get everything she could, and now that Lou's financial resources were drained was planning on ditching him, getting out while the getting was good. So Flower was genuinely surprised when he saw Tawny's image repeated again and again in the photographs, a woman only a few years younger than Lou and twenty to thirty pounds overweight, always wearing the same frowzy sack-like dresses when she wasn't displaying her thunder thighs in Bermuda shorts, her hair lank and her doughy face marked by a permanent deep wrinkle set between her eyes.

Flower dropped the wallet and settled back in his chair when Lou stopped speaking, guessing that the abrupt silence meant Lou's phone call was finished. In a moment, Lou stalked into the kitchen area, a hangdog expression on his face and his shoulders slumped in defeat until he noticed Flower. Then he pulled himself together. He went to the chair across from Flower, tossed the cellular phone underhanded onto the table, seated himself, and resumed cleaning the revolver with quick, efficient movements of his hands.

"What's up?" Lou asked with studied indifference.

"Just been fishin'. You should try it. Every time I ask ya if ya wanna go with me, ya always say no."

"Yeah, I went fishin' once. My dad dragged me and my brother out to some lake in the ass-end of nowhere one time, and the wind was blowin' about a hundred miles an hour the whole day long. We never caught a thing. Like to froze my ass off. I never went fishin' again, and don't see any reason to start now, thank you very much."

"Ya could swim, if ya don't wanna fish. Or go sightseein'. Go into town and meet the natives. Rent a dirt bike and check out the desert."

"Not gonna be enough time to mess with it," Lou said curtly. "I plan on takin' this guy out, and then headin' back to the U. S. of A. I take care of this guy, and I'm outta here. The way I see it, I either get him when he comes out of his bar to go home at night, or I get him at the house. If I do him behind the bar, then I'm gonna hafta sit there and wait for him because he don't always leave at the same time. But if I do him at home, I've gotta worry about witnesses. There's the daughter, and he's got servants runnin' in and out. I don't think any of the help actually lives there, but who can tell? I gotta think of which way's gonna give me the best chance of gettin' outta here once I'm finished, is all."

"Hold it, hold it, hold it," Flower objected.

"Ya gotta problem with that?"

"Yeah, as a matter of fact, I do. Ya can't just go around shootin' people."

"Why do ya think Jack sent me here?" Lou replied angrily. "The guy ripped Jack off big-time, and Jack's gotta do somethin' about it, or other people get the idea they can do it, too. The guy brought it on himself, Flower. He pissed in his bed—now let him drown in it."

He slapped the cylinder of the revolver into place with a snap.

"And why do ya think Jack put me in charge of things here?" Flower responded. "I'm the one who says whether ya waste him or not, remember? I'm the one who decides. There's already been one hasty decision made that turned out to be a major screw up, so let's not be so quick to make another one."

"Ya blamin' what happened on me? Ya weren't doin' any complainin' that night when ya thought he was a *bandito* gettin' ready to back-shoot us and jack the RV, I'll tell ya that. And if I hadn't plugged him, where'd we be right now? I was carrying an unregistered gun, and that means one to five years in a Mexican prison—*and* confiscation of the vehicle it's found in. Zero tolerance for firearms violations, man. We'd both be in a fine fix right now if I hadn't wasted him."

It was something that'd occurred in the Baja desert on their way to San Estaban. Unable to find an RV park, they'd pulled off the highway to an isolated stretch of side road to boondock for the night. They came across an apparently abandoned car with both its doors wide open that straddled both lanes so they couldn't get around it. They stopped and got out of the RV to see what they could do about moving the car out of their way. From behind them, the sound of a slide chambering a round into a semiautomatic pistol took them unawares.

"Turn around!" a man's voice commanded them in Spanish.

Flower didn't understand the order, but he followed Lou's lead; they both raised their hands in the air.

The man who'd ambushed them was short and gaunt, his clothes hanging off him like rags draped on a scarecrow. He had skin the color of mahogany, and deep hollows scooped beneath his brows in which dark wells of blackness smoldered. He shouted at Lou and Flower again in Spanish. Flower spoke out of the side of his mouth to ask Lou, "What'd he say?"

"He wants us to walk off the road. Into the desert."

"Tell him we just stopped to help him. We'll give him a hand gettin' his car off the road. Give him a ride into town if he needs it. Tell him we weren't tryin' to jack his car, for God's sake."

The man with the gun yelled, "*Silencio!*"

"He said shut up," Lou muttered sideways.

"Yeah, I figured that much out," Flower answered *sotto voce*.

The man with the gun took a step closer, and shouted again.

"What's he want now?" Flower said to Lou.

"He says we're to get off the road. Over that way. To the right. He'll be walkin' behind us, he says."

"That's reassuring."

The man with the gun yelled again.

"What's that?"

"He said shut up. This time he wasn't polite about it." Lou switched to Spanish to address the other man. He spoke for a minute, and then the gunman answered him. Flower didn't have to ask for a translation; Lou interpreted as soon as their exchange was over.

"He says he's a cop. Says he wants us off the road for our own safety. And we're supposed to keep our hands up in the air for *his* safety, until he's satisfied were just innocent bystanders."

The man with the gun yelled at them one more time.

"He says to stop wastin' time. If we don't do what he says and get off the road, he's gonna shoot us in the legs to make sure we're not able to make any trouble for him."

"Yeah, he sure talks like a cop," Flower said. "We'd better do it."

Flower turned and started walking; out of the corner of his eye he saw that Lou was following suit. They left the pool of light cast by the RV's headlights and stepped off the asphalt and onto the sand. They dodged prickly desert plants that grew in clusters: *dátillos* ten to fifteen feet tall with nine-inch dagger-like blades for leaves, and organ pipe cactuses.

"Ya think this guy's really a cop?" Flower muttered to Lou.

"I think we're gettin' bullshitted to keep us quiet, so we do what he says. He gets us off the road, he can kill us with no trouble from pain in the ass drive-by witnesses. Then he jacks the RV."

Flower slowed to match Lou's pace, dragging his feet as much as possible. "Ask him if that's his car on the road."

Lou spoke over his shoulder to the gunman.

"He says shut up," Lou reported. "This guy's no cop."

Flower glanced around at the wilderness they were marching deeper and deeper into.

"How much farther we supposed to go?"

Lou asked the man.

"He says until he tells us to stop. Probably where our bodies'll be far enough off the road they won't be found for a few days."

"This's insane!" Flower said. "How'd he get out here if that wasn't his car?"

"Good question."

"Maybe he's workin' with partners, and they got a car. They stopped this car back here for drug runnin', or something. The people who were in the car ran away on foot, his partners took their car to follow 'em, and he's the one they left to watch the abandoned car in case the others circle back. Whattaya think?"

"I don't think he's a cop at all," Lou said. "I think he's gonna waste us and jack the RV."

The Mexican shouted at them, and by this time even Flower knew what the words meant: shut up.

They walked beneath a boojum, a desert plant resembling a tall, skinny upside-down carrot forty feet high. Its trunk tapered slowly to a point at the top, where it put out branches as thick as a pencil and only slightly longer.

Lou muttered, "I'm gonna get something in my shoe in a second. I'm gonna stop to get it out. Move between me and ass-bite here when I do. Got it?"

"What are ya gonna do?"

"Just step in front of me. Do it now."

Lou gave a yelp of pain, came to a sudden halt, and bent over to poke his fingers into his shoe. Flower promptly spun around to face the armed man and shifted over a step to the right, blocking the gunman's view of Lou. The self-proclaimed cop wasn't happy with the new tableau, and he raised his free hand as if to slap Flower out of the way so he could see what Lou was doing.

Lou stepped to Flower's side with the .38 in his own hand, and an orange and yellow flash six inches long shot out of the muzzle. Another followed it, then another. The Mexican dropped to the earth at Flower's feet; his gun fell from his limp fingers and went skittering away into the darkness.

"Jesus fucking goddamn Christ!" Flower said.

When they had a chance to search the abandoned car and found the gaunt man's ID in the glove compartment, it was Lou who said, "I'll be go to hell—I guess he really was a cop!"

Almost a week later, as they sat at the table in the RV, Flower had to agree with Lou's assessment of what'd taken place. "All right," Flower said. "Under the circumstances, it was probably the best thing we could've done. But we don't have our backs to the wall where we gotta make a snap judgment now. We got time to figure things out. And Jack isn't payin' ya to indiscriminately kill random people on the off chance ya might get the right one."

"Jack's not gonna pay me nothing till I kill the prick heisted his money!"

"Now ya got to the root of the problem," Flower said.

"What the hell's that supposed to mean?"

"I don't think this Ernest Tavia's the guy who took Jack off all those years ago."

Lou was incredulous. His jaw dropped as he goggled at Flower. "Whattaya mean, he's not the guy? What kind of bullshit's this?"

"I mean, I don't think he's the one. I think it might be a mistake."

"What are ya doin' to me here, Flower? He looks just like the picture Jack gave us."

Lou stood and stomped to the cabinets in the galley. He pulled the doors open and pushed things aside. "Where's that picture again, anyway?"

"I know about the picture—"

"Here," Lou announced as he pulled a sheet of paper out and presented it to Flower. "Here—look at this. That's him. Right there. Who's this, if it's not him?"

The fourth- or fifth-generation photocopy of a California driver's license with the name Patrick Lott on it'd been blown up again and again so that the face filled most of the 8 1/2 by 11 inch sheet.

"Yeah, it looks kinda like this Ernest Tavia," Flower allowed.

"Right!" Lou stabbed his forefinger at the face triumphantly.

"But it looks like about ten other guys I know, and I don't think any of them are the one Jack wants to find, either. This picture's fifteen years old. And it's a bad picture to begin with. It's a driver's license picture, for God's sake!"

"Yeah? Well, he's sure done all right for himself with his RV park and his bar. He showed up twelve years ago and starts buyin' businesses right and left. Twelve years ago—right after he took off with Jack's money. And then he shows up in Mexico—where else's he gonna go to hide out after stiffin' Jack Kilby? And he's got enough cash to start makin' major purchases like that—where'd that money come from, huh? How's this not the right guy?"

Lou picked up the revolver, clicked open the wheel, and began picking bullets from the box and sliding them into the cylinders.

Flower was unconvinced. "So what are ya gonna do—kill everybody ya can find in Mexico who bought businesses twelve years ago? I bet there are thousands of guys—thousands of Americans, even—who bought businesses in Mexico twelve years ago. And we don't know that this Lott went to Mexico when he rabbited. Hell, he could've gone to Bali. He could be on the Riviera. For all we know, he may never've left L.A. Maybe he got run over crossing a street before he could do anything with the money. Just 'cause somebody paid for a business in Mexico, doesn't make him the one we want.

"Besides, no one here ever heard of Patrick Lott. This guy's Ernest Tavia, according to the Mexican authorities. All of his licensin', all of his taxes, his tourist card, everything's under the name Ernest Tavia. There's no connection I can find between Ernest Tavia and Patrick Lott. And here's another thing, something I didn't tell ya. When I talked to him the other day, when he called me into the back room to have a heart-to-heart? It was 'cause he's all hot and bothered about us goin' around askin' questions about him. Yeah, he's pushed out of shape about that, but he didn't say word one about Jack Kilby and workin' as a bagman and doin' a fade with the cash. No, the only thing he's concerned about is, we might be private detectives lookin' into something about his kid. If you ripped Jack Kilby off and were on the run for it, would ya be worryin' about private dicks trackin' down your kid, or would ya be layin' awake at night sweatin' bullets 'cause Jack was gonna find ya sooner or later and pop a cap in ya? I ask ya, Lou, does that sound like somebody who ripped Jack off?"

"If he was stupid," Lou sullenly muttered. He lay the gun down.

"Yeah. If frogs had wings, they wouldn't drag their asses when they hopped. And if flies didn't, they'd call 'em 'walks.'"

"Goddamn it!" Lou shouted, slamming the palm of his hand on the table so hard the can of oil fell over and the pistol jumped an inch into the air before it dropped back with a clatter. "I need this money, Flower! I need this job!"

"There's nothing I can do about that. I was sent here to do a job myself, and that's what I'm doin': my job. Which's to make sure we find the right guy."

Lou bit his lip, then he repeated hollowly as he stared at nothing, "I need this money."

Flower shook his head and pushed himself up from the table. "Tough titty. You're just gonna hafta suck it up."

He took two steps toward the hallway. When he heard a deep roar that sounded like "Eeeeeeeaaaaah!" coming from behind him, he had just enough time to spin halfway around before Lou pounced on him and dragged him to the floor.

Lou's fists wildly pummeled Flower as Lou's weight kept him crushed beneath it.

"Goddamn it, Lou! Get off me!"

Lou's fist smashed into Flower's neck with a powerful rabbit punch.

"I need this money! Why ya do this to me, Flower? Huh? Why? Why?"

Lou punctuated each question with a new blow. Flower put both his hands out beside him on the floor and managed to push the combined weight of himself and Lou up and over, throwing the other off of him. Quickly, Flower scrambled across the floor and pitched himself on top of Lou, wrapping his arms around Lou's to keep him from renewing his attack. Lou, though shorter than Flower, was heavier and more strongly built, and he fended Flower off with his left arm though his right was trapped in Flower's hold. He drew back his left hand and punched the fist into Flower's face. The blow was too weak to do much damage, but effective enough to bat Flower's head back a few inches. Flower struggled with the writhing Lou, trying to control him by wrestling him to the ground again, but Lou squirmed and kicked and struck with the fist of his left hand, keeping Flower from linking his hands around Lou's arms and neck to put him in a half-Nelson.

"I'll kill ya!" Lou hissed as he fought to free himself. "I'll kill ya!"

Lou staggered upward to his feet carrying Flower with him. He pushed and pulled and struck at Flower until Flower could no longer keep his arms in place above Lou's shoulders; they slipped so that Flower was clinging to Lou's sternum; Lou squirmed farther from his grasp inch by inch, and soon Flower was holding Lou around the waist, trying to force him to the ground while Lou smashed at his forearms, though he had to swing his own fists around behind him to get at Flower since Flower'd spun around to clutch him from the rear.

"I'll kill ya!" Lou shouted.

He thrust himself backward in an effort to smash Flower into something solid and thus break his grip. Flower fell against the table, and the metal weld that held it to the floor snapped and the table collapsed when both men crashed on top of it at the same time. Flower lost his grip on Lou, and the two men flew in different directions, Lou ending up sprawled next to the counter that supported the microwave/convection oven while Flower lay by the door of the reefer cabinet four feet away. The gun, spilled when the table broke then kicked by a flailing heel, skittered over the floor toward Lou.

From their positions on opposite sides of the kitchen, Flower and Lou both watched the revolver spin like a lopsided top across the linoleum until it came to rest only a few inches from Lou's right hand. Flower could see the gleaming brass ends of the rimmed cartridges in the gun's cylinders from where he sat.

Lou stared at the gun dully for several seconds, as though he'd forgotten what it was for. Then he raised his head and looked directly at Flower and said, "I got no money, Flower. I got no money at all. Ya been asking me why I don't go out and do something while I'm here in Mexico? Why I don't go fishin', or rent a three-wheeler, or buy some stuff to take home as souvenirs? I got no money. I'm flat broke. If it weren't for the fish you been catchin', I wouldn't be able to eat. I got bills, man. I got bills, and my wife, she don't wanna live like this anymore, dodgin' the bill collectors all the time, the car about to get repoed, the kids wearin' clothes she's gotta buy at Goodwill and garage sales. She's gonna leave me, I know it. She's gonna leave me."

Lou's eyes were tearing up. He was shaking his head from side to side. An electric charge ran through Flower, and he thought: He's losing it. He's cracking up—and he's got the gun.

An adrenaline rush gave Flower heightened perceptual acuity: he hyperkinetically shifted his gaze from point to point, first watching Lou's face, then moving his eyes down to watch Lou's hand and the gun beside it, then quickly glancing around to find a possible weapon of his own.

"Look, man," Flower said. "I didn't realize things were like that for ya. I thought we were here on vacation. Isn't that what Jack said? At least we'd get a vacation outta this, if nothing else? Sure he did. But if ya got no money, how can this be a vacation for ya? Ya haven't had any chance to relax. You're all wound up. Tense. Tight. Ya need to have some sort of fun while you're here."

Flower leaned forward and propped himself up on his hands and knees, all of his attention now focused on the gun ahead of him though he kept his eyes on Lou. With the intensity of a cat stalking a bird, he moved slowly toward Lou, speaking soothingly as he did so.

"I tell ya what, Lou. Ya don't have any money? I'll get ya some money. I don't have a lot, but I got enough with me I can front ya some, enough so ya can do something while we're here. How'd that be? Ya can go into town, blow off some steam, maybe get laid? Huh?"

Lou's eyes remained dull and lackluster, but his face showed some slight interest in what Flower was saying.

"Let's make it a business deal, whattaya say?" Flower reached out and rested his hand on the pistol, though he didn't pick it up. "I'll buy this from ya. What's it worth? Maybe three hundred? Four hundred? Let's say four hundred. I got that much I can spare. I'll give ya four hundred for it, and that'll give ya enough to do something before we head for home. Okay?"

Lou said nothing; he made no move to interfere when Flower picked up the gun.

"Then, if ya wanna buy it back from me when you're on your feet again, I'll have it waitin' for ya. Just reimburse me, and I'll give ya the gun back, no problem. Like pawnin' it without interest payments, ya see? Like a loan between friends. Yeah, a loan between friends! I'll get ya the money right now. Okay?"

Flower rose to his feet in an awkward lurch, wobbling slightly until he regained his balance, taking the pistol with him. He went to the wardrobe off the narrow hallway and dug through one of his bags from which he pulled out his money pouch. He counted out a sum of money in pesos, then returned to the galley, carrying both the money pouch and the gun.

Lou was on his feet again, standing amid the wreckage of the kitchen's furnishings.

"Here ya go, man," Flower said as he handed Lou the bills. "That's a little more than four hundred dollars at the current rate of exchange."

Lou spiritlessly lifted his hand and accepted them.

"Ya gonna be okay, man? Ya all right? Why don't ya do what I said, get yourself cleaned up and head into town. I can drop ya off. Remember, I'm gonna be drivin' south today. Overnight trip. Catch some fishin' farther down where the fish've gone for the winter." Flower pantomimed casting with a rod, making noises to imitate a reel spinning out. "Hey, Lou! I got an idea! Why don't ya come along? I got extra rods ya can use, get ya out in the sun and the surf, get your mind off your troubles. Whattaya say? No? Not for you, huh? Well, I'm gonna take a shower and get my things ready for the trip. I'll be back tomorrow sometime, don't wait up for me!"

Flower's smile stayed on his face until Lou turned away and listlessly walked to the door. The greedy gulls that'd landed to feed on the guts of the fish Flower'd cleaned a few minutes earlier screeched and flapped their wings to ascend in a panic when Lou stepped outside. Once Lou was gone, Flower looked to the ceiling and breathed a sigh of relief.

"That boy's wrapped too tight!" was Flower's final judgment.

He searched through the rubble scattered across the floor until he found the holster for the .38. He slid the pistol into the leather sheath, then took the gun, the holster, and his money pouch to squirrel them all away in the luggage he'd already set aside to take with him on his fishing trip in order to make sure Lou couldn't get his hands on the weapon while he was away.

CHAPTER 7

Lott wandered restlessly from room to room in his empty house on the Day of the Dead. Although his employees at the RV park and the bar worked the holidays, he always gave the cook, the maid, and the handyman the first two days of November off so they could commemorate with their families at their own homes. Morinda was in town making last-minute preparations to spend the night at Maria Elena's house; on the second day of the month, when adults who'd died were memorialized, she was expected to return home.

He paced back and forth, unable to find anything to occupy his mind other than his worry about the two detectives who'd come to San Estaban looking for his daughter. It'd been three days since he'd offered the bribe money to the one named Flower, offered to pay him twenty-five thousand dollars if he'd leave him and his daughter alone, leave them to live their lives in peace, tell Denise he hadn't been able to find Morinda after all. But since their meeting at Snidely Whiplash, Lott'd heard nothing from him. He'd seen both Flower and the other detective named Lou on occasion since then, but not to speak to. Flower was fishing on the beach every morning, and Lou sometimes drove their small car to town to refill their propane tank. They were still staying in the RV park, but Flower gave no indication he planned to accept Lott's proposition.

As time wore on, Lott's anxiety grew. With every passing hour, he became more uneasy. He wondered if he should try going over to the RV and confronting Flower face to face, demanding to know what the detective was going to do. But every time he considered it, he rejected the idea. He'd already put his cards on the table, already made his offer. To do anything more'd be to reveal his desperation, to show Flower just how much he wanted this deal to go through—a bad bargaining maneuver. The best thing, he repeatedly reminded himself, was to wait for Flower to make the next move.

He tried not to think about what he'd do if Flower turned him down. If the detectives reported to Denise that Morinda was found, legal complications'd result that could prove extremely costly, and emotionally devastating for Morinda as well. Lott had no intention of giving his daughter up without a fight, even though he knew his legal position was weak; in fact, criminal charges of some sort might be brought against him. But that didn't matter. He was convinced he'd done the right thing twelve years ago when he'd taken Morinda from Denise, and he'd given Morinda a chance in life she'd never've had if she'd stayed with her mother.

In the back of his mind he'd sketched out the ghost of a contingency plan of what to do should Flower decline his overture: instead of allowing Morinda to face the onslaught of lawyers and police and social workers and everyone else who'd get in on the ensuing legal battle, Lott'd send her away to school. He'd send her to Europe, put her in a private boarding school, and then let them try to locate her to implement their extradition proceedings or whatever it'd take to get her out of Switzerland. Such an act'd complicate matters even more for Denise and whatever government agencies she had on her side; the whole mess'd then involve not only American and Mexican courts, but Swiss courts as well. He had only a vague idea of how he could take care of Morinda's proof of citizenship in order to get her a passport, but he was reasonably certain a way could be found. Many people were born in Mexico without birth certificates, and a record of baptism could be forged that'd establish her background sufficiently to satisfy Mexican government officials, as long as he was willing to pay the *mordita*, the bite. It could be done.

But the best, the easiest, the most gratifying solution to the problem'd be for Flower to acquiesce in the deception, to agree to tell Denise that Morinda was still missing and that the Ernest Tavia and his daughter who were living in San Estaban, Baja Norte, Mexico, had nothing whatsoever to do with Patrick Lott and Denise's daughter from Los Angeles, California, the United States of America. But that decision was Flower's to make.

Lott went to the window of the living room that looked across the RV park. He pulled the curtain back and peered out. He could see the big RV the detectives'd arrived in sitting at the edge of the lot, but he saw no sign of either of the men who lived in it.

"Damn!" he muttered and let the curtain fall back into place. He paced into the dining room.

He'd tried to tell Flower what kind of woman Denise was, the sort of woman he intended returning Morinda to. He thought he'd gotten through to the detective, but apparently he hadn't fully conveyed the state of Denise's degeneracy, failed to convince Flower of how totally unfit Denise was as a mother, or even as a human being. Whenever specific memories of Denise arose, Lott's mind filled with disgust and anger, especially when he thought of his beautiful and brilliant daughter being taken from him and turned over to the waste of human life he considered Denise to be.

He rested his hands on the dining room table and glanced at the altar Morinda'd made. It was covered with candles and the traditional *papier-mâché* skulls and skeletons; Morinda was in the process of placing the finishing touches of the bread of the dead, fruits, and vegetables as offerings for the mother she believed to be deceased. Lott usually let his gaze pass over the shrine without really seeing it, but now he paused to ponder it. He'd never refused Morinda the right to mourn her mother, to think of her mother in whatever way she chose, and Lott'd never said anything in his daughter's presence that was negative about the crack-addicted prostitute Denise was in actuality. Whenever Morinda mentioned her mother, Lott struggled to maintain a diplomatic silence. Now, he studied the shrine to Denise with scorn and bitterness.

"If ya only knew, kiddo," he said aloud.

He stalked again to the living room window and glanced through an opening in the curtain one more time. He was just in time to see Flower stepping out of the RV, and his heart leaped.

"This's it!" he told himself.

Flower walked toward Lott's house, and Lott cackled. He almost rubbed his hands together in anticipation. He had the money ready for Flower; he had more than enough. The day after he'd broached the possibility of a payoff to the detective, Lott drove to Ensenada and cleaned out the contents of the safe-deposit box he maintained at the branch office of the Multibanco Comermex there. He'd returned with far more than the twenty-five thousand he'd promised Flower, just in case; he was prepared, if necessary, to turn over his entire life savings if that was what it'd take to keep Morinda out of her mother's clutches. He'd placed the cash in a suitcase he'd taken with him for that purpose, and then stashed the money in the floor safe built into the concrete foundation of the house beneath his desk in the study. He was ready for Flower, and he watched in eager anticipation as Flower left the RV.

His elation abruptly turned sour when he saw Flower wasn't coming to the house after all, only picking up his fishing rods and loading them into the small Japanese car he and Lou'd brought with them. Flower then disappeared into the RV, and came out again carrying two pieces of luggage that he stowed in the rear of the car. In a few minutes, Flower drove away. Lott kept his eyes fixed on the empty parking spot for several long seconds, as though Flower might return at any moment and Lott wanted to be waiting for him when he did. After a while, he realized it wasn't going to happen, and he let the curtain fall.

He was at the point that he was like a coiled mainspring given too many tightening twists.

He curled his right hand into a fist and smacked it into the open palm of his left.

"Son of a bitch!"

He glanced wildly about the room for something to break. He stepped toward a shelf that held glass figurines and raised his hands to tear it off the wall. Before he got to it, he had a better idea. He turned and stamped into the dining room. Morinda's shrine to her mother for the Day of the Dead waited around the corner.

He gripped the edge of the nearest box and hurled it across the room. It smashed into the wall on the other side with a clatter. He grabbed the next box in line; it'd been pulled several feet out of place when he tossed the first aside because the boxes making up the pyramidal altar'd been covered with a single long, white tablecloth. Lott picked it up and dashed it to the polished hardwood floor. The fragile handmade *papier-mâché* mementos that'd been spread over it crumpled into unrecognizable lumps. Apples, gourds, peppers, and loaves of bread rolled when they landed; Lott ground them beneath his feet. He angrily kicked furniture, boxes, and food items out of his way, then slumped into a chair at the eight-place dining room table. He sat contemplating in unabated rage the wreckage he'd created. His mind's image of himself shrank into something very small and seething, as though he'd been reduced to nothing more than a pair of tiny red eyes glaring balefully at the world from the blackness at the bottom of a very deep well. He sat like that for a long time.

He didn't stir even when he heard the kitchen door open and bang shut. Morinda called from the next room, "Dad! Dad!" She pushed her way noisily into the dining room, excitedly crying, "Dad! Wait till you see—" Then she lowered her voice to something less than a shout when she saw him sitting in the darkened room. "Oh, there you are. Look! Is this cool, or what? I got it for . . ."

She held up a dancing Catrina puppet, a skeleton dressed in the height of French couture with flowers and feathers stuck in her floppy hat that was a popular decoration for the Day of the Dead; the puppet had strings attached to its wrists and ankles that bent at the appropriate joints to caper about as they were pulled and released. When she finally noticed the shambles of her altar, she let the limbs of the skeleton droop.

"What happened?" she asked in shock and dismay. Her eyes went wide to take it all in.

"I got sick of lookin' at it," Lott said harshly.

"You?" Her lower lip sank; her eyes widened even further. "You did this?"

Morinda knelt beside one of the boxes to which the length of tablecloth still clung, her hair sweeping the floor. She moved the tablecloth aside to pick up one of the *papier-mâché* fragments that'd once adorned the shrine. It fell apart in her hands, crumbling into pieces that dropped next to where the dancing skeleton puppet lay.

Tears formed in the corners of her eyes. In a quavering voice, she turned to Lott and said, "Why do you hate her so much?"

Lott said nothing. He continued to view the world from the depths of his well through hot, red eyes.

"Every time I try to talk to you about my mother, every time I try to find out anything about her, you get so cold, and you act like you've gone to some far away place that I can't follow you to. And now you do this. Why do you hate my mother? You must have loved her once, didn't you? When she was alive, you must have loved her, or why did you marry her? Why did you have me? What did she do to make you feel like this about her? Is it because she died? Is that what made you like this? Did you turn so cold about her after that?"

As if spitting a bad taste out of his mouth, Lott said, "Your mother's not dead!"

"What?"

"She's not dead! I only wish she was. It'd be better for everybody if she would just die. Better for everybody—includin' her."

Morinda was struck dumb. She could only stare at her father from her place on the floor.

"Those guys, those guys in the forty-five footer. Flower and his buddy. They're private detectives. Your mother hired 'em and sent 'em to find you. That's why they're here, that's why they've been askin' questions all over town. Your mother's lookin' for you. That bitch, Denise, broke every deal we ever made between us!"

"She's alive?" Morinda said in a whisper.

Lott rubbed his hands over his face.

"Listen, More," he said, "I'm thinkin' about sendin' ya away to school. To Europe. To a boardin' school. Honey, I want ya to start gettin' ready. In a couple of weeks, I'll make the arrangements. Ya should start gettin' the things ya wanna take with ya together now, though. Gettin'—"

"My mother's alive? Why did you tell me she was dead?"

Weakly, Lott said, "Honey, I never said she was dead. That was something one of your *nana*s told ya when ya were little. She didn't know, but she assumed, 'cause your mother didn't live with us. Now, we hafta figure out what we can do about it. To keep Denise from getting hold of ya again. That's why I want ya to get ready to go, why I'm sending ya to school. You'll board there, and they'll get ya ready for college. We'll find a good school to enroll ya in, one where ya—"

"You lied to me," Morinda said softly, as though speaking to herself. Then, more forcefully, she declaimed, "You lied to me!"

"No, honey, I didn't lie to ya. I never—"

"You lied to me! You let me believe my mother was dead when you knew she wasn't! That's the same thing as a lie!"

"More, please, listen to me—"

"A lie of omission is as bad as a lie of commission. You told me that yourself. Either way, it's a lie, you said." She held Lott in her gaze for a moment, then she rose from the floor to stand. "You lied to me!"

"More, honey, it was—it was for your own good. It was better for ya to believe your mother was dead. Dead and gone. So ya wouldn't think about trying to see her, to meet her. So ya wouldn't be tempted into wanting to—to go back with her."

"For my own good? Better for me? No, no, no—it was for *your* own good! It was better for *you*! You wanted to keep me hidden from my mother! You wanted to keep my mother hidden from me! Because you're afraid I might love her more than you! So, like a coward, you went sneaking away from her, and you lied to me, in order to keep the two of us from ever knowing each other!"

"That's not true."

"What do you know about what's true? You've lied to me my whole life! You've told me nothing but lies!"

"More, stop it!"

"And now you're going to tear me away from my home, from my friends, and send me off to some school a million miles away, all so you don't have to share me with my mother. All for yourself! So you won't have to do what's right! To do what I want, what my mother wants! Just so you can have everything your own way!"

"Let me explain, okay? Just let me explain."

"I don't want to hear any more of your explanations! I don't want to hear any more of your lies!"

Lott stood up and said, "All right—that's enough. Stop it! Stop it right now! We have a situation here, and we're gonna hafta deal with it. So you'd better get yourself ready for goin' away to school. You will be goin', so ya better get used to the idea."

Morinda spun on her heel and marched out the swinging door that led to the living room. Lott went after her, calling to her back, "Wait a minute, young lady! Hold it right there! More! Wait, Goddamn it!"

She strode angrily to her bedroom and vanished inside. Lott stopped a few feet into the living room. He heard banging sounds coming from Morinda's room, as though she were throwing her possessions around in a fit of rage. A few minutes later, when she stepped into the hallway, she was carrying the utility bag she normally used as an overnight carryall.

She swept past him without glancing at him, saying in an icy voice, "I'm going to the Marias."

"You remember what I said!" he said to her retreating figure as she stamped to the exit. "About gettin' ready to go to school!"

"I remember everything you've ever said to me," Morinda said without looking around. "I wish I could forget."

She opened the door, stepped outside, and yelled, "I hate you!"

She slammed the door behind her.

CHAPTER 8

It was late the next afternoon when Flower returned from his fishing trip to the south. He pulled the car into the RV park and headed to the back part of the lot, searching for the outline of the forty-five-foot RV to guide him to the proper space. He turned down what he thought was the right lane, saw nothing where the RV should've been, and assumed he'd gotten off somehow. He drove to the end of the cul-de-sac to turn around, then headed back slowly the other way, scrutinizing every mobile home and recreational vehicle parked in each space he passed till he came to the very last—there was no place farther to go, so he doubled back again. He finally had to admit that the RV he and Lou'd been living in was simply not there. The space it'd occupied was empty.

Frowning in consternation, Flower stopped the car. He got out and walked around the vacant site, examining the ground as though the RV might've been misplaced behind a bush or a rock.

He went next to the RV park's office where he and Lou'd checked in when they first arrived. There was a young Mexican man dressed in stark black and white—white long-sleeved shirt, skinny black tie, and black slacks—behind the counter. He told Flower that Lou'd checked out with the RV the day before. From what the man said, Flower concluded Lou waited only a few minutes after Flower left with the car before taking off himself. Flower left and drove into San Estaban.

Outside the CONASUPO, Flower saw the cryptic word LADATEL printed on the side of a pay phone, so he knew it'd accept his TELNOR calling card. He pushed the buttons for the direct-dial international long-distance call. When it went through, Flower heard a hum, followed by a wavery high-pitched clarion playing three notes, then a female contralto voice on the line saying, "We're sorry. Your call cannot be completed as dialed. Please check the number and dial again."

As soon as the message was finished, Flower started to speak, talking over the recording as it repeated itself. "It's Flower. Get back to me at," and he gave the international access code for Mexico, the area code, and the number of the pay phone. "It's 3:16 in the p.m. Monday, November second. I'll be here for another half hour, and then I'll try again if I don't hear from ya. The number again is," and he repeated it before he hung up.

Flower'd wondered why Jack Kilby used such an elaborate method for screening his calls: you left a message on an answering machine that never identified itself as an answering machine; instead, it was designed to make the uninitiated believe they'd reached a disconnected number. Then Kilby'd call you back from a pay phone several blocks away from his office at the Delaware Club. He'd once asked Kilby why he didn't use a beeper instead, and Kilby said, "'Cause I wanna know who I'm talkin' to. Ya get a number on a beeper, and it could be from anybody who's got twenty-five cents burning a hole in their pocket and this phone number to play around with. With the answering machine, it blows off wrong numbers and telemarketers right off the bat, and I can hear a voice, so I know it's somebody I really wanna talk to."

Flower had to admit there was a method to Kilby's madness.

The phone rang within only a few minutes, and Flower scooped up the receiver before the echoes of the first shrill trill ended.

"Yeah."

"Flower," Jack Kilby's gruff bass voice said. "Ya know what that jamoke Lou's up to?"

"That's what I'm phonin' about, Jack. I left him alone overnight, I went down south to get some fishin' in, and when I got back, he was gone. Took off with the RV. Checked out of the RV park yesterday, must've been just after I left."

"Ya left that lunatic by himself?"

"I didn't know the guy needed a keeper, Jack."

"Why the hell'd ya think I sent ya with him? You were supposed to keep an eye on him. If Lou had a brain, he'd take it out and play with it. That's why I sent you along, to do the thinkin'. All Lou was supposed to do was the heavy liftin'."

"Jack, before we left ya told me, 'Flower, go to Baja, take a trip on me. Ya can relax, unwind, do some fishin'.' That's what ya said, Jack."

"C'mon, Flower, ya know me—I'm a Dutchman, it's not what I say, it's what I mean!"

Jack issued his bark of a laugh.

"You're German, Jack? I didn't know that."

"*Plattdeutsch*. My mother's whole side of the family. Like Lou. The son-of-a-bitch."

"Well, it's Lou I wanted to talk to ya about, Jack. He's not here anymore. I dunno what happened to him. He just up and vanished."

"Yeah, I know. The fool-fucker's in Tijuana."

"Ya talked to him?"

"Hell, no, I didn't talk to him! I got a message from some guy at somethin' called *Procuraduría de Protección al Turista*. He said that's spic for 'Attorney General for the Protection of Tourists.' Says that asshole Lou told him to get hold of me when they arrested him. They picked him up at the border when he tried to get back across. Seems he didn't have the car with him that ya towed over behind the RV, and they keep a real close eye on stuff like that. Ya take a vehicle in, ya gotta take it out again. So they pulled Lou over and hemmed and hawed for a while, tryin' to figure out what they were gonna do about this nuisance. Kept him at a border checkpoint for about two hours before they realized Lou didn't have enough brains to figure out all they wanted was a bribe, and they finally booked him on some bullshit smugglin' charge for takin' the car over and sellin' it."

Flower thought of the last time he'd seen Lou, and the pathetic scene when Lou admitted he didn't have any money to live on, and the four hundred dollars he'd paid Lou for the gun. He wondered if Lou even had enough money left after filling up the tank of the RV to offer a decent amount for the *mordita*. He shrugged it off: if Lou'd been carrying the gun on him when they arrested him, he'd be facing a prison term of one-to-five-years for unlawful possession of a firearm instead of the easy-to-beat smuggling charge.

"I've got the car," Flower said.

"Well, thank you Jesus!" Kilby said with heavy sarcasm. "That's another thing I wanna know about. Where do you guys get off rentin' some Goddamned RV the size of the *Queen Mary* on my American Express card? I let ya take a vacation in Baja on my money, I didn't think you'd pay me back this way!"

"I didn't have anything to do with that, either, Jack. Lou showed up to get me, he already had the RV. I thought ya knew. I figured you approved it."

"Unbelievable! I'll kill that fuckin' Lou if he ever gets out of there alive!"

Flower listened to Kilby rant for another minute about Lou's profligate ways. Then Kilby changed direction and said, "All right, let me hear the bad news all at once. Did Lou finish the job I sent you guys on before he took off for the Great White North?"

"No."

"Swell. Why not?"

"I dunno if this's the guy you're lookin' for or not."

"What's the story?"

"He kind of looks like this Patrick Lott, but the only thing ya gave me to go on's a driver's license picture that's fifteen years old. It could be him, but it might not be, ya know? So I started asking around town about him. He showed up here in San Estaban for the first time twelve years ago. He had enough cash to buy the RV park, and a year later he bought a *cantina* that he's had remodeled and rebuilt and turned into a really nice place."

"Well, that fits—the prick takes off with a shitload of my dough twelve years ago, and he sets himself up in Beanerville."

"But there's a few things that don't fit, Jack. Nobody here's ever heard the name Patrick Lott."

"How tough is it to change your name? He'd hafta be an idiot—he'd hafta be Lou, for God's sake!—not to change his name."

"Okay. But there's something else. He's got a kid."

"Uh-huh. They know what causes that now, Flower. Jesus Christ, so he got some bitch knocked up? What's that got to do with anything?"

"No, Jack, he had the kid with him when he arrived here in town. She was about two years old then. Ya told me he didn't have a wife or a girlfriend or any kids when he worked for ya. Isn't that what ya said? No connections. So where'd this daughter of his come from? If it's the same guy, is what I mean."

Kilby sighed. "I dunno, Flower. It's all a mystery to me. I don't guess it makes much difference, anyway, now that Lou's flown the coop. Even if it's the guy, there isn't much can be done about it till I get somebody else down there to take care of it."

"If it's the guy," Flower said, "if he's this Patrick Lott you're lookin' for—how much'd ya offer Lou to do the job?"

"Too damned much, I can tell ya that right now."

"I mean it, Jack. What's the job worth?"

"Why are you so interested?"

"I was just thinkin'—I mean, I'm already here. Lou left his—his equipment with me. I could do it, if it turns out this's the guy. If the price's right."

"You? No, no, that's not—naw."

"Why not?"

"I sent you along to do the thinkin', 'cause God knows Lou ain't no mental giant. I wanted you to figure out if this guy's the one I'm lookin' for, 'cause I didn't want Lou gettin' the wrong guy. But I sent Lou to do the job, ya know? 'Cause let's face it, Flower, you ain't no tough guy."

Flower's hand tightened on the receiver. "Whattaya mean?"

"I mean, you're not gonna be able to do a job like that."

"Ya don't think so?"

"C'mon, Flower, get real! There's guys who can do that kind of stuff, and there's guys who can't. And you can't. There's nothin' wrong with that. It's not to say ya aren't a man, or something. It's just that ya aren't cut out for that kind of work. I appreciate that, and I accept it. It's the way it is. Don't mean I think any less of ya, okay? I sent ya along 'cause ya got brains. Ya can keep things from goin' haywire. From gettin' outta hand. That Lou, he was likely to run wild." Kilby barked another laugh. "Like he already did!"

"Ya don't think I could do it?"

"Do what?"

"Take care of this job."

"Jesus, Flower, give it a rest, will ya? Ya aren't the kind of guy who can do things like that. I never asked ya to. I only wanted ya to keep a handle on old Lou, to run things the right way, run 'em the way I would if I was there, okay? I don't expect ya to do nothing else."

"How much?" Flower persisted. "How much were ya gonna pay Lou for this job?"

"Man, ya don't give up, do ya? Twenty-five. Lou was in for twenty-five."

"Is that offer still open? Twenty-five if I finish the job? If it's the guy, and I follow through?"

"Sure, Flower. If this's the guy, and you take care of it, you get the twenty-five."

"Plus the grand for the work I've done so far?"

"Plus the grand I already told ya I'd pay."

"And the rest of it? Ya said half of whatever I can collect of the money he ripped ya off for, right?"

"Just like a collection agency," Kilby assured him. "Half of whatever ya can get from him's yours. Keep in mind that you're gonna hafta get any money from him before ya earn the rest—ya won't be able to get it from him after."

Flower was doing sums in his head: the thousand dollars he'd already earned simply for accompanying Lou to Baja and asking questions about the missing Patrick Lott and Ernest Tavia; the twenty-five thousand dollars he was being offered by Tavia in the mistaken belief that he was a private detective searching for the guy's daughter; twenty-five thousand dollars more for killing Tavia if he found proof that Tavia was in fact Patrick Lott;

and, as a possible *lagniappe* that might turn out to be worth more than the rest combined, half of whatever money Lott/Tavia'd squirreled away that Flower could retrieve.

"Don't worry about sendin' anybody else, Jack," Flower said. "I'll take care of the whole thing myself."

"Okay, okay. I'll give ya your shot at it, Flower. Do whatever you're gonna do. One thing, though."

"Yeah, what's that?"

"You'd better give me another call before ya head home. Before ya try to make it over the border. If they took Lou in for tryin' to get across without the car, they're probably gonna stop you for tryin' to make it without the RV. Give me a call and we'll work something out."

"Right."

He hung up the phone and considered what precisely to do next. There were several hotels in San Estaban, so he could always find a place to stay. But it'd depend on Ernest Tavia whether he'd need to remain in San Estaban or not. If Ernest Tavia wasn't Patrick Lott, then there was still a chance to make twenty-five thousand dollars by promising to forget Tavia's existence, something Flower could do quite easily. And if Ernest Tavia was in fact Patrick Lott, there was only one way to establish the connection, and that was by meeting the man and talking to him, since no one else in town seemed to be able to provide any information that could confirm or disconfirm the man's erstwhile identity.

He drove slowly past Snidely Whiplash, looking for the owner's car, which was always to be found in the rear parking lot whenever Lott was at the bar; it was nowhere to be seen. So Flower returned to the RV park. The car was not visible at the house attached to the RV park's business office, either, but the garage door was closed and there were lights visible around the curtains in the windows in front of the attached house. Flower stopped. He flipped open the glove compartment and reached inside for the zippered money pouch he'd stashed there before he left on his trip south. He was puzzled at first when he felt the excess weight of the bag, and he couldn't account for it until he recalled having put the .38 he'd bought from Lou inside. He was about to take the gun out and leave it, but then he shrugged and slammed the glove compartment's lid shut.

Lott answered the door when Flower rang the bell. His hair was uncombed and he seemed disoriented, as though he'd just been awakened from *siesta*, or been drinking all day. When he arrived at the entryway, his eyes were vague and unfocused, and his expression was sullen, as though he resented being dragged away from whatever he'd been involved in prior to Flower's showing up. But when recognition of his visitor dawned, Lott's demeanor changed. His eyes brightened and his lips cracked into a broad smile. His happiness radiated from him in a warm glow that was almost palpable to Flower standing three feet away.

"I thought you'd gone," Lott said. "I thought ya took off yesterday."

"Not me," Flower said. "I sent Lou on ahead with the RV. Like I told ya, he doesn't have anything to do with this business between us, so he doesn't need to be here."

Lott's delight became even more apparent. "You're gonna take my offer?"

"That's what I'm here for. Ya said to catch ya here or at the bar. I went by the bar—"

"C'mon in, c'mon in! Sorry about the mess. I gave the maid and the rest of the help the day off. Yesterday, too. Holidays here in Mexico, ya know. Here, have a seat. Sit down. Take a load off."

"Things are pretty quiet around here, then, huh?"

"Yeah, it's just me rattlin' around in the house. Morinda's stayin' at a friend's. So I'm bachin' it for a couple of days. Look, ya want a drink? I can get ya one if ya want. No? Okay, okay. Let me know if ya change your mind."

"The other day when we were talkin', ya said ya wanted me to forget—certain things. Which I'm willin' to do. I've decided to drop the whole inquiry. Lou, he doesn't know anything to tell anybody. I made sure of that. He's already gone north, and I'm about to drive up to TJ and then back into the States myself, so I thought I'd come over and talk to ya about it."

Lott laughed. "Ya wanna get paid! Naturally. That's what I promised ya. And I've got it, the money's here. Twenty-five thousand, in cash, American money. Don't want ya to hafta make a stop at a *cambio* to exchange it before ya leave Mexico! Ha, ha, ha. Nosirreebob! I'll get it for ya. Just sit back, relax. Wait right here."

Lott hustled out of the living room and propped open the swinging door that led to the hallway. He vanished into a room off the corridor, leaving its door open. Flower could hear him rummaging around; then he heard a heavy piece of furniture being moved across the floor by fits and starts.

"Ya need some help?" Flower yelled.

"No, no," Lott's faint voice called in return. "Stay where ya are. Be with ya—" and Lott grunted "—in a minute." He grunted again.

"Ya know," Lott shouted, "when you guys came here to San Estaban, you and Lou, and ya were askin' questions about me and my business? Askin' my bartender and the other people who own shops around Snidely Whiplash? I thought ya were thinkin' about settin' up your own bar here in town and were checkin' out the competition and how things worked."

"Is that right?" Flower shouted.

"Yeah. Had me worried. There's really not enough of a tourist trade here to support more than one American-style bar. And if you guys moved in, it'd seriously cut into the profits of Snidely Whiplash."

"I can see how that'd bother ya."

"It wasn't till I talked to *Licendiado* Flores that I realized you guys are detectives."

"Talked to who?"

"Victorio Flores, the Notary Public. Ya know, the lawyer."

"Oh, yeah. Him."

"He kinda let it slip ya were interested in the name Patrick Lott."

Flower leaned forward in his chair. The money pouch lay on his lap, and his stomach ground into the pistol. He shifted the pouch forward so it rested on his knees.

"He told ya that, did he?"

"I don't guess it matters, now, that he's the one who let the cat outta the bag. Since we've agreed to take care of things this way. But, yeah, it was Flores told me. And when he said the name Patrick Lott, I knew. I haven't used that name in a lot of years. So I knew Denise must've hired you guys."

"It's been twelve years or so since ya went by Patrick Lott, hasn't it?"

"Something like that. What surprises me's that Denise could remember my name after all this time."

"Some people have long memories," Flower said.

"Well, Denise was doin' crack back then. She usually couldn't remember her *own* name from one day to the next. Hang on, okay? I'll be with ya in just a sec."

"No problem. Take your time."

"I'm putting this into a money belt for ya. Make it easier to carry."

"Thanks. That'll be a help."

"Ya know, when your friend left with the RV yesterday, I thought you'd decided to pass my offer up. I thought—I thought ya were gonna report everything to Denise even after what I told ya about her. To send Morinda back to her mother. But then ya showed up this afternoon. And I knew I hadn't been wrong about you. I knew I had ya pegged right."

"Had me pegged?"

"Sure. I knew you were a nice guy, Flower. I could see it in ya. I could tell you were a nice guy."

"That shows on me, does it?"

Lott's voice grew stronger as he passed out of the room he'd been in and returned to the hallway. "Sure it does. It shines through, no matter how much ya try to hide it. Ha, ha, ha."

Lott walked into the living room with a padded money belt draped over his shoulder. His laughter died when he saw Flower waiting for him with the .38 held in his right hand, the barrel leveled at his heart.

A single shot erupted. A burst of red blossomed on Lott's shirt, and Lott crumpled to the floor.

Flower stepped across the room to take the money belt from Lott's lifeless body. He retraced the path Lott'd taken, turning into the room Lott was in during their shouted conversation. A throw rug was shoved from its place at the center of the room and left in a pile against one wall, a large wooden desk of black cherry was pushed aside, and the hinged metal disk of a floor safe remained flung open. Flower quickly went to the round hole built into the concrete foundations of the house. There were stacks of hundred dollar bills within it. He glanced around the room. Sitting in a built-in closet he saw a suitcase. It felt light when he picked it up, and it proved to be empty when he opened it. He started feeding the packets of bills from the safe into the suitcase until he'd transferred them all. There were so many that he felt he ought to count them, to make sure there was truly as much as he believed there to be by rough measure. But he knew he'd be putting himself at risk by lingering in the house with the body of the man he'd killed, and he forsook the pleasure of determining exactly how much his half'd be. He unslung the money belt from his shoulder and dropped it in with the rest.

He returned to the living room, superstitiously keeping as far away from the dead body as he could, and put the gun into its holster inside the money pouch. Carrying the suitcase in one hand and the money pouch in the other, he slipped outside and made his way to his car, satisfied that, once again, he'd proved them all wrong.

He drove back to San Estaban, stopping at the same public telephone in front of the CONASUPO he'd used earlier that evening, and he placed the same identical call. When the misleading recording finished telling him he'd reached a number that was not in service, he repeated his name and the number of the pay phone, gave the time and date, hung up, and waited. The return call came in only a few minutes.

"It's all taken care of, Jack."

"What does 'all' mean?"

"'All' means 'all.' He admitted he was the one you were lookin' for. I took care of it. And—I got the money."

"Ya did it? Ya sure? Everything clean and neat? No messy loose ends lying around?"

"It's done, and it was done right. Don't worry."

"It's not me that's gotta worry about it, my boy. Ya say ya collected some money, too? How much?"

"I haven't had a chance to count it yet, Jack. But I can tell ya this—it's bigger than a bread box."

"Got a rough guess as to the amount?"

"How much can ya fit in a good-sized suitcase? In stacks of hundreds?"

"Mexican pesos? Or real money?"

"Ben Franklin's picture on the front."

"Yeah, okay. That's what I wanna hear. Now, look, you're gonna have some trouble at the border. Same trouble that *schmuck* Lou had. Because ya went in with an RV and a car, ya gotta come out with an RV and a car, as far as the greasers are concerned. So here's what you're gonna hafta do—"

"Oh, shit."

"What's the matter?"

"Jack, I'm gonna hafta get back to ya. I've got a bit of a situation developin' here."

"Cops?"

"No, nothing like that. Not yet, but it might get to that point if I don't do something fast. I'll call ya later."

"Right. Okay. Ya take care of that money, kid. Don't let it get confiscated by some taco-bender cops, ya hear me? And phone before ya try crossin' into the States. I got some ideas on that."

"Sure, Jack, sure. I gotta go."

Flower hung up, thinking furiously. His mind began to churn up possible solutions to the problem as soon as he noticed Morinda walking toward him carrying a nylon utility bag by its strap. She had her head bent to the ground, as though she was profoundly unhappy about having to go where she was headed. She'd already passed Snidely Whiplash, and her ultimate goal must be her house, Flower thought. He'd assumed from what Lott said that neither the servants nor his daughter were supposed to return until the next day, after the two-day celebration of the Day of the Dead. That'd've given him plenty of time to get far away from San Estaban before the body was discovered and the search for the killer began. Since Lou'd checked out of the RV park the day before, and Lott'd believed

Flower'd gone at the same time, Flower hoped that'd confuse the issue until he was safely on the other side of the border. But if Morinda was to find her father this same night, the search'd start too soon, and might catch Flower in its dragnet.

His eyes were fixed on Morinda as she approached, and he was a bit discomfited when she lifted her head and spotted him at the pay phone; he was thoroughly unnerved when she turned her steps toward him and boldly walked to where he stood. The wild thought flashed through his mind that she already knew what he'd done to her father and was coming to confront him about it. He wanted to run, to hide, but he was unable to do anything besides stand frozen in place like a bird paralyzed by the sight of a snake.

"You're a detective," she said baldly when she got to within speaking distance. "My father told me you're a detective, that my mother sent you to find me."

"That's—that's right," Flower managed to stammer.

"Then you must've met my mother. You must've talked to her. When she hired you."

"Sure. Sure."

"I've never met her. I've never known my mother. I didn't even know she was alive until yesterday. All these years, I thought she was dead. Can you tell me—can you tell me about her? Can you tell me what she's like? My father, he doesn't want me to know anything about her. And he doesn't want me to see her, ever. He's the one who made me believe she's dead. He's—he's going to send me away to school, to get me away from her, so you'll never be able to find me again. So my mother'll never be able to see me. In the next few weeks, he said, he's going to send me to another country. So I won't be able to meet my mother. That's why I wanted someone to tell me—something about her. Anything. Just—what color is her hair? Does she look like me at all? Does she—does she miss me? Does she want to see me again as much as I want to see her? Anything. Anything."

"Your father," Flower began, and then he stopped to clear his throat. "Your father—he's plannin' on sendin' ya away, is he?"

"He's going to spirit me out of the country," Morinda assured him with complete seriousness, adopting the romanticized vocabulary of the novels in which she'd read about such things. "To Europe, he said. To conceal me at a convent school. Where I'll be held incommunicado. Until I can escape."

"Your mother—how bad do ya wanna meet her?"

"Oh, more than anything!"

"Really? 'Cause this may be your last chance. If your dad does what he says he's gonna do, we may never be able to get ya to her. He sends ya to some place like that, we—I mean your mother, I work for your mother—may not be able to find ya there, or get ya out, even if we can locate ya. Ya wanna meet your mother?"

"Yes!"

"I'm goin' to Los Angeles for a rendezvous with her right now. I'm leavin' tonight. Ya wanna go with me? Ya wanna see her? I can take ya to her."

Morinda's resolve faltered. "Right now?"

"I gotta get word to your mother as soon as possible about this new development in the case," Flower extemporized. "Let her know your dad's about to ship ya to Europe. So maybe she can find ya whenever ya get where you're goin'. Or stop your dad from gettin' away with it. It won't be easy, but I know she'll do anything she can to find ya. She's sick at heart about all this, about not bein' able to talk to ya, to see ya. It's really tearin' her up inside. Has been for years. I just tried to call her, but she's—she's not anywhere I can get through to her by phone. I'm gonna hafta meet her face to face to tell her about all this. So if ya wanna go with me to Los Angeles to see her, I'll make a place in the car for ya. It's up to you."

"I couldn't tell my father . . ."

"That's right. Ya couldn't tell him. He'd scream like a stuck pig if he thought ya were gonna hook up with your mother. He'd never let ya go, ya know that. He doesn't want ya to see your mother. Ever."

"Yes. I know." Hesitantly, she asked, "Do you have to get your RV?"

"No. We'd be takin' the car. Lou took the RV north yesterday, so he won't be along for the ride, either. I know that won't break your heart."

"He's—strange."

"He's off the wall. But he won't be around to bother ya, I swear."

Morinda scrutinized the ground, deep in thought. Then she brought her head up defiantly and said, "I'll go. I'll go with you. To Los Angeles. To my mother."

"Ya ready to roll right now?"

"Yes," she answered brightly, then her face fell. "But how long will we be gone? I don't have enough clothes. What about food? Money—I don't have any money."

"Don't worry about clothes or food or money. The trip'll take at least a couple of days, but I'm authorized by your mother to spend whatever it takes to bring ya to her. I'll pay for your meals and your other expenses, don't worry about that. But there's something else I gotta talk to ya about. Once we start, there's no turnin' back. Ya can't decide ya wanna go cryin' to your dad. Ya can't wimp out and make a phone call to tell him where ya are. Ya can't do anything that'll let him know how to find ya, 'cause I'm goin' way out on a limb to help ya with this. I could get in a lot of trouble doin' this for ya, and if ya aren't gonna back me up, then forget it before we start. Okay? You're either on the bus, or you're off the bus. Get me? If you're not gonna go through with this the whole way, then don't play like ya are. So—what's the story? Ya ready to head north to meet your mother?"

"Yes. I'm ready. I won't change my mind. I'm grateful for what you're doing for me, and I won't do anything to get you in trouble for it. I promise."

"Okay, good. Is this your only bag? Then throw it in the back and climb on in. We're outta here."

CHAPTER 9

When they got to Tijuana, Flower registered them in a hotel, getting a room for each of them. He warned Morinda again about calling her father, and then he went out to take care of some business after giving Morinda a thousand pesos so she'd be able to purchase any clothes and food and incidentals she might need. He drove to a public phone five blocks away and placed yet another call to Jack Kilby's answering machine. He waited for nearly half an hour for the call to be returned.

"What the hell were you guys doin' down there, Flower?" were the first words out of Kilby's mouth when Flower picked up the receiver.

"Whattaya mean?"

"I mean they bumped up the charge on Lou. No more smuggling some lousy car into the country—now it's a murder beef. They're saying he wasted some cop. A nark. Ya know something about this shit?"

"I know something about it, yeah. It's a long story."

"Then tell it to me later. Right now, the important thing's ya got trouble big time when it comes to crossin' the border. Mexican cops are lookin' for ya, and they've got ya pegged as a cop killer. They gotta search goin' on for ya and the car you're drivin'. Ya still have that car, don't ya?"

"Yeah."

"Dump it. Where are ya now?"

"I'm in Tijuana."

"Perfect. Drive it over to some side street, park it in the shadows, leave the keys in the ignition and the doors unlocked, and walk away from it. It's insured, so I'll report it as stolen to the rental company."

"Okay. How do they know about the car? And about me? Did Lou spill his guts."

"Lou didn't hafta tell 'em anything. Ya filled out a tourist card when ya first got there, remember? They found some tire tracks where the dead cop's body was found, and they matched 'em to the RV when they got Lou. But Lou's probably told 'em everything he knows by now, anyway. Ya know how Mexican cops interrogate ya? They don't just slap ya around a little bit like they do up here. They waterboard ya, only they don't use water. They got this method, see. They put ya in this chair that's got no back to it. And they hold your head back. Then they bring in this bottle of soda, and they shake it up good before they dump it down your nose. I talked to a guy they did it to once, and he said it feels like your drowning—only ten times worse, 'cause it takes longer. They leave ya alone for a while after that, then they come in and start to ask ya questions. If ya don't answer 'em the way they think ya should, they give ya the soda pop treatment again. And they keep doin' it till ya come around to their way of thinkin'. Yeah, Lou's probably ratted ya out, but ya can't blame the guy."

"Should I rent another car?"

"Flower—listen to me. They got your name. They got your description. They think you're a cop killer. You're in a country where they got no Bill of Rights. They got the Napoleonic Code down there, which means you're guilty until proven dead, once those Mexican cops get hold of ya. Ya need to go underground. Ya speak Spanish, don't ya?"

"No. Lou was doin' all that."

"That's gonna make it tough. Real tough."

"I got somebody with me. She speaks Spanish."

"Ya got a girl with ya? Jesus, Flower, are ya crazy? The last thing ya need right now's some bimbo along for the ride. Ditch her."

"Not that kind of girl, Jack."

"They're all that kind of girl. Get rid of her."

"Ya got any ideas about how I can get back into the States?"

"We're workin' on it up here. Tell me, did ya get a chance to count that money?"

"No. Not yet."

"Well, how much does it weigh? Can ya tell me that? Just a ballpark figure."

"I dunno . . ."

"Ten pounds?"

"At least. Probably more like fifteen or twenty. But that's a guess, don't hold me to it."

"And it's in hundreds, ya said?"

"Yeah. All hundreds."

"Okay. Okay. That's what I need to know. If ya can head south again as far as Ensenada, we think we can get ya out by boat . . ."

Flower only half listened to Kilby's words. He was preoccupied by a consideration of Kilby's last few questions: Kilby seemed far more concerned with how much money Flower was bringing with him than with Flower's rescue. It seemed to Flower that Kilby'd been trying to figure out whether saving him was worth the time and effort before he suggested the escape route by way of Ensenada. And if Kilby was willing to abandon him to the tender mercies of the Mexican legal system should helping him prove to be more trouble than it was worth according to a benefit/cost analysis, then Kilby could very well be setting him up: why bother bringing him back to the States when doing so'd involve Kilby in harboring an international fugitive, if instead he could just pay someone to take Flower far out to sea and leave his body where it'd never be found. Especially if that'd save Kilby what he owed Flower for the hit on Lott as well as the recovery fee for the cash. That Kilby considered the money to be the main priority, Flower had no doubt. Warning signals went off in his mind.

". . . It'll take a couple of weeks to get this set up, but we can probably get ya out of Mexico and back here to L.A.," Kilby ended his peroration. Flower blanked most of the details out while Kilby spoke, so he paid attention only when Kilby finished.

"Thanks for the offer, Jack, but I think I'm gonna pass."

"What the hell are ya talkin' about?" Kilby growled.

"I'm talkin' about findin' my own way out of Mexico. I think I can do it from TJ, and make it home faster than a couple of weeks. I don't like the idea of layin' low in Mexico that long. Too much can go wrong."

"Flower, don't even think about runnin' out on me with that money. Ya know what happened to the last guy who tried it." He laughed grimly. "Ya should—you were the one who *did* it to the last guy who tried it!"

"You'll get your half, Jack. Provided I make it across, that is."

"You'd better make it, is all I can say. Ya got the Mexican cops to face if ya don't. Either the Mexican cops, or me. I don't know which one of us'd go easier on ya, them or me, but I'd sure hate to face a choice like that."

"I'm gonna dump this car, like ya said. I'll phone ya again in a couple of days. Sooner, if I can find a way over before then."

"Stay in touch, Flower. And don't lose my money."

"It's half mine, Jack," Flower reminded him.

"What ya do with your half, I don't much care. Don't let anything happen to my share, is what I meant."

"Yeah. Sure. I'll be in touch."

Tijuana wasn't like San Estaban. Tijuana wasn't like Ensenada. Tijuana wasn't like anyplace Morinda'd ever been before.

Since NAFTA'd gone into effect, Tijuana'd become a flourishing manufacturing center with numerous *maquiladoras* or foreign-owned factories that worked in shifts ceaselessly, twenty-four hours a day, seven days a week, to produce quantities of television sets, trucks, electronic parts, furniture, cargo containers, and garments, giving it one of the highest *per capita* incomes of any city in Mexico. Yet even so, signs of abject poverty could be found everywhere, cheek by jowl with ostentatious displays of newly acquired wealth, much more destitution than Morinda'd ever seen in San Estaban, or in the busy seaport of Ensenada.

After Flower disappeared to take care of his other affairs, Morinda also left the hotel in order to shop. The streets were jammed, the atmosphere intoxicating. Everywhere she turned, there were people selling fresh cheese, cotton candy, tamales, and warm bread from horseback, on foot, or out of cars equipped with loud speakers; they vied with the beggars for the disposable income of the better-off native inhabitants and especially the numerous *turistas*. She bought her dinner of two *churritos*, fried sticks of bread dough and chile, from one of the vendors with pushcarts who plied the narrow, grungy streets of the town.

When she returned to the hotel, Flower was waiting for her. He met her downstairs in the lobby and said, "Your dad's notified the state police and the *federales* that you're missin', and they'll be searchin' for ya at the border checkpoints. Let's go upstairs and we'll talk about what we're gonna hafta do."

Morinda lay the clothes she'd bought on her bed without bothering to unwrap them or take the labels off.

"How are we going to get to my mother?" were her first words to Flower once they were alone.

"We're gonna hafta do it the old fashioned way," he said. "Sneak across with the wetbacks."

"*Hijole*!" She shook her head. "That's really dangerous."

"If you're up to it, that is. It depends on how bad ya wanna meet her."

"Oh, I'll do it! It's just—it's going to be hard."

"I won't lie to ya, it's not gonna be fun and games." Flower's mouth was set in grim determination. "But I'm willin' to give it a try, to get ya to her. So I guess you can make some sacrifices, too."

Morinda felt guilty. She'd been whining about what she'd have to go through when it was only necessary because of her in the first place. She knew that Flower, if he didn't have her with him, could simply drive across the border with no hassle and be home in Los Angeles in a few hours without having to endure the discomfort and danger of an unauthorized entry into the United States.

"I didn't mean it that way," she told Flower contritely. "I know this is something you're doing to help me."

Flower's forbidding expression remained unchanged for a few seconds, but then he smiled and said, "Forget it. There's been a lot of pressure on both of us lately. But if we work together, we'll both make out okay."

"So what do we do first?"

"I'm not real sure," Flower admitted. "It's not like I've ever been an illegal alien before. I heard somebody say most of the smugglers hang out at the bus station, the Central Camoniera. Maybe we should try there and see what we can come up with. Most of these guys speak English, I hear, but I'm gonna need ya along to translate just in case. Can ya handle that?"

"I'm ready. Whatever we need to do."

"Good. We'll take a taxi. There's a cab stand outside the hotel, I think."

"What happened to your car?"

Flower looked to the window and off into the distance. "I returned it to the rental agency. They've got a franchise here in TJ. Since we can't take it over the border anyway, I thought it'd be easier to get rid of it now. In case we find somebody to take us across right away."

They went downstairs and hailed one of the ubiquitous green Volkswagen beetles with the front passenger seat removed that serve as taxis in Mexican cities. Morinda told the driver in Spanish where they wanted to go, and he took them to east Tijuana.

They didn't even have to go inside the bus terminal. Loitering around the outer walls were dozens of men who murmured the magic words, "Los Angeles," as people walked past. These were the *talones*, recruiters for the smugglers who actually take undocumented Mexicans and Central American nationals into the United States. The *talones* have to work exceptionally hard, since they're paid piece work and receive only a flat rate of so much per person they recruit, and November's the slowest time of year for them: during the late fall and early winter, most of the illegals who'd been in the U.S. are returning home with the money they made there, or with Christmas presents for their families; not many want to make the journey going the other way during this season. Nevertheless, Flower and Morinda ran into trouble from the very start.

The *talones* approached Morinda with their offers to get her over the border, but when it became obvious that Flower was with her, they grew suspicious and played stupid, refusing to answer any of the questions Flower put to them through Morinda.

"You're a *huero*," Morinda explained. "They think something's wrong when you're here asking about crossing over. Let me try it by myself. You wait, and I'll find out something."

"They're gonna realize I'm with ya at some point," Flower said. "We've gotta find somebody who's willing to take me, whether I'm a *huero* or not. What the hell's a *huero*?"

"It means an Anglo," Morinda said, not bothering to tell him it was a derogatory term used along the border in the same way that an Anglo might call a Mexican a spic. "I mean, I'm a *huero*, too, but I don't look like one. You? You're white bread."

"Okay, let's do this. You talk to somebody, find out whatever ya can. But this's what we're lookin' for: we don't wanna get shipped over to Tecate. We wanna cross here, directly from TJ into San Diego. I've heard about that Tecate crossin' through the mountains and over the desert, and we're not plannin' on hikin' a hundred miles on the Goddamned Bataan Death March! And we're not goin' coach—we expect to travel first class. Tell 'em not to worry, we can pay for it. But we don't get dragged over in a van stuffed with thirty-five other people and everyone of their kids along for the ride. We wanna go with just the two of us on the trip. And we're willin' to pay. Here, here's a hundred." He gave her five twenty-dollar bills in American money. "That's to pay for information, to let 'em know we mean business."

"Okay. Let me see what I can find out."

Flower remained halfway hidden in the shadows of the bus station, and Morinda trawled the perimeter of the building. After ten minutes, she rejoined Flower. She handed back the unused portion of the cash he'd given her. He didn't bother to count the money before he thrust the bills into his pocket.

"I only needed twenty dollars. I could've gotten him to talk for ten, though."

"What'd he say?"

"To take *me* across, he wanted two thousand. When I told him there was another person, he said three thousand for both of us. When I said you were American, the price doubled: six thousand."

"Pesos?"

"Dollars."

Flower whistled through his teeth, but he said, "Okay. I can live with that."

"But we'd still have to go to Tecate."

Flower shook his head vigorously. "No way, José. Too many people get killed tryin' to get over from Tecate."

"I asked him if there wasn't someone who knew how to get people across here. That's when I had to pay, to get him to talk. He said there's a man named Febo. Febo has some kind of arrangement with the Border Patrol and takes people over from Tijuana. He said we should talk to this Febo."

"Great. Where do we find Febo. Is he around the bus station?"

"No. He gave me the name of a *cantina* where Febo hangs out. It's in the Zona Norte, he said."

Flower made a face. "Well, it can't be helped, I guess. The Zona Norte. Let's get down and dirty."

They took another taxi from the cab stand outside the bus terminal. Morinda asked the driver if he knew where the *cantina* was that the smuggler's recruiter'd named, and he nodded and sped away with his two passengers in the rear as though he'd gone to that exact address a thousand times before. He drove with great confidence, but their route soon took them off the major traffic arteries and as they plunged into the Zona Norte red-light district they wound through numerous back-alleys and narrow gaps between buildings that didn't appear to be designed for automobiles at all until they came to what looked like a vast earthen field with buildings scattered randomly across its surface in no set order through which the taxi made its way by meandering around the walls of tarpaper shacks and hovels constructed of scrap lumber.

The taxi came to a stop outside a ramshackle structure of adobe with a *palapa* roof surrounded by strings of blinking Christmas-tree lights. Music, loud but tinny as though coming from a two-inch speaker on a radio that had the volume control turned up to maximum, issued from the open front door. It was *norteña* music, a style popular in northern Mexico, and Morinda recognized the song as a *narcocorrido* or ballad about life in the drug underworld. It told the story of a daring band of drug dealers who brazenly defied the law, lived fast, died young, and left gruesomely hideous corpses when they were massacred in an ambush set up by the inept and cowardly police who could never've caught them without their having been betrayed by one of their own.

Flower paid the cab driver and he and Morinda entered the place. They stopped just inside the door, waiting for their eyes to adjust so their vision could penetrate the dingy, smoke-filled atmosphere. By the time their sight adapted to the dim interior, the song'd come to an end and a radio announcer began babbling. The bar was only a set of planks nailed together stretched across two sawhorses; behind it was a shelf holding several partially full liter bottles along with a boom box, the two speakers stretched about ten feet apart for sound separation. There were dozens of men—all the patrons were men, except for a few obvious prostitutes who sat on the laps of customer's and shared their drinks—sitting at rough wooden tables.

"God, what a shithole!" Flower muttered.

He went to the bar with Morinda following in his wake. The bartender was a seedy little man with a mustache and a cast in his right eye that turned the iris the color of milk. His sleeves were rolled up to his elbows, revealing remarkably hairy forearms. He asked Flower what he wanted without saying a word, merely flipping his chin up in inquiry.

"What do they got to drink?" he asked helplessly, turning to Morinda.

Morinda posed Flower's question to the bartender in Spanish, then told Flower, "They don't have anything besides beer, some cheap tequila, Mexican brandy, and *aguardiente*."

"What's *aguardiente*?"

"Homemade whiskey. Moonshine. Don't drink it," she warned. "The only thing you'll want to order here is beer—in the bottle. Not in a glass. The same water they tell you not to drink is the water they use to wash the dishes with, too."

"Okay. Beer. *Cerveza*. Tell him I want it in the bottle, like ya said."

Morinda spoke to the bartender in Spanish. The bartender asked her a question, and she answered him. She turned to Flower and said, "I got a beer for me, too. He seemed to expect it. I'm not going to drink it, I'm just telling you why you're going to be paying for two."

"Drink it if ya want," Flower said. "When he comes back, ask him if he knows somebody named Febo."

The bartender returned with two chilled bottles of Tecate beer. Flower glanced at the labels and said, "It figures," then tossed a ten-dollar bill on the plank table and waited while Morinda asked about Febo. The bartender said nothing, simply picked up the bill Flower left and made change out of his pocket.

"Tell him the change's his if he can tell us who Febo is," Flower said.

Morinda translated, but the bartender merely cocked his head so that only his dead eye was aimed toward her, and he still said nothing. With his good eye, he gave Flower a contemptuous look, holding him in his sight for several long seconds, then turned away from the pair of them.

"What was that about?" Flower asked Morinda.

Morinda ignored him. She turned around to face the customers sitting at the tables and shouted in Spanish, "Does anyone know Febo? Where can I find Febo? Is Febo here? And does he want to make some money?"

An advertisement for an American brand of coffee was playing over the boom-box speakers.

From across the barroom, from the back and out of the darkness, a man said, "*Febo esta aquí!*"

Flower peered into the smoky air like someone trying to find his seat at a theater after the movie starts, then pushed his way through the crowd of bodies seated at the intervening tables. Morinda came after him.

"Where's Febo?" Flower shouted over the music that'd started up again on the radio. "Are you Febo?"

There were three men sitting at a solid rectangular table. It had no tablecloth. The three had shot glasses in front of them, and a bottle lacking a label made of brown glass sat in the middle of the table. A metal ashtray was piled high with crushed cigarette butts, and the men kept lighted cigarettes in their mouths. Each of them wore a cowboy hat; each wore a brightly colored long-sleeved shirt made of polyester that resembled silk; the first three buttons at the top of their shirts were left unbuttoned so their chests were exposed in V's to several inches below their sternums; the sleeves of their shirts they kept rolled above their elbows. One wore a Saint Christopher medallion around his neck, the other two had chains with crucifixes on them as necklaces.

The one who'd called to them was young, no older than his early twenties, and he was strikingly handsome. He had a deep cleft in his chin. His lips were set in a near-pout. The musculature of his arms was noticeable because he had the arm nearest Morinda draped casually over the back of his chair: his powerful biceps and triceps were clearly defined, and they looked rock solid.

Flower said, "I'm here to talk business. Maybe we could have some privacy. Tell him that," he said to Morinda.

She stepped up beside Flower and translated his words into Spanish. Then she told Flower Febo's reply, putting it into English.

"He says these are his *socios*, his partners. He wants to know what business you want to talk about."

"Tell him we're trying to get to Los Angeles."

Morinda interpreted. The three men at the table began to talk among themselves, speaking rapidly and interrupting one another with snickers and sounds that weren't words. They spoke in *caló*, the Mexican Spanish underworld argot used by thieves, drug dealers, and pimps; it was difficult for Morinda to follow since it differed so much from standard Spanish, but she could tell they were discussing her. One of the words she caught was *puñetero*, hot or sexy.

"Hey!" Morinda shouted, slamming her open palm on the table so hard it made the pile of butts in the ashtray jump and then collapse. "We're here on business, so don't waste our time! Are you the Febo who can take us to Los without having to go to Tecate, or aren't you?"

The men fell silent, and Febo for the first time paid serious attention to her, but it gave Morinda no sense of accomplishment. Febo ran his eyes up and down her. It made her skin crawl.

"I'm the man who can do—whatever you want, *chica*," he said in an inviting, insinuating tone.

His friends sniggered, but said nothing.

"Just tell me what it is you want me to do," he said, then after a pause a heartbeat's length, added soulfully, "to you."

191

"First of all, I want you to listen—to me," Morinda said, mocking him. His salacious expression didn't change. He moved his eyes from one part of her to another, without ever looking at her face. "Can you get us across so we don't have to go to Tecate to get around the fence? And if so, how much will it cost?"

Negotiation began in earnest at that point. Neither of Febo's *socios* entered into the conversation, and Morinda ceased to interpret what was being said for Flower's benefit; she knew Flower's minimum expectations, and providing a sentence-by-sentence translation'd only interfere with her bargaining. Febo remained slouched in his chair, his body language indicating he was bored with the whole affair. Occasionally he made reference to the silent Flower by flicking his head in that direction. Flower didn't know what was being said about him, though he could discern the word *maricón*, and later he thought he was called by the word *canijo*.

Morinda's voice grew louder, more argumentative, and finally, when she seemed to be cutting off any further discussion by loudly pronouncing, "No! No! No!" and slashing the air for emphasis with her arm, Flower put his hand on her elbow and pulled her aside.

"What's goin' on? What's he sayin'?"

"He says he can do it. He says he can get us across, under the fence and past the lights and the dogs. But he wants ten thousand dollars. I told him he's out of his mind."

"That's fine. Tell him I'll pay it."

"No, no, I can get him to take less. I'll get him down to five or six."

"It's not worth the aggravation it's causin'. Or the attention we're attractin'. Tell him I'll pay the ten thousand. When can he do it? Tonight? Tomorrow night? When?"

Morinda was indignant. "You can't pay him ten thousand dollars just because that's how much he's asking for, Flower! That's only the price he starts with to get the bargaining going. Flower—he *expects* to haggle over the price. He wants to haggle. So let me haggle. He'll have more respect if I do."

"Listen, I know I'm supposed to give a damn about these Third-World customs, and I know I'm comin' across like the Ugly American, but I'm tired of this crap. Tell him we agree to his price, and let's get on with it. When do we go, and where do we meet to do it? Can ya ask him that? Please?"

Morinda sullenly and reluctantly conveyed the message to Febo, who gave no hint that he was either disappointed the negotiations hadn't continued any longer than they had or that he was enjoying his triumph. He ran his tongue over his lips as he surveyed Morinda's body, his demeanor one of languid lubricity.

"He says it won't be tonight," Morinda said to Flower. "Maybe tomorrow night. But maybe not until the night after, or even the night after that. These things take time, he says, because he has to set things up. Going across is more difficult since the Border Patrol began their crack down. He says we should come here tomorrow night after it gets dark and he can tell us if we can go then. He says he wants you to pay him the ten thousand now."

Morinda spelled it all out, repeating the words as exactly as she remembered them. After Flower overruled her in her attempt to reduce Febo's price, her feelings'd been hurt and she refused to take any further responsibility beyond giving as precise an interpretation of what was said as she could. She hoped Flower recognized that she was no longer lending any assistance beyond the bare minimum; she wanted him to know she resented his rejection of her help.

"He wants the whole nut up front?" Flower said, and snorted derisively. "Yeah, and people in hell want ice water! Tell him I'll be here tomorrow night, and if it's a go at that time, I'll pay him half, five thousand dollars. He'll get that before we start. He gets the other half when we're on the other side. And to sweeten the deal, I'll give him two hundred now, as a sort of deposit, to let him know I'm serious."

While Morinda repeated in Spanish what Flower'd said in English, Flower pulled two hundred-dollar bills out of his pocket and laid them on the table, stretching them and unwrinkling them and finally letting them lie.

Febo brought his cigarette to his lips and left it dangling from the corner of his mouth. His eyes squinted against the stinging smoke, and he said, "Okay. Okay." But he made no move to pick up the money.

"We got a deal?" Flower asked Morinda.

She nodded her head, and Flower left the table, struggling to get through the press of people in the bar, Morinda trailing him. As they went, "*Chica!*" a man's voice called from behind. Morinda stopped and cocked her head to the side. It was not Febo who said it, so it must've been one of his *socios*. The same voice called out, "*Chupar es mi verga!*"

The flush that rose to her cheeks was not visible in the dim light inside the *cantina*. Morinda tightened her lips but said nothing in reply, and she walked away, stonily refusing to look at any of the people around her. Flower left his empty bottle of Tecate on the bar. Morinda, who hadn't even taken the cap off hers, did the same, and they went out the open door into the night.

CHAPTER 10

Once they'd gotten far enough away that the bar's radio no longer drowned out their voices, Flower stopped and said, "What was that he said to ya at the end? When we were leaving? One of 'em shouted something."

"Nothing," Morinda said, blushing again at the reminder. "They were just—being stupid. They think that's what they have to do to be *machos*."

"It sure sounded like an awful lot to be nothing," Flower said, searching Morinda's face. "Okay. It was nothing. But when ya were talkin' to old Feeble and the sociopaths, he said a couple of things about me. He called me a few names, didn't he?"

"He called you a *maricón*," Morinda admitted. "It means a—"

"Yeah, a fag. I know what that means. What else? He called me something besides that. What was it?"

"I think he was trying to see if you really didn't speak any Spanish. He called you that to see if you'd react."

"What?"

"He said you were a *canijo*."

"What's that?"

"It means something like—" Morinda had to pause to consider for a moment. Then she said, "A wimp?"

Flower tilted his head and contemplated the stars overhead.

"He thinks that because I did the talking," Morinda explained. "To them, the man should do the talking and the woman should be quiet and do what she's told. It doesn't mean anything. They think they're *picudos*, tough guys. That's all. Don't go back in and start trouble with them," Morinda pleaded. "They carry knives. I heard them talking about it."

"Start trouble? Why would I start trouble? They think they're hard asses and I'm a pussy? That's fine with me." He laughed, put his thumbs inside the waist band of his slacks and ran them back and forth a few times. "That's exactly what I want 'em to think."

There were no taxis anywhere nearby when they left the *cantina*, and they walked a long way before they reached a paved street. They passed through a cluster of shacks made of old wooden garage doors in which families were living; Morinda could tell they were homes by the clotheslines outside on which hung dozens of dresses, pairs of pants, and shirts small enough for children. The odors of fried corn flour and baked beans filled the air, vying with the stench of stagnating water and human waste for predominance. Groups of men with hard, sullen faces sat on the porches of decrepit sheds passing bottles between them; they stared at Flower and Morinda with dull eyes. Other men stumbled and staggered from the pools of shadow attached to one building on their way to another.

More frightening than the obvious drunks were those human forms that flitted between hiding places, moving purposefully with stealth and cunning. Morinda couldn't help but throw uneasy glances at their shapes, although Flower seemed indifferent, and he walked without bothering to lift his eyes, always scanning the ground ahead of him in order to avoid the crater-sized potholes. He only showed fear once, and that was when an animal they couldn't see threatened them with a deep growl, and then a large pariah dog ran out from the deep shadows beside a hovel made of adobe and weathered scrap wood. Flower stopped in place as soon as he heard it, and Morinda reflexively grabbed his left arm. His whole body tensed; his right arm went up, his hand clutched at something he carried under his jacket, and Morinda heard several metallic clicks. But the dog went slinking by, keeping its eyes fixed on them as it crossed to the other side of the open space, and Flower relaxed. He dropped his hand to his side, and Morinda released her hold.

A few minutes later, they came to an actual paved street where they found a taxi that took them to their hotel.

The next morning, Morinda went by herself to the hotel coffee shop for breakfast. She didn't want to bother Flower if he was sleeping, so she didn't go to his room until after noon. Although the DO NOT DISTURB sign was still on the outer knob when she got there, she ignored it and knocked anyway.

She heard rustling sounds coming from the other side, then footsteps thudding across the floor. Flower's muffled voice said through the door, "Who is it?"

"It's me. Morinda."

Flower pressed an eye to the peephole; the eye withdrew, the chain latch rattled, the door swung back.

"C'mon in," Flower said. "Close it behind ya."

The bed was unmade and the trash can hadn't been emptied. The television was on an English-language station broadcast from San Diego. One of the chairs set around the table near the picture window was pulled out and a hand towel from the bathroom was spread in front of it. There were lumps underneath the terrycloth.

Flower went to his place at the table and threw the towel aside revealing a revolver, along with a small black cylindrical brush, a can of 3-in-1 oil, and the gleaming brass shell casings of six cartridges set on their bases. Flower returned to cleaning the handgun.

"I came to see what you're planning to do for lunch," Morinda said. She sat in a chair across from Flower, but she didn't take her eyes off the gun. She was fascinated by it. In all her life, she'd never seen a real gun up close, only the ones on television and in the movies.

"I'm gonna be goin' out in a few minutes to take care of some things," Flower said as he ran the brush through the length of the barrel, coring it as Morinda would've cored vegetables. "So I'll grab something to eat on the fly. Hey, did ya have enough left to get breakfast this mornin'? Jesus, I didn't even think about that! Sorry, kid, I—oh, good! Good! I'll give ya some more cash so ya won't starve before I get back."

He set the gun on the table and pulled open the drawer of the night stand next to the bed. With one hand, he took out a sheaf of bills and spread them like the cards of a poker hand on a clear space beside him. Flower returned to reaming the barrel with the brush.

"How are ya fixed for clothes? Did ya buy enough yesterday to get ya through another day? Well, you'll probably need to get another pair of shoes, at least. If Feeble and his buddies do what they're supposed to, we'll hafta do some hikin' through some pretty rough terrain. A few miles, anyway, before we cut back into San Ysidro and catch some transportation. So you're gonna need some boots or tennis shoes. And you'd better wear Levi's or something like that tonight, just in case. The weather report says we got a few days of Indian summer, so it should be mild tonight. Good weather to be outdoors. Take a thousand pesos. Go ahead. Get what ya need."

Morinda pulled the bills apart and picked out several. She slipped them into her pocket.

"We'll head over to that dive to meet Feeble around six," Flower continued. "That oughta get us there before dark."

Flower squeezed the can of oil, letting a brown spot appear on a square piece of cloth he held under it.

"I've been thinking," Morinda said. "Maybe we should find another *coyote* to take us across. Maybe we shouldn't rely on this Febo . . ."

Flower rubbed the cloth over the working parts of the revolver. The pieces gleamed as the oil filmed on their surfaces.

"Why not?"

"Do you think we can trust him?"

"What's he gonna do? If he doesn't show up tonight, I'm only out two hundred bucks. And a lot of wasted time. Then we're right back to square one, the same as we'd be if I dumped old Feeble and went looking for another *coyote*."

"Well . . ."

"What is it? You're worried about something. Did ya hear 'em say something? Anything I should know about?"

"I told you, I told you last night—they carry knives. They were talking about them. About their knives. Why do they carry knives if they're not going to use them?"

"Same reason I carry a gun—so I don't *have* to use it," Flower answered blithely. "Besides, I'm not worried about a knife. I can outrun a knife. Let's see if they can outrun a .38—I'll even give 'em a head start."

He laughed harshly at his own joke.

He fitted the pieces of the weapon together, held it aimed at the door, and said, "Point and click—just like the mouse on a computer."

She frowned and turned away. "There's things about Febo that bother me. The way he talks. He and his friends—"

"Let 'em talk," Flower said dismissively. He cracked the wheel of the handgun open and began feeding cartridges into the cylinders. "The

Arabs have a saying: 'The village dogs bark, and the caravan passes on.' Let Feeble and his butt-buddies bark as much as they want. As long as they get us over the line and into the States, what do you care what they're barkin' about?"

"I don't like going into that place," Morinda said. "I don't like the way Febo looks at me."

Flower stood and slipped the gun someplace under his clothes so smoothly that Morinda couldn't tell where it went. He took his warm-up jacket from the foot of the bed and put his arms into the sleeves.

"You'd better get used to men lookin' at ya," Flower said. "I've gotta go out for a while. To make a phone call. It's gonna take some time. Ya don't hafta hang around waitin' for me, but we'll be leavin' around six, like I said, so be in your room by then."

He crossed to the door, opened it, and stepped over the threshold before he paused halfway in and halfway out.

"If he does anything besides look," he said as he frowned thoughtfully while leaning around the barrier of the door, "let me know."

Then he left.

Morinda went out of the hotel a few minutes later. First, she made her way to a shoe store and bought a pair off athletic shoes. Then she wandered aimlessly around the streets. She dreaded having to return to the sleazy *cantina*, a place she knew no respectable woman'd ever enter, only prostitutes, which was why Febo and his *socios*'d treated her with such contempt the night before. She could only expect more of the same when she went there again. And if the arrangements were settled, then tonight she'd be making the difficult and dangerous crossing into the United States, a journey at the end of which she'd at last find her mother, and though she wanted that, wanted it more than anything, there was a part of her that feared this leap in the dark, and she felt a strange and inexplicable foreboding about the voyage through chaos she was about to make.

Lonely, and growing increasingly more uneasy about what would happen that night, she stopped at a *bodega* and bought a TELNOR calling card. She took it to a public phone and pushed the buttons for the number of her father's bar in San Estaban, the most likely place he'd be at this time of day, but when Guillermo the bartender answered, she lost her nerve and hung up without saying a word. Then she called Maria Elena's house.

The maid, Consuelo, answered. Morinda lowered her voice an octave to disguise it and asked hoarsely for Maria Elena.

"She's not at home right now," Consuelo said. "May I tell her who called?"

"This is Teresa Aguilar," Morinda said, using the first name that came to mind. "I'm a friend of Maria Elena's from school. When do you expect her back?"

"Oh, she should be home later this afternoon. You could try again then."

Morinda thanked her and hung up.

Feeling lonelier than ever, she returned to the hotel to sit in her room and wait for Flower to come for her.

He arrived with a grocery sack tucked in one arm. When she let him in, he carried it to the bed and set it down.

"Did ya get those shoes?"

Morinda looked at her feet and knocked her heels together like Dorothy with the ruby slippers.

"Oh, yeah. Tenny-runners. Good." Flower examined her legs and said, "Levi's are good, too. We'll head over and find Feeble in a minute."

"What about my clothes? The one's I bought—"

"Dump 'em. You can get more when we get to the States. No sense takin' more weight than we hafta. But I'm worried about water. Could ya carry a canteen? We might need it if we get stuck someplace and can't get to civilization for a while."

He opened the sack and pulled out a pair of two-quart canteens. They each had cloth straps and were covered on their fronts and backs with a furry fabric that could be soaked for evaporative cooling of the metal containers. He took them into the bathroom and filled them under the tap in the bathtub, wrapped them in bath towels he pulled off the towel rack, then put them back into the paper sack he'd brought them in. He handed the bag to Morinda; the full canteens gurgled as they shifted when she tucked them under her arm.

Flower stopped at the front desk to check out and regain the suitcase he'd deposited in the hotel safe. Morinda wondered what the suitcase held that was so important Flower'd take it with him when he insisted they travel as light as possible. She gave only a little thought to the matter, however, for her mind turned to Febo and his friends at the *cantina*, and the cloud she'd been under all day darkened even more.

After she and Flower boarded a taxi and she told the driver where to go, Flower surprised her. As if he'd been reading her mind, he said, "I don't want ya to go into that place. That *cantina*. I didn't know it'd be such a dump. When we get there, you wait outside, and I'll find Feeble."

Half-relieved, but at the same time dismayed when she thought that her chance to finally meet her mother might be jeopardized due to her squeamishness, Morinda protested weakly, "But you'll need me to translate."

"Oh, I think old Feeble's English's good enough to tell me if we're goin' tonight or not, and that's the only thing he's gonna hafta do."

"What if—?"

"Ya worry too much," Flower said. "I've got old Feeble figured out. There's nothing he's gonna do that I'm not already two steps ahead of him."

Flower leaned back in the seat's cushions with such an air of confidence that Morinda relaxed, feeling better than at any other time that day.

Set against the cracked stucco wall of a tottering building a hundred yards or so away from the *cantina*, there was an old-fashioned phone booth, though the glass in the door'd been smashed and never replaced. Flower told Morinda to order the taxi driver to stop there. Morinda got out with the grocery sack and its contents, and Flower said, "Wait here for me. This shouldn't take long."

The taxi drove off, then stopped in front of the *cantina*. From where she stood, Morinda could see Flower get out of the VW bug lugging his suitcase after him. He paid the driver. She watched the red and blue jacket he wore disappear into the *cantina*'s open doorway.

Morinda thought about the rigors of a border crossing at night. In preparation, she set the grocery sack and its two full canteens on the shelf below the telephone, stretched the collar of her blouse to loosen it, lifted her hair from the nape of her neck, and tucked it inside her clothing so it was out of the way.

Idly, she put her hands in her pockets and when her fingers struck the hard edge of her phone calling card, she took it out. It seemed like a good idea, since this might be her last day in Mexico, to tell someone goodbye. She again dialed Maria Elena's number. Consuelo answered as she had the first time Morinda called, and once more Morinda gave her name as Teresa Aguilar in her husky voice.

"*Bueno?*" Maria Elena said when she came to the phone. Morinda knew her friend was suspicious, not having any idea who "Teresa Aguilar" could be.

"Maria Elena?" she said. "It's Morinda."

"Morinda! *Hijole*! Where are you? Are you all right?"

"Of course I'm all right, but I can't tell you where I am. I called earlier, but you weren't home—"

"No, I was at church. My sisters, my mother, we were all at church," Maria Elena said. Then suddenly she grew agitated, and she added, "We lit candles for you!"

"Why would you light candles for me?"

"For you, and for your father!"

"Why? What's happened? Is my father okay?"

"Don't you know?" Maria Elena's tone became increasingly more shrill. "Morinda, your father—he's dead!"

"Dead?" Morinda asked, stunned. "What do you mean?"

"It's true!" Maria Elena insisted. "He's dead! He was shot! Murdered! And the night it happened was the night you left our house to go home! And that same night, you disappeared! We didn't know what happened to you! We thought you might have been taken!"

"Shot? Who would shoot my father? It doesn't make any sense. There's got to be some mistake."

"The safe in the floor was open. At your house. And there was nothing inside it. Somebody killed your father and took his money. Robbed him. The police have been there, they found fingerprints. That Flora—he's the one they're looking for. They think he's the one who killed him. He killed another man, a policeman, too. Morinda—"

Morinda jumped as a hand touched her shoulder; another hand reached across her other shoulder and the fingers at the end of it clicked the phone dead. She dropped the handset and spun around.

"Time to go," Flower said. "Feeble and his buddies are waitin' on us."

He lifted the sack with the canteens from off the shelf before he stepped aside to give her enough room to get out of the booth. She hesitated. Febo's handsome face came into view from the direction of the *cantina*.

He paused a few feet behind Flower, raised his muscular arms, intertwined the fingers of his hands on his neck, and stretched, the polyester fabric of his shirt expanding and his well-muscled chest showing through the V of its unbuttoned top. His two *socios* followed. They also came to a halt. Everyone was waiting for her. Morinda took one step out of the booth. Flower moved next to her and clutched her arm. As they walked, her elbow struck the hard metal of the gun under his jacket. Febo went ahead of them, Flower marched along at Morinda's side, and the other two fell into place behind them.

In the evening dusk, the mesas between Tijuana and San Diego stood out against the electric lights that burned brightly on both sides of the border, and Morinda could see the dark wall that divided the two countries. It was made from carbon steel landing mat panels each twelve feet high that once served the American military as runways on temporary air bases but that'd been given a new function in recent years: to keep the people of the south from going any farther north along a fourteen-mile-long strip separating Tijuana from San Diego.

The small group walked for several blocks until they came to a pickup truck with a camper shell covering its bed. The name of the truck was painted on its side: in English, the words meant THE QUEEN OF HEAVEN AND HOME. Febo told Morinda and Flower to get in the back before he and one of his *socios* clambered into the cab. The other of the smugglers accompanied the two into the rear of the truck where they sat on a wooden bench stretched across the covered wheel-well on the driver's side.

Morinda's mind was in a roil as the group drove through the slum that stretched between Febo's hangout and the borderline, and she tried to think of what she should do, what she *could* do. The news that her father was dead struck her like a hammer blow between the eyes, but the idea that Flower was his murderer transformed her mental and emotional state from stupefaction to near hysteria.

The first thought that arose in her mind was that she'd gotten Maria Elena's message wrong. She'd only had a chance to speak to her friend for a brief moment, and she hadn't had a chance to verify what she thought Maria

Elena said by asking her to repeat it or ground it in some sort of context so she could be sure she was hearing it right. Their phone conversation was cut off too soon. News of the death of her father—the murder of her father!—was something so horrendous that it demanded validation beyond a mere mention in a foreshortened telephone call.

Perhaps Maria Elena had the facts wrong. How would she know the conclusions of the police in a murder investigation? She was only a fourteen-year-old girl, after all, and thus not the most reliable source of accurate information on something of this kind. On the other hand, she was the daughter of the *delegado*, and as far as the authorities knew she was the last person in San Estaban to see Morinda before she disappeared from the town, vanishing on the heels of her father's death by gunshot, if that was in fact what'd occurred. So the police would've questioned Maria Elena, and as her father was the *delegado*, they'd keep him informed of the progress of their investigation, so actually Maria Elena could be extremely knowledgeable.

And Flower had a gun! He carried it on him even now; she'd felt it when she bumped her elbow into it. She remembered him cleaning it at the hotel, when she'd thought it perfectly natural—all American detectives carried guns on TV and in the movies. But Flower packed a gun for a totally different reason than what he'd said; he didn't use it for protection, he used it to kill people, people like her father.

Another thought struck her like a revelation: the suitcase Flower carried with him, the one he was at such pains to protect—that was her father's! Morinda once remarked to him how much it looked like her father's suitcase, and Flower said it was a common brand. But they weren't just similar—they were identical! Flower took it after killing her father. He put whatever he stole from her father's safe in it, and that was why he made sure to keep it secure in the hotel safe when they checked in.

It was those two pieces of incontrovertible physical evidence—the gun and the suitcase—that convinced her. She knew deep in her heart it was only her desire *not* to believe that led her to entertain doubts in the first place. She had to accept it as the truth—Flower'd murdered her father. The question was, what was she going to do now?

She should run! She should escape! But where could she run to? Flower was no longer holding her arm, but he walked right beside her, and she knew he carried a gun—the same gun he'd used to kill her father. He could shoot her if she tried to get away. He'd probably only taken her along when he left San Estaban in order to keep her from discovering her father's body, and kept her with him as a convenience because she was able to translate for him. But when he no longer needed her, he'd no longer have any reason to keep her alive. As soon as they were in the U.S., he could afford to get rid of her, and he'd eliminate her as a bad risk, a witness who needed to be silenced. He'd leave her body in an arroyo where it might never be found by anything other than the wild animals that scavenged there.

There were Febo and his *socios*. They carried knives. Would they help her if she appealed to them? More likely they'd help Flower! The things they'd said both about her and to her the night before let her know they'd never give her any assistance. And they were in Flower's pay, so they'd do what he told them to do, even keep her from running away if she tried.

If she did run, and Flower didn't shoot her, and Febo and his friends didn't stab her with their knives, where could she go? She looked desperately out the back of the truck at the tumbled-down shacks and decaying businesses around her: would any of the people in any of these places have any sympathy for her, or would they be more likely to side with toughs and killers like Flower and Febo? The only answer she could find to this question told her there was no hope for her in the Zona Norte, or in the slums of Colonia Libertad that spread out from the red-light district to the international boundary line.

She was trapped. There was nothing she could do but continue with Flower and the others to the fence, make her way across the border, and seek an opportunity to escape once she was in open country, or, if she couldn't do it then, hope Flower wouldn't kill her before they reached San Diego, where she might be able to slip away. It was the only chance she had, she realized, and the only way out of her dilemma was to go along with the original plan, and above all else not let Flower know that she now knew he'd murdered her father, for if he ever discovered she was on to him, he'd kill her to keep her quiet. As long as he believed she was ignorant of what he'd done in San Estaban, he had no reason to kill her right away, and he might let her live—at least long enough for her to manage to get away.

They arrived at a construction site where a large new factory was going up. Even at night, work continued as crews of laborers used banks of stadium lights just like those on the San Diego side of the border that lit up the wilderness areas surrounding the city. The site was like an anthill, with workers in hard hats scrambling over the whole surface and the skeleton of the five-story structure and eighteen-wheel big rigs rolling through. The pickup they rode in was only a drop in the ocean of manic activity.

Morinda could only see where they'd already been out the back as they passed through until they drove by the twenty-foot wall of a security barrier and finally stopped at a tension membrane temporary construction shelter. They heard Febo and his companion getting out of the cab, and the smuggler in the rear indicated Morinda and Flower should also climb down from the pickup's bed.

Three armed men dressed in uniforms holding rifles at port arms and carrying pistols strapped to their hips blocked the entrance to the tent-like shelter. Febo spoke to the security guards, who seemed to recognize him and acted as if they expected him there. They waved him and the four others with him into the building as if they wanted the group to get inside and out of sight quickly. One of Febo's *socios* said to Morinda and Flower, "*Andale! Andale!*" They hurried inside as they were instructed.

The interior of the building was the size of an airplane hangar. It was completely empty. Their footsteps echoed noisily through the open space as they followed Febo to the center of the shelter. There in the middle of the concrete floor was a hatchway large enough for a person to easily fit though. Febo kneeled down and pulled the door of the hatch open by a metal ring handle. The passage led to a stairway of wooden risers. Febo let the man who'd ridden with him in the cab of the truck go down first, then waved for Flower and Morinda to go next, and finally he and the second of his companions went into the dark hole before the hatch was pulled shut behind them.

Once they were all in the tunnel, one of Febo's group turned on the string of electric lights to illuminate their way. Bare 100-watt bulbs were spaced every ten feet along the ceiling. They went down steps to a depth of 80 feet before they reached the bottom. The lights continued down the stairway and down the entire length of the tunnel, perhaps a hundred yards. The tunnel was over a yard wide, and two yards high. Flower had to bend over slightly as he walked through it, but no one else had any difficulty getting through. The walls of the passage were framed with two-by-four wooden studs. Morinda noticed an occasional drainage device and ventilation hose. It all seemed very professional.

There was a two-inch-wide line painted around the four sides of the tunnel in bright yellow paint at a certain point. As they went by it, one of Febo's friends said, "*El linde.*" Mentally, Morinda translated: The border.

They were now in America.

CHAPTER 11

They came out of the ground in *El Norte*, the North, hidden from view by four or five irregular piles of steel pipe and sections of railroad track chained together to form temporary vehicle barriers to stop smugglers and drug runners from escaping pursuing Border Patrol agents on the U.S. side. Each was so heavy it could only be moved with a forklift or a front-loader.

Morinda's impressions of what happened after that bled into one another, and they were as distorted and unreal as the phantasmagorical images of a fever dream.

Helicopters with glaring searchlights passed over the dark, towering mesas and deep fissures of the arroyos, the stark contrast of brilliant searing light sweeping across the night-shaded landscape making it seem that a hunt was taking place on the surface of the moon. When the helicopters' prop wash was no longer audible, and the traffic on the nearby highway diminished for a moment, Morinda heard dogs barking and radios playing music drifting up from Colonia Libertad, the slum section of Tijuana they'd left behind. Once the helicopters' searing searchlights were gone, she could see to the north the shadowy forms of scrub oak, cholla cactus, and mesquite.

Febo said something in a peremptory tone to his *socios*, and they disappeared into the darkness, moving furtively. The group was safely beyond the secondary fence that was a back-up to the primary fence. This was an angled two-piece wall, vertical up to ten feet and then extended at an angle facing the south to keep climbers from the Mexican side from scaling it. Morinda didn't hear what Febo ordered the other two to do, but she understood they were being sent out as *checadores*, scouts, to watch for Border Patrol agents who might be in the area. The scouts'd go through the fence first, and the *coyote*, Febo, would bring the *pollos*, Flower and Morinda, after them. This was standard operating procedure.

Flower dragged his suitcase and canteen with him, and the three ran, Febo in the lead. Febo proceeded confidently and expertly, loping easily to follow the worn footpath through the dense ground cover, sticking to the densest parts of the shadows and never bothering to check to make sure Morinda and Flower were keeping up with him. The *coyote* had no trouble avoiding the jagged rocks and nasty clusters of desert plants that seemed to leap out of the darkness directly into Morinda and Flower's path so that they had to constantly twist and dodge at the last second to avoid knee-high walls of sharp-edged stones and waist-high clumps of bristling needle-like spikes, and the two *pollos* found themselves bumping into each other and having to hold one another up for support. Without daring to speak a word, they eventually worked out a symbiotic division of labor so that while Morinda kept her eyes on the *coyote* to see where he was leading them, Flower watched the ground ahead to guide them away from obstacles, and sometimes they silently exchanged jobs. Several times when Morinda's arm prodded Flower, or he held her up when she tripped over the uneven ground, she felt the heavy metal lump of Flower's revolver, and she was reminded that she was running with a murderer, a man she expected to kill her as soon as he no longer needed her.

Febo disappeared behind a boulder, and he didn't come into view again. By that time, the *coyote* was more than ten yards ahead of his *pollos*. First Morinda, and then Flower, rounded the massive rock; they slowed, halted, and peered into the darkness seeking any trace of their guide. Only when they heard an exhalation like a snake's hiss off to the side did they turn and catch a glimpse of Febo, crouching in the shadows. He waved them over to where he squatted. When Flower tried to ask a question, Febo scowled and slashed a hand through the air, cutting him off.

The three waited as noiselessly as they could for what seemed to Morinda like fifteen or twenty minutes. She was thankful for the respite, which gave her a chance to catch her breath after the dash from the tunnel, but it was terrifying to cower in the middle of nowhere, hiding in the darkness with only a knife-wielding thug and the gun-bearing killer of her father as company. She could hear shouts in Spanish, but they were distant and indistinct, carrying across the bleak lunar landscape like the disembodied voices of wandering ghosts. Several times she heard the faint cracks of faraway gunshots. Once she heard a woman's scream, high and shrill; it lasted for five seconds before it suddenly ceased, the abruptness of the ensuing silence more horrifying than the cry that preceded it.

From much nearer, two sharp clicks resounded, as if one rock was being struck against another. Febo's head cocked sharply to the right, the source of the noise, as if he'd been waiting for it. But he made no move to leave their hiding place until the same double click of stone on stone came again. Then he stood, motioned his *pollos* forward, and the three made their way up the slope at a slower pace than before. Morinda realized the clicks'd been a signal sent to Febo by one of his *socios* telling him it was safe to proceed.

They reached the crest of the hill. For hours after that they hiked up inclines, scrambled down the craggy walls of arroyos, and skirted the bases of mesas. Morinda kept track of their compass bearings as best she could as she sought an opportunity to flee the two men she'd come to think of as her captors. But until they got closer to San Diego, Morinda knew she'd have to remain with Febo. If she got separated from her guide, she might never find her way out of the wilderness; and dying of thirst and exhaustion, or lingering on in agony after breaking her neck by stumbling into an unseen crevice, would be a far worse fate than the relatively easy death by gunshot she could expect from Flower.

Febo was angling to the northeast, as far as she could tell, which meant they were heading away from the lights of both Tijuana and San Diego. She assumed this was in order to skirt the area most intensely patrolled by the Border Patrol. But their path soon cut back toward their primary objective: north.

Morinda never saw either of the two associates of Febo's who acted as *checadores* after they left them on the American side of the fence, nor did she ever see anyone else in the foothills making the perilous crossing, but once she heard a voice calling from a distance, "*Vengan acá!*" "Come here!" And on two occasions Febo stopped, motioned for Flower and Morinda to wait, and walked ahead for several minutes to turn his head slowly from side to side as he listened for something; then he banged rocks together and listened further, trying to communicate with his scouts. She didn't hear any response to these signals, and both times it happened, after a short while Febo gave up and waved for the *pollos* to rejoin him.

They were beyond the flight path of the helicopters, and they'd seen no Border Patrol units in some time. A cylindrical mountain of rock thrust skyward from the earth, standing between them and San Diego. Jagged peaks with steep slopes covered by wild anise and manzanita shrubs spread around them in the three directions Morinda could see; the air was redolent of the musky odor of the desert plants.

Febo came to a halt one more time and motioned Morinda and Flower to remain where they were. The *coyote* then walked ahead until he could no longer be seen in the darkness, not even as a ghostly shade. Morinda and Flower kept still. They listened for the clicking of rocks, but they heard nothing except for the distant noises coming from the hunters and the hunted.

Morinda stood five feet away from Flower, her arms folded while she nervously rubbed one hand over the elbow of the other arm. Flower grew increasingly more anxious as time went by and Febo didn't return. He stood in one place for the first few minutes, but soon began to pace, strutting forward in the direction Febo'd gone and then returning before he turned and walked back, shifting the suitcase from hand to hand. After dozens of such trips, Morinda heard him mutter impatiently, "Where the hell'd he go?"

Flower then sidled close to Morinda and said in a hushed voice, "Where'd he disappear to? Did ya see?"

Morinda shook her head.

"I don't know what he's tryin' to pull. He's been gone almost an hour. He can't be tryin' to ditch us—he hasn't been paid the other half of his money yet." Flower stretched out his left arm to reveal the watch he wore on his wrist. He peered at the dial; the numbers and the hands glowed faintly. He dropped his arm and said, "I'll give him a few more minutes."

He peered around at the rugged terrain and added, "We get lost out here, and—"

They both jerked their heads about when they heard a rustling in the nearby bushes.

"Febo?" Flower called in a stage whisper.

There was no answer.

Flower slipped his canteen off his shoulder and set it down. Then he took several cautious steps forward.

"Febo? Is that you?"

He reached inside his jacket and brought out his revolver. The oiled metal gleamed in the starlight. Soon, Morinda could see Flower only dimly as a dark form that stood out by contrast against the slightly lighter background of the manzanita shrubs. Flower stepped off a dozen stealthy paces.

"Febo?"

Morinda slid her own canteen off her shoulder, letting it lay in the dirt. She recrossed her arms in front of her, the fingers of one of her hands worrying the neckline of her blouse.

Flower's figure dimmed to imperceptibility, so that Morinda couldn't say for sure what'd happened to him: whether he'd gone too far away for her to discern him any longer, stepped off the pathway into the dense vegetation, or gone down an arroyo in pursuit of the source of the rustling sound.

It was the perfect opportunity for her to escape, she realized, except that she was totally alone and lost in the most desolate and hostile terrain she'd ever been in. She had no light to see by other than that of the moon and the far-distant stars, and there were still many miles of wilderness to cover.

She raised her hand to her mouth and bit her thumbnail.

She fully expected to hear a gunshot shatter the placid stillness any moment, and she hunched her shoulders and held her breath in anticipation. She silently promised herself that as soon as the pistol went off, she'd run, whatever the dangers. She scouted around her and saw a streak of white winding through the darker vegetation, marking what must be the footpath they were following, and she decided that that was the way she'd bolt the very instant she heard the crack of a bullet.

But the gun never fired. Instead, she heard a much softer, gentler sound that insinuated its way into her consciousness so slowly that she couldn't tell when she first noticed it: dry manzanita scraping against cloth, and shoes scuffling on dirt. In a moment, she matched the noises to a moving figure that coalesced out of the night and the darker shadows clinging to the barrier of shrubs.

A man's figure carried a suitcase in one hand and a gun in the other, yet it didn't move with Flower's gait. As it approached, Morinda noticed the form was shorter than Flower, and broader shouldered. It was Febo.

"Where's Flower?" she asked.

Febo came within arm's reach of her and stopped, stooping sufficiently to lower the suitcase to the ground, then raising himself again to his full height. Morinda lowered her hands to her sides when something warned her that Febo's sudden appearance carrying Flower's gun and the suitcase, with Flower nowhere in sight, might mean the fulfillment of her worst possible scenario.

Febo moved closer to her so he was standing less than a foot away. It struck her that, although she knew Flower'd killed her father and was planning on killing her, nevertheless she'd been relying on him to protect her from Febo.

She stumbled backward a step to put a safe distance between her and the *coyote*, but the *coyote* lifted the hand that held the gun and rested it on her shoulder, stopping her from retreating any farther. She turned her eyes toward the pistol only a few inches from her head.

"Don't run, pretty one," Febo said in Spanish. "Don't run, and I won't have to cut you open like I did that stupid *huero*, that *pinche gabacho*."

"Flower . . ." she began, but she couldn't complete the thought. She raised her head to fix her gaze on the features of Febo's handsome face.

"Flora?" Febo said. He waved his empty hand dismissively through the air. "*Un maricón sin vergüenzo*! But now he's dead."

Terror-stricken, Morinda couldn't move. She was held in thrall like a rabbit caught in the talons of a hawk. She was constantly aware of the heavy butt of the pistol that Febo pressed against her shoulder. When the weight of the gun fell away as Febo bent to lay the weapon on the ground, Morinda found she'd been holding her breath—for how long, she couldn't say—and she forced out one long sigh, then held her chin up to the sky and sobbed. The act released her from the marrow-freezing dread that'd kept her transfixed.

She spun on her heel and ran in a mindless panic. She managed to take only three steps before Febo reached her. The fingers of his hands clutched at her clothes, jerking her back so violently that both her feet were lifted in the air, the neckline of her blouse pulled so tight against her throat that it strangled her. Febo twisted the collar even tighter, coiling the material so it felt like a noose as he grappled her to his body.

From over her shoulder, he shoved his face next to hers and whispered into her ear, "I can fuck you alive, pretty one. Or I can fuck you dead. It doesn't make much difference to me. But it might make a difference to you. It'd be so much nicer—for you—if you were alive to feel it, *chica*."

Morinda was familiar with the vulgar Spanish word *chingar*: as she knew, it was a transitive verb, one that took an object. But only at that moment, and for the first time in her life, did it occur to her—even as a possibility—that she herself could be the object the verb might take.

When Flower regained consciousness, he was surrounded by darkness, and he was in agony. The pain was indescribable, and came from too many sources for him to count. The greatest was centered on his stomach. He put his hands up to touch the spot, and he felt the haft of the knife Febo'd left in him. He couldn't recall in detail what'd happened, but he remembered Febo lying in wait for him, and the *coyote* plunging the knife into him again and again, driving Flower to the ground and then leaving after the final thrust of the blade into Flower's abdomen. Flower raised his gun at the first hint of Febo's treachery, but he'd been unable to swing it into position before the knife pierced his chest, numbing his arm and turning the muscles on the right side of his body to jelly, causing him to drop the pistol before he ever got a chance to use it. He blacked out, then, only to wake up to a world of hurt.

He made a feeble attempt to remove the knife, giving it a tentative tug: he found it was firmly lodged within his flesh, and it'd take much more effort to remove it than he was willing or able to expend just then. Merely touching the knife's haft sent excruciating shock waves through him as the attached blade jiggled within him, causing damaged nerve endings to scream for relief; to pull the knife out'd be a nightmare. Besides, the blade might be the only thing that kept his blood from gushing out of the gash the knife'd cut.

Flower swallowed and nodded his head, though the movement was little more than a waggle of his chin. He let his hands fall off the knife's bone handle and ran them weakly up his torso. He winced when his fingers encountered the gaping lips of a wound. He paused then, resting up. After a few seconds, he moved his hands again, stopping at each of half a dozen places where the knife'd entered and been yanked out. Finally, he lay still to regain his strength.

After a few minutes, he lifted his hands to look at them. They were slick with a thick, wet coating.

Dully, Flower realized he was bleeding out. The flow of blood from the numerous wounds was too copious for it to stop on its own. In a short time, he knew, he'd lose consciousness again from the loss of blood pressure, and then he'd die.

Above him, the stars in the night sky twinkled. They were distant and uncaring, unconcerned that the most significant event in the universe—Flower's universe, the only universe he'd ever directly experienced—was about to take place, the culminating event of its history, that which'd bring it to an end, collapsing space and time and all that they contained into a single pinpoint that displaced nothing in any direction, either of extension or of duration. And yet another universe, which'd always run parallel to that which Flower inhabited, the universe of objective reality that possessed a shadowy, secondary being in relation to the much truer existence of Flower's subjective life, would continue to run on after Flower's more authentic world ended.

The stars themselves were proof of that. They'd burned at vast distances for thousands, even millions of years before his own birth, and they'd continue to burn for thousands and millions of years after his death. They had nothing to do with the world Flower'd known and familiarly lived within, the true world of his inner life. They were part of the natural order that sometimes impinged upon the private kingdom within him, but which never had any solid connection with the internal workings of the meaningful universe—the sphere of events that took place within his mind.

Many of the stars he now saw were already dead, Flower knew. The light from them started from their sources many thousands of light-years away, and the stars that sent the light out'd exploded into novas or their nuclear fires'd faded and then grown so dim they couldn't even maintain themselves many, many years before, and what Flower was seeing now were events that occurred long ago, the last remains of a dead theater, like watching old newsreel footage. Perhaps someone, some conscious being living on a planet circling a living star some hundreds of thousands of years hence, would use a telescope powerful enough that it could focus upon the earth, and that observer'd view Flower's death taking place years and years after its actual occurrence. And it'd have as much meaning for the being that then watched it as it had now, ultimately, in the grand scheme of things . . .

None whatsoever.

For many years, Flower'd sought to find some sort of meaning in life. It'd never revealed itself to him. Life was a pointless struggle, a journey going nowhere, lacking destination, purpose, and value. No matter what he did, it simply didn't matter; to do nothing, to remain totally inactive, made as much sense as doing any particular thing, when it was viewed philosophically rather than practically. Looking at life with detachment, *sub specie aeternitatis*, was like seeing the world with one eye closed: everything appeared two-dimensional, so that everything seemed equidistant, nothing stood out as foreground against a background; everything was, from the cosmic point of view, weary, stale, flat, and unprofitable. In the final analysis, nothing mattered.

Flower's contemplation was interrupted by a signal from the external universe of objective reality. The world intruded itself into his brooding thoughts in the form of a human voice. From some distance away, he heard a man crooning, "Ooh, *lindalita!*" Only slowly, and as a result of some considerable mental effort on Flower's part, could he identify the voice as Febo's. It was strange that Febo should be speaking within the range of his hearing, and he turned this fact over and over in his mind as he attempted to grasp its significance.

He heard Febo speak again, saying something in Spanish.

It was then that Flower's mind snapped into focus like a telescope that's been set on 1000X to scan the empyrean realm of the skies suddenly switched to 10X and turned to view what was taking place in a window across the street. An abrupt shift in his attitude accompanied the change in perspective: though nothing ultimately mattered in the grand scheme of things, Flower realized, some things might still be of immense importance in the quotidian realm of day-to-day events.

The thought passed through his mind: "Febo thinks I'm dead. He thinks he killed me."

The idea galvanized him to action. By sheer dint of will, Flower lifted himself up on one elbow and flipped himself over. The move caused his entrails to shift, and as his bowels coiled they passed across the edge of the blade stuck into their midst, intensifying the agony he'd thought was already at the maximum he could endure. When he finally fell forward on his hands and knees, he opened his mouth to scream, but the cry was stifled by a thick gob of blood he coughed up into his throat and spewed out of his mouth. He gagged and choked until his throat was clear, and by then he was too weak to utter a sound. The blood looked black to him as it spurted out and dropped to the earth.

Febo relaxed his hold on Morinda's blouse, and she could breathe again. She sucked in air in a series of gasps. He continued to hold her in place, forcing her against his own body. He put the palm of his left hand out and covered her right breast with it. Then he let both his hands range freely over her. He slid his hand inside her blouse and slipped his fingers under the cup of her bra. "Little *pechos*," he said, appraisingly. "Little *tetas*." He folded his hand so that the thumb, forefinger, and middle finger pinched the nipple of one breast between them. She hissed in pain.

"Ooh, pretty one," Febo said. He slid her bra strap off her shoulder and kneaded the breast it revealed with one hand while the other he ran down her belly, across the rough denim fabric of her jeans, then shifted around so that it slithered underhanded between her legs. Morinda closed her eyes and shuddered.

The hand that groped her crotch was removed, but Morinda still did not dare to look. The zipper of Febo's pants came undone; the metal buckle of his belt jingled when the tongue rattled against it.

"Get down on the ground," Febo ordered.

He gave her no time either to comply or to resist; she was dragged backward with a lurch, causing her to sprawl supine on the powdery earth. Febo stood over her, his pants down round his ankles. She lay at his feet, stunned and paralyzed with fear.

Febo dropped on his knees beside her. His fingernails dug into her flesh beneath the waistband of her pants, ripping at the material on either side of the fly without bothering to undo the top button. He tore savagely until the flaps came loose, and he yanked her pants down, pushing them to her knees, then forcing them even farther until they were around her ankles. She tried to cover herself, and then to cling to her panties. It did no good. With ridiculous ease, he removed her protective hands and renewed his assault when he tugged at the elastic waistband of her panties, pushing them to her ankles along with her jeans. She writhed in pain as his fingernails ripped at the flesh of her waist and thighs. His manic efforts left gashes on her vulva, and new scrapes on her thighs as well.

Once he'd stripped her from belly to ankles, Febo inched toward her, taking mincing steps as he duckwalked on his knees. He bent her legs at the knees and pushed them apart. Morinda tightened her thighs, fighting Febo's efforts to force himself between them. He brought his hand up to her vulva, his thumb on one side of the sensitive tissues while his fingers clamped the other and squeezed them together with tremendous pressure. Morinda squealed but did not relax the muscles locking her legs together. He continued to crush the handful of flesh until she screamed. She could no longer bear it, and she allowed her legs to go limp.

Febo inched his pelvis and his tumescent penis toward her. He put one hand on her face to cup her jaw, and she twisted her head away to escape its hold. She failed in this as well. He clutched her chin in his grasp, and leaned his weight on it as he pressed himself into her, grinding the other side of her face into the dirt. Her eyes were turned to her right, the same side on which Febo had set the gun, and she could see the weapon laying only a few feet from her. Febo half sighed and half grunted at the same time Morinda felt something tear inside of her. She had a wild, incoherent thought: "Dear God, something inside me's burst! My appendix is ruptured! Not now! Not now!"

Feeling she had nothing left to lose, she whipped her right arm up and bent it at the elbow, trying to work her hand around to grasp the butt of the pistol. Her arm flailed as she attempted to twist it into the unnatural position it'd have to assume in order for her to take control of the gun.

Pain surged through her one more time as Febo partially withdrew then lunged into her again. His thrust drove her whole body backward so she was nearer the gun. She could now brush the butt of the weapon with her fingernails. She renewed her efforts, willing herself to dislocate her own arm if necessary in order to grasp the weapon. The tips of her fingers came within a fraction of an inch of clutching the trigger guard. She lifted her hand and swung it over and back one more time, confident she'd succeed on the next try.

Her heart broke as Febo's arm extended his much larger hand, plucked the gun from the ground, and carried it away, placing it more than a foot away from the fingers of her outstretched hand. He left the pistol where Morinda could see it, tantalizingly close but just out of her reach.

Flower panted like an animal from the exertion. He rested for as long as it took to reclaim his strength, then shifted his weight so he was held up solely by his left arm, allowing him to raise his right hand to grasp the haft of the knife. The arm bearing the weight of his upper body trembled, then shook almost uncontrollably, as he slowly drew the blade of the knife out of his belly. His face twisted and contorted while he fought to keep silent; he knew any outcry he made'd only fill his mouth with more blood and choke him. His teeth ground against each other with so much force he thought they might shatter. When the tip of the knife exited the puncture wound at last, the folds of flesh that'd encompassed it gave a slight pop. His white intestines and more black blood dropped out of the hole the knife'd plugged.

Flower released the knife from his grip. With trembling fingers, he used his free hand to pick up the length of bowel that oozed from the hole in his belly; after a long struggle, he forced it back inside and then managed to zip his jacket up far enough to keep his entrails from falling out and dragging in the dirt. He paused to rest on his hands and knees for a few minutes. Blood continued to drip from the open wounds the knife'd gouged in his chest. It pattered on the ground below him like rain on a rooftop.

Tentatively, he set the hand he'd used to collect his innards back on the ground to help prop himself up. It dropped on the smooth bone haft of the knife, and his fingers curled around it. He rested on all fours, swaying arrhythmically and panting heavily, but his ragged breaths soon turned to wheezing sobs. He coughed and choked on blood. After a while, the nausea passed and his mind cleared.

He could no longer see the stars. But that didn't matter. If life itself had no meaning, nevertheless there were things within life that did.

"He thinks I'm dead," he told himself. "He thinks he killed me."

Driven by that thought, Flower began to crawl.

CHAPTER 12

Morinda gazed up at the stars. Pain coursed through her every time Febo thrust himself into her. At first she'd groaned at each assault in a counter-rhythm to the grunts Febo made, but her body grew numbed after a time and the feeling became a steady throbbing ache more than a series of sharp pangs, and her thoughts turned more to the humiliation of being raped than to the physical suffering. The coarse way he'd exposed her breasts and then handled them as though he were buying fruit at the marketplace. The demeaning way he'd talked about their small size as though she had no understanding of the words, as though she were only an animal being judged at a fair. The way he'd stripped her, then mauled her to get her to move her legs apart for his benefit, leaving her with no pride at all when she was forced to aid him in his use of her, reducing her ultimately to something far less than human at the same time he was engaging in the most intimate act possible, touching his skin to hers and putting his flesh inside her, doing it without her permission, against her will, with no care that she not only didn't want him to do it, but that she hated it, loathed it, and felt so degraded by the experience that nausea welled up like hot lava in the pit of her stomach.

As the rape proceeded, a new idea arose: Febo'd no reason to leave her alive when he was finished with her; therefore, she had only a few minutes to live.

The realization made her turn icy cold from the inside out.

His mind dulled by the continued loss of blood, there was only one conscious thought that went round and round in Flower's mind like a Buddhist prayer wheel carrying its single message, and certainly it was the only thing that impelled him to force himself onward: "He thinks he killed me. He thinks I'm dead."

Flower gave no consideration to what he was going to do; he was no longer lucid enough to formulate a plan of any kind. After he emerged from the shallow arroyo Febo'd left him in, he used the grunts and pants he heard to guide him. Flower instinctively guessed he had at most another minute during which Febo'd be sufficiently distracted. He knew he was weakening with every passing second, and the physical exertion needed to get him near enough to Febo was causing even more blood loss, but he forced himself to keep going anyway. When he could see Febo's naked buttocks rising and falling in time with the groans, he roused himself to get his eyes to track, and from then on he used both sight and sound to guide him.

Febo cried out, "Uh, uh, uh," preorgasmically as Flower approached.

The nerve endings at the jagged edges of his numerous wounds tortured him with every movement he made, and stomach acid spilled agonizingly into his body cavity whenever his entrails coiled, but he somehow found the strength to alternate his hands and knees in a progressive creep forward. His vigor ebbing steadily, he could only drag himself along, slowly inching ahead the one hand that held the knife, followed by an infinitesimal shift forward of the knee on the same side of his body, then after he'd locked his advance elbow so that it wouldn't collapse under him, he lurched the opposite hand up another inch or two and planted it before painstakingly hauling up his other knee. All the while, his head wobbled like a jack-in-the-box on his neck.

His mind steadily lost clarity, but never its sense of purpose. He concentrated almost solely on Febo's grunts and the undulations of Febo's body. The knowledge that the man who'd left him for dead was nearby, and that he was closing in on him, drove Flower on.

Flower held the blade of the knife up as he neared Febo from the side. He didn't deliberately try to sneak up on his prey, to keep the knife from clinking against the ground or a rock as he crawled and thus giving Febo a warning; his bodily reactions were functioning on something like automatic pilot. When he arrived a few feet from where Febo stiffly held his head parallel to the earth with his arms spread out supporting himself above the body of Morinda while he grunted with each thrust of his pelvis, "Uh, uh, uh," Flower paused so as not to alert the man he was stalking with no conscious thought whatsoever. It was more an intuitive act sprung from sly animal cunning than anything else.

Ponderously, with an extreme effort of will, Flower shifted his weight off his hands so that he was kneeling. With great labor, he brought his head and torso erect. He lifted his right arm. It felt rubbery, as though it'd been dosed with Novocain. He found he didn't have the strength to keep the knife under control with just the one hand, so he brought the other up to lift the blade above his head. He teetered in place, wavering from side to side. Raising his arms stretched the torn ligaments and muscles of his chest and abdomen, and he sucked in his breath as the multiplied pain seared through him.

His exertion also caused the wounds in his abdomen to sigh and wheeze, air being forced out of the ruptures in his body cavity. The noises attracted Febo's attention; his head snapped to the side, and he caught his first glimpse of the danger he was in.

"*Chingao!*" Febo exclaimed. He whipped his left hand through the dirt, scrabbling for the pistol he'd put there to keep it from Morinda's grasp.

Flower's eyes blinked, widened, then narrowed as they tried to focus. Febo's sudden movements were just a blur to him.

The *coyote*'s own eyes grew wide with fear, and their whites became visible all around the irises. He desperately slapped at the dirt, seeking the gun.

Flower plunged the knife down.

Febo shrieked. The hand that'd been groping for the .38 was transfixed, the blade piercing its flesh and the numerous fine bones to hold it in place as the tip buried itself deep in the earth under it.

Spent, Flower fell forward and collapsed, his head only a few inches from that of the *coyote*. His hand found the gun Febo's'd unsuccessfully sought. Almost languidly, he raised it. He swung its muzzle toward the side of Febo's head.

Flower's strength continued to drain away. The gun waved loosely back and forth in his grip. Febo stared in agony and wide-eyed wonder at the hilt of the knife that pinned his hand. Flower leaned forward and pressed the pistol's barrel into Febo's temple, which brought Febo's full attention to the weapon.

Flower opened his mouth to speak. His tongue moved through blood as thick as gelatin, spitting droplets into the *coyote*'s face as he attempted to articulate the words, "Die, you shitbag!"

Morinda never noticed Flower as he came crawling out of the darkness, not even when he paused beside her and Febo to bring the knife up to striking position. The first indication she had of his presence was when Febo shouted in surprise and then floundered about, trying to grab the gun. The agonized, almost inhuman screech Febo gave when the knife pierced his hand shocked her.

Morinda watched as Flower placed the revolver to Febo's head. Flower coughed and sputtered as a black liquid spilled from between his lips, and she heard him mumble something she couldn't make out. And then the gun exploded like a clap of thunder only an inch from her ear.

A wet spray stung her eyes. Febo's body shuddered, collapsed, and then lay still on top of her and within her.

At the blast, Febo was transformed into a limp and cloying lump, a mass of unanimated flesh and bone and blood that held her to the earth, but which did so with no more purpose than would a sack of potatoes that might've fallen upon her. It nearly drove Morinda mad: as horrible as being raped by the living Febo'd been, this being raped by the dead was infinitely worse.

She put her hands up to the *coyote*'s shoulders and pushed. The idea that the dead man's still tumescent penis remained inside her revolted her and gave her the determination to heave Febo's body away; the weight shifted as it lurched to the side until its shoulder slumped on the ground. Although the crown of its head turned toward Morinda, it was impossible for her to see its eyes: the upper half of the face was transformed into a dark mask of blood.

Once Febo's upper body no longer pressed her down, she was able to lever her legs out from under the lower half of it by bucking and kicking. Febo's lifeless arm remained stretched across her, the palm of its open hand touching her bare thigh, and then the body's fingers caught in the cotton panties where they were bunched at her ankles. Morinda pumped her legs until the hold of Febo's dead hand loosened, and finally she managed to escape its reach and it fell into the powdery dirt along with the rest of Febo.

She struggled to her feet, pulling her panties up as she unsteadily swayed from side to side in an effort to keep her balance. She let her panties go and put her arms out to keep from tipping over, then glanced down to find her underwear again. Shooting pains ran through her between her legs. She was bleeding from inside; dark trails of her own blood ran down her legs.

"Oh, my God!" she whispered. She pulled her panties up, using the bunched cloth like a rag to sop up as much of the wetness as she could, then she tugged up her jeans to zip and button them.

The two sides of her blouse hung open. She looked at her chest. Her breasts were bare. She cast her gaze around her crazily, and her eyes caught a streak of white that lay cast aside in the dirt. Her bra'd been torn off her at some point during the rape, the buttons of her blouse likewise ripped off, and she'd never noticed.

Her attention turned back to the men at her feet. She staggered backward, away from them, and as she did so lifted her hands to her head and rubbed her fingers through her hair, sobbing. She brought her hands away again.

Her fingers were stuck together. She raised them in front of her. They were dark, wet, shining.

Her hands were covered in blood, though whether it was her own, or that of Flower, or of Febo, she had no way of telling. Raising one of her hands to her eyes to wipe away the stinging tears that poured out of them, she felt something thick and viscous on her cheek. She wiped the back of her hand across it and tried to see what clung there when she moved it to within a few inches of her eyes: it was dark, with white chunks mixed in with it, and she knew it must be something the bullet'd turned Febo's head into.

She dropped to her knees and began to sob uncontrollably, her mind having reached the end of its tether. Hopelessly, she wailed, "Help me! Help me!"

The hot nausea welling up from the pit of her stomach returned. She bent over double to gag, but nothing came out. A second retching spasm started, and she closed her eyes and whimpered to herself, "None of this is me. *I'm* me. This is me. I'm in here. I'm me. I'm right here. This is me. I'm right here. None of this is me."

In a few moments her dry heaves ended, and the nausea passed.

She lifted both her hands to her face and rubbed as hard as she could at her cheeks, her chin, her neck, everywhere she could think the blood and the brains might've landed. She cleaned her hands by picking up clods of dirt and scrubbing with the coarse grains. One of the canteens was only a few feet from her. She crawled to it, unscrewed the cap, and poured water over herself, splashing it on her face and rubbing the gore and the grime off as best she could. Then she staggered back to where the two men lay.

Febo she knew was dead: she'd felt him die while he was still within her. Much of his head was missing, and what was left was covered in black blood.

Flower didn't move; his limbs were sprawled in awkward, unnatural positions. He lay prone, his gun still clutched in the grip of one hand.

Morinda forced herself to touch him so she could turn him over. His jaw was slack; his mouth drooped and his tongue fell out over his lips. His eyes were open, and he stared vacantly at the stars overhead. Morinda put her fingers at his chest to feel for a heartbeat. She felt nothing.

"Flower?" she said in a thin, distant voice.

There was no response.

She shook his shoulder. "Flower?" she tried again, and shook him one more time.

She heard a male voice in the distance calling, "*Andale! Andale!*" telling someone else to hurry, hurry! It had to be one of Febo's *socios* yelling to the other. She'd no way of knowing how far away the men might be, but the idea that they were in the same small canyon she was in, that they were using the same trail she was on, that they were rapidly closing in on her and would find her here with the dead body of their partner swept over her and drove her to do the things she couldn't otherwise've done.

It was in a state of near-hysteria that Morinda stooped and pulled Flower's fingers apart so she could take the gun. She clutched it in her hand with her forefinger pressed along the barrel. "Point and click," she said to herself. "Just like the mouse on a computer." She glanced wildly around at the trail in both directions. She saw no one coming from either way, yet. She stood anxious guard for a few seconds, but she heard no more of the shouts.

Terror clicked her mind into hyperclarity. She conceived a plan in a split second. She knew she couldn't go back to Mexico. There was nothing for her there, now that her father was dead. She knew there were many miles left to go to get to San Diego, and that the dangers of the border crossing wouldn't be completely over until she made it there. So she'd need the gun to protect herself along the way. But there were other problems she'd have to face once she got to civilization. For one thing, her clothes were ruined, and she was covered in blood, which meant people were going to ask questions as soon as they saw the state she was in. She needed to do something about her appearance, and the easiest thing was to cover herself.

She went to Flower's corpse. With a great deal of effort, she propped Flower's body up, resting its shoulders against her shins so that she could hold its neck in place with her knees long enough to pry the warm-up jacket off. She had to put the pistol on the ground by her feet so she could use both hands to get the body into position and then unzip the front. Once she took the jacket off, she held it up so she could examine it. There were no tears, no stab wounds, to be seen in it. And it was long enough that it'd hang below her waist. She stuck her arms into the sleeves.

She searched Flower's jacket pockets for a wallet and any money he'd been carrying, but she found nothing. She next ran her hands into the pants pockets, turning them out as she did so. She found keys, some coins that she set aside with the gun, a stick of chewing gum that she ravenously ripped the paper and foil off and tried to chew but which crumbled into dust in her mouth it was so ancient. But she found no wallet and no money.

She next went to look over Febo's body, to search it for whatever she could find that might help her. It was in Febo's pants, crumpled down around his feet, that she found Flower's wallet, which had a thick wad of bills in Mexican and American money inside, some credit cards, a drivers license, and a few personal pictures. Into the left hand pocket of the warm-up jacket she slipped Flower's wallet and the loose coins, and the gun she wedged in the other pocket so she could easily get to it if she needed it.

Finally, she went to the suitcase Flower'd stole from her father. She lifted it by its handle, pulling it on its end. It was heavy, as though it was full of clothes. She snapped first one latch, then the other. The lid dropped down. She expected the clothes inside to be held in place by the interior straps, so when the loose contents came pouring out, she gasped in surprise. Then when she realized what it was the suitcase held, she fell silent with wonder.

It was money. Thick packets of money. Scores of them, piled now around her feet.

She picked up one of the bundles and brought it close to her face. It was made up American Federal Reserve Notes, all of them hundred-dollar bills.

The packet was a half-inch thick and held together with rubber bands. She dropped it and picked up another. It, too, was American money, also hundred-dollar bills, and the stack was just as thick as the first one. There were many other bundles, each one the same thickness and each made up of hundred-dollar bills. She couldn't even guess how much money there was, but she knew it was a lot, much more than she'd ever seen in one place in her life.

She'd previously considered the probability that the suitcase was filled with the money Flower'd taken from her father, but actually seeing it in front of her filled her with amazement.

She heard one rock click against another; then they clicked again, and again. It was the same signal she'd heard given to Febo earlier that night, and she knew Febo's partners were coming.

She hurriedly gathered the spilled packets and shoved them inside the suitcase along with a padded belt that'd dropped out on top of the cash. When she'd returned all she could find after a hasty search, she snapped the lid shut, hefted the bag in one hand, hurriedly grabbed the full canteen, threw it over her shoulder, and started hiking away from the scene, following the dimly visible trail that circled around the mesa heading north.

She didn't look back.

PART THREE

CHAPTER 1

Morinda paused briefly to examine the Moderne façade of the single-story building where the taxi left her off. One corner of the structure lacked the customary right-angle juncture and instead was molded into a rounded curve, the windows formed of 9 by 9s and 13 by 13s of translucent glass blocks, and a band of solid blue tiles two and a half feet high ran along the base of the front. According to the sign outside, it was the home of five businesses: two attorneys, a modeling agency, a real estate broker, and Hudspeth Investigations.

As soon as she came in from the street entrance, she stepped into a central reception area. A woman in her mid-twenties with short blond hair wearing a pant suit sat behind a large desk surrounded by two massive photocopying machines the size of refrigerators laid on their sides, a computer linked to a laser printer, and three filing cabinets. On a corner of her desk was a telephone with numerous buttons and lights set into its casing along with a caller ID box. She was speaking into the handset when Morinda stopped in front of her. While the receptionist was busy, Morinda looked around.

Offices faced onto the lobby. Many of their doors were wide open. Through one, she could see a bald man wearing a pair of reading glasses halfway down his nose dressed in a white long-sleeve shirt with thin blue stripes and a pair of old-fashioned red suspenders sitting at a huge mahogany desk where he pored over a book as thick as an unabridged dictionary. Behind him were shelves running from floor to ceiling filled with books, each and every one of which was almost precisely as thick as the others, and all covered in the same oxblood-colored bindings. Through another open door, she saw a woman in a conservatively styled navy blue dress speaking animatedly to a man standing across from her; the woman lectured while pointing to something on display on an easel behind her that Morinda couldn't make out. A cul-de-sac corridor directly ahead of Morinda led to more offices, and dozens of beautiful girls and young women in tight, short dresses showing yards and yards of the skin of their shoulders, legs, and thighs crossed from one side of the passages to the other with the graceful gait of gazelles.

One door to the left side of the receptionist's desk was closed. Across its frosted glass window were printed the words "HUDSPETH INVESTIGATIONS, Dennis Hudspeth, Prop."

The blonde receptionist pressed a button on her phone, hung up the receiver, turned to Morinda with a smile, and said, "May I help you?"

"I came to talk to Mr. Hudspeth, please."

"Is he expecting you?"

"I don't have an appointment. I didn't know I needed one."

"He's got someone with him right now. Let me check to see if he can fit ya in. Hold on."

She picked up the handset and pushed a button. "Dennis? There's someone here for ya . . . No, without an appointment. Will ya see her? . . . How long do ya think it'll be? . . . Okay, I'll let her know. Do ya want me to ring ya back? . . . Okay. Will do."

After she set the receiver down, she said, "Mr. Hudspeth can see ya as soon as he's finished with the client he has now. It might be ten or fifteen minutes. Is that all right? Great! What's your name?"

"Morinda Tavia."

"How do ya spell that?"

Morinda spelled both her first and last names for the receptionist, who jotted them on a notepad.

"Have a seat over there and I'll call ya as soon as he's ready. It'll be just a few."

Morinda sat and waited. A tall, thin man with an apricot-colored sweater thrown across his shoulders and the arms tied around his neck hustled to the reception area carrying a sheaf of papers, his pointed-toe dress shoes clacking on the marble floor as though they were fitted with taps. As soon as he reached the blonde receptionist, he passed the loose pages to her and said, "Amber, I need a hundred copies of each of these. There's no rush, any time in the next five minutes'll do."

She took the sheets and set them on a much larger stack of paperwork beside one of the photocopy machines. "It's not gonna happen, Jerry."

"Of course it'll happen," Jerry blithely asserted. "You'll *make* it happen. Why else do we pay you the inordinately high salary we do if not to make things like this *happen*?"

Amber smiled cheerily at him and said, "Because I hold this madhouse together, and without me you'd all be doing business out of the trunks of your cars?"

"It's rather gauche of you to mention it, especially since it happens to be true. Don't I show you how much I appreciate you? Didn't I send you a dozen orchids last Secretary's Day? Hmm?"

"No."

"Well, shame on me! But it's the thought that counts, and I'm thinking about it right this second, so that should more than make up for it." He waved his hand in the air magisterially, then looked at the papers he'd brought to her. "Why can't this be done?"

"One of the copiers's on the fritz, and the repairman can't get here until this afternoon."

"Oh, Lord!" he said, rubbing his temples. "Why didn't I listen to my mother and go to dental school? Well, anyway, let me know when they *are* finished so I can get on with making a living." He saw Morinda out of the corner of his eye, and he turned his head to stare at her. He appeared even more beset than he had earlier as he clack-clacked across the floor toward her.

"Uh, Jerry—" Amber called to his back.

He paid no heed. He spoke directly to Morinda. "You're late. This cattle call was set for ten o'clock. That's when the big hand's on the twelve and the little hand's on the ten. If that's too difficult for you, perhaps you should go digital."

"Jerry—" the receptionist tried again.

Again, he paid no attention. He raked his gaze up and down Morinda and said, "Where's your portfolio? You didn't bring it, did you?" He raised his eyes to heaven. "Why me, Lord?" He snapped his eyes back down. "Why is it the ones who look like this are always brain dead? Their heads are so empty they'd collapse in on themselves if they weren't held up by their over-inflated egos! Some slightest degree of professionalism—is that too much to ask?" He sighed dramatically. "Apparently it is. Anyway, you need to—"

"Jerry!" the receptionist snapped. "She's not here to see you, Jerry. She's waiting to see Dennis Hudspeth."

Jerry's mouth hung open for a second.

"Oh, I *am* sorry!" he gushed when he overcame his surprise. "I am *so* embarrassed I could just drop through the floor! A thousand pardons! I'll go to my office and slap myself, and that'll save *you* the trouble." His eyes narrowed and one side of his mouth moved up a fraction of an inch. "Tell me, are you signed with anybody? Don't worry about it if you are, we have lawyers here in the building who can get you out of any bogus contract you might've been duped into signing by one of those bloodsucking fly-by-night agencies who are just exploiting you after all! Have you done any runway work? Where've you appeared? Nothing? Nowhere? Ever? Lord have mercy, you must be the last virgin left in Los Angeles! But don't let that worry you, it certainly doesn't worry me! The first thing you need to do's get a portfolio made up. A portfolio's a *sine qua non* in this business. *Sine qua non*, that means—"

"I know what *sine qua non* means," Morinda said. They were the first words she managed to squeeze in.

"Well, scare *me*!" Jerry raised one hand to his chest and rested the tips of his fingers against it. He wore a gold ring set with an ostentatiously large blue jewel on the middle finger. "I can see you're not just another pretty face! She has *this* appearance, and she's actually read a book or two! Will wonders never cease? Anyway, you absolutely *must* have a portfolio. It's how this business's done! Any professional photographer'll know what's required, you can go to anyone in town. I can recommend a good one."

He took an ivory card case out of his shirt pocket and extracted a business card from it. He clack-clacked back to Amber's desk to pick up a pen, and began writing on the back of the card.

"He's a *good* photographer, not a great one. The best part's that he *knows* he's only good, so he doesn't overcharge. Tell him I sent you, and he'll treat you right." In a singsong, he added, "He'll treat you right, he'll treat you left, he'll treat you anyway you let him—so don't let him!" He tittered as if his words meant something more than what Morinda could decipher. He passed the card to her. A name and an address were handwritten on the otherwise blank side; on the obverse was printed "THE LYON'S DEN—JERRY LYON, MODELS' REPRESENTATIVE AND TALENT AGENT EXTRAORDINAIRE" beneath a stylized line drawing of a lion tamer holding a whip and a chair.

"Get your portfolio and come back. Definitely come back! We can do *business* together, girlfriend! And promise me—absolutely *swear* to me—that you will not change! I mean, change *nothing* about yourself! If I

239

want anything about you changed, I'll do it myself. I like this Third-World look you've cultivated—it works for you. The problem with most girls your age is they wanna make themselves up to look like thirty-five-year-old hookers. And every woman I know who *is* thirty-five tries to make herself up so she looks like you do on the natch. They'd *kill* to have skin like this! At least you don't have an addiction-to-make-up problem to overcome. But do *not*—repeat, do *not*—get collagen injections, do *not* have implants, do *not* have anything enlarged or shortened or moved to another part of your body! And please, oh, please, do *not* have your hair butchered into some God-awful fright wig that one of those overpriced, no-talent bitches in every Beverly Hills salon will try to talk you into! Please, no!"

He put his hand out to Morinda's shoulder and lifted up the mass of her long black hair, allowing the strands to filter through his fingers as he released them.

"My God! It's like fine *silk*! It's stunning! It's perfect! It'll drive men mad with desire! And, false modesty aside, I *know* what drives men mad with desire! What's your name again?"

"Morinda Tavia."

"Morinda Tavia," he repeated after her, looking thoughtfully off to the side. "Morinda Tavia. Tavia," he waved his hand in the air, as if brushing dirt aside. "That does nothing. It's plebeian. But Morinda—Morinda. That has possibilities. Have you ever considered working under just your first name? No last name? Well, think about it. Get your portfolio ready. And *call* me! We'll discuss this name thing when we have a contract ready. How old are you?"

"Fourteen."

"Good age. Best time to start. But too young to sign a legally binding contract. So you'll need to bring one of your parents. Mother, father, legal guardian, whatever. If they give you any flak about it, let *me* talk to them! I'll explain the kind of money you could be making, and—pfft!—all objections to your career'll vanish, I guarantee it!"

He put his hand out and Morinda shook with him before he turned and scurried away, looking back at her long enough to call, "*Ciao!*"

Feeling as though she'd inadvertently stumbled into the path of a tornado, been picked up and swirled around for several minutes, only to be abruptly dropped back to earth without warning, Morinda examined the card she'd been given. When she raised her head again, the blonde secretary was smiling at her in sympathy.

"Jerry's not always like that. It's just that he's bit distracted today. He's got a big show coming up, and he's off his feed." She cast her eyes over her shoulder, then confided, "Usually he's worse."

The phone on her desk rang, and Amber took the call. "Hudspeth Investiga—sorry, Dennis, I was talkin' to someone out here and didn't notice it was an internal call . . . Yes, she's still waitin' for you . . . Oh, I don't think she was bored, exactly. But she did get quite an earful. She was exposed to a full two minutes of Jerry . . . No. No, honestly. He tried to recruit her . . . No, I mean he *really* tried to recruit her. He practically dragged her into white slavery as a runway model right here in front of God and everybody."

She listened to whatever was said on the other end of the line, looked at Morinda's face and said, "Wait till ya see her," almost singing the words.

When she hung up, she pointed at the HUDSPETH INVESTIGATIONS door and said brightly, "You're up."

"Should I knock, or . . . ?"

"Walk right on in. He knows you're comin'."

As often happened when Morinda was around adults, she had the feeling they had access to some secret to which she was not privy, and that they were talking over her head about the mystery while she could grasp only a small part of what they were referring to. She entered the detective's office and closed the door behind her.

She'd found Hudspeth's name and address in the Yellow Pages of the phone directory the day before. After leaving Flower and Febo's bodies in the foothills, she'd trudged until dawn until she came across a *raitero*, a driver for hire, who was preparing to take a truckload of illegals to Los Angeles. She paid to join them, and arrived later that afternoon on Alvarado Street, where she bought a full set of false identity documents from an underground printing shop other *pollos* on the truck led her to. Then she faced the problem of finding a motel willing to rent a room to a teenager. She was repulsed by several desk clerks before she decided she needed an adult to accompany her. She found a homeless man who agreed to get her registered in a room for a week in exchange for a payment of a hundred dollars, and she spent the next few days recuperating from the ordeal of the border crossing.

The previous evening, she'd flipped through the pages of the phone book to look for a private detective. She chose Hudspeth Investigations out of the myriad listings for two reasons: it was located on a street she was familiar with, since it was only a few blocks from her motel (although its address turned out to be at least twenty blocks north of where she was staying, and she had to take a cab to get there), and because its quarter-page ad was the first one she noticed that mentioned "Skip Tracing—Missing Persons." As soon as she saw those words, she put the tip of her finger on the page and left it there for a moment, almost memorizing the rest of the ad and not bothering to look any further.

When she entered the detective's office, she saw a man in his mid-fifties sitting behind a desk while he typed at a computer keyboard. He had brown hair that was thinning in front and graying all around. He squinted at his work through a pair of glasses with black frames. A cigarette smoldered in a glass ashtray on the desk beside him. He finished what he was entering into the computer, lifted both hands with his fingers curled as though he were a concert pianist, plucked one final key with the ring finger of his right hand to end his keyboarding with a flourish, then turned to smile at Morinda. She smiled back, and walked a few steps closer. The man stood halfway up out of his chair, indicated the three chairs available on the other side of his desk with a wave, and settled in again to wait for her to be seated. She edged into the chair on the far right and sank into the padded leather.

"I heard ya had a run-in with Jerry Lyon out front," he said. "Sorry about that. Jerry can be a little—overwhelming." He chuckled.

Morinda held up the piece of cardboard she carried. "He gave me his card."

"I bet he did! Jerry may come on a little strong, but once ya get to know him, he's a good guy. He's intense, but he doesn't mean any harm, which's more than I can say for a lot of people. I'm Dennis Hudspeth. What can I do ya for?"

"My name is Morinda Tavia, Mr. Hudspeth—"

He held up his hand palm outward in a stop gesture and shook his head. "Call me Dennis, please. This's L.A. Nobody calls anybody 'mister' here."

"Okay," Morinda said. "Dennis. I saw in your ad—in the Yellow Pages, that's where I saw it—that you find missing people?"

"Well, I try to."

"I'm looking for my mother."

"All right," Hudspeth said. He picked up a pen and drew a yellow legal pad on the desk top toward him. "I'm gonna take some notes while we talk. Don't think I'm not payin' attention to what you're sayin' just because I'm writin'. I'll follow ya, don't worry. You're name was spelled how? M-o-r-i-n-d-a? Okay. And the last name was—T-a-v-i-a. Good. Got it. Now, your mother—how is it she came to be missing?"

"I never knew her. I was raised by my father. I always thought—because my father, he let me think it—that my mother was dead. Until a few days ago. And then my father admitted to me that—that she's alive."

"And he wouldn't tell ya how to find her? Or he doesn't know where she is either?"

"I'm not sure."

"Can ya ask? It might take care of your problem without havin' to involve me. It could save ya some money if he'll tell ya what ya wanna know."

"I don't think he knew. And there's another problem besides. That's the second thing I want you to do. I need you to find out about my father. I heard—I heard from someone else that he's been killed. It would've happened the day after I saw him last, I think. I'm not sure. But I wanted you to find out if that's true or not. That he's dead."

Hudspeth lifted his head. "I'm sorry about your father. If it happened, I mean."

"That's the other thing. I want to know what happened to my father. And I want to find my mother."

"This thing about your father—if it happened, if he was killed—it would've been in the papers. Have ya checked the obituaries? Did it happen here in L.A.?"

"No. This was in Mexico. We lived in Baja Norte. In a small town called San Estaban. That's where it would've been."

Hudspeth scrutinized her face more intently than he'd done previously. He said, "I hadn't thought to ask—are you a Mexican citizen?"

"No. I was born in America. In Los Angeles, is what my father said. That's why I've come here to look for my mother."

"Okay. It's not that big a deal, but it could complicate things if ya were a Mexican national, maybe. Your father was American?"

"Yes."

"And your mother? American, too?"

"I'm—not sure. I don't know. My father, he never talked about her. I always thought it was because they'd fought, or that he came to hate her. That they might've been separated or divorced—before she died. That was when I believed she was dead, you see. But whenever I mentioned her, he'd turn very cold. Like he hadn't heard what I said, you know? He pretended he hadn't even heard me speak of her. Like she never existed."

"I see. What was your mother's name. Did he ever mention that?"

"Denise."

"Same last name as yours? Tavia?"

"Ye-e-e-s. I—think so. But I don't know for sure."

"Hmm. Do ya have any relatives ya can get hold of? Especially relatives on your mother's side. Grandparents, aunts, uncles, cousins? Anything?"

"No."

"How about on your father's side? Anyone who might've stayed in touch with your mother?"

"No. We were always by ourselves. No relatives ever visited, and we never visited any of them. My father never mentioned any."

"Ya never got a card on your birthday? Or at Christmas?"

"I don't remember ever getting any. Except from my father. And my friends. And my nannies, when I was real young. Never from anyone else."

"Nannies?"

"Yes. When I was growing up. They took care of me."

"Is—was your father wealthy? Rich?"

"No. He owned a recreational vehicle park. And a bar. But he wasn't rich."

"I was just wondering because of the nannies."

"In Mexico, lots of people have servants. Not only rich people. We always had a maid, a handyman, and a cook. And the nannies, too, when I was little."

"So your father owned businesses in—what was the name of the town again? San what?"

"San Estaban. It's in Baja Norte."

"How long did he own the RV park?"

"I don't know. Since I was little. But he didn't really own it. Foreigners can't own land in Mexico within thirty miles of the coast, so it's held in a *fideicomiso*, a trust, that's good for fifty years. He put in a lot of things Americans like in the RV park, so we got a lot of tourists staying there. And the town started getting more and more Americans coming to it, so my father bought a *cantina* in town that he made over into an American-type bar. They're different than *cantinas*. Women go into bars and drink. Respectable women can do that in an American bar. Not in a *cantina*."

"Let me get the names, addresses, and phone numbers of both the businesses your father owned."

Hudspeth wrote them down.

"Ya said ya believed your mother was dead, but your father told ya different a few days ago. Is that right?"

"Yes."

"What finally led him to tell ya she was alive after all these years? I mean, why now? Did he think she was dead and he just found out different, or what? Did he get a letter or a phone call from her?"

Morinda shook her head. "Two men came to town. They stayed at our RV park. They were asking questions around town about me, and about my father. My father thought they were detectives sent by my mother to find me. That's when he told me she's still alive."

"He *thought* they were detectives lookin' for ya? But they weren't?"

"No. I don't think so."

"Were they Mexican?"

"Oh, no. They were American."

"Do ya know their names, by any chance? I can check to see if they're licensed operatives."

In her mind, Morinda heard the voice of Maria Elena calling to her over the phone, "That Flora—he's the one they're looking for. They think he's the one who killed him." And an image of Flower's body sprawled beside that of Febo, the man who'd raped her, flashed into her memory.

"I don't remember," she said brusquely.

Hudspeth stretched his arm out so that his sleeve came away from his wrist, and he checked the time on his watch.

"Okay, I think I've got enough here to get started with. Now, let's talk business. Do ya have a legal guardian who'll be taking care of the payment for this?"

"No. I'll pay it myself. If you can tell me how much it'll cost—"

"That's the next thing. I wanna warn ya—private investigation doesn't come cheap. I don't want ya to fall out of your chair when I tell ya my price. Ready? It's two hundred dollars a day. Plus expenses."

"Plus expenses?" Morinda said. "What sort of expenses?"

"Well, in your case it'd probably be mostly long-distance phone calls, faxes, express mail delivery. But if I had to go outta town overnight on your case, then food and lodging, plane tickets, taxi fees, and anything else I needed to pay for on the way'd be charged to ya. But I wouldn't do anything like that without clearing it with ya ahead of time. And you'd get an itemized printout of anything I billed ya for."

"So, how much do I give you now?"

"As a retainer? Oh, five hundred'd get things rolling. And when that's used up, I'll let ya know, and ya could pay me a few hundred more. We could do it like that."

Morinda reached into the pocket of her new suede jacket, one she'd bought at a boutique the day before to replace the warm-up jacket she'd removed from Flower. She took out a roll of bills and held them in her hands.

"How long do you think it'll take? To find my mother?"

Hudspeth pursed his lips and blew air out. "It's impossible to say. It could be only a day or two. Or it could take weeks. That's why I said, pay me a couple of hundred and come back in a few days. I'll be able to tell better how things stand then."

Morinda peeled off several of the bills and gave them to Hudspeth. He counted them, folded them, pulled out a drawer on the side of the desk, opened a metal cash box inside, dropped the money there, and closed the drawer again.

"I'll have Amber give ya a receipt before ya go. But there's some things I wanna tell ya so ya won't be upset if they come up later. None of this may ever apply to you, but I want ya ready for it if it does. Okay?

"First of all, ya should be prepared to hear some bad things about your mother. I'm not sayin' ya will, but it's possible I'll find things out about her ya may not like to hear. Ya haven't seen or heard from her in a lot of years, and sometimes people get involved in some pretty nasty sorts of affairs.

"Second, this's a missing persons case. About 14,000 people in this country turn up missing every year. The vast majority of 'em vanish for one very good and simple reason: they wanna be missing. They made a conscious and deliberate choice to disappear. Some of 'em have debts no honest man can pay, so they run away from the bills. Some find their marriages or their home-life unbearable, and they can't think of any other way out but to run. Some get tired of the humdrum and go off looking for adventure under another name. But they all have that one thing in common: they don't wanna be found. So it might happen that your mother won't think you're doing her any big favor by locatin' her. She might be extremely unhappy about the whole situation. Again, I'm not sayin' that's the way it'll play out, but ya should be ready for it if it does.

"The last thing I want to mention's that ya should be ready for complete failure. I may never be able to find your mother. I have a pretty good success rate on missing persons cases, but there are no guarantees.

"I'm sorry if I sound negative, but ya should be aware of the possibilities. None of these things I've mentioned might turn out to be the case. With any luck, everything'll go fine, we'll track your mother down in a short time, she'll be overjoyed to find ya again, and your lives together after the reunion will be hunky-dory. Hope for the best, but plan for the worst.

"Now that that's outta the way, let me explain to ya how I'm gonna go about this. I'll start with your father and what happened to him. That sounds fairly easy. I can report to ya on that if you'll call or come in—what's today, Thursday?—make it Monday. I'll tell ya what I've found out then. About your mother, I'll start with public records. Your birth certificate. Oh, by the way—what's your birth date?"

She gave it to him, and he wrote it on the legal pad.

"Good. Okay. First, I search for your birth certificate. That'll give me your mother's maiden name. With that and whatever information I can find on your father, I should be able to dig up a marriage license. I'll do some background search on your father and see if I can cross-link him to your mother. Once I've got a Social Security number or an old address or something for her, I can start to hook her into the information network, establish a paper trail, and sooner or later, we'll find out where she is now. Okay?"

"Okay."

"That's about it."

Morinda rose from the chair as Hudspeth stood up from his.

Hudspeth escorted her to the exit. On the way, he said, "By the way, it may be none of my business, but you're carryin' a lot of cash on ya. I dunno how things are in San Estaban, but here in L.A. that's very dangerous. If I were you, I'd get a bank account and put that money in it. Or bury it in a coffee can in the backyard if ya don't trust banks."

Morinda didn't reply, but she wondered what the detective'd say if he knew about the money in the suitcase she'd taken from Flower. She'd already developed the same concerns about her own safety and that of the money that Hudspeth voiced, and two days before bought a pair of work gloves and a trowel at a gardening shop. After dark, she called a cab and had it take her to the beach, carrying the suitcase with the money belt and the .38 revolver stowed inside. She had the driver let her off at a pier, and she walked along the strand for over an hour until she was far away from any signs of city life. At a place where there were no buildings or artificial lights visible, and she hadn't seen another person for more than twenty minutes, she stopped. She was sure she could later identify the site because of a peculiar rock formation against which the ocean's waves crashed. She dug until she had a hole a few feet deep that was big enough to hold the suitcase. She dropped it in and covered it up, keeping only a few thousand dollars out of the hoard, a sufficient amount to get her through the next few weeks, she figured. It was this money that Hudspeth noticed when she took it from her pocket to pay him.

Hudspeth went with her to the receptionist's desk. He asked Amber to write a receipt for the amount of the retainer Morinda'd given him. She did so in a large receipt book, then tore out a slip like a coupon that she handed to Morinda.

"Could ya schedule an appointment for her for Monday? Whenever I have free that fits her schedule," Hudspeth said.

Amber checked an appointment book and asked Morinda if she could return at eleven o'clock Monday morning.

Morinda thanked them both before she left the building.

Amber said to Hudspeth, "She's pretty, huh?"

"Gorgeous," Hudspeth agreed.

"What's she like?"

"Oh, she's a real sweetheart," Hudspeth said. Then his face fell in on itself in a frown. "But there's about a dozen large, gaping holes in her story."

Still frowning, he returned to his office, closing the door behind him.

CHAPTER 2

Some time after Morinda left his office, Hudspeth told Amber he was going home for lunch, asking her to call him on his cell phone if anything came up that required his immediate attention.

He was two blocks from his house when he noticed the van parked in his driveway. He could tell it was a commercial vehicle by the custom printing on the side, although he couldn't quite make out what it said since the sliding door on the driver's side was open. Hudspeth pushed his glasses up his nose with one finger and squinted at the lettering. Eventually he made out enough of the telescoped words to tell the van belonged to a locksmith. He knitted his brow.

By the time he got within a block, he could discern the figures of three men on his front porch. The locksmith knelt to work on the doorknob, and the others hovered over him. Hudspeth didn't know one of the observers, but the second one was his twenty-three-year-old son, Stuart. As soon as he recognized him, Hudspeth unconsciously began grinding his teeth together.

The heavyset locksmith, dressed in blue jeans held up by a leather belt, a work shirt, and a baseball cap, worked bent over the lock until he suddenly stood and shouldered his way between Stuart and the other man just as Hudspeth made the turn into his driveway. Stuart shuffled around to watch the locksmith go to his van, and when he saw his father driving up, he slid his hands into his back pockets. Hudspeth slammed the door of his car, locked it, and walked to the porch.

"What are you doin' here?" he demanded of his son without ever actually looking at him.

Stuart took a few steps forward to meet his father. He wore an amiable grin. "Hey! Ya know what they say: 'Home's the place where, when ya gotta go there, they gotta take ya in.'"

Sourly, Hudspeth said, "I don't think breakin'-and-enterin's exactly what Robert Frost had in mind when he wrote that."

"Yeah, I was kind of surprised my key wouldn't work, too. Ya have the locks changed, or something?"

"You're damned right I had the locks changed!"

Hudspeth avoided eye-contact with his son. He sidestepped and went around Stuart to the porch. He glanced to the right as he passed the van. The locksmith was inside, working at a bench built in to the rear cargo space, gauging the pins and tumblers of the new cylinder he was preparing.

"Would ya let him use your key?" Stuart asked his father. "It might make it easier for him if he could just copy it."

"Not really!" the locksmith shouted. He shifted around on the box he used as a seat so he could look out at both the father and son. "I'm almost finished now, and doin' it this way helps me stay in practice. I'd have to charge ya the same, anyway. 'Cause of the time I put in. I'm almost done."

"I don't wanna interfere with your work," Hudspeth said with a heavy irony that the locksmith didn't detect and Stuart ignored. "Would it bother ya if I open my door?"

"Naw, go ahead," the locksmith said.

Hudspeth jingled the keys he'd carried in his hand since taking them out of the car's ignition. The same key worked on the dead bolt and the Yale lock in the faceplate. Hudspeth released both, then swung the door back and entered the house. Stuart followed him in.

"How'd ya get him to let ya in?" Hudspeth asked.

"My driver's license still shows this address on it, so I told him I lost my key. How come ya changed the locks?"

Hudspeth looked directly at his son for the first time. "'Cause I thought that'd be enough to keep you out. I didn't realize you'd find a way around it so easily," he said coldly. "What am I gonna hafta do—move and not leave a forwardin' address?"

"Ah, c'mon, Dad!" Stuart's smile faltered, then returned in a watered-down version, and finally shifted into a thin grimace. "Don't be like that."

"I don't want ya here, Stuart. The last time ya stayed here, things disappeared. Valuable things. Things I wanted to keep. Oddly enough, they stopped disappearin' as soon as I threw ya out."

"I don't know anything about that, I swear—"

"After ya left, people were calling here. At all hours. At three o'clock in the morning, sometimes. In the beginnin', they wanted to talk to you. Then, later, they left messages for ya. They said they wanted their money, Stuart, and if they didn't get it, they were gonna come here and take it. I had to change my phone number. Have my number unlisted."

"That was a misunderstandin', Dad. That whole thing's cleared up now."

Hudspeth said nothing; for a long time he regarded his son as though he were watching a balance beam shift and wobble, waiting to see which side it'd finally come down on. When he broke the silence, it was to say, "Good. I'm glad to hear you've taken care of something."

"Yeah, well, it's behind me, okay? Dad, this's Elliot. Elliot, my dad."

Elliot was the man who'd been standing on the front porch with Stuart when Hudspeth drove up. Elliot carried an attaché case that bulged like a python digesting a rabbit, looking as if it was about to pop open at any moment from the internal pressure. He was much older than Hudspeth's son, but younger than Hudspeth himself. He looked about forty, had longish light brown hair that wasn't of any fashionable length, only in need of a haircut that it hadn't had in several months. His nose was red, the corners of his eyes filled with rheum. Elliot didn't offer to shake hands with Hudspeth when Stuart introduced them; he merely nodded his head.

"Listen," Stuart said, "I just came over to see if ya could help me out with something. Okay? I got into a little bit of trouble, and I need to borrow some money. I can pay ya back in a couple of weeks, I only need it to get me over the hump. I'll give ya the key he's makin' so ya don't think I'm gonna be buggin' ya permanently, and I'll be outta your hair for good, I promise, if ya could help me out this one time."

"Ya said a minute ago ya had that problem taken care of. Another lie, I assume?"

"No, no, no! *That* problem *was* taken care of. I swear, I paid it off. I won big at the track. A trifecta came in for me, and everybody got paid off, everybody was happy. Ya can ask Elliot."

"So what happened? Why do ya need more money?"

Stuart shrugged, gave his "I'm-a-baaaad-boy" smile, and said, "I lost it all back."

"Pathetic," Hudspeth said, not disguising his distaste. "How much are ya into 'em for this time?"

The sunlight streaming through the windows glinted off Stuart's eyeballs as he nervously moved them around the room, never letting his gaze settle long on any one object.

"Forty grand."

Hudspeth refused to be shocked by the enormity of the amount. He'd heard his son's debts enumerated before, and though they'd never reached quite this sum, they'd climbed progressively higher so that Hudspeth knew someday they had to scale to the rarefied heights they'd now achieved. He tightened his lips and watched his son for a few seconds. "Forty thousand dollars's more than your life's worth, Stuart."

"Yeah, that's what *they* tell me."

"Ya knew it was gonna come to this sooner or later. It's what cops refer to as 'victim induced homicide.' Even when ya win, ya keep bettin' your winnin's until ya lose. And then ya beg, borrow, or steal more money to bet even more. Until ya lose that, too. It's inevitable, Stuart. And these people ya owe the money to? They know you're a degenerate gambler, that you'll continue to fork over to 'em every dime that ever passes through your hands. Until finally they'll come to the conclusion that the goose can no longer lay any more golden eggs. That the only thing the goose's capable of producin's goose shit. And that's when they're gonna hurt ya very seriously. I really think it's time, Stuart, that ya went to live with your mother."

"In St. George? Do ya know what it's like there, Dad?"

"Eat, drink, and be merry, for tomorrow you may be in Utah," Elliot intoned sententiously.

"No horse racin' in Utah? No card clubs? Is that the problem?" Hudspeth asked remorselessly.

"There's not even any dog tracks in Utah, are there?" Stuart turned to Elliot, seeking the opinion of an expert.

"Nothin' in Utah," Elliot stated as an authority. "Can't even lay money on the pups. No harness racin', either. There might be bingo parlors . . ."

"Stuart, you'd better get used to it. I'd say you've worn out your welcome here in L.A. Your bookies are gonna get repaid, one way or the other. If they can't get it from ya in cash, they'll take it out in satisfaction. And I don't want ya here anymore. Go to Utah, get straightened out, get over this gamblin' disease, and stay alive in the process. It's a win-win situation for ya, Stuart."

Stuart scrunched his face into a *moue* and shook his head.

Hudspeth lifted his hands and dropped them again in frustration. "I should've known better than to try to talk ya into bein' a winner, Stuart. You're like every other degenerate gambler in the world—you'll keep playin' until ya lose, no matter what it takes."

"That's right, that's right," Elliot said. "I've been talkin' to him and talkin' to him till I'm blue in the face. Tryin' to get him turned around on this. Tryin' to get him to be a *winner* for once in his life."

"Elliot has a business proposition he wants to tell ya about, Dad."

Hudspeth wrinkled his nose as if his son'd thrust a handful of rotting garbage under it. "What kind of business proposition?"

Elliot dropped to one knee on the hallway carpet and opened the snaps of his briefcase. The attaché was filled to overflowing with racing forms, tip sheets, paperback books that described different gambling systems, and a ream of computer paper covered with serried rows of numbers. He took out the stack of folded sheets and stood, leaving the briefcase laying at his feet.

"I'm lookin' for an investor with fifty thousand dollars in venture capital," Elliot explained. "This isn't one of those pie-in-the-sky schemes."

He stretched the spreadsheets out between his two extended hands so both he and Hudspeth could refer to the ranks and files of numerals dimly recorded there by a dot-matrix printer. "I spent six months working in the UCLA library on this. It took me six months to iron out the wrinkles," he said. "Six months. But I found the key. It's all here. If I play any fifty-fifty payoff game—any game the bet's even or odd, or black or red—I've got a 5 percent edge on it. Laws of chance say it should only happen 50 percent of the time. I can win 55 percent." With the pedantic over-precision of the true mathematical crank, Elliot looked Hudspeth straight in the eye and admitted, "Actually, it's only 4.874 percent, but I round it off to five 'cause it's easier to explain that way.

"It's all here in black and white. Look," he said, emphatically pointing at numbers here and there on the page, many of which were highlighted and underscored in ball-point ink with hieratic marginalia of obscure meaning jotted beside them. "This's a sample computer-generated run of random numbers, and ya can see the difference between the odd and the even—which should work out according to orthodox probability theory to an exact fifty-fifty split—is off by 5 percent. That 5 percent represents the bias in the system, in any system of so-called random events. It's there, ya can see it, and I can use it to beat any even-odd game."

Hudspeth prodded his glasses up his nose with his index finger. "I'm no mathematician, but I think there are a lot of people who've worked out the probabilities on things like this. How is it you've been able to find a way to beat the house that nobody else's ever been able to?"

"I told ya, it took me six months of research to put this together. Six months." Elliot tapped his finger on the printout. "Here's the proof, right here. Look, look, right here. Ya can see what I'm talkin' about . . ."

Hudspeth attempted to follow Elliot's unbelievably complicated explanation of his discovery for the first minute Elliot forced it upon him, but then his eyes glazed over and his attention wandered.

"So why are ya here trying to convince me you're a genius?" Hudspeth interrupted once again. "If you've got this surefire scheme, why aren't ya in Vegas makin' big bucks at the craps table?"

"It only works on fifty-fifty gambles, or something close to fifty-fifty odds," Elliot said. "I told ya that. That's what I've been goin' over with ya here."

"Okay, so why aren't ya in Vegas at the roulette wheel breakin' the bank?"

Elliot was patient. He looked Hudspeth squarely in the eye, and his manner remained professional and businesslike. "This computer program proves it'll work. A friend of mine with a random number generator set up this program, and these are the results. Six thousand numbers, and with my system I came out ahead 5 percent better than chance says I should. This proves it."

"But why do ya need *my* fifty thousand dollars to do this?"

Elliot's composure remained unfazed. It occurred to Hudspeth that if Elliot worked half as hard at selling door-to-door as he worked at hawking his gambling scheme, he wouldn't need to gamble—he'd live quite comfortably on his commissions. Hudspeth shook his head almost imperceptibly to refocus on what he was being told.

"I tried this system once before. I hit a streak of bad luck. That's why I went broke that time. And that's when I realized I need at least fifty grand as a back up, just in case."

"I thought your system guaranteed ya a 5 percent advantage?"

"That's exactly what it shows here. But that doesn't do much good on each and every bet; it only gives an advantage on a long string of even-odd wagers. A bad streak of luck can wipe anyone out, unless they got enough to ride it out until—" he tapped his forefinger on the printout "—until the inherent bias shows up. That's when it pays off. It has to. It's inevitable, if I make the bets, and the more bets I make, the more that 5 percent bias comes into play."

"That's what I don't understand," Hudspeth said. "Why don't ya use your system in a lower stakes game, say, one where you're only betting nickels and dimes? You've got your advantage of 5 percent, which should let ya get ahead no matter what, until you'll have your own fifty thousand dollars to bet with. Then ya go to Vegas and make your fortune."

Elliot shook his head. Sadly, but stoically, he put his computer printout back in the attaché case and used his whole body's weight to force the lid down so he could lock the snaps. He acted as though he were used to being treated harshly by an uncaring world.

When he stood up again, he asked Stuart, "Could ya slip me a few bucks for cab fare? I used the last of mine to get us here, ya know."

"Hey, Dad, could ya give Elliot fifteen bucks? That's what it cost us for the ride."

"Where'd ya come from? Hollywood Park?" Hudspeth asked acidulously.

His son's face showed only the slightest trace of chagrin. "I don't go to Holly Park anymore. There's some guys there, ya know? I go to Santa Anita, now."

Hudspeth turned to face Elliot while he fished in his pocket. He brought out a handful of change and carefully plucked a few of the coins out. He put those he'd separated into his left hand and tried to give them to Elliot. "Here's a buck and a half, Elliot. That's what the fare is on the city buses. There's a bus stop two blocks over. Remember to ask for a transfer."

Elliot ignored the proffered money. He glanced around the room, speaking to Stuart but not looking at him. "I've gotta get back to Arcadia. There's someone there who's interested in my idea, and I don't wanna miss him. I've gotta go, man. I'll see ya around, okay?"

Elliot took his bulging briefcase and left. Stuart didn't seem embarrassed that his friend simply walked out, leaving him alone with his father.

"Ya think ya wanna invest in Elliot's project, Da?"

"Don't call me 'Da.' It was cute that ya couldn't say 'Dad' when ya were four. It's not cute anymore."

"So what should I call ya? Huh? 'The *pater*,' maybe, like I'm some prep-school twerp?"

"I'd be happy if ya didn't call me anything that lets people know we're related."

"Should I call ya Dennis? Dennis. How's that, Dennis. Is that better, Dennis?"

"My friends call me Dennis. You can call me Mr. Hudspeth."

The locksmith entered the hallway and deferentially paused a few steps away. Stuart glanced toward him and asked, "Finished?"

"All done. Who gets the bill?" he said, casting his eyes back and forth between the Hudspeths. Stuart immediately turned to his father.

Hudspeth exhaled a deep breath, and said, "Wait till I find my checkbook."

Hudspeth insisted that the two new keys be given to him, and he pocketed both of them, pointedly ignoring his son's silent request for one until Stuart finally lowered his extended hand.

When the locksmith was gone, Hudspeth said, "Look, Stuart—"

"First names, now? I don't think we should get that familiar. Ya want me to call ya Mr. Hudspeth, you can call me Mr. Hudspeth, too. Yeah, that's what we'll do—we'll call each other Mr. Hudspeth."

"Okay, Stuart, you win. Ya can call me Dennis. Just not when anybody else's around, okay? They might get the wrong idea."

"Whatever's right, Dennis."

"And if you're moving back in here, there's gonna be some ground rules. No drugs of any kind in my house. I catch ya doin' drugs, you'll be out of here so fast it'll make your head spin. Understood? And I don't want the phone calls to start up again. I don't want your bookmakers calling here lookin' for ya, and I don't want loan sharks callin' here. Got that? And I want ya to keep your flake friends away from me. That means Elliot. Don't bring him over here after this. Okay?"

"Sure, Dennis. Anything ya say."

"Another thing. Do ya have a job right now? Any sort of gainful employment? Anything that's got nothing to do with defying the law of averages, I mean?"

"I'm between jobs, Dennis."

"Yeah. But to be 'between' means you'd actually hafta've had a job at some point in the past. Since you're 'at liberty,' you're gonna be workin' for me. I'm puttin' ya on the payroll so I can recoup your room and board and whatever else you're gonna end up costing me. How's your Spanish? Can ya still speak it? I need ya to make some phone calls to Mexico for me. When ya finish with that, you're goin' to the County Clerk's office to hunt me up a birth certificate. After that, we've gotta run down some data bases on the Internet. And then I'll give ya some more to do to keep ya off the streets and out of trouble."

"Okay, Dennis."

"And stop calling me Dennis. I'm your father—God help me!"

"Right, Dad."

"One last thing, Stuart."

"Yeah, Dad?"

"Don't ask me to bail ya out of this trouble you're in. I don't have forty thousand dollars I can afford to throw down a rat hole. You're gonna hafta deal with this problem on your own. I can't help ya, Stuart. Not again. And that's final. Get me?"

"I get ya, Dad. In other words, you're throwin' me to the wolves. I'm hangin' over the precipice by my fingernails, and you're stompin' on my hands."

"Not in other words, Stuart. Those are the exact words I had in mind. And I'm glad to hear you're not bitter about any of this."

CHAPTER 3

Morinda spent her days at a branch of the Los Angeles County Library near her motel. To Morinda, this was a place of wonder. The town of San Estaban was too small to support a library or a book store, so all the books she'd ever read came from other sources: some were given to her by her father, but as she'd grown older she'd mostly bought her own, usually selecting them from Amazon.com and having them sent by mail, though her father'd taken her to book stores in Ensenada a few times. And her tutors loaned her many of their books. She'd never been inside a public library before arriving in Los Angeles, and she was overwhelmed by the experience on her first visit.

The branch she went to, they told her, was a small one, nowhere near as large as the central library downtown, but still it was an amazing place. There were books *everywhere*. It had every kind of book, novels and histories and biographies and studies of different subjects, and she was free to walk between the shelves and take whichever ones she wanted, and if one book wasn't something she wanted to read right then she could put it away and find another, or if she wanted to she could take it with her to the carrel and get lost in it until it was time to go to eat. It was like being in paradise.

At first, the library intimidated her. She stared blankly at the rows and rows of volumes on display, not knowing how they were arranged and so unable to even begin seeking what she might want. Her bewilderment must've been obvious, for a woman librarian stopped and asked if she could help her. The woman was young, in her mid-twenties, and she wore a dress that fell to her ankles and large glasses with plastic frames. Morinda, caught off guard by the question, stammered that she wanted books in Spanish! It was the first thing she thought to say, and she blushed as soon as the words were out of her mouth at how stupid they sounded, but the librarian only said, "This way. I'll show ya," and led her to a section of English translations of works that'd originally been written in Spanish, and critical studies of writers from Spain, Mexico, Argentina, Chile, and other parts of Latin America.

The woman told her, "If ya need help with anything, just ask," and left Morinda alone with the treasure trove.

She'd lived in Mexico most of her life, but her reading'd been restricted for the most part to the works of American and English writers. She knew that Latin America also had a rich literary history, but she'd never sampled much of it. Now she dipped into the well, and found new wonders.

She picked out a book called *Love in the Time of Cholera* by Gabriel García Márquez, took it to a carrel, and read it without stopping until five hours later when, driven by pangs of hunger, she had to quit for an hour. She hurried to take up where she'd left off in the astounding book that was about love in everyone of its manifold forms. She finished it the next day, and returned to the shelves for more by the same author. She tried *One Hundred Years of Solitude*, only to be disappointed. It wasn't the same as the first one of his she'd read; it seemed tedious, and the "magic" incidents that peppered the story just silly.

It was when she came across a slim volume entitled *Ficciones* by Jorge Luis Borges that she discovered the *real* magic she'd always been looking for in her reading. She was in awe. She was intoxicated, and she was addicted. She never knew that anyone'd written such things—that anyone *could* write such things. When she left the library that evening, she floated. Her mind'd entered another dimension, one far removed and far more strange and beautiful than the ordinary reality she lived in. She wanted to stay in the world Borges created forever. To return to the mundane realm of her everyday existence after having been exposed to the sublimity of Borges's imagination was an awful letdown.

The library was closed on Sundays and she had to pass up a visit on Monday in order to keep her appointment with Dennis Hudspeth. Her single most important goal still awaited her, and she couldn't be distracted from the search for her mother by even such heady diversions as Borges offered, no matter how enticing they might be. She caught a cab and made her way to the detective's office.

Amber, the blonde receptionist, was behind the front desk and smiled as Morinda entered the building. She seemed to recall Morinda very well as she didn't even wait for Morinda to mention her appointment before she said, "Morning! I think Mr. Hudspeth's waitin' on ya, but let me make sure. You'll probably go right in."

She picked up the phone, pushed a button, and said, "Dennis? Your eleven o'clock's here. Should I send her in? Okay. Comin' at ya!"

She smiled at Morinda yet again as she placed the receiver on the hook. "They're ready for ya. Go ahead."

Hudspeth was seated behind his desk. He had a burning cigarette in his hand; smoke curled from the corners of his mouth, drifting languidly to the ceiling.

There was another man in the office with him. He was younger, perhaps in his early or mid-twenties, and he was thinner than the detective, with dark hair and a look of affable enthusiasm on his boyish face. He wore Levi's and a T-shirt underneath a sports coat with the sleeves shoved above his elbows. He sat in one of the three chairs spread in a semicircle in front of Hudspeth's desk and twisted the swiveling chair around so as to face Morinda when she entered. He gave her a genial grin while he rocked his chair back and forth an inch at a time, pushing against the floor with his planted foot.

"Have a seat," Hudspeth said and motioned her toward a chair. "Morinda Tavia, this's my son, Stuart."

"Hi," Stuart said.

Morinda gave him a shy half-smile and nodded.

"Stuart's gonna sit in with us, if that's okay with you. Stuart's done most of the investigation work on your case so far, so he knows everything we've talked about."

"Okay."

"Before we get goin' on this," Hudspeth said, "I wanna remind ya of what I told ya the last time. That this investigation could turn up things that are—troubling. Things about people ya love and care about that ya might not wanna know. Things that might be ugly or disturbing. A lot of times when I come across facts of that kind, and they don't have anything to do with the reason a client hired me to begin with, I put 'em aside and don't bother to tell the client what it is I've learned 'cause there wouldn't be any point to it. It'd just cause 'em unnecessary pain.

"There are some things we've found that may bother ya if we tell 'em to ya. I want ya to know that up front, because we've run into some real roadblocks in your case, and we're gonna need ya to answer some more questions before we can continue, I'm afraid. So we're gonna hafta tell ya what we already know if ya wanna go any further with this. What it boils down to is, we can file away this information we have so far, and ya won't need to hear any of it. But if we do that, we'd pretty much hafta give up the search for your mother. I can't think of any way to proceed without gettin' some clarification on these other matters that've come to light. It's up to you, Morinda, where we go from here."

Hudspeth lifted his cigarette to his lips and inhaled deeply.

"I want to find my mother," Morinda said without hesitation.

Hudspeth blew smoke out of his nostrils, leaned forward, and crushed the butt of his cigarette out in the ashtray on his desk, stabbing it into the bottom five times before he spoke again.

"All right, let's start with your mother. We're havin' a real problem getting anywhere with that. Stuart's been at the County Clerk's office and the Hall of Records lookin' for your birth certificate, and he hasn't been able to find anything so far. Do we have the birth date right? Let's double-check that to make sure we're not on a wild goose chase."

He picked up a legal pad and read the date she'd given him, asking if it were correct.

"Yes," she said.

"And your father told ya that ya were born in Los Angeles?"

"Yes."

"We can't find a birth on that day under the name Morinda Tavia recorded in Los Angeles County."

Morinda frowned as if Hudspeth were accusing her of deceiving him.

Stuart spoke up to say, "I've been through the lot, and I can't find anything. But, hey, a lot of people say L.A. when they mean anyplace that's close, ya know? People in Upland and Rancho Cucamonga say they live in L.A., and that's San Bernardino County. Sometimes people talk about Santa Ana or Garbage Grove like it's L.A. instead of Orange County. Or they call Ventura part of L.A. What I'm gonna do next, I'm gonna check out birth registries in San Bernardino, Orange, and Ventura counties. And if I don't turn up anything there, I'm gonna go to Kern, Buenavista, Riverside, and San Diego counties. Just on the off chance. I've sent to Sacramento to have 'em check statewide, but that could take a while."

The older Hudspeth took over from his son. "Now, without knowin' your mother's maiden name, or a Social Security number, or a last known address—something we can tie her to—we're limited in what we can do. The best way to proceed without something like that's to work backward from somebody we *do* have some information about, and see if we can cross-link the two of 'em at some point. That's why we went ahead with a background check on your father. This's where some of the—" Hudspeth lifted his hands from the desktop where they'd lain since he'd crushed out his cigarette, raising them in a gesture of surrender "—disturbing aspects of what we've discovered arise. It's up to you if ya wanna hear about this. Ya could—ya could let the whole thing rest."

"No. I want to know. Whatever it is, I want to know. I understand my father's dead. I know he was murdered. Anything else you have to tell me couldn't be any worse than that."

"Then let's start there." The elder Hudspeth flipped open a file folder that lay in front of him and picked up the top sheet of paper. "Ernest Tavia was killed in the late afternoon or evening of November second of this year. His body was found the next morning by a servant who works in the house. He'd been shot to death by a single bullet from a medium-caliber weapon, probably a .38, but the slug was too distorted to tell for sure and the shell casing wasn't recovered at the scene. The motive for the murder is believed to be robbery. There was a floor safe in the den that was open with the rug that usually covered it pulled back. The safe was empty, so it's assumed the contents of were removed. The police in Mexico are currently looking for a man named Flower Child Ashland—" Hudspeth released his hold on the paper he was referring to, raised one hand to his glasses, and took the spectacles off his face. "Is that right?" he asked Stuart. "Flower Child?"

"That's what they told me over the phone," Stuart assured him.

"Flora," Morinda said in a low voice. "Yes, that's—yes, that's right."

"Ya know him?" Hudspeth said, turning his attention to her.

"He—he stayed in our RV park. I checked him in. I talked with him a few times. He's the one—the one my father thought was a private detective."

"The one whose name ya couldn't recall?"

Morinda looked shamefaced, and hung her head, unable to meet Hudspeth's gaze and continue to claim she'd ever forgotten a name like Flower Child.

Hudspeth put his glasses back on and used the paper in the file folder as a prompt. "This Flower Child Ashland left fingerprints inside the house, on the door knob and on the floor safe. He disappeared from San Estaban about the same time the murder occurred. And he's also wanted as a suspect in the murder of a Baja Norte state policeman that took place October 27 of this year. They have another man in custody they think was also involved in that killing, a Lou Helmholtz. The state police are still looking for Ashland, apparently. They're also looking for—you."

Morinda's head jerked upward. She'd been peering at the floor, but at Hudspeth's words, she shifted her eyes from place to place in the room in agitation.

"Ya seem to've disappeared from San Estaban the same night the murder took place, and they think ya might've been kidnapped by this Ashland fellow. They'd also like to hear anything you've got to tell them that could help in their investigation of the crime."

"I don't know anything about it!" she almost shouted.

"Whoa, whoa!" Hudspeth held one hand up. "I'm just relayin' a message. It's not even a message—I'm only tellin' ya what the cops in Mexico want from ya."

"Are you—are you going to send me back to Mexico? Are you going to turn me over to the police?"

"Me? Why would I do that?"

"You said, you said that the police want to talk to me . . ."

"Well, they do. But the Mexican police don't have any jurisdiction here. There's nothing they can do to ya unless they charge ya with a crime, and then they'd have to extradite ya. But the Mexican government and Mexican cops don't have any authority over me. The only person I have any obligation to in this matter's you. You're my client, not the cops in Baja.

"However, I'd advise ya to get hold of the Baja Norte state police. Let 'em know you're still alive, so they don't waste a lot of time, effort, and money searching for ya as a kidnap victim. Or thinking they can find this Ashland guy by tracin' ya. And answer any questions they have that can help 'em find the killer. There—I said it. Now I'll just shut up and mind my own business."

Morinda regained her composure and asked, "Is that everything?"

"No. There's a couple of other pieces of information to pass along. But one more time, Morinda, I'm gonna give ya a chance to walk away from this. Do ya really wanna know these things?"

"I want to find my mother. My father's dead. I need to find my mother."

Hudspeth and Morinda locked eyes for a moment, as though plumbing each other's depths. Finally Hudspeth's gaze faltered, and he rubbed his thumb and forefinger on the bridge of his nose beneath his glasses.

"All right, I tried," he said wearily. "The man known as Ernest Tavia—probably *wasn't* your father. Not your real father, your biological father, the man who impregnated your mother."

"What do you mean?"

"Let's begin at the beginning. Ernest Tavia wasn't his real name. The Baja police sent a fax of his fingerprints to the FBI once they determined he was an American citizen, and the FBI promptly informed 'em that the true name of the man the prints belonged to was Patrick Lott. He apparently assumed the name Ernest Tavia twelve years ago when he first showed up in Baja. He was Patrick Lott when he lived in the United States, but they're the same person. He was in the U.S. Army for three years, so his fingerprints are on file. It's the same man, Ernest Tavia and Patrick Lott.

"Before he joined the Army, while he was still a college student, he was exposed to the mumps. Most people get the mumps when they're kids, and after that they develop an immunity so they never catch it again. Which's good, especially in the case of men, because if a man gets it when he's an adult, it can cause sterility. Men who catch the mumps as adults a lot of times aren't able to produce sperm, and they aren't able to have children. Patrick Lott, Ernest Tavia, whatever name ya want to think of him by—he got the mumps when he was twenty-one. He was treated for it at the clinic on the campus of UCLA, where he was attending school at the time. It made him sterile. He couldn't possibly've had children six years later when ya were born, or nine months before that when ya were conceived."

"That can't be right," Morinda said weakly.

"It was confirmed by a medical examination he took a few years later, after he was admitted to the VA hospital in Long Beach. That was after he was honorably discharged from the service. The diagnosis: incapable of fathering children. Now, the medical records I have are accurate and detailed—don't ask me how I got hold of 'em, because I won't tell ya. But this information's straight from the files of the university clinic and the Veterans Administration. Or the Department of Veterans Affairs, whatever the hell they call it now. Of course, it's possible mistakes were made by the attending physicians, or at the laboratories where the analyses of his sperm were conducted."

Stuart interjected, "Aren't there ways of testing paternity? Blood tests and DNA?"

"There are certain blood types that are incompatible, so they can screen out certain people as possible parents of a child. But that's kind of a hit-or-miss procedure. Ya hafta factor in the blood type of the mother and that of the possible father to find out whether or not the child's blood type can be produced from the two of 'em. In some cases, but by no means all, it can prove that someone couldn't possibly be the father. And the polymerase chain reaction or PCR testing, that's done by checking the DNA of the child and the mother, factoring out the mother's contribution and leaving only the DNA contributed by the father, or *vice versa*. Either way, we'd have to have a sample of the mother's blood or DNA to start with. We can get what we need for Lott, or Tavia, from the autopsy. But we'd still have to find the mother."

271

"Ya know," Stuart said, "if he knew he was sterile—and he had to, he got the original report on his condition and then confirmation two years later—maybe he and his wife decided to conceive by artificial insemination. How common was that fourteen years ago?"

"I dunno," Hudspeth said. "We could try prying some information out of sperm banks and fertility clinics, but it wouldn't be anywhere near as easy as gettin' things from the VA. People who work for fertility clinics are a lot better paid than VA hospital staff. Bribes wouldn't come cheap, believe me."

"There's always the possibility she was adopted," Stuart went on. "Couple who wanna kid, but they know the husband can't produce sperm, they decide to adopt. That'd explain why I can't find a birth certificate, too."

"Maybe. But once we get into adoption, things get even tougher. Confidentiality laws on adoptions are strict—"

Morinda withdrew into herself as the Hudspeths spoke to one another. The discussion about her father's murder'd been no worse than she'd imagined it'd be; she'd had a chance to harden herself, to accept whatever the detective might tell her about his death. But having it dropped on her that her father—the man she'd always believed was her father—was in fact *not* her father, was too much. It was like being socked in the gut from her blind-side, a treacherous and unexpected sucker-punch that made her stomach churn. Acidic bile crawled up into her throat.

Abruptly, she stood up. She whipped her eyes around the room, looking at nothing. The elder Hudspeth paused in the middle of speaking to his son, stopping in mid-word. Both the detective and Stuart turned toward Morinda. She stood in place, swaying slightly from side to side.

"Are you okay?" Hudspeth asked solicitously.

She took one step forward, and then promptly stepped back again. She felt her equilibrium crumbling; she was tottering like a building on a rotten foundation.

"I feel sick—" she managed to choke out. "Sick."

She stepped around the chair she'd been sitting in and rushed to the door. She pulled at the knob several times before she remembered to turn it; then, leaving the door ajar, she dashed out of the office. Her steps clattered on the marble floor of the lobby.

As soon as she turned to leave, Hudspeth stood. Stuart pushed himself from his chair a second later. They both remained in place watching Morinda's retreating figure.

"Maybe ya could go and make sure she can find her way to the restroom," Hudspeth suggested.

"Yeah, sure," Stuart replied, and with long, loping strides he followed in Morinda's wake.

Three paces into the lobby, he stopped to survey the open space between him and the ladies' room across the way. There was no sign of Morinda. Wondering that she could've made it so quickly to the lavatory, he went to the receptionist's desk. Amber was on the phone when he arrived, and he waited for her to finish her call, all the while scanning the lobby in an effort to spot his client.

Amber hung up and turned her attention to Stuart.

"Did ya see where she went?" Stuart asked.

"The one who came out of your dad's office? Yeah, straight out the front. What'd you guys do to her, anyway? She went—"

Stuart charged to the exit, down the steps, and on to the sidewalk, looking first to the left, and then, when he saw no sign of her there, to the right. There were only a few pedestrians to block his view, and twenty yards away he spotted a flash of blue the same shade as Morinda's blouse'd been. Keeping her in sight to make sure she didn't evade him, he hurried up the street.

She was leaning against the sandstone wall of a bank, her shoulders and chest heaving as she breathed spasmodically, tears streaming down her face.

"Hey," Stuart said when he got near. "Hey," he said again. It was as much as he could think of to say. He pulled up several feet from her, not knowing what to do.

Morinda had her arms folded across her chest. She lifted one hand to wipe her cheek, brushing her right eye to clear it. She continued to sob, her face contorted, as she cried, "I have to belong *some*where!"

"Hey," Stuart repeated stupidly. He'd always felt helpless when faced with a crying woman. The only means of dealing with them he'd ever found effective was to give them a hug, but Morinda's body language—her arms crossed in front of her—didn't invite that sort of familiarity. Stuart scratched his head.

"Look, let's go—"

He glanced hastily around him. The few passersby turned reproachful glares from the weeping Morinda to Stuart; they obviously considered him the villain in whatever melodrama they concocted in their imaginations to explain the scene. The public scrutiny made Stuart feel even more feckless.

"There's an ice cream parlor over here. Let's go there, have an ice cream, and talk about it. Okay?"

Morinda sniffled, and she ran her finger under her nose.

Stuart reached out to her and gently took her elbow. "C'mon, we'll get ice cream," he said coaxingly. "Things always look better with ice cream. It takes the sharp edges off. C'mon."

Morinda allowed herself to be led away without showing any enthusiasm. Stuart kept his hand on her arm to guide her; she might've walked into traffic, or bumped into lampposts, if he hadn't directed her.

The ice cream parlor's décor was *faux* Parisian of the Toulouse-Lautrec period, the color scheme pink and white, the tables and chairs made of curlicue wrought iron like something to be found on a wedding cake. Stuart led Morinda to a chair and asked her, "Whattaya want? They got sundaes here, and banana splits, ice cream floats. Ooh, how about that one?" he said, examining a picture of a confection behind the sales counter. "My God! Two bananas, four scoops, chocolate syrup, whipped cream, sprinkles, and cherries on top! Ya want one of those?"

"I don't want anything," Morinda said dismally. She'd stopped crying, but the tears she'd so bitterly wept were scarcely dry on her red, swollen cheeks.

"Like every woman I've ever known," Stuart said. "They tell ya they don't want anything. Then they pick and nibble at yours until they've eaten half of it, so ya don't get enough yourself. Is that what you're gonna do to me?"

"No!" Morinda insisted. "I don't want any! Unless—unless it looks really good. Then I might have—a little."

"Okay," Stuart agreed magnanimously. "If it'll make ya feel better, ya can take as much of mine as ya want."

He went to the counter and returned a few minutes later with a scaled-down version of the dessert pictured on the poster. There were two plastic spoons thrust into the ice cream. Morinda listlessly picked up the one nearest her, but she didn't begin to scrape tiny shavings off and carry them toward her mouth where she could lick them with the tip of her tongue until Stuart'd already swallowed three enormous spoonfuls from his end.

As he ate, Stuart eased into what he hoped was a comforting mode. "Ya really shouldn't think of it as a completely bad thing, that you're adopted or whatever. That he wasn't your real father."

Morinda morosely used her spoon to skim the surface of the banana split several times, accumulating whipped cream, chocolate syrup, and vanilla ice cream in microscopic amounts at each pass before raising it and delicately touching it to her lips.

"He raised ya. He took care of ya. He seems to've given ya a good life. He gave ya an education. He must've loved ya a lot to do all that."

"He made me think my mother was dead," Morinda said harshly.

"Maybe ya should put this thing into perspective. One of the things I heard when I called San Estaban was that he left a will he wrote a couple of years ago and filed with some lawyer down there. You're the sole beneficiary. Ya inherit everything. I guess that means the RV park, the bar, a house, a car, I dunno what else. So he's left ya in pretty good shape, financially."

"He *lied* to me!" Morinda objected. "He lied to me all my life! Giving me those things, that doesn't make up for doing that, does it?"

"Well, maybe he meant to tell ya—ya know, when ya were old enough to understand it."

"I'm old enough now," she said with cast-iron conviction.

"Sure, sure, but what I'm sayin' is, maybe he didn't wanna tell ya when ya were younger. He planned to tell ya, he wanted to tell ya, but a good time to bring it up never came around. He knew ya were old enough to hear about it, but he was busy, and you were busy, and the two of ya never got together when it seemed like a good time to go into it. And he didn't feel like there was any real pressure to do it because he didn't know he was gonna—ya know, that he was gonna get killed. He probably figured he had a lot more years to take care of things, and he'd've said something about it to ya then, and the two of ya could hash the whole thing out. But then it turned out he didn't have as much time as he thought, and—and ya found out about it this way instead of the way he probably wanted ya to."

Morinda was implacable. "He lied," she said.

"Well, honesty's a—a very overrated quality."

This assertion, baldly state, brought Morinda up short. "How can you say that?"

"It's not as good a thing as some people think. It kind of depends on what the truth is," Stuart said. He'd ceased shoveling mounds of dessert into his mouth; he held his spoon in one hand and thrust it into the air for emphasis. "My dad, he doesn't hide the truth from me. He doesn't pull any punches. He lets me know the truth straight out. He hates me."

To Morinda, this was a revelation. She'd never heard anyone say such a thing before, never suspected she'd ever actually meet someone who could honestly claim his father hated him. "Why does he hate you?"

"I dunno." Stuart's expression changed. He was no longer the amiable extrovert; his thoughts seemed to turn inward, something he didn't seem to be used to. "I try to do what he wants me to do. I—I try to do the right things. But it never seems to work out. Everything I do, I screw up. I don't mean to. I don't want to. It just happens that way. Other people, it's easy for them. They know what to do, they don't have to think about it, they just do what's right. But me—I try and I try. But I can't seem to connect. I think I'm doin' what I should, but it turns out to be wrong. And I never know why. Nobody'll tell me, or if they do, it doesn't make any sense to me. So I keep doin' these things, and my dad, he keeps givin' me that look—that look that says how disappointed he is in me. Because I don't measure up. Not that I don't measure up to some ideal son he wishes he had: I don't measure up to bein' even a normal, average person. I'm substandard, is the way he thinks about me. I'm a scrub. A reject. And I dunno what to do to change."

Stuart'd been staring out the window as he spoke. Now he looked at Morinda to ask, "Do you remember the last time you were happy? When everything was good for ya?"

Thinking Stuart was trying to maneuver her out of her self-pity by some clumsy psychological ploy, Morinda dismissively answered, "Yes, of course."

She was wrong in her guess of what Stuart was getting at, however, for he said flatly, "I don't. Every time something comes into my memory about my life, it's some instance of failure, some defeat, some embarrassment or humiliation. Those are the only times I can ever recall really well. I can't remember anything else. I've failed at everything, is the way it seems to me. Oh, sure, I can think of times I did things that are supposed to be a success—I won ribbons in school, and got awards, and people told me good things about myself, and like that. But none of those things seem to matter. None of those are the important things. And I have to go deliberately lookin' for those memories before I can dredge 'em up to begin with. The memories that always float to the top of my mind on their own are the other ones, the dark ones, the painful ones.

"So I don't blame my father for judgin' me the way he does. He's seein' me the way I am. I am a screw-up. I only wish somebody'd be able to tell me what it is I'm doin', what it is that keeps me from—from bein' like everybody else. 'Cause I try. I try. I watch other people, and I think I'm doin' the same things they are, actin' the way they'd act in the same situation. But it never works out that way. I always do it wrong, and it turns out a mess. That's how things've always been for me."

Stuart, who'd been staring at nothing, suddenly returned to the here-and-now. "How did we get off on this, anyway? I'm supposed to be cheerin' ya up, not makin' ya even more depressed."

"Do you want the rest of this?" Morinda asked.

"No. I think I've had too much already."

She considered the remainder of the dessert in the chrome salver ruefully, then stuck her spoon into it and shoveled a large portion into her mouth.

"Not too fast," Stuart warned. "It'll give ya a headache."

"You sound like my dad," she said without thinking, and then she remembered that her father was dead, and that he wasn't truly her father anyway. It made her sad, but she was beyond tears.

CHAPTER 4

The day after her meeting with the Hudspeths, Morinda returned to the library. As usual, the place became a freeform social center for several hours in the afternoon when the elementary and middle schools were dismissed, with swarms of teenagers and younger children using the Internet computers, skateboarding in the parking lot, sleeping, doing their homework, eating, talking on cell phones or to each other *viva voce* in the cubbyholes, in the carrels, and at the tables. The librarians didn't even attempt to keep them quiet. Morinda tried to ignore the raucous crowd around her. She was reading another book by Jorge Luis Borges, this one called *El Aleph*. The stories in this collection were just as good as those in *Ficciones*, and she was distracted only occasionally when the noise grew exceptionally shrill.

If she'd been fully conscious of her surroundings, she would've noticed when the volume of the chatter abruptly diminished, and then died completely; and that several of the older kids picked up their backpacks, slung them over their shoulders, and slyly slipped away. But intent upon the Borges book, she was unaware of the change until she heard a jangling that sounded as though Marley's ghost'd materialized right next to her.

She tore her eyes away from the page and glanced to the side to see a woman wearing dozens of metal bracelets on each of her wrists and a nicely tailored dress suit; the expression on her unsmiling face was one of set determination. Morinda'd never seen the woman before, so her first thought was that she was a new addition to the library staff.

"You're in the library a lot, aren't ya?" the woman asked. She folded her arms across her chest and her many bracelets clinked against one another.

Morinda said, "I come here—to read."

"You're here everyday, they say. Sometimes all day long. Why aren't ya in school?"

Morinda's mind went blank, and she could think of nothing to say that wouldn't sound like an absurd lie. Her confusion grew even greater when she heard the squawk of another woman's voice electronically amplified and distorted followed by a burst of static that came from behind the woman interrogating her; then a man's natural baritone voice spoke saying only, "Ten-four." A large policeman was talking into the microphone of a radio clipped to the loop on one shoulder of his blue uniform as he walked up to stand beside the officious woman. The policeman carried a clipboard in one hand. His leather belt and holster squeaked as he walked.

"I'm a truant officer," the woman said. "And you're supposed to be goin' to school. What school are ya enrolled in?"

"I—I'm not enrolled in any school. Not any school here. I just moved."

"Your parents should've taken care of that right away. As soon as they got here. What's your home phone number?"

"There's no phone," Morinda said in a tiny voice.

"No phone in the home? How can I contact your parents? One of 'em must have a phone where they work. Or does a neighbor have a phone?"

"No. No. There's no phone."

"Where do ya live?" the woman asked. "We'll take ya there and talk to your parents."

"I don't live with my parents," Morinda said desperately.

"Ya in foster care? Living with relatives—grandparents, or an aunt or uncle?"

Morinda searched the faces of the teenagers and younger children around her who watched the proceedings in silent wonder. But she could expect no help from any of them; none of them knew her as anybody other than a face they'd seen a few times, but with whom they hadn't even a nodding acquaintance since Morinda always made a point of sticking strictly to herself.

Standing beyond the ragged ring of spectators was the librarian who'd led Morinda to the shelves of Spanish-language books the first day she'd visited the library. Morinda'd passed her many times since then, and they always smiled at each other as their paths crossed. Morinda knew the librarian could do nothing to rescue her; she sought only to find concern and sympathy from someone she'd formed at least a tenuous bond with. Her eyes lingered on the librarian's face, searching for some degree of compassion there.

The librarian watched Morinda for a moment, but then she turned away. It was almost furtive the way the librarian refused to meet her eyes.

The words of the truant officer arose in Morinda's memory: "You're here everyday, they say. Sometimes all day long."

And she knew then who it was who'd betrayed her.

Heartsick, she made no protest when the truant officer took one of her arms and the uniformed policeman took the other and they escorted her out of the library to put her into the rear of a patrol car.

Unable to convince Morinda to tell her where she lived or who she lived with, the truant officer transferred her to the custody of the Department of Human Services as a runaway. The place she ended up had rooms as small as cells, shatterproof glass and bars on the windows, and doors that locked and unlocked electronically, emitting a buzz whenever one of the uniformed guards—although they insisted upon being called matrons—entered or exited, but which the internees couldn't control;

none of the inmates could come or go from any room in the building without being conducted by a matron.

She was taken to a county hospital and given a medical examination. The female doctor said nothing about the cuts, abrasions, and bruises she found on Morinda's thighs and vulva, but she spent a long time making notations on her paperwork after completing the gynecological checkup, taking much longer to record those notes than any other portion of the exam. Morinda was too embarrassed to ask any questions about what the doctor found.

At the detention facility, she was fed in a cafeteria. The food was bland and undercooked. She was reminded repeatedly by the food preparation staff, by the matrons, and by large signs posted around the cafeteria: TAKE ALL YOU WANT, BUT EAT ALL YOU TAKE.

She was given a bed in a dormitory. Nearly all the thirty beds in the long hall were filled. None of the girls who occupied the dorm paid much attention to Morinda when she arrived; they spent most of their time braiding each other's hair and gossiping. There was nothing there to read, and only a few games, most of which were missing too many essential pieces to be of any use.

One morning after breakfast, Morinda was escorted by a matron to a room that was outfitted Spartanly, the only furnishings being two metal chairs and a bare metal table bolted to the floor. There was a window of thick sheets of glass with chicken wire sandwiched between them; it looked out upon an expanse of green grass that ended at a concrete basketball court. The basket at one end had a net made of rusty metal links; that at the other end was missing its net completely. Beyond the concrete apron was a tall hurricane fence topped with razor wire on an angled extension arm. When the matron left and the door lock buzzed then clicked behind her, Morinda went to the window.

She was looking wistfully at the blue of the sky beyond the chain link enclosure when the door buzzed again. Reluctantly, she left the sad little view to face the new arrival.

It was a woman in her mid-thirties with her hair cut at her shoulders in a severely utilitarian manner, scissored straight across and lacking curl, either natural or artificial. She wore a minimum of makeup and her skin was rather coarse. Her khaki-colored pant suit looked a little like something a meter-reader or a delivery person'd wear as a uniform, though the sleeves of the jacket were flipped back to reveal the bright purple sleeves of her blouse. Her fingernails were unpolished and probably'd never been manicured. She had a no-nonsense air about her as she briskly entered the room carrying an open case folder in her hands; she skimmed the contents of the file while she walked, glancing up every few seconds to judge the distance left to go to reach the chair on her side of the table. When she got there, she dropped into the seat and without looking at Morinda said, "Sit down."

Morinda took the three paces to the empty chair and sat. The woman across from her examined the papers inside the folder furiously, as though she were angry at them for some reason, as she said, "The results of your medical exam are in. Good news: you're not pregnant, ya don't have any sexually transmitted diseases, and you're clear of HIV. Ya dodged a bullet, sister."

While the newcomer was preoccupied with her reports, Morinda closed her eyes for a moment in silent thanks.

"The bad news is," the woman went on, "your ID's as phony as a three-dollar bill. But it says you're fourteen-years-old, which matches your appearance, and if you're fourteen, you're supposed to be in school. You're supposed to be livin' at home, not runnin' wild in the streets. And ya had close to seven hundred dollars on ya when we picked ya up—not what most parents give their kids for lunch money. You've got some problems, toots."

The woman finally deigned to lift her eyes from the folder and actually act as though Morinda were visible.

"Is that why you're keeping me in jail?" Morinda asked.

"This isn't a jail." The woman's tone of voice was like her expression, hard and cynical. "This facility's maintained by the Department of Human

Services for the temporary custody of minors. I'm a social worker, not a prison guard."

"I'm locked in, and I can't get out. I eat the food you give me. I sleep where you tell me I have to. I dress in the clothes you dole out. I eat and sleep and dress when you tell me to do it. I can't do the things I want to do without your permission. It's a jail. Oh, you don't mind putting me in a jail," Morinda said, paraphrasing her father. "You just resent it when I point out to you that that's what you're doing."

"It's not a jail. You're bein' kept in this facility for your own good. Because you're too young to take care of yourself."

"I didn't ask you for your help, did I? I was doing just fine on my own."

"Just fine?" the woman said sarcastically. "You're seriously tellin' me you were doin' *just fine* by yourself? You were raped—do ya remember that? Did ya bother to report it to the police, or were ya doing so fine all on your own that ya didn't think ya had any obligation to help protect other women from having the same thing happen to 'em? And how've ya been livin', that things are so fine, anyway? Ya were clean and neatly dressed, which means you're not on the street. Who've ya been stayin' with? Ya been shackin' up with your boyfriend? Maybe some older guy? Ya had almost seven hundred dollars in cash. Is he pimpin' ya already? Was that how ya came to get raped—some trick got too rough for ya to handle? And your pimp wasn't around to take care of things?"

Morinda blanched at each of the accusations the woman threw at her. Each imputation hit her like a slap across the face.

"Right now, we don't even know your real name. We wanna contact your parents to tell 'em you're okay. Why don't ya give me their phone number so I can let 'em know you're not lyin' dead in some alley with your throat cut? It might spare 'em a lot of pain and misery, if they knew ya were alive."

Morinda, still reeling from the shock of the social worker's charges against her, couldn't respond. She was dumbfounded.

"C'mon! The game's over! Ya ran away, ya got caught, so now it's time to head home and face the music. Why'd ya leave, anyway?"

Morinda didn't answer.

"Your parents try to break ya and your boyfriend up? Wouldn't let ya smoke dope in your bedroom with your friends? They expect ya to actually do some work in school? What?"

Morinda remained silent, staring morosely at the wall beyond the social worker's head.

The social worker's tone softened almost to the point of being unctuous. "Or was it something more serious? Were ya bein' abused? It could've been physical, you've got a lot of marks and scars on ya. Or maybe sexual. Was somebody at home forcing ya to have sex? Was your father rapin' ya?"

Morinda's outrage, once fervid, now turned frigid. She withdrew into herself, implementing the *Ley de Hielo* as she'd seen *Señor* Ramirez, Maria Elena's father the *delegado*, do on one occasion. In Mexico, it's considered impolite to contradict another person, nor do officials want to disappoint someone who's requesting their assistance, so many times Mexican bureaucrats will tell petitioners whatever it is they think they want to hear; but in order to protect themselves from future recriminations, when an importuning citizen becomes too insistent, the official will set his face in a mask and refuse to speak a single word, no matter what entreaties the applicant might make. This was the *Ley de Hielo*, "the Law of Ice."

Thereafter, no matter what inquiries, no matter what insinuations, no matter what threats the social worker made, Morinda remained stoically and stonily silent, her face fixed straight ahead, willing herself to remain cold, hard, and immovable.

After a time, the social worker realized she was getting nowhere, and she gave up in disgust. She pushed herself from the table, stomped to the door, and tapped on the glass in the window until a matron came to let her out. Morinda continued to stare at the same spot on the wall she'd chosen to focus her eyes upon even after the social worker left. She kept her mind concentrated on the specific flyspeck she'd selected there until a matron came to take her away.

She wasn't returned to the dormitory. Instead, she was taken to a tiny room painted institutional green with a single narrow window of shatterproof glass in the handleless door facing onto the corridor. There was a steel-framed bunk bed bolted to the concrete floor set flush with one wall that allowed three feet of open space between its edge and the wall opposite. Morinda had the room to herself, and she reflected on the fact that the living space she had here was about the size of the closet she'd once told Mrs. Blowfeld she lived in at home. The environment inside the cell was not even as intellectually stimulating as the dorm'd been, except there was reading material provided here: a stack of much-thumbed comic books lay in the corner on the floor.

Morinda put her shoulders against the wall and let herself slump to the ground. With her knees drawn up, she closed her eyes and fantasized being someplace else—anyplace else. Abject and despondent, as far as she could tell she had only one thing left to look forward to: a visit by Melmoth the Wanderer, who'd offer to exchange places with her; she'd be free to leave if she'd only agree to sacrifice her soul as Melmoth the Wanderer'd done, and lived to regret. Wondering which fate she might choose if Melmoth ever did appear, she stayed beside the bed until a matron came to escort her to the cafeteria when lunch was ready.

CHAPTER 5

Sitting in his father's car at the back of the parking lot of the Delaware Club, a business legally licensed for wagering at card games in the city of Gardena on the west side of the Los Angeles metropolitan area, Stuart checked his appearance by twisting the neck of the rearview mirror on its swivel to reflect different patches of his face, head, and throat, the only parts of himself visible in the range of the narrow rectangle. An out-of-place lock of hair required only a patting down with his fingers. When he thrust his forehead within two inches of the mirror's surface, a blemish ballooned monstrously, but Stuart could do nothing about it except worry for a few seconds and then squeeze the white head of the pimple with a fingernail until it popped. On his Adam's apple he found a cluster of black bristles an eighth of an inch long that he'd missed when he shaved that morning; he edged the Windsor knot of his tie up to cover the telltale hairs.

He got out of the car and examined his clothes. The tie he'd borrowed from his father's rack'd worked out better than Stuart had any right to expect when he took five tries to get it tied correctly earlier that morning: the wider end hung an inch longer than the narrower end at the bottom, which was all Stuart knew or cared about the proper look of a tie anyway. His blazer, which he'd also appropriated from his father's wardrobe, was too big across the shoulders, and the sleeves dangled over his wrists, but he'd seen movies in which Tom Cruise's clothes looked worse-fitted, so he felt he was within a safe margin-of-error on that score.

Robert L. Gaede

His slacks were fine. They were inexpensive, but they were new, and he'd been able to select them himself, so he knew they were at least in fashion, and they fit him. They were cheap because he'd had to con his father out of enough money to buy them the day before.

He'd driven one of his father's two cars to the office, and the elder Hudspeth'd driven the other. They stopped at a service station as they'd arranged ahead of time, and his father paid by credit card to have both cars filled up. While they waited for the attendant to finish pumping their gas, Stuart angled for his father to surrender at least one of his credit cards to him.

"I'm goin' out to San Bernardino and Riverside to check the County Clerks' offices for birth certificates on that Morinda Tavia today. I may need to fill up again."

His father wasn't an easy mark. The elder Hudspeth said, "The Ford's got an eighteen-gallon tank. It gets twenty miles to the gallon in town, twenty-three on the freeway. My suggestion'd be, don't go more than three hundred and sixty miles round-trip, and you'll be fine."

"C'mon, Dad. I'm gonna be gone all day. I gotta eat."

His father gave him a cool look and said with even colder sarcasm, "I fail to see why." And he refused him the credit card. Instead, he passed Stuart a twenty-dollar bill.

"Twenty bucks?" Stuart asked incredulously. "For breakfast, lunch, and dinner? Ya think we're still livin' in the Depression, Dad? How can ya eat on twenty bucks these days?"

Of course, his father was able to tell him precisely how it could be done. "Denny's for breakfast. Even with a tip, that's less than six. You're goin' out to San Bernardino? There's a restaurant out there called Lou's Cafe that has a lunch special ya won't believe. Only $4.99, and ya won't be able to eat everything they serve. For dinner, hit the Sizzler."

Stuart should've known better than to challenge his father on a point of niggardliness. The elder Hudspeth prided himself on being able to sniff out the least expensive places to eat, and the cheapest motels to stay in, the quality of which was above fast food and flophouses, in any town he'd ever passed through. He had a built-in homing device that unerringly led him to bargains. He bragged about it.

So Stuart managed to finagle no more than the twenty from his father. He had twenty of his own, and he put the two together to purchase a pair of slacks at Penny's. It left him with no money to actually buy any food during the day, but he knew of a bar that served chicken wings and another that served cold cuts during Monday Night Football when the buffet tables got very crowded and the bar's staff couldn't tell whether he'd ordered a drink at the bar or not. So he just had to make it through the day until four when Happy Hour began. He'd done it before, many times.

He finished his self-inspection with his shoes, noting the layer of fine dust that'd settled across the toes veiling the high gloss he'd shined them to. He raised one foot and rubbed the tip across the back of the opposite pant leg, then did the same with the other. He didn't worry about leaving dust streaks on the backs of his slacks; he only cared about first impressions, and what people thought of him after he left didn't matter.

Satisfied that he'd made himself as presentable as possible within the confines of his budget, he straightened his shoulders to display confidence, and walked under the brightly lit marquee into the glittering lobby of the Delaware Club.

The interior décor was designed to dispel any notion that this was a sleazy gambling den or lowlife haunt; the club's appointments were tasteful, expensive, and immaculately clean. The carpeting was plush, and everywhere Stuart looked his eye was caught by the lambent surfaces of gleaming brass, spotless glass, and varnished wood. Framed prints lined the walls, each depicting a different scene of an Edwardian-period English private club in which card playing was a prominent feature.

Stuart stepped briskly past the bar, then along a terrace that skirted the main room, which was divided into two sections. On one side were dozens of tables at which men and women were engaged in straight poker, low-ball, pan, and blackjack. Their chips clicked together as the cards were dealt and bets placed. On the other side of the room, separated by brass railings and a drop in the floor level of three feet so that a set of stairs was needed to go between the two areas, were tables slightly larger than those at which blackjack was played though designed after the same pattern, having room for seven players who sat opposite the house dealer; each was surrounded by scores of Asians animatedly wagering at Pai Gow, a gambling game played with a 32-piece set of dominoes with their dots mostly white, although some were colored red, the distinction made according to some arcane formula that to Stuart's mind was incomprehensible, as were the rest of the rules of the game. As usual, there were far more people at the tables on the east side of the room than there were those playing the more traditional Western games.

Stuart glided past it all, continued along a corridor where the terrace ended, made a left turn, and proceeded down another hall until he came to an open door. He read the metal sign that marked it: CLUB MANAGEMENT. He paused a few steps away, brushed lint off his blazer, re-straightened his tie, muttered to himself, "It's show time!" and entered.

The room resembled a lounge more than an office. There was a large wooden desk to one side, but it was unoccupied and had absolutely nothing on its surface; it might've been a stage prop. The long wall on the opposite side of the room and the short wall ahead of Stuart were dominated by matching sofas with low coffee tables set in front of them. There was a passthrough into another room between the arms of the couches. Two men dressed in tailored suits were seated at the closest ends of the sofas, one with his left leg crossed over the right, the second with the ankle of one foot resting on the knee of the other. They were in the middle of a conversation that Stuart's arrival interrupted. They both looked up, rose to their feet, and stepped forward as though to courteously greet Stuart, but in a way that insured they blocked Stuart's access to the walkway.

"Are ya lost?" one of the men asked politely. "There's no tables back here. They're all up front."

Stuart cleared his throat and said, "I came to see—"

Another man stepped out of the room behind the two guards holding a cigar in his right hand. He stopped and peered over the shoulders of the men who'd intercepted Stuart. Stuart recognized the newcomer immediately as the manager of the Delaware Club, a nattily dressed, thin-lipped man with a nose shaped like a pair of needle-nosed pliers named Al Thibodeaux. Thibodeaux studied Stuart's face for a few seconds, then his thin lips stretched like the rubber of an expanding balloon into a half-smile when he recognized him.

"How's your car?" Thibodeaux asked. His tone was solicitous, as if he truly cared, but the supercilious upward turn of his lips at their corners made his expression into as near a sneer as possible without it being blatant. "Haven't had any more trouble with the battery, have ya?"

A month before, prior to its repossession, Stuart'd parked his car in the lot of the Delaware Club one night when he had no money to pay for a motel room. He made sure he was in the darkest, most inaccessible, most out of the way spot, right up against the retaining wall near the dumpsters where no one else ever went. He was asleep in the front seat, his coat wrapped around him and the windows fogged into opacity by his breath, when he was aroused suddenly by a uniformed security guard who tapped on the windshield. Stuart told him a story about his car's battery being dead, and that he was waiting a few minutes to see if it'd come back to life; the guard laughed and said a dead battery was gonna stay dead until it got charged and went into the club to get some jumper cables, returning with them a little later to find Stuart driving out of the lot and into the street, waving to the guard as he left and rolling down his window to call out, "Hey! It charged up again, just like I thought it would!" From the corner of his eye, Stuart saw Thibodeaux come out of the club's glass doors to stand by the security guard as Stuart exited the grounds. He hadn't encountered the manager of the Delaware Club since then, but clearly Thibodeaux'd heard the whole story.

"Well, actually, the truth of the matter is—I sold it," Stuart replied to Thibodeaux's query about his car. "Yeah, I decided to do something about the old cash flow situation."

Thibodeaux continued to grin, showing a series of sharp little teeth. "I bet ya got a good price for it, car with a battery that's self-chargin' like that."

Stuart laughed along with Thibodeaux to take the sting out of the dig and said, "Oh, well, I sold it to a friend, so it wasn't a matter of makin' a killin' on it."

"Whew!" Thibodeaux said. He raised his cigar to his lips and took a puff. "Sellin' a used car to a friend! That's a good way of gettin' rid of the car—and the friend!"

Thibodeaux edged farther into the room, moving between the guards who stepped aside to let him by. When he was facing Stuart with the others no longer intervening, he came to rest with his hands crossed in front of him at the wrists and said, "So, what can we do for ya?"

Stuart found the situation more intimidating than he'd anticipated. He assumed he'd meet the management while he and they were seated at a table or a desk, not by having to explain himself to Thibodeaux flanked by two apparent bodyguards standing in the middle of a room. The standing was the worst aspect of it, since it told Stuart he was expected to present his case without delay, so he wouldn't be allowed the leisurely pace to unfold his argument that he'd counted on. Instead, he was under the gun. He spoke hastily.

"Yesterday—ya may've heard about it. Ya probably did, you're the manager, ya must've heard what happened to me yesterday when I was at the poker table? I, uh, I had a problem—ya know, with the busboy. The barmaid brought me a drink. And then the busboy came over to clear the table next to me. And the barmaid brought me the wrong drink. Only I didn't notice it until she'd gone, and so I mentioned it to the busboy and asked him to get the barmaid back or replace it or whatever. And, uh, he, uh, he turned on me, started yelling at me in Spanish, cussin' me out. In Spanish. Said, '*Chingu to madre*,' called me a *pendejo*, and a *pinche cabrón*, a buncha stuff like that."

Thibodeaux began to nod his head toward the end of Stuart's narrative, as if he'd finally made the connection. "Oh, yeah. The pit boss mentioned that incident. So that was you, was it?"

"Yeah, that was me."

A booming voice called from out of the space beyond the wall formed by Thibodeaux and the two guards. "What the hell's this about, anyway?"

Thibodeaux and the two henchmen quickly craned their necks to look behind them. Thibodeaux's expression changed from smug snideness to unctuous diffidence.

"Just a public-relations problem, Jack!" Thibodeaux called back. "Customer had a run-in with an employee yesterday!"

The man who'd shouted filled up the walkway. He was well over six feet tall, and he carried a lot of bulk. His body was massive, and though he was past sixty years of age, he still generated an aura of physical power that was menacing. His hair was white and short-cropped, but showed no pattern baldness. His face displayed the signs of dissipation, indications that although his huge frame'd once been formidably strong, it'd been exposed to too much nicotine, too much alcohol, too much cocaine, and too much of the constant debilitating search for sex with too many different partners over the years to maintain itself as anything like the smoothly functioning machine it'd been at its peak. His face'd acquired fleshy layers of flab, with deeply engrained lines etched into the forehead and cheeks; his nose was crisscrossed with burst capillaries; his eyelids drooped heavily. He looked as though he had a permanent hangover that kept his face fixed in a glower. He looked like the Picture of Dorian Gray.

Stuart knew who he was: Jack Kilby, the owner of the Delaware Club, and reputedly head of the largest sports book operation on the West Coast. Stuart's indebtedness to Kilby's operation was minimal, on the order of a few hundred dollars, which was the only reason he dared to beard this particular lion in his den.

"So I heard," the gruff growl of the big man said. "Who's this Goddamn busboy? What's his name?"

He lifted his oversized hands as if he intended to pick the busboy up and snap him in two pieces with them.

"Kid named Pedro," Thibodeaux said.

"Get him in here. Get him in here, now!" the big man ordered.

"We didn't keep him on, Jack. Not after that. He was fired."

The big man continued to scowl, and he ground his teeth, as though pondering whether it'd be worth his while to track the errant busboy down in order to lay hands on him. After a moment, his frown relaxed slightly and he said to Stuart, "Okay. The punk mouthed off to ya, and we shitcanned him. It'll be tough on his wife, but she should've known better than to marry the asshole. Of course, it'll be tough on his kids, too, and it's not their fault their father's a jerk-off. But, hey, what are ya gonna do?"

"So he's not workin' here any more," Thibodeaux's oily voice slid into the opening left by the big man's silence. "He'll never get out of line with ya again, believe me."

"The worst mistake we ever made was givin' those greasers long-handled hoes to replace those short-handled ones," Kilby said jocularly. "That's when they started to walk upright. Made 'em think they were human!"

He barked a laugh. The two guards laughed easily along with him; Thibodeaux also made a show of appreciating the big man's wit, while all the time he was snickering he was shifting his eyes from side to side. Stuart chuckled politely, then raised his hand to his mouth to cover a cough.

Kilby said, "I hope that gives ya some satisfaction, Mister—sorry, I didn't catch your name?"

"Hudspeth. Stuart Hudspeth."

The big man put out a huge paw to shake with Stuart; Stuart felt it engulf his own hand. Kilby didn't attempt to crush bones, as Stuart half-feared he might; he seemed to understand the physical power that was at his command, and consciously reined it in.

"Jack Kilby, glad to meet ya. Sorry about your trouble with the punk yesterday. Glad we could satisfy ya. Don't wanna lose your business."

Kilby dropped Stuart's hand and was about to turn away, clearly thinking the problem resolved.

Stuart saw he was losing momentum, and he jumped in with, "But I'm not satisfied, Mr. Kilby."

The big man's frown returned in full force. He swung his broad shoulders back around so he was facing Stuart, and he shifted his weight from one foot to the other, balancing himself. "Huh? What's that?" he rasped.

"Well, this guy, this guy who worked for ya here—here at the Delaware Club. He went after me pretty good out there. In front of other customers. In front of my friends. Told me off, cussed me out. It was pretty embarrassing."

"He did it in Spanish, didn't he?" Kilby asked. "How many people out there even understood what he was sayin'? 'Cept for the rest of the kitchen help."

"I dunno, Mr. Kilby. *I* understood what he was sayin'. I think most people around here know what *pendejo* means. And it—it was demeaning. To me, I mean. Bein' called a bunch of dirty names by a busboy. When I couldn't do anything about it."

"Why couldn't ya do anything about it?" Kilby asked. "You're a man, aren't ya? He did it to me, I'd've broken the cocksucker's neck for him."

Stuart shrugged helplessly. "I didn't wanna do anything—ya know, disrespectful. In your place of business and all."

Thibodeaux's lips retracted in a grin.

Kilby said, "So whattaya want me to do? What *would* satisfy ya? Ya want I should go find old Pedro, drag him down here, and let ya slap him around some? Huh?"

Kilby sought appreciation from his cronies for this joke as well. The two guards chuckled softly; Thibodeaux's smile broadened.

"For the humiliation I suffered," Stuart said, ignoring the smirks on the faces of the men around him, "I think I'm owed compensation."

"Compensation?" Kilby said. "What kind of compensation?"

"I was thinkin'—I thought five thousand dollars'd be—would be about right. For what I was subjected to. Everything considered."

Thibodeaux let out a sputter of stifled laughter around the cigar he'd clamped in his teeth. It came and went so fast it sounded almost like a cough. The two guards let their faces go blank, as though waiting for instructions from Kilby on how they should respond. Kilby put one of his fists into the palm of his other hand, rubbing the knuckles while he considered Stuart for a long moment.

Without taking his eyes off Stuart, Kilby said in a low growl, "Jimmy, ya know where those ten-dollar chips are? The new stack I just had brought in?"

"Sure, Mr. Kilby," the man on his right said.

"Bring me some of those, would ya?"

"How many ya want?"

"Just bring a handful, all right?"

The man disappeared into the back room.

Kilby said, "Al, ya have some of those tickets for complimentary drinks on ya?"

Thibodeaux kept his cigar in his mouth and slapped his hands on the breasts of his coat, then reached into one side and took slips of paper out of an inner pocket. He gave them to Kilby.

"Each one of these's good for a drink from the bar," Kilby said as he riffled through the packet with his thumb. "There's gotta be—I dunno, fifteen or twenty of 'em here." He passed the tickets to Stuart.

The man who'd gone to fetch the chips returned with some clamped between the thumb and the fingers of one hand. They were the standard blue chips with the logo of the Delaware Club imprinted on them that served as ten-dollar markers. Kilby nodded his head, indicating that the man should give them to Stuart. He did, and Stuart's hands were both full, one with free-drink tickets and the other with poker chips.

Kilby then turned his back on Stuart and lumbered into the rear office. The two guards returned to their old places by the couches, though they continued to stand, not seating themselves. Thibodeaux took Stuart by an elbow and escorted him to the exit, explaining unnecessarily, "Those chips are good at any table in the house. Drink passes can be redeemed at the tables or at the bar. Enjoy."

It'd all turned out as Elliot told him it would when Stuart detailed his plan to his friend while they both stood along the home stretch at Santa Anita with the rest of the railbirds who were admitted free to observe the morning workout of the horses running in the afternoon races.

"A woman gets coffee that's scaldin' hot served to her at McDonald's, she burns her lip or somethin', and a jury awards her, like, a hundred grand," Stuart reasoned. "Or some guy finds a cockroach in his Whopper at Burger King and he gets paid off like he won the lottery. So there I am, gettin' cussed out by a busboy. I mean, that's not even an accident, that's one of their employees goin' outta his way to treat me like dirt. So I figure I go to 'em and ask for five grand, 'cause they gotta realize I could get a lot more if this ever went to a jury, ya know what I'm sayin'?"

Elliot only shook his head slowly and said, "Not a good idea, Stu."

Nevertheless, Stuart felt obligated to give it a try. He respected Elliot for his knowledge of the recondite mathematics of probability, but he considered Elliot too caught up in abstruse matters of the mind to have any real grasp of how things actually worked at the level of everyday give-and-take. Yet Elliot's analysis of the situation proved to be prophetic after all.

Stuart was disappointed, but not chagrined. He'd given it his best shot. He'd failed, but he'd gone down swinging; he could feel pride in the fact that he'd stood up at the plate and done his best. That was something, at least.

He shuffled out of the CLUB MANAGEMENT office and took a few steps. He heard the men behind him speaking. Kilby's plangent baritone called across the room, "What a jamoke!" Thibodeaux's reedy tenor was easy to identify, and he spoke next, saying, "Where do they come from?" Kilby answered, "Good question. But I got a better one: why don't they go *back* there?"

The sycophants of the court laughed, then Kilby said, "Trey, I want ya to get up to the People's Republic of Santa Cruz. Check and see if there's a flight up there. If not, drive. Flower's parents live in that hippy-dippy insane asylum. Get up there and talk to 'em. See if they heard anything from their kid recently."

As soon as he heard the name Flower mentioned, Stuart halted. He spun around on his heel and eavesdropped in earnest.

"First one guy takes off with my money. Then I send that fuckin' Flower to Mex-spic-o to find *him*, and *he* takes off with it, too! I wish I'd never left Chicago. Everybody I ever trusted out here in California's ripped me off. I'm startin' to think—"

Stuart interrupted Kilby's diatribe when he returned to the lounge, crossed the room, and stood behind the two guards who now had their backs to him. They'd taken up positions at the passthrough to listen as Kilby issued orders. Thibodeaux was in the inner office with Kilby, puffing on a cigar and sending billows of smoke out. When Stuart got as far as he could without bumping into the guards, he could see Kilby's ugly, angry face addressing his henchmen. He looked even uglier, and even angrier, when he noticed Stuart.

"What?" he barked.

"I'm really sorry about disturbin' ya in the middle of your discussion, but I couldn't help overhearin'—did ya say ya were lookin' for a guy named Flower?"

CHAPTER 6

After lunch, Morinda was returned to her solitary cell where she lay down on the lower bunk, placing her arm across her eyes. She was alone for less than an hour before a matron came for her. This matron kept her black hair cut mannishly short, and she wore even less makeup than the social worker who'd interrogated Morinda that morning. She was forty pounds overweight, most of the excess concentrated in her shoulders and upper arms. She lumbered like a bear when she walked. Her breasts showed virtually no horizontal thrust outward from her body; they had little contour, but sagged with no definition apart from the form of the woman's upper body. She carried a ring holding a mass of jingling keys on a metal clip that swung from a belt loop on her uniform pants.

She was the subject of much talk by the other girls in the shelter, though Morinda'd never had any direct dealings with her. During the time she'd been housed in the dormitory, a black girl braided Morinda's hair and fixed the long tresses with bobby pins, and while she worked she talked about this matron, calling her "a bull-dagger bitch" and "a diesel dyke." Morinda's knowledge of English slang was somewhat limited, and she'd never heard these terms before, but she knew from the reactions of the others in the dorm who heartily agreed with the black girl's judgment that this particular matron was cordially despised by the other inmates of the detention facility.

When she came to get Morinda, she called from the doorway, "Let's go, girly. Up and at 'em," in a husky voice.

Morinda silently rose and followed the matron out of the cell and along the corridor. They stopped at the elevator, and the matron pushed the button to go down. As they waited, the matron said, "Won't tell 'em who your parents are or where they live, huh?"

Morinda didn't answer. When the elevator arrived, she stepped in, and the matron clumped aboard after her. The doors slid shut.

The matron grabbed Morinda's ear lobe between her thumb and forefinger and jerked her head toward her chest. It was done without warning, and the pain was agonizing. Morinda ground her teeth together to keep from crying out.

"When I ask ya a question, I expect an answer, girly," the matron said in the same gruff voice. "Ya understand that?"

She gave an extra twist to Morinda's ear.

"Yes!" Morinda yelped. "Yes! I understand!"

"Good."

The matron released the ear and allowed Morinda to rub it while she pressed the button on the wall panel marked B for the basement in which the underground parking lot was located. When she'd done so, she pointed a meaty finger at Morinda and said, "Ya can pull that silent treatment B.S. on those wuss social workers, but it don't cut no ice with me. I've worked with enough of you surly, sullen, spoiled teenage brats. I've got a zero tolerance level for crap—I don't take any, so don't try to give me any. And if ya want sympathy, I can tell ya where to find it—it's in the dictionary between 'shit' and 'syphilis.' I'm supposed to take ya to the hospital for some more X-rays, so on the way there and back let's pretend that you're a kid and I'm an adult. If ya can remember that, we won't have any more trouble like what just occurred."

Tears welled up in the corners of Morinda's eyes, more from resentment and frustration than from the physical pain. Her face was flushed red from the humiliation. The matron must've been satisfied with the demonstration of her power over her charge the ear wringing provided because after that she limited her interactions with Morinda to barking directions and prodding her with a thumb in the small of her back to get Morinda to go where she wanted her to. Once they arrived at the hospital, they used the elevator to climb to the sixth floor where the X-ray Unit was located.

The X-ray technician was male and young, barely more than twenty. He tried to put Morinda at ease. "We'd like to take another series of X-rays because there's a small—well, we're not quite sure what it is, but there's a spot of some kind on your right lung that showed up in that last set of pictures we took of you. We wanna make sure it isn't anything to worry about."

Morinda'd felt some anxiety about the doctors requesting more X-rays to supplement the original set they'd taken, worrying that they might've found something wrong with her after all, but she relaxed when she heard the explanation. The strange spot on her lung—she'd been through this before. The last two times her father took her to have physical examinations, the doctors asked for a second set of X-rays because of the strange mark there—it could be tuberculosis, they said, or cancer, or a tumor. But each time they took duplicate X-rays, they later reported it was nothing to be concerned about after all, only a shadow, nothing malignant. This'd be but another chapter in the continuing saga of her mysterious spot.

The technician sent Morinda behind a curtain to remove her blouse and bra and slip on a hospital gown. When she'd changed, she stepped out from behind the curtain. The technician wore a thick, padded apron hung over his shoulders; it fell to below his groin. He took Morinda by the elbow to move her in place in front of the X-ray machine.

"Uh-oh," he said as his hand touched her hair. "Ya have bobby pins in here?"

She lifted her hand and ran her fingers over her locks. "There's a lot of them," she admitted.

"Yeah," the technician said. "Not a good idea having those things in the way of the rays. Could ya take 'em out? Or—wait a minute, let's do this.

Could ya, ya know, lift your hair up and keep it up, out of the way? Try that."

Morinda picked her tresses up and held them above her head. "Like this?" she asked.

"Hmm. Yeah, that'd work, but I dunno if it's gonna give us the same profile shot we had the last time if you've got your arms up like that. It might lift the lungs too high. Hey, I know! Let me get ya a towel, and ya can wrap your hair up, maybe. Like my sister does when she gets outta the shower."

He scurried from the room. He was back in a few seconds with a white towel in his hands. He gave it to her and she swathed her head in it like a turban.

"Good. Perfect," the technician said. "Just step in front of the plate here, and we'll take the first shot face forward. Press yourself against the plate. That's right. Okay. Hold it, don't move."

A thick cord ran from behind the massive piece of equipment to a control box in the technician's hand. He took the box with him and stepped behind a lead screen with a narrow slit of opaque black glass set into it. Morinda heard a buzz like that of the doors at the detention facility; the technician popped out from behind the screen and had her turn to the side and lift her arm so he could take some profile shots as well.

"All done," the technician told her. "I'll take these over for processin', and then we'll get 'em to the doctor, and the doc'll let ya know what he's found out. Ya can change over there behind the curtain. Just leave the gown on the hook."

The technician left. Morinda was about to do as the technician said, go behind the curtain and put her clothes on, but then she realized—at no time had her matron escort ever been in the room with them. She couldn't recall seeing the matron since they'd arrived at the nurses' station of the X-ray Unit. Curious, Morinda went to the doorway and inched her head out to peer down the corridor. The matron was there, leaning over the counter with both of her fleshy forearms resting on it and talking animatedly to a pair of nurses in starched white uniforms.

Reflexively, Morinda snatched her head back inside as soon as she glimpsed the matron's burly figure. The matron hadn't so much as glanced at her when she stuck her head out, so she tried it again. She thrust her head far enough beyond the door jamb to be able to spot the matron, then she put it out even farther, so that her shoulders and then her torso were well into the hall.

The matron gave no sign she noticed Morinda.

Morinda stepped into the corridor. She kept her face toward the matron. The matron still didn't look at her.

Morinda spun on her heel and started the other way.

She expected at any moment to hear the foghorn bellow of the matron commanding her to halt. But she made it to the end of the corridor where it abutted another passage running the other way, and she vanished around the corner.

Her heart raced and her pulse pounded by the time she reached an elevator. She pushed the button to go down, and held her breath while she waited. The doors slid open, and no one'd yet tried to stop her. There were people in surgical scrubs and nurse's uniforms on the elevator; none gave her a second glance. The number 1 on the control panel was lit up—someone'd already pressed the button for the ground floor.

The elevator cage stopped on the second floor. No one got off, but two more people who looked as though they'd been to visit a patient got on. Then the elevator dropped to the first floor. Those inside struggled to exit at the same time a crowd tried to push themselves on.

Morinda found herself in another corridor. At one end of the hall she saw a large, well-lit open space with people dressed in ordinary streetclothes rather than green surgical scrubs and starched white nursing uniforms passing to and fro. One woman came out of a glassed-in partition from the right carrying a bundle of brightly colored flowers, and Morinda guessed she'd just left the gift shop after purchasing a bouquet. She remembered the gift shop was in the foyer of the hospital, off to the side just as one entered. She walked toward it.

Patients stood in the doorways of their rooms, dressed in hospital gowns the same as the one Morinda wore, though most of them lacked pants. One or two shuffled past her going in the opposite direction, not saying a word or paying any special attention to her as they went by, and this made her more confident.

She left the hall and entered the hospital lobby: on one side was the gift shop, to the other was the admitting desk. A pair of sliding glass doors that opened and closed automatically by photoelectric eye, an inner and an outer barrier set eight feet apart forming a vestibule, led to a long cement causeway beyond the confines of the medical center that ran all the way to the sidewalk paralleling the street. A uniformed security guard stood five feet outside the exit, one foot propped up on a metal bike rack while he smoked a cigarette and chatted with a female nurse who was also smoking. Morinda watched the guard closely as she neared the exit, but he remained intent on his conversation.

Morinda paused for a moment, glanced behind her to see if anyone at the admitting desk seemed disturbed by someone about to leave who was dressed in a gown that was clearly hospital issue. No one gave her a second look. She turned and moved again toward the exit. She stepped into the photoelectric beam that triggered the inner door to slide open.

Over the public address system came the woman's voice Morinda'd been hearing since she arrived at the hospital, and which she'd previously ignored completely. This time the voice said, "Mr. Strong, to the lobby. Mr. Strong, to the lobby." The fact that the announcement mentioned the lobby made Morinda wary. She threw another glance over her shoulder at the admissions desk: the women who worked there suddenly grew animated, and they looked anxiously around as if seeking the source of some unspecified trouble.

Outside, the security guard dropped his foot to the ground, turned away from the nurse he'd been talking to, and removed a flip phone from his shirt pocket. He put the phone to his head and spoke a few words. Then he stared quizzically through the glass of the outer door, his eyes pointed straight at her, it seemed to Morinda. He started moving, heading purposefully in her direction.

Morinda changed course, veering to the left, heading out of the foyer and into the corridor that began just past the admitting desk. A sign on the wall told her she was going toward Pediatrics, Ophthalmology, and the Prosthetics Laboratory. She deliberately slowed her pace, forcing herself to walk at a normal gait, and tried not to show her panic. When she got to a point where the hallway joined another, she turned, stopped, and peered back around the corner: the security guard'd stationed himself on the inside of the sliding doors and was scrutinizing the faces of all those who exited.

She continued down the corridor that branched to the left, then made another turn as soon as she reached a T-intersection. She went by an unattended cart with stacks of medical supplies including tongue depressors, alcohol wipes, and bandages still wrapped in their sterile packaging piled on it. The idea of disguise occurred to her, and she quickly grabbed a large bandage and took it with her. As soon as she reached an open door, she came to a halt. It led to a semiprivate room with two beds separated by a portable screen; a wide wooden door at the back was marked RESTROOM. Only one of the beds was occupied: an elderly woman had the television mounted on the wall turned on, but she wasn't watching it; she seemed to be asleep. Morinda went in and, without acknowledging the existence of the patient, crossed between the foot of the bed and the TV to get to the restroom. She went straight to the mirror over the sink.

When she saw her reflection, she hardly recognized herself. She'd forgotten about having put her hair up in the towel when she was in X-rays. With her hair covered and her head wrapped like a swami, she looked totally different.

She ripped the package open and took the bandage out. It was a three-inch-by-six-inch pad of gauze that came with adhesive already attached. She hastily stuck it on her face, covering her jaw, cheek, one eye, part of her forehead, and a side of her nose. She cocked her head from side to side, using her unblocked eye to check her appearance. Satisfied, she left the restroom, walked boldly past the patient in her bed, and went into the corridor again.

There was an empty wheelchair sitting beneath a schematic diagram of the hospital's layout on the wall. She stopped to examine the map, trying to decide where she'd gotten herself and how she could find another exit from the building. Unfortunately, the map had no YOU ARE HERE indicator. After some searching, she figured out approximately where she was, and she spotted the location of the Emergency Room, which was also on the ground floor. She put the sole of her shoe on one of the footrests of the wheelchair as she pored over the diagram, and when she leaned forward to read the names of the other units in the immediate vicinity of the ER, the wheelchair skidded away from her and she fell on her hands and knees on the linoleum tiles. She used the wall for support to pull herself up. The wheelchair crashed into someone behind her, and Morinda, red-faced with embarrassment, began to apologize profusely.

The person who'd been struck by the runaway wheelchair was a girl not much older than Morinda dressed in a red-and-white striped pinafore with a bib that covered a white dress. The girl smiled broadly as she pushed the wheelchair back to Morinda.

"Don't apologize, that's all right," the candy-striper said in a thick Southern accent. "These contraptions take some gettin' used to before ya get the hang of 'em. Where were ya trying to get to? Climb in, and I'll take ya wherever ya want."

Morinda started to protest that she didn't need any assistance, but then thought better of it. "Thanks," she said as she sank into the wheelchair. "I'm tryin' to get to the Burn Clinic," Morinda said, having seen that the Burn Clinic was right next to the Emergency Room.

"Have ya there in a jiffy," the candy-striper said. Her voice was so cheery that she almost chirped. "Ya just sit back and enjoy the ride. When I first saw ya with your hair all gone like that, I thought ya must be in chemo.

But I guess ya lost it in the fire. How did ya come to get burned like that, anyway?"

"We don't have to go through the lobby, do we?" Morinda said demurely as they approached the place where the corridor joined with the passage back to the entrance where the security guard waited. "I don't like all those people—how they stare at me."

"Oh, I'm sorry! I shouldn't've mentioned it. Me and my size sixteen triple-E mouth! No, hon, we don't hafta go that way. I'll just take ya around the other way. I am so sorry! Forget I said anything to make ya feel bad, will ya please?"

"Oh, no. I don't don't mind *you* asking about it. You're very nice to help me like this. So I know you don't mean any harm. No, really, I don't mind talking to you about it. You see, what happened was, I was with my uncle, and he was filling the gas tank of a lawnmower from this big can, and I was standing nearby watching. But he was too close to the pilot light of this water heater. It was in this shed, and he didn't know it was there, and the gasoline fumes caught fire and exploded."

The candy-striper bent to catch a glimpse of Morinda's face, and said, "And you're so pretty! Will they be able to do anything about your face?"

"Oh, sure! They say there's a fifty-fifty chance. And if you add fifty and fifty, that makes a hundred, and you can't do any better than that."

"That's right, hon," the candy-striper said. "That's the way to look at it. You'll do fine."

"They've been sending me to counseling, and they say that even if they can't fix my face, there's still hope for me. Faceless people have an organization, and there are many jobs that faceless people can go into: radio announcer, telemarketing, employment on the Internet. All sorts of things."

"You're so brave!" the candy-striper said with breathless admiration.

"Oh, you don't have to be brave to stand up to a lawnmower!" Morinda said. "It was only a little one, the kind you push in front of you. Now, if it'd been a big riding lawnmower, *that* would've taken courage!"

The Burn Clinic had a small waiting area with a few chairs scattered around its walls. No one was at the reception desk when they arrived. The candy-striper said, "Will ya be okay here by yourself? Ya want me to get ya anything before I go?"

"No, thanks. I appreciate you helping me get here."

The candy-striper maneuvered Morinda's wheelchair next to the wall, then came around to the front. She bent down with her arms open to give Morinda a hug. This was the sort of unwanted physical contact that Morinda normally would've repulsed, but the candy-striper'd been nice to her, and Morinda felt she owed the girl something for that, and for having listened to her lies so credulously, so Morinda hugged her in return.

"Good luck, hon," the candy-striper murmured before she left.

Morinda waited for the candy-striper to disappear around the corner before she pushed herself out of the wheelchair and scurried out of the Burn Clinic. The ER was only a little way farther along the hall. She knew it as soon as she reached it: a gurney was rushed past her by two paramedics who were joined by several ER staffers dressed in scrubs who shouted at each other as they hurriedly kept pace with the supine patient. Morinda scooted out of their way to let them get by; they rammed through swinging doors at the end of the corridor and out of her sight. Other patients lying on gurneys, moaning in pain and rolling their eyes to the ceiling as they waited to be attended to, crowded the narrow hallway. Morinda decided to go the same way the paramedics'd come from, and she soon came to a set of swinging doors that had AMBULANCE ENTRANCE ONLY! painted above them in large red letters.

No one attempted to stop her as she shoved through them. She found herself outside the hospital in a cavernous carport where dozens of emergency vehicles with red-and-white light bars were parked in total disarray. She walked up the slope of a driveway that took her out to the street. Once she reached the sidewalk, she ran.

The main entrance of the medical center faced a major boulevard, but the ER in the rear of the building was near a residential neighborhood that consisted of lower-middle-class homes set on quiet tree-lined streets. Not knowing how extensive the search for her might be once it was realized she'd escaped, she thought it best to stay off the main traffic arteries until nightfall. It was only mid-afternoon when Morinda made it to freedom, so she still had several hours before she dared show herself on a large street. She headed north, without a clue as to where she was going.

She walked past one house where a man in his mid-twenties wearing a ribbed white tank-top undershirt was washing his car in the driveway; he studied Morinda with a long curious look as she went by while a stream of water gushed out of his garden hose on to the lawn. Morinda didn't turn her head to look back at him, but she came to the conclusion that the disguise that'd worked so well for her in the medical center was drawing stares outside the hospital. When she was out of sight of the man with the hose, she began to peel the bandage off her face. Then, reminded by a breeze blowing from the south that the gown she wore left bare an open strip of flesh down her back, she took the towel from her head and shook her hair out, running her fingers through the ends to untangle the worst knots in it before draping the towel lengthwise over her shoulders, flinging her hair over it, and letting it hang behind her like a cape.

She walked for a dozen blocks. She came to a four-way stop and off to her left spotted a small strip mall a few blocks away. She turned her steps in that direction.

Her initial exhilaration and euphoria at having successfully eluded her pursuers faded, and she began to think about more practical matters; specifically she was worried about where she was going to sleep and what she was going to eat. The money she'd been carrying prior to her detention'd been taken by the authorities at the facility "for safekeeping," as they told her. They couldn't legally confiscate her property, but they wouldn't allow any of the detainees to keep more than ten dollars on them at any given time since it was assumed it'd lead to thefts and conflicts, or be used for gambling and contraband. So she'd had to go to the bursar whenever she wanted money to spend in the candy and soda machines or at the commissary, and ask for some more of her money to be issued. Fortunately, she'd gotten a fresh infusion of cash the day before, and she still had some of that left. She turned her pockets inside out, and counted the bills and change she found. It came to seven dollars and seventy-six cents. She'd left more than six hundred and fifty dollars behind when she fled, though she had no intention of returning to claim it. Of course, she had much more than that buried in her cache under the sand at the beach, but she dared not dig it up until after dark. And even after she had the suitcase that contained the money she'd taken from Flower, she'd be in the same position she'd been in when she first arrived in Los Angeles: no respectable motel was likely to rent a room to a fourteen-year-old without an adult accompanying her.

She turned the problem over in her mind as she walked until she arrived at the shopping center. By the time she reached a pay phone, she'd made her decision. She flipped through the Yellow Pages to find the number she wanted, then fumbled coins out and dropped two quarters in the slot.

"Hudspeth Investigations," Amber's voice cooed.

"This is Morinda Tavia. I'd like to speak to to Mr. Hudspeth, please, if he's in."

"Oh, hi! I don't think Dennis's here, but Stuart's holdin' down the fort. Ya wanna talk to him?"

"Yes."

"Hold on, let me buzz him and I'll put ya through. Just a sec."

She waited for a full minute, listening to a Muzak version of the Rolling Stone's "Street-fighting Man," then Stuart's voice came on the line.

"Morinda!"

"Yes, it's me."

"Where've ya been? We've been hopin' you'd come in or call or let us know how we could get hold of ya. We didn't have an address or a phone number for ya, ya know, and we've got some information I think you'll wanna hear."

"About my mother?"

"Yes! We found her!"

"This is true?"

"Absolutely! We found her! I spoke to her, told her about you, and she's real anxious to talk to ya. She's here in Los Angeles. She wants to meet ya. Is that okay with you?"

"Yes! Oh, yes!"

"Listen," Stuart said, his voice taking on a more somber tone. "Listen—she wants to meet ya, but there's a problem."

"What sort of problem?"

"Well, like I said, she's here in L.A. That is, she's in L.A. right now. But she may not be able to stay here very much longer. She may hafta leave."

"Where is she going? I can go anywhere. I have nothing to keep me here."

"It's not that she wouldn't want ya to go with her, but she's—well, she's in some trouble. So she might not be able to take ya along when she goes, is the thing. And if she can't square this trouble she's in, she may hafta disappear in a big hurry. She may hafta skip town, is what I'm sayin'. She may hafta get gone so fast that—well, she may not be able to see ya at all, is what it comes down to."

"What kind of trouble is she in?"

"She owes some people—some very bad people—a lot of money. I guess she had to borrow money for something important, and she couldn't get it from a regular financial institution, so she had to get it from some loan sharks. And she couldn't pay 'em on time, so now they're lookin' for her. And if they find her, they're gonna hurt her."

"How much—how much money does she need?"

"I'm not certain," Stuart said. "A lot."

"I have money. I can give it to her."

"That's a real nice offer, Morinda. I'm sure she'd appreciate it. But we're not talkin' about the kind of money you might be able to come up with. It's not the kind of money ya might've saved from baby-sittin'."

"No. I have a lot of money."

"How much are ya talkin' about?"

"Thousands. Many thousands."

"Thousands of what?"

"Dollars."

"Ya—you're not kiddin', are ya?"

"No. It's the truth. I have it. I'll give it to her."

"Are ya talkin' about the money you'll inherit in Mexico? That's not gonna help. That'll be tied up in court for years, probably."

"No! I have money here in Los Angeles, right now."

"You're not walkin' around with that kind of cash on ya, are ya?"

"No. But I can get it. I can get it tonight. After dark."

"So ya don't have it right this minute?"

"No."

"But ya can get it, ya say? Ya can get it tonight?"

"Yes."

"You'd be willing to do that? To get the money and bring it to your mother? Give the money to her so she can get out of this trouble she's in?"

"Of course. What else would I do? She's my mother!"

"Boy, this's gonna be a big load off her mind, I tell ya! She's been worried sick—mostly 'cause she wanted to find you, and she thought that if she had to vanish, she might never see ya again. This'll make her so happy! Ya can't imagine how happy this is gonna make her!"

Stuart went on, "My dad's outta the office right now, and I'm kinda waitin' on your mom to phone in. She's gonna call sometime this afternoon to let us know what she's plannin' on doin', and when she does I'm gonna tell her what ya told me. I'm sure she'll wanna get together with ya as soon as possible, now that she won't have that other thing hangin' over her head. Ya say ya can't get the money before dark?"

"No. It'll have to be tonight before I can get it. But I can meet her and give it to her—when? When can I meet her?"

"I think I can probably set it up for tonight, if that's all right with you."

"Yes! Oh, yes! Tonight! How soon?"

"That depends on you. How soon can ya get the money?"

Morinda did a quick calculation: darkness fell fairly early in mid-November, and she could take a bus across town to the beach where she'd stashed the money so that the sun'd be down by the time she got there. But then she'd have to take a cab to wherever the meeting was supposed to take place, and driving across Los Angeles could take some time.

"Where? Will we meet in your office?"

"Not a good idea," Stuart said. "Let me give ya an address. It's kind of close to downtown. Do ya have something to write with?"

"I can remember it. Go ahead."

Stuart told it to her twice, and she repeated it back to him for confirmation.

"That's it. Could ya get the money and be there by, say, ten o'clock?"

"Yes. I'll be there."

"Oh, and ya probably shouldn't phone here again. Your mom'll be tryin' to get through, and I don't wanna miss her call. Okay?"

Morinda laughed. "No! Don't miss her call! Tell her—tell her that I have the money for her! Tell her I've been looking forward to seeing her—again—very, very much and for a long, long time! And thank you! Thank you for finding her!"

CHAPTER 7

"What the hell's this?" Kilby said. He had his head tilted back as he looked around the vast empty space within the building.

"Wild, isn't it?" Stuart asked.

The four men'd gone only a few steps into the structure. Stuart, who guided the others, was pleased by Kilby's reaction. He acted like a five-year-old showing his older brother something extraordinary who's gratified to find his sibling's properly awed.

Thibodeaux's response was less satisfying. Although Thibodeaux allowed his jaw to drop and he swept his eyes around the building's interior much as Kilby did, Stuart knew he was doing nothing more than aping his boss's demeanor; if Kilby'd appeared jaded, acting as though he'd seen the same sight a thousand times before, Thibodeaux would've followed suit.

The third man with them didn't seem unimpressed; he simply expressed no interest—in anything. He was as old as Kilby, but he was shorter than average height, and his shoulders were hunched and the flesh on his neck and throat'd wrinkled with age so that with his sharply beaked nose he resembled a snapping turtle sticking its head tentatively out of its shell, or perhaps withdrawing it after having taken a cursory examination of his surroundings. He languidly moved his head about in slow motion, the corners of his mouth turned down in a permanent expression of disdain.

"There's a bunch of these things around downtown L.A.," Stuart burbled. "Nobody knows how many of 'em there are."

"Man!" Kilby said. "From the outside, it looks like an ordinary buildin'. Like a real office buildin', or something. Ya could drive right past the place and never know it wasn't filled with people doin' business in here."

"Yeah, that's the whole idea. They got these façades put up so they blend in with the rest of the scenery. Anybody goin' by sees just another buildin' like every other one on the block. But it's only a front. There's nothing inside but these."

Stuart waved his hand at the oilfield pump jacks that moved up and down like giant bloodsucking insects. There were several of them in a row on the level on which the three men were standing, and more on a terraced hillside fifteen feet above their heads at the far end of the cavernous structure. The building itself was ten stories high, sufficient to cover the single towering oil rig: there was nothing else within the walls but the constantly ascending and descending grasshopper pumps and the rotary rig drill surrounded by the skeletal framework of the derrick.

"Ya know," Kilby said, "I've lived in this fuckin' city for thirty-five years, and I never knew there was anything like this."

Stuart beamed with pride.

"Ya know about these things, Gene?" Kilby asked the man with the tortoise head.

Gene Templeton, the owner of the bookmaking operation in which Stuart'd invested large sums of money he'd seldom been able to pay, lethargically swung his whole head around to face Kilby, as though his eyes were fixed and incapable of moving independently. His down-turned mouth remained set in its wonted scowl.

"It's like everything else in this sewer of a city," he said. "All fake. Nothings what it looks like. It's all silicone and plastic and capped teeth. It's all bullshit. When's the last time ya felt real tits on a woman?"

317

Kilby barked a laugh and said, "When's the last time ya felt a woman's tits *period*, ya old fart? The last time you got laid, they hadn't even invented silicone yet."

"Aah," the old man snapped and slowly craned his head away so his eyes were no longer aimed at Kilby.

"My dad's got a security business," Stuart explained. "It's a sideline for his detective work. He's got the contract on this place. That's how I know about it. That's how I got us in here—I gave the guards the night off, reassigned 'em elsewhere. So we could use this place for the meetin'."

"When's this money supposed to show up?" Templeton said. "I ain't got the whole night to take the scenic tour of L.A.'s finest shitholes. I mean, the only reason I'm here at all's Jack said you'd set something up so ya could pay off what ya owe. I'm only here 'cause Jack okayed it."

"Hey! Don't make it sound like I gave this the Good Housekeepin' Seal of Approval, or something, Gene!" Kilby interjected. "I never said I give any of this my endorsement. But when the guy came to me and told me he could get me my money back, I gave him the same deal as anybody else—he's in for half of whatever he collects. From what I heard, his share's gonna be plenty, enough to get him out of your pockets for what he's lost, so I told him you'd have to be let in on this arrangement, too. So there's no question later about me and him bein' in cahoots, ya get my drift? I wanna be up front with ya about him comin' in to this lump sum all of a sudden, Gene, so ya don't think I'm part of some scheme to snake ya out of what he owes ya. On the other hand, if he's just strokin' me and can't deliver as promised—" Kilby considered Stuart with a glare "—then the unfortunate accident he's gonna have involving his kneecaps may keep him from ever bein' able to repay any of his debts."

"Won't matter much," Templeton said sourly. "He don't pay off, he's gonna end up the same way. Whether you do it or I do it, it's the same difference."

"How can ya be sure she's even got the money Lott took ya off for, Jack?" Thibodeaux asked. "That happened a lotta years ago. Lott probably spent what he stole a long time ago. He had to. So how do ya know she's got what he took?"

"Flower said on the phone he was bringin' back a shitload of money. He said he had some girl interpreting for him down in Mexico. I figured she was, ya know, a woman—what ya call a girl, not some kid. But it turns out this's the one he was with. And she's gotta have the cash Flower was carryin', or where else did it go?"

"So why's she supposed to be showin' up here tonight?" Thibodeaux said. He puffed on his cigar.

"Her mother disappeared when she was little," Stuart said. "She thought Flower was a private detective her mom'd hired to find her. Then it turned out Flower wasn't a detective after all. That's why she hired me and my dad when she got to L.A. To locate her mother. So I told her we'd found her mother, but her mom needs a lotta money to pay off a loanshark. She's bringin' the cash with her tonight 'cause she thinks her mom's gonna be here."

"That's low," Kilby said. "Tellin' a kid she's finally gonna meet her mom, then ya stiff her, and it's all to pay off your own markers. You're a degenerate, ya know that?" To Templeton, Kilby said, "Hey, Gene, did ya ever do anything that low?"

Templeton's face with its permanently imposed glower was impossible to read on its own terms alone; it made him seem as if he disapproved of everything. In answer to Kilby's question, he said, "I never let myself get into a position where I had to."

Kilby cast an appraising eye upon Stuart and said, "Me neither."

"So where is she?" Thibodeaux said. "She wants to help her mom out so bad, why ain't she here already?"

"Ya sound nervous about something, Al," Kilby said. "Relax. You're not out anything if she don't show. It's no skin off your ass."

319

"She'll be here," Stuart assured the others. "She said she had to wait until after dark to get it, and then she'd be comin' straight here. It's early yet, I told her ten o'clock. She's got fifteen, twenty minutes."

Stuart's voice was strained, revealing his own anxiety to anyone who cared to listen closely.

"I'm not worried," Templeton said. "It's not my kneecaps."

"It won't be mine, either," Stuart insisted. "She'll be here. And she'll have the money with her. And everybody's gonna get paid. Everything's gonna be fine. Just fine."

It was not obvious who he was trying to convince by his show of certitude, the others or himself.

An explosion erupted, echoed, then reechoed through the vast space of the building's interior, filling it and then rebounding on itself again and again so that it was impossible to tell from where it originated. The four men whipped their heads about as soon as the crash sounded, searching for its source, and only after several seconds did they all four turn to face the tiny, distant figure of Morinda standing on the high earth terrace next to the derrick behind a two-foot-high concrete overflow trough filled with crude oil. She held a pistol in both her hands, a faint wisp of smoke still issuing from its muzzle. A suitcase rested on the ground beside her. She said nothing even after she had the undivided attention of the men on the lower level. They kept their eyes fixed on her as though they expected to hear her begin a sermon at any moment.

No one spoke until Stuart finally called up to her, "Morinda! Hi! How long—how long've ya been here?"

Morinda didn't immediately reply. She studied Stuart from her place above him for a moment, and when she did break her silence, it wasn't to answer his question, but to pose one of her own.

"Where's my mother?" Morinda demanded. She had to shout in order to be heard over the throbbing diesel engines and plaintive moans of the pump jacks. "You said she'd be here!"

"There's been—there's been a slight problem! She got held up! These guys—these guys I'm with, they got something to do with it! Listen, why don't ya come down here so we can talk?"

Morinda made no move whatsoever. She remained frozen in place, staying silent while holding Stuart in her steady, implacable gaze.

"Well, let me come up there, then! To talk! Okay? I'll come up and explain everything to ya! So you'll know what's happenin', all right?"

Morinda gave no reply. She continued to examine Stuart, her expression impenetrable.

Stuart turned to address the men on either side of him, lowering his voice to say, "I'll get this whole thing straightened out. I'm gonna go talk to her, okay?"

"It's your show," Kilby said. "It's your show—but it's my money. Don't forget that."

"I won't."

Templeton stuck his neck out of his collar an inch and hissed sibilantly in Stuart's direction, "Kneecaps-s-s."

Stuart nodded without looking at Templeton. Then he left the group and walked to the iron staircase that ran up the glacis of the terrace to the upper level. His shoes clanged against each of the thirteen metal runners. The rich, tangy petroleum odor grew thicker as he approached the open pool of crude oil by which Morinda waited.

When he was within a few feet of her, Stuart stopped and said, "How'd ya get in, anyway? Oh, yeah, I forgot I'd unlocked that rear door, too. What's with the gun?"

Morinda never took her eyes from Stuart's.

"Where's my mother?" she repeated.

"I, uh, I didn't bring her with me."

"That doesn't answer my question, Stuart. That doesn't tell me where she is."

"I know." Stuart ran his tongue over his lips. "Look, ya need to know who this is with me. The big guy—that's Jack Kilby. He runs one of the biggest sports books in California. That's a bookie operation, where people make bets on football games and basketball? Your dad—Ernest Tavia, Patrick Lott—he used to work for Kilby. He used to pick up the money from the different bookie joints around the state, and then he'd bring it here to L.A. to give to Jack. Except one day, he didn't. He didn't bring the money back. And he disappeared. That was twelve years ago. Ya with me so far? Twelve years ago he ran off with Jack Kilby's money."

"I don't believe my father stole money," Morinda said flatly.

"That's the thing—it doesn't matter if it's true or not, and it doesn't matter what you or I believe. It's what Jack Kilby believes that's important. And he believes your dad ripped him off. A few weeks ago, some friend of Jack's was passing through Baja on vacation, and he happened to see your dad in San Estaban. He mentioned it to Jack, and Jack sent some people down there to find out if it was really Patrick Lott, the thief—the guy Kilby thinks was a thief—who he's been lookin' for all these years. The ones he sent, that was Flower and his partner. They went to Mexico to locate your father, find out if he used to go by the name Patrick Lott, recover the money he took off with, and—"

Stuart licked his lips once more, this time glancing nervously over his shoulder toward Kilby. When he returned his attention to Morinda, he said, "That guy Flower called Kilby a couple of times from Mexico, so Kilby knows he was bringin' the money he got from your dad with him. He knows ya must've gotten the money from Flower somehow. He wants that money back. And he doesn't care much what he has to do to get it. Ya understand what I'm saying?

"That's why I thought it'd be best if I gave ya a chance to—to return the money to him instead of having him take it from ya, the way Flower got it from your dad. 'Cause he'll keep lookin' for it, and he'll keep lookin' for you, until he gets it back. He's gonna recover what he lost, no matter what. That's why I set up this meetin', so you two can work things out without ya havin' to worry about somebody like Flower comin' after ya. Ya see why I did it?"

Morinda coolly contemplated Stuart for a long time, during which she remained absolutely silent. Finally she said, "There are three of them. Why are there three of them?"

"The one guy, the one with the cigar, that's Al Thibodeaux. Your dad worked directly under him when he was with Kilby's operation. I don't know why he's here now, but he got real hot and bothered when he heard about you. He pushed and pushed until Jack told him he could tag along, mostly to get him to shut up, I think."

"What about the other one? The grandfather?"

"He's—he's not really part of the same agenda. Believe it or not, he's the one I'm the most scared of."

"Why?"

"He's here 'cause—well, 'cause *I* owe *him* a lot of money. Let me be completely honest, okay? Kilby told me if I could get ya to turn the money over to him, not only will that get *you* off the hook, but I'm supposed to get half of whatever I can recover for him. That's the same deal he had with Flower—whoever gets the money back, they get half. So I thought I could get at least the money I owe to Gene Templeton. To save myself." Stuart started to look ill. "Jesus, Morinda, he's got guys who break people's kneecaps! Ya know how much that hurts? Ya ever seen somebody try to walk after they had their kneecaps broken? Ya gotta go through years of therapy, and it doesn't always fix 'em even then." Stuart's voice became strident. "I hafta pay this guy off! I don't have any choice!"

Morinda's imperturbable, unyielding expression didn't change. She watched Stuart with the same pitilessness she'd maintained since she'd announced her presence with the gunshot. Finally, she spoke to ask, "How much do you owe him, Stuart?"

"Forty grand. Forty thousand dollars. I don't have it. My hand to God, I don't have it. He's gonna—"

Stuart's words ceased abruptly as he swallowed a sob. Tiny tears'd formed in the corners of his eyes. Without speaking, he appealed to Morinda. She didn't react in any perceptible way.

"Go back with them, Stuart," Morinda told him. "Go down there so I can talk to all of you at the same time. It'll be easier that way."

"Can ya help me? Please?"

"Go back down," she coldly replied. "I'll talk to all of you at once."

Stuart's shoulders slumped in dejection. He shook his head, not so much to indicate a negative but because he had nothing to turn his eyes toward that offered him any hope. He left her, slowly trudging to the metal stairs, then stepping from one riser to the other using the handrail to support himself. He made it only halfway down before Kilby's plangent baritone called out, bringing Stuart up short.

"So what's the word? We ready to negotiate, or what?"

Stuart stopped on the middle of the staircase, lifting his head to answer. But Morinda interjected before Stuart gathered enough courage to speak.

"You killed my father!" she called to Kilby. Even though it was difficult to convey nuance by means of a shout, it seemed to be a simple statement of fact rather than an accusation.

"Whoa! Wait a minute!" Kilby said. "I don't know what line of bullshit this guy's been feedin' ya! I never killed nobody! What's this about?"

"My father's name was Ernest Tavia! You knew him as Patrick Lott! You sent Flower to kill him!"

"No, no, no, that's not the way it was! You're dad, he took me off for a lot of dough! I wanted to get my dough back! Flower went to Mexico for that, nothing else! To get the money! The way I figure it, Flower went nuts when he got down there! Too much sun, or too much tequila, or something! He killed your dad, and then he planned on takin' off with my money himself! I never sent nobody to kill nobody, not your dad or anybody else! That's not my style!"

"Stuart says he owes you—you, not you—forty thousand dollars!" Morinda called out next, addressing Templeton. "That you're going to have him beaten up if he doesn't pay you!"

Templeton didn't deign to reply. He contracted his neck inside his collar and stared balefully from his hiding place with his reptilian eyes.

"You! The other one! You made a deal with Flower to pay him half the money he got from my dad! You made the same deal with Stuart! Is that right?"

"I'd pay the same to a collection agency—half of whatever they can get back for me! Yeah, Flower was gonna get half! Until he decided he'd rather take it all! Him—Stuart—he's in for half, for bringin' ya here tonight! That's the deal we cut!"

"But he hasn't delivered the money to you! Isn't that what you're paying half for, to have the money given to you?"

"That's right! Once the dough's in my hands, that's when we divvy it up! Only way of doin' business I know!"

"So if I give the money to you, half of it's mine? Is that the way it works?"

Kilby blinked his eyes, then he grinned appreciatively. "It's a standin' offer, kid! Whoever puts the money in my hands gets half! Flower, Stuart, you—I don't care who it is! The finder gets the finder's fee!"

Morinda lifted the revolver in her right hand, letting the men on the lower level see it clearly. She carried the suitcase in her other hand, taking it to the concrete trough. She set it on the angle of a corner so it balanced, then flipped the snaps to open the lid. She took out packets of bills and placed them on a metal plate covering the end of the trough closest to the onlookers. She doled the packets out in two separate piles, one on the right and the other on the left, with a wide space between them—she first placed a packet on one, then a packet on the other, and so on, until she'd emptied the suitcase. The bills having been divided equally in two, she lifted the suitcase up so the lid dropped and swung it around so Kilby could see it was now empty.

"There was a money belt, too!" Morinda called. "Flower was wearing that! But I already mixed that money in with the rest, so this's everything! You can see there's two piles here! One's yours, and one's mine! Okay?"

Kilby said, "Hey, kid! How stupid do ya think I am? I don't know how much ya got there! Could be anything! I'm not gonna buy a pig in a poke! I'll come up there, take a look at things, see what you've got! Don't get trigger-happy, now, I'm only gonna—"

"No! You don't come here until I'm gone! You take what I'm giving you! If it's not everything I said it is, then you can do what you were going to do anyway—come looking for me! To kill me! Like you killed my father!"

"I told ya, I never killed your dad! If ya keep talkin' like that, I'm gonna get real pissed! Now, I'm comin' up to check out the situation—"

Morinda let the suitcase fall from her hand and grabbed a bundle of bills. She held it over the trough of crude oil.

"The pile on this side? This one's yours! So this—this is part of *your* half!"

She dropped the bills into the black liquid in the trough. It plunked when it struck the surface, then vanished to the bottom beneath two feet of opaque crude.

"Jesus, kid!" Kilby shouted. "Ya got no respect for money, ya know that?"

"If you have any respect for *your* money, you'll do what I tell you to do!" Morinda answered.

"All right! All right!" Kilby said. He stepped backward two paces as a placating gesture. "How much is there, can ya tell me that?"

"I don't know! I never counted it! But you can see how many bundles there are! The bills are all hundreds!"

"What you've got there, is that everything Flower had with him?"

"Most of it! I had to use some to get here, and to live on!"

"Ya weren't staying at the Ritz, were ya?"

"No!"

"How much do ya figure ya spent?"

"A couple of thousand! About that!"

"Okay! Let's not worry about it, then! What's a few grand between friends?"

From the side where he stood on the metal steps, Stuart cried out, "Morinda! Is there anything ya can do—for me?"

"My mother—where is she, Stuart?"

"She's—she's with my dad! We found her! Like I told ya, we found her! Ya can meet her tomorrow! Okay? Okay? Can ya help me? Please?"

Morinda shouted to the group on the lower level, "He owes forty thousand! Is that how much it is?"

"Yeah, yeah," the old man below her said, not bothering to raise his voice.

"Ya old fart, tell it to *her*, not to me," Kilby said, then he shouted to Morinda, "Yeah, that's what it is! Forty grand!"

"I think we should pay it!" Morinda said. "The two of us! Half and half! Share and share alike! I'll put up twenty thousand, and you put up the rest!"

"What?" was as much of a protest as Kilby could articulate.

"You wouldn't have gotten any of this if Stuart hadn't brought us both here tonight! That's worth twenty thousand from you!"

"Him? He's nothing to me! You wanna pay his debts, knock yourself out! But not with my money, ya don't!"

Morinda picked up another packet of bills from the stack she'd earlier identified as Kilby's. She held her arm out straight and let the bundle fall into the trough of oil.

She looked down on Kilby with her features set impassively and called, "Your half keeps getting smaller!"

Kilby appealed to Thibodeaux and Templeton. "Do ya believe the balls on this kid?"

Morinda reached once again to Kilby's pile, and Kilby threw his hands up in the air and said, "I'm getting nickeled and dimed to death here, I swear to God!" To Morinda, he shouted, "All right, all right, already! I'll pay the other half of what he owes! Just—just stop throwin' my money away, okay!"

"You, the other one! Are you satisfied? If I leave twenty thousand here, will you take his word that he'll pay you the other half?"

Templeton surprised Kilby, Thibodeaux, and Stuart then. It was the first time any of them'd ever seen him smile. His lips withdrew from his yellow, broken teeth, and he croaked, barely loud enough to carry to where Morinda stood, "Sure, sure! Jack's good for it, no problem!" He shook his head in wonder. "Ya know, they say if ya live long enough, you'll see everything. But I never thought I'd ever live long enough to see the day somebody got the best of Jack Kilby in a business deal."

Kilby thrust his lower jaw forward an inch. "Yeah, you laugh, ya old fart! But I'd like to see how you come out if ya ever had to haggle with this kid!"

Kilby cocked his head to the side as he considered what he'd just said, then he turned to face Morinda again. She'd finished stuffing her own pile of bills back into the suitcase, leaving the twenty thousand dollars she'd promised to help settle Stuart's account. She was stripping off the rubber bands holding the bundles that were Kilby's.

"Hey!" Kilby called out. "Hey, kid!"

Morinda closed the latches of the suitcase before she stood and attended to what Kilby had to say.

"Ya wanna job, kid?"

Morinda didn't answer. Her face gave nothing away about what she was thinking.

"Uh, Jack," Thibodeaux said from the side. "What kind of job were ya thinkin' about givin' her, Jack?"

"I dunno. About any damned job she wants. She'd probably browbeat me into givin' it to her, anyway, no matter what it was."

"But, Jack—can ya really trust her? I mean, she's the kid of this guy who ripped ya off, remember? Ya couldn't believe anything she says."

"Christ, Al, relax, will ya! It's not like bein' a thief's hereditary or something. I'm startin' to wonder about you."

"I was just lookin' out for your interests, Jack," Thibodeaux said.

Kilby returned his attention to Morinda. He shouted, "I'm serious, kid! Ya ever need a job, ya look me up! I could find a place for ya—no trouble at all! Ya could be makin' six figures a year, easy! Ya ever need work, ya come to me!"

"Your money!" Morinda said, pointing to the stack remaining on the edge of the trough. "I've taken the bands off the bundles and I'm going to throw it down there to you! That should keep you busy picking the bills up long enough to let me get out of here without having to worry about you coming after me! And remember—I've still got this!"

She held the gun up one more time.

Kilby grimaced. "Nobody's gonna come after ya, kid! Ya don't hafta do that!"

"I probably don't have to!" Morinda said as she set her suitcase behind the stack of cash. "But I want to!"

With a sweep of the suitcase, she sent the loose bills flying. They slowly fluttered and drifted to the ground. Thibodeaux ran forward to grab them out of the air, though without much success; then he stooped to pick them up as they started to come to rest.

Kilby lifted his hands in the air in surrender and muttered in resignation, "Yeah, well, that's the way it goes—first your money, then your clothes."

Stuart still stood on the metal stairs. He called to Kilby, "Ya meant that, what ya said to her about a job? 'Cause I could sure use a job with ya!"

"You?" Kilby said disgustedly. "I wouldn't hire *you* to lead blind turkeys out to shit!"

CHAPTER 8

Morinda waited until after nine the next morning to make her phone call. She knew that no one'd be in the office until then. There was a large clock on the wall of the open-twenty-four-hours doughnut shop she'd spent the night in. As soon as the hands showed five minutes after the hour, she wearily picked up her suitcase and went to the pay phone on the corner at the end of the block. She flipped through the Yellow Pages to find the number, dropped two quarters in the slot, and pushed the buttons.

"Hudspeth Investigations," Amber chirruped when she answered.

"I'd like to speak to Dennis Hudspeth, please."

"May I tell him who's callin'?"

"This is Morinda Tavia."

"Hi, Morinda Tavia! Hold on a sec."

Hudspeth took the call as soon as it was transferred to him.

"Morinda," he said in a dispirited voice drained of life.

"Yes, hello."

"I heard about what happened last night. Stuart told me. He told me everything. At least, I hope it was everything."

Hudspeth paused. Morinda allowed the interlude to stretch out. Finally Hudspeth said, "I am so ashamed of what my son did. I am so sorry."

"Yes."

"Nothing like this'll ever happen again. I promise you, it will not happen again."

"Yes."

"Ya hafta believe me. My son—I don't know what to say. I'm sorry."

"About my mother—" Morinda cleared her throat, then continued. "About my mother. Stuart said last night—he said you'd found her. That she's with you."

There was a silence from Hudspeth's end of the line. After several seconds, he said, "Stuart told ya that?"

"He said he was going to bring her with him last night. That's why I went to the address he gave me. But she wasn't there. So I asked him where she was. And he said that she was with you. That I could meet her today."

"Oh, God! Morinda, I—I don't know what to tell ya. It's not possible for me to even imagine what was goin' on in Stuart's mind for him to say something like that."

"So that—that wasn't true."

"No. We haven't found your mother. We haven't been able to find any trace of her as yet."

She'd been fighting to keep her voice under control, and now for the first time during their conversation it broke into a quaver. "I thought maybe—I was hoping maybe—that part—that that part wasn't a lie."

"Oh, man!" Hudspeth's voice was hollow, as though it were too small to fill up the void he found himself speaking into. "I—I don't know what to say. Except—except that I'm gonna make this up to ya. I'm gonna do everything I can to do the right thing for ya, Morinda. I'm gonna keep lookin' for your mother. I'm not gonna give up. I'll do whatever I can to make up to you for what my son did. I'll keep lookin', and if she's out there, somewhere, I'll find her. Okay? And this isn't gonna cost ya another dime, I swear. I'll work for free, and I'll do anything I hafta do to find your mother."

Her voice cracked as she said, "It doesn't matter."

"What? I couldn't hear ya. We've got a bad connection."

She breathed in through her nose in a sniffle. She made an effort to pronounce her words clearly. "It doesn't matter."

"Don't—don't talk like that. Of course it matters. She's your mother. Ya wanna find where ya came from. And I'll keep lookin' for her."

In the thin, tremulous pitch her voice'd been reduced to, she said, "Where you come from—that's not so important. It's not as important as where you're going."

"Look, you're not thinkin' straight, Morinda. I'll find your mother for ya, or find out what happened to her. I'll keep lookin'. At no cost to you. No cost. I'll make it up to ya. I'll do it. I promise ya."

"It doesn't matter," she said. "It never mattered."

"Don't talk like that, okay? It *does* matter! Don't say it doesn't. Don't tell me it doesn't matter, 'cause I know better. Please, don't say that. Don't say that again."

"Okay," Morinda said, her throat so constricted that the words came out high-pitched and strained. "I won't."

She gently slipped the telephone receiver onto its hook.

She lifted her head, closed her eyes, and said, "None of this is me. I'm me. I'm right here. This is me."

When she'd finished the recitation, she bent her knees to pick up the suitcase. The pay phone began ringing. Leaning to one side with the weight of the bag, she walked away. The phone rang again and again. She walked faster, then faster still, until she was running to escape its sound.

The air brakes farted and squealed as the Greyhound bus moved ahead in line behind the other vehicles and finally drove across the bridge that spanned the tiny river between the United States city of San Diego and the Mexican city of Tijuana. The bus halted on Mexican soil and the passengers disembarked, lining up at the checkpoint to have Mexican immigration officials process their paperwork. Signs in both Spanish and English were prominently posted informing those entering the country that anyone staying in Mexico longer than seventy-two hours or traveling farther than twenty kilometers from the border required a Form FMT. Since the bus's final stop was at Cabo San Lucas, most of those on board needed the tourist cards, which were actually pink slips of paper.

Morinda waited her turn. When she got to the head of the line, she answered the questions the young immigration official with the head of coal-black hair asked her in English.

"You are an American citizen?"

"Yes."

"Do you have proof of citizenship and a picture ID?"

"Yes."

She presented the second set of forged documents she'd acquired on Alvarado Street in Los Angeles that verified she was Morinda Tavia, daughter of Ernest Tavia, born in Los Angeles, California, fourteen years before. She also passed across forged letters signed by both her parents granting her permission to enter Mexico to pursue her education there.

"You are planning to go to school in Mexico?"

"Yes." Morinda switched to Spanish to add, "There are several private schools I'm going to look at while I am here. And then I'll decide which one I will attend."

"There are many fine schools in Mexico." The young man behind the counter looked up at her. "Your Spanish—it's extremely good."

"Thank you."

"I can barely detect your accent. You speak Spanish almost like a native Mexican."

"Thank you. I've worked very hard at it."

He passed back the documents she'd given him to examine along with the pink slip of her tourist card. "This is only good for 180 days. If you want to stay longer than that, you'll have to cross over and get another one." He shrugged his shoulders, indicating this was a routine matter, then smiled and said, "Welcome to Mexico, *señorita*. Enjoy your stay. And good luck with your studies."

When she returned to the bus, she sat next to an old Mexican man with white hair who was napping with his head turned sideways toward the window. He wore black dress slacks and a white dress shirt with iridescent mother-of-pearl buttons he kept buttoned right up to the collar. He must already've taken care of his business with Immigration and Customs, Morinda thought, since he remained asleep until the bus was fully loaded and pulled onto the road. Then the old man jerked his head up and looked owlishly around.

The bus entered the terminal in east Tijuana. Morinda was interested to see how the place looked in the daylight from the vantage of a seat high up on a bus rather than the way she'd last seen it, at night, on foot, when she and Flower'd searched among the *talones* to find a way out of Mexico.

By the time the bus reached the Transpeninsular Highway, the old man'd introduced himself to Morinda. He did so very formally and with great dignity. Morinda was charmed by the old man's gallantry and formal manners, and found herself speaking to him quite easily of the feelings that'd been pent up inside her for the past few weeks, although she couldn't tell the stranger the entire truth about everything that'd taken place during that time. Nevertheless, it was much easier talking to this man she'd never met before and'd most likely never see again than it would've been trying to say the same things to someone she knew more intimately. When she told her traveling companion she was going to San Estaban to make the funeral arrangements for her father, the old man said, "That is very sad. I am very sorry to hear of his passing away. But he was very fortunate to've had such a beautiful and intelligent daughter. I am certain he was proud to've had you as the jewel of his life. He must've been a very good father to've had such a daughter."

"He was a very good father," Morinda said. "But I was a bad daughter."

"Is this true?" the old man said, his frost-white eyebrows arched in surprise.

"I argued with him the last time I saw him. I told him I hated him. And I ran away from him. In order to chase after a dream. A dream he told me was a lie. But I didn't believe him. I ran away, and he—he died while I was gone. So the last thing I ever said to him was that I hated him. Which was a lie. I didn't hate him. I loved him. I still love him. And then after I ran away, I found out this dream I had, I found that it was just a dream, nothing more. There was nothing there when I got there, nothing real, just like in a dream. So it was all for nothing. I did a terrible thing, and I hurt him, and now I can't tell him that I was wrong, and beg him to forgive me, because now he's—now he's dead."

Only when she paused to take a breath and found her breath nearly stopped, and she sniffled with the intake, did she realize that she was crying again. She reached up to brush away the tears that rolled down her cheeks.

The old man pursed his lips pensively, all the while looking straight ahead rather than at Morinda. When he spoke, he continued to stare at the back of the seat in front of him.

"I have had many children," he said in his stately way. "My first child was a daughter, and she was a great joy to me. When she was born, every day I was happy to be alive just so I could hold her in my arms. When she grew older, I would smile just to see her smile. I would laugh whenever I heard her laugh. When she was a little girl, every night she would wait for me to come home from work, and she would run to me and throw her arms around my legs and cry, 'Papa! Papa!' when I walked in the door, and I would pick her up and swing her around and then put her on my lap as soon as I sat down so she could tell me all the things that had happened to her that day. And when she started to school, we would sit at the kitchen table for hours every night working on her arithmetic and her reading. And she would always want me, her papa, to be the one to help her with her work, no one else. I was so proud that I was the one she loved so much.

"But after a few years at school, the work she did was beyond me. I could no longer help her with it. And, a few years later, she no longer brought her friends home for me to meet. And she was no longer in the house when I got home from work—she was out somewhere with her friends. And then sometimes she did not come home at night at all. And she got into trouble, trouble with the law. And she was taking drugs. Yes, drugs! And I didn't know what to do with her anymore. So I told her: Leave my house. Leave, and never come back as long as you are doing these things. Never come back, I said to her. And I forbade her brothers and sisters to mention her to me ever again. She was dead to me. And I made my heart hard against her, so that I would never think about her, that I would not care what happened to her. Because she was already dead. To me, she was dead.

"So when she died, died the real death, a year after I had thrown her out, I told myself that it meant nothing to me. I told myself that she had been a bad daughter to me, and I could not care that she had taken too many drugs one night and died from them." The old man made the sign of the cross. "And for many years, I pretended that I did not care. But, of course, deep in my heart I did.

"Only recently I have come to realize what a mistake I made. I thought of her as a bad daughter. But for so many years she had been a very good daughter. She brought me much happiness, and she made me very proud. It was only for a little while that she was a bad daughter. Does that wipe out the many years she was a good daughter? Does that cancel out everything else that went before, just because it came at the end? No. No, nothing can make those many years of her being a good daughter go away. Nothing except the mistakes a bad father makes can do that.

"My wife, she is dead now, too," and the old man crossed himself again. "Every year on the Day of the Dead I set a place for my daughter, and on the second day I set a place for my wife."

He fell silent for a long moment, his eyes burdened with care. "It's not good for a man to live longer than his children. Every year I set a place for my daughter on the Day of the Dead. But I would rather that she was alive, and I was the one who was gone, so that she would set a place for me."

He turned his head and solemnly contemplated Morinda for a moment before he said, "Do you wish to be a good daughter to your father, *mija?*"

"I wish I had been, yes."

"You still can be. If you will remember him on the Day of the Dead."

"I always will."

"The dead return to us on the Day of the Dead. If you set a place for your father, he will come back to you. And then you can tell him the things you want to say to him. Tell him just the way you have told it to me. Tell him of your love for him. Ask for his forgiveness. And, because he is a good father, he will forgive you. But tears only make the way back slippery for the dead when they return. So you must not cry, *mija*."

"I know," she said, though her tears wouldn't stop.

The old man offered her a handkerchief, which she accepted. She held it clutched in her fist to wipe her eyes until she'd cried herself out.

There was no bus station in San Estaban, so Morinda was let off on a turnout on the soft shoulder of the highway near the road that went into town. There she kissed the cheek of the old man to say goodbye, regained her suitcase, and walked the half mile into San Estaban. A breeze blew salt air from the ocean; gulls soared overhead.

A few people turned to stare at her as she went past, but she met no one she knew so she didn't stop to speak to anyone. She went to the home of the Marias, dropped her bag on their doorstep, and rang the bell. The maid, Consuelo, answered the door. It took her a few seconds to recognize Morinda, but when she did, she threw her hands up in the air and shrieked Morinda's name before she rushed forward to enfold her in her arms as though she were the long-lost prodigal.

Morinda smiled weakly and let herself be hugged and bussed on both cheeks. The maid's cries brought the other members of the household hurrying to see what the commotion was about, first Maria Gabriela and Maria Teresa, then Maria Isabella, Maria Magdalena, and Maria Sophia, finally Maria Elena and *Señora* Ramirez. All of them crushed around Morinda, alternately celebrating her return, expressing their condolences over the death of her father, and wondering what'd happened to her since she'd disappeared after spending the night with them weeks before.

"Are you really back?" Maria Elena wanted to know. "Are you here to stay for good?"

"Yes," Morinda said. "I'm going to stay here in San Estaban, at least until I decide which school I'm going to go to."

"All of your father's affairs, they are tied up by the court," *Señora* Ramirez said. "The house is sealed up. The businesses are closed. They are yours, according to your father's will, but since you are underage they have been put into a trust. It's all mixed up with lawyers and judges! It's a mess!"

"I'll have to find someplace to live, then," Morinda said.

"Find a place to live!" *Señora* Ramirez was indignant. "What are you talking about, you silly thing? Isn't there anything inside that head of yours? It's a wonder I love you so much, you're such a goose! You always have a place to live. Here with us. Of course you'll live with us, *mija!*"

And she walked away carrying Morinda's suitcase as if the matter was settled.

Morinda started to follow *Señora* Ramirez inside when a thought occurred to her. She halted and asked, "Does this mean I'll have to change my name to Maria Morinda, to become one of the Marias?"

The girls who stood around her looked at each other, then they turned to Morinda and chorused gleefully, "Yes!"

Morinda shrugged, and accepted her fate. "Okay," she said.

With the sound of her sisters' laughter ringing in her ears, Morinda entered her new home.